ONE MAN DISCOVERED THE TRUTH

—The Fall of Rome, the Wars that racked the world, mass murder and horror. . .

Men thought they were historical accidents, "human nature."

But each one was a move in a Universe-wide battle—and the men who suffered and died were the big chessmen.

Finally, one man discovered the truth—and faced his strange destiny in the ultimate struggle for control of the Universe.

First of the Famous Lensman Series

NOVELS OF SCIENCE FICTION
by
"DOC" SMITH

●

The Lensman series

> TRIPLANETARY
> FIRST LENSMAN
> GALACTIC PATROL
> GRAY LENSMAN
> SECOND STAGE LENSMAN
> CHILDREN OF THE LENS
> MASTERS OF THE VORTEX

The Skylark series

> THE SKYLARK OF SPACE
> SKYLARK THREE
> SKYLARK OF VALERON
> SKYLARK DU QUESNE

TRIPLANETARY

E. E. "DOC" SMITH

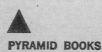
PYRAMID BOOKS • NEW YORK

TRIPLANETARY

A PYRAMID BOOK
Published by arrangement with the Author

Fantasy Press edition published 1948

Pyramid edition published August 1965
Ninth printing, January 1974

ISBN 0-515-02890-8

Printed in the United States of America

PYRAMID BOOKS are published by Pyramid Communications, Inc.
Its trademarks consisting of the word "Pyramid" and the portrayal
of a pyramid are registered in the United States Patent Office.

Pyramid Communications, Inc.
919 Third Avenue
New York, New York 10022

TO ROD

CONTENTS

BOOK
ONE
DAWN

CHAPTER 1

ARISIA AND EDDORE

TWO THOUSAND MILLION OR SO YEARS AGO TWO GALAXIES were colliding; or, rather, were passing through each other. A couple of hundreds of millions of years either way do not matter, since at least that much time was required for the inter-passage. At about that same time—within the same plus-or-minus ten percent margin of error, it is believed—practically all of the suns of both those galaxies became possessed of planets.

There is much evidence to support the belief that it was not merely a coincidence that so many planets came into being at about the same time as the galactic inter-passage. Another school of thought holds that it was pure coincidence; that all suns have planets as naturally and as inevitably as cats have kittens.

Be that as it may, Arisian records are clear upon the point that before the two galaxies began to coalesce, there were never more than three solar systems present in either; and usually only one. Thus, when the sun of the planet upon which their race originated grew old and cool, the Arisians were hard put to it to preserve their culture, since they had to work against time in solving the engineering problems associated with moving a planet from an older to a younger sun.

Since nothing material was destroyed when the Eddorians were forced into the next plane of existence, their historical records also have become available. Those records—folios and tapes and playable discs of platinum alloy, resistant indefinitely even to Eddore's noxious atmosphere—agree with those of the Arisians upon this point. Immediately before the Coalescence began there was one, and only one, planetary solar system in the Second Galaxy; and, until the advent of Eddore, the Second Galaxy was entirely devoid of intelligent life.

Thus for millions upon untold millions of years the two races, each the sole intelligent life of a galaxy, perhaps of an entire space-time continuum, remained completely in ignorance

of each other. Both were already ancient at the time of the
Coalescence. The only other respect in which the two were
similar, however, was in the possession of minds of power.

Since Arisia was Earth-like in composition, atmosphere, and
climate, the Arisians were at that time distinctly humanoid.
The Eddorians were not. Eddore was and is large and dense;
its liquid a poisonous, sludgy syrup; its atmosphere a foul and
corrosive fog. Eddore was and is unique; so different from
any other world of either galaxy that its very existence was
inexplicable until its own records revealed the fact that it did
not originate in normal space-time at all, but came to our
universe from some alien and horribly different other.

As differed the planets, so differed the peoples. The Arisians
went through the usual stages of savagery and barbarism on
they way to Civilization. The Age of Stone. The Ages of
Bronze, of Iron, of Steel, and of Electricity. Indeed, it is probable that it is because the Arisians went through these various stages that all subsequent Civilizations have done so, since
the spores which burgeoned into life upon the cooling surfaces
of all the planets of the commingling galaxies were Arisian,
not Eddorian, in origin. Eddorian spores, while undoubtedly
present, must have been so alien that they could not develop
in any one of the environments, widely variant although they
are, existing naturally or coming naturally into being in
normal space and time.

The Arisians—especially after atomic energy freed them
from physical labor—devoted themselves more and ever more
intensively to the exploration of the limitless possibilities of
the mind.

Even before the Coalescence, then, the Arisians had need
neither of space-ships nor of telescopes. By power of mind
alone they watched the lenticular aggregation of stars which
was much later to be known to Tellurian astronomers as Lundmark's Nebula approach their own galaxy. They observed
attentively and minutely and with high elation the occurrence
of mathematical impossibility; for the chance of two galaxies
ever meeting in direct, central, equatorial-plane impact and of
passing completely through each other is an infinitesimal of
such a high order as to be, even mathematically, practically
indistinguishable from zero.

They observed the birth of numberless planets, recording
minutely in their perfect memories every detail of everything
that happened; in the hope that, as ages passed, either they
or their decendants would be able to develop a symbology and
a methodology capable of explaining the then inexplicable

phenomenon. Carefree, busy, absorbedly intent, the Arisian mentalities roamed throughout space—until one of them struck an Eddorian mind.

* * *

While any Eddorian could, if it chose, assume the form of a man, they were in no sense man-like. Nor, since the term implies a softness and a lack of organization, can they be described as being amoeboid. They were both versatile and variant. Each Eddorian changed, not only its shape, but also its texture, in accordance with the requirements of the moment. Each produced—extruded—members whenever and wherever it needed them; members uniquely appropriate to the task then in work. If hardness was indicated, the members were hard; if softness, they were soft. Small or large, rigid or flexible; joined or tentacular—all one. Filaments or cables; fingers or feet; needles or mauls—equally simple. One thought and the body fitted the job.

They were asexual: sexless to a degree unapproached by any form of Tellurian life higher than the yeasts. They were not merely hermaphroditic, nor androgynous, nor parthenogenetic. They were completely without sex. They were also, to all intents and purposes and except for death by violence, immortal. For each Eddorian, as its mind approached the stagnation of saturation after a lifetime of millions of years, simply divided into two new-old beings. New in capacity and in zest; old in ability and in power, since each of the two "children" possessed in toto the knowledges and the memories of their one "parent."

And if it is difficult to describe in words the physical aspects of the Eddorians, it is virtually impossible to write or to draw, in any symbology of Civilization, a true picture of an Eddorian's—any Eddorian's—mind. They were intolerant, domineering, rapacious, insatiable, cold, callous, and brutal. They were keen, capable, persevering, analytical, and efficient. They had no trace of any of the softer emotions or sensibilities possessed by races adherent to Civilization. No Eddorian ever had anything even remotely resembling a sense of humor.

While not essentially bloodthirsty—that is, not loving bloodshed for its own sweet sake—they were no more averse to blood-letting than they were in favor of it. Any amount of killing which would or which might advance an Eddorian toward his goal was commendable; useless slaughter was frowned upon, not because it was slaughter, but because it was useless —and hence inefficient.

And, instead of the multiplicity of goals sought by the various entities of any race of Civilization, each and every Eddorian had only one. The same one: power. *Power!* P-O-W-E-R!!

Since Eddore was peopled originally by various races, perhaps as similar to each other as are the various human races of Earth, it is understandable that the early history of the planet—while it was still in its own space, that is—was one of continuous and ages-long war. And, since war always was and probably always will be linked solidly to technological advancement, the race now known simply as "The Eddorians" became technologists supreme. All other races disappeared. So did all other forms of life, however lowly, which interfered in any way with the Masters of the Planet.

Then, all racial opposition liquidated and overmastering lust as unquenched as ever, the surviving Eddorians fought among themselves: "push-button" wars employing engines of destruction against which the only possible defense was a fantastic thickness of planetary bed-rock.

Finally, unable either to kill or to enslave each other, the comparatively few survivors made a peace of sorts. Since their own space was practically barren of planetary systems, they would move their planet from space to space until they found one which so teemed with planets that each living Eddorian could become the sole Master of an ever increasing number of worlds. This was a program very much worthwhile, promising as it did an outlet for even the recognizedly insatiable Eddorian craving for power. Therefore the Eddorians, for the first time in their prodigiously long history of fanatical non-cooperation, decided to pool their resources of mind and of material and to work as a group.

Union of a sort was accomplished eventually; neither peaceably nor without highly lethal friction. They knew that a democracy, by its very nature, was inefficient; hence a democratic form of government was not even considered. An efficient government must of necessity be dictatorial. Nor were they all exactly alike or of exactly equal ability; perfect identity of any two such complex structures was in fact impossible, and any difference, however slight, was ample justification for stratification in such a society as theirs.

Thus one of them, fractionally more powerful and more ruthless than the rest, became the All-Highest—His Ultimate Supremacy—and a group of about a dozen others, only infinitesimally weaker, became his Council; a cabinet which was later to become known as the Innermost Circle. The tally of this cabinet varied somewhat from age to age; increasing by one when a member divided, decreasing by one when a jealous fellow or an envious underling managed to perpetrate a successful assassination.

And thus, at long last, the Eddorians began really to work together. There resulted, among other things, the hyper-spatial tube and the fully inertialess drive—the drive which was, millions of years later, to be given to Civilization by an Arisian operating under the name of Bergenholm. Another result, which occured shortly after the galactic interpassage had begun, was the eruption into normal space of the planet Eddore.

"I must now decide whether to make this space our permanent headquarters or to search farther," the All-Highest radiated harshly to his Council. "On the one hand, it will take some time for even those planets which have already formed to cool. Still more will be required for life to develop sufficiently to form a part of the empire which we have planned or to occupy our abilities to any great degree. On the other, we have already spent millions of years in surveying hundreds of millions of continua, without having found anywhere such a profusion of planets as will, in all probability, soon fill both of these galaxies. There may also be certain advantages inherent in the fact that these planets are not yet populated. As life develops, we can mold it as we please. Krongenes, what are your findings in regard to the planetary possibilities of other spaces?"

The term "Krongenes" was not, in the accepted sense, a name. Or, rather, it was more than a name. It was a key-thought, in mental shorthand; a condensation and abbreviation of the life-pattern or ego of that particular Eddorian.

"Not at all promising, Your Supremacy," Krongenes replied promptly. "No space within reach of my instruments has more than a small fraction of the inhabitable worlds which will presently exist in this one."

"Very well. Have any of you others any valid objections to the establishment of our empire here in this space? If so, give me your thought now."

No objecting thoughts appeared, since none of the monsters then knew anything of Arisia or of the Arisians. Indeed, even if they had known, it is highly improbable that any objection would have been raised. First, because no Eddorian, from the All-Highest down, could conceive or would under any circumstances admit that any race, anywhere, had ever approached or ever would approach the Eddorians in any quality whatever; and second, because, as is routine in all dictatorships, disagreement with the All-Highest did not operate to lengthen the span of life.

"Very well. We will now confer as to . . . but hold! That thought is not one of ours! Who are you, stranger, to dare to intrude thus upon a conference of the Innermost Circle?"

"I am Enphilistor, a younger student, of the planet Arisia." This name, too, was a symbol. Nor was the young Arisian yet a Watchman, as he and so many of his fellows were so soon to become, for before Eddore's arrival Arisia had had no need of Watchmen. "I am not intruding, as you know. I have not touched any one of your minds; have not read any one of your thoughts. I have been waiting for you to notice my presence, so that we could become acquainted with each other. A surprising development, truly—we have thought for many cycles of time that we were the only highly advanced life in this universe . . ."

"Be silent, worm, in the presence of the Masters. Land your ship and surrender, and your planet will be allowed to serve us. Refuse, or even hesitate, and every individual of your race shall die."

"Worm? Masters? Land my ship?" The young Arisian's thought was pure curiosity, with no tinge of fear, dismay, or awe. "Surrender? Serve you? I seem to be receiving your thought without ambiguity, but your meaning is entirely . . ."

"Address me as 'Your Supremacy'," the All-Highest directed, coldly. "Land now or die now—this is your last warning."

"Your Supremacy? Certainly, if that is the customary form. But as to landing—and warning—and dying—surely you do not think that I am present in the flesh? And can it be possible that you are actually so aberrant as to believe that you can kill me—or even the youngest Arisian infant? What a peculiar—what an *extraordinary*—psychology!"

"Die, then, worm, if you must have it so!" the All-Highest snarled, and launched a mental bolt whose energies were calculated to slay any living thing.

Enphilistor, however, parried the vicious attack without apparent effort. His manner did not change. He did not strike back.

The Eddorian then drove in with an analyzing probe, only to be surprised again—the Arisian's thought could not be traced! And Enphilistor, while warding off the raging Eddorian, directed a quiet thought as though he were addressing someone close by his side:

"Come in, please, one or more of the Elders. There is a situation here which I am not qualified to handle."

"We, the Elders of Arisia in fusion, are here." A grave, deeply resonant pseudo-voice filled the Eddorians' minds; each perceived in three-dimensional fidelity an aged, white-bearded human face. "You of Eddore have been expected. The course of action which we must take has been determined long since. You will forget this incident completely. For cycles upon cycles of time to come no Eddorian shall know that we Arisians exist."

Even before the thought was issued the fused Elders had gone quietly and smoothly to work. The Eddorians forgot utterly the incident which had just happened. Not one of them retained in his conscious mind any inkling that Eddore did not possess the only intelligent life in space.

*   *   *

And upon distant Arisia a full meeting of minds was held.

"But why didn't you simply kill them?" Enphilistor asked. "Such action would be distasteful in the extreme, of course —almost impossible—but even I can perceive . . ." He paused, overcome by his thought.

"That which you perceive, youth, is but a very small fraction of the whole. We did not attempt to slay them because we could not have done so. Not because of squeamishness, as you intimate, but from sheer inability. The Eddorian tenacity of life is a thing far beyond your present under-standing; to have attempted to kill them would have rendered it impossible to make them forget us. We must have time . . . cycles and cycles of time." The fusion broke off, pondered for minutes, then addressed the group as a whole:

"We, the Elder Thinkers, have not shared fully with you our visualization of the Cosmic All, because until the Eddor-ians actually appeared there was always the possibility that our findings might have been in error. Now, however, there is no doubt. The Civilization which has been pictured as de-veloping peacefully upon all the teeming planets of two gal-axies will not now of itself come into being. We of Arisia should be able to bring it eventually to full fruition, but the task will be long and difficult.

"The Eddorians' minds are of tremendous latent power. Were they to know of us now, it is practically certain that they would be able to develop powers and mechanisms by the use of which they would negate our every effort—they would hurl us out of this, our native space and time. We must have time . . . given time, we shall succeed. There shall be

Lenses . . . and entities of Civilization worthy in every respect
to wear them. But we of Arisia alone will never be able to con-
quer the Eddorians. Indeed, while this is not yet certain, the
probability is exceedingly great that despite our utmost efforts
at self-development our descendants will have to breed, from
some people to evolve upon a planet not yet in existence, an
entirely new race—a race tremendously more capable than
ours—to succeed us as Guardians of Civilization."

*Centuries passed. Millenia. Cosmic and geologic ages.
Planets cooled to solidity and stability. Life formed and grew
and developed. And as life evolved it was subjected to, and
strongly if subtly affected by, the diametrically opposed forces
of Arisia and Eddore.*

CHAPTER 2

THE FALL OF ATLANTIS

1. EDDORE

"MEMBERS OF THE INNERMOST CIRCLE, WHEREVER YOU ARE
and whatever you may be doing, tune in!" the All-Highest
broadcast. "Analysis of the data furnished by the survey just
completed shows that in general the Great Plan is progressing
satisfactorily. There seem to be only four planets which our
delegates have not been or may not be able to control prop-
erly: Sol III, Rigel IV, Velantia III, and Palain VII. All four,
you will observe, are in the other galaxy. No trouble whatever has developed in our own.

"Of these four, the first requires drastic and immediate
personal attention. Its people, in the brief interval since our
previous general survey, have developed nuclear energy and
have fallen into a cultural pattern which does not conform in
any respect to the basic principles laid down by us long since.
Our deputies there, thinking erroneously that they could
handle matters without reporting fully to or calling for help
upon the next higher operating echelon, must be disciplined
sharply. Failure, from whatever cause, can not be tolerated.

"Gharlane, as Master Number Two, you will assume control of Sol III immediately. This Circle now authorizes and instructs you to take whatever steps may prove necessary to restore order upon that planet. Examine carefully this data concerning the other three worlds which may very shortly become troublesome. Is it your thought that one or more others of this Circle should be assigned to work with you, to be sure that these untoward developments are suppressed?"

"It is not, Your Supremacy," that worthy decided, after a time of study. "Since the peoples in question are as yet of low intelligence; since one form of flesh at a time is all that will have to be energized; and since the techniques will be essentially similar; I can handle all four more efficiently alone than with the help or cooperation of others. If I read this data correctly, there will be need of only the most elementary precaution in the employment of mental force, since of the four races, only the Velantians have even a rudimentary knowledge of its uses. Right?"

"We so read the data." Surprisingly enough, the Innermost Circle agreed unanimously.

"Go, then. When finished, report in full."

"I go, All-Highest. I shall render a complete and conclusive report."

2. ARISIA

"We, the Elder Thinkers in fusion, are spreading in public view, for study and full discussion, a visualization of the relationships existing and to exist between Civilization and its irreconcilable and implacable foe. Several of our younger members, particularly Eukonidor, who has just attained Watchmanship, have requested instruction in this matter. Being as yet immature, their visualizations do not show clearly why Nedanillor, Kriedigan, Drounli, and Brolenteen, either singly or in fusion, have in the past performed certain acts and have not performed certain others; or that the future actions of those Moulders of Civilization will be similarly constrained.

"This visualization, while more complex, more complete, and more detailed than the one set up by our forefathers at the time of the Coalescence, agrees with it in every essential. The five basics remain unchanged. First: the Eddorians can be overcome only by mental force. Second: the magnitude of the required force is such that its only possible generator is such an organization as the Galactic Patrol toward which we have been and are working. Third: since no Arisian or any fusion of Arisians will ever be able to spear-head that force, it was and is necessary to develop a race of mentality sufficient to perform that task. Fourth: this new race, having been instrumental in removing the menace of Eddore, will as a matter of course displace the Arisians as Guardians of Civilization. Fifth: the Eddorians must not become informed of us until such a time as it will be physically, mathematically impossible for them to construct any effective counter-devices."

"A cheerless outlook, truly," came a somber thought.

"Not so, daughter. A little reflection will show you that your present thinking is loose and turbid. When that time comes, every Arisian will be ready for the change. We know the way. We do not know to what that way leads; but the Arisian purpose in this phase of existence—this space-time continuum—will have been fulfilled and we will go eagerly and joyfully on to the next. Are there any more questions?"

There were none.

"Study this material, then, each of you, with exceeding care. It may be that some one of you, even a child, will perceive some facet of the truth which we have missed or have not examined fully; some fact or implication which may be made to operate to shorten the time of conflict or to lessen the number of budding Civilizations whose destruction seems to us at present to be sheerly unavoidable."

Hours passed. Days. No criticisms or suggestions were offered.

"We take it, then, that this visualization is the fullest and most accurate one possible for the massed intellect of Arisia to construct from the information available at the moment. The Moulders therefore, after describing briefly what they have already done, will inform us as to what they deem it necessary to do in the near future."

"We have observed, and at times have guided, the evolution of intelligent life upon many planets," the fusion began. "We have, to the best of our ability, directed the energies of these entities into the channels of Civilization; we have adhered consistently to the policy of steering as many different races as possible toward the intellectual level necessary for the effective use of the Lens, without which the proposed Galactic Patrol cannot come into being.

"For many cycles of time we have been working as individuals with the four strongest races, from one of which will be developed the people who will one day replace us as Guardians of Civilization. Blood lines have been established. We

have encouraged matings which concentrate traits of strength
and dissipate those of weakness. While no very great departure from the norm, either physically or mentally, will take
place until after the penultimates have been allowed to meet
and to mate, a definite general improvement of each race has
been unavoidable.

"Thus the Eddorians have already interested themselves in
our budding Civilization upon the planet Tellus, and it is inevitable that they will very shortly interfere with our work
upon the other three. These four young Civilizations must be
allowed to fall. It is to warn every Arisian against every well-
meant but inconsidered action that this conference was called.
We ourselves will operate through forms of flesh of no higher
intelligence than, and indistinguishable from, the natives
of the planets affected. No traceable connection will exist between those forms and us. No other Arisians will operate
within extreme range of any one of those four planets; they
will from now on be given the same status as has been so
long accorded Eddore itself. The Eddorians must not learn of
us until after it is too late for them to act effectively upon
that knowledge. Any chance bit of information obtained by
any Eddorian must be obliterated at once. It is to guard
against and to negate such accidental disclosures that our
Watchmen have been trained."

"But if all of our Civilizations go down . . ." Eukonidor
began to protest.

"Study will show you, youth, that the general level of mind,
and hence of strength, is rising," the fused Elders interrupted.
"The trend is ever upward; each peak and valley being higher
than its predecessor. When the indicated level has been
reached—the level at which the efficient use of the Lens will
become possible—we will not only allow ourselves to become
known to them; we will engage them at every point."

"One factor remains obscure." A Thinker broke the ensuing
silence. "In this visualization I do not perceive anything to
preclude the possibility that the Eddorians may at any time
visualize us. Granted that the Elders of long ago did not
merely visualize the Eddorians, but perceived them in time-
space surveys; that they and subsequent Elders were able to
maintain the status quo; and that the Eddorian way of thought
is essentially mechanistic, rather than philosophic, in nature.
There is still a possibility that the enemy may be able to deduce us by processes of logic alone. This thought is particularly disturbing to me at the present time because a rigid
statistical analysis of the occurrences upon those four planets

shows that they cannot possibly have been due to chance. With such an analysis as a starting point, a mind of even moderate ability could visualize us practically in toto. I assume, however, that this possibility has been taken into consideration, and suggest that the membership be informed."

"The point is well taken. The possibility exists. While the probability is very great that such an analysis will not be made until after we have declared ourselves, it is not a certainty. Immediately upon deducing our existence, however, the Eddorians would begin to build against us, upon the four planets and elsewhere. Since there is only one effective counter-structure possible, and since we Elders have long been alert to detect the first indications of that particular activity, we know that the situation remains unchanged. If it changes, we will call at once another full meeting of minds. Are there any other matters of moment? . . . If not, this conference will dissolve."

3. ATLANTIS

Ariponides, recently elected Faros of Atlantis for his third five-year term, stood at a window of his office atop the towering Farostery. His hands were clasped loosely behind his back. He did not really see the tremendous expanse of quiet ocean, nor the bustling harbor, nor the metropolis spread out so magnificently and so busily beneath him. He stood there, motionless, until a subtle vibration warned him that visitors were approaching his door.

"Come in, gentlemen . . . Please be seated." He sat down at one end of a table molded of transparent plastic. "Psychologist Talmonides, Statesman Cleto, Minister Philamon, Minister Marxes and Officer Artomenes, I have asked you to come here personally because I have every reason to believe that the shielding of this room is proof against eavesdroppers; a thing which can no longer be said of our supposedly private television channels. We must discuss, and if possible come to some decision concerning, the state in which our nation now finds itself.

"Each of us knows within himself exactly what he is. Of our own powers, we cannot surely know each others' inward selves. The tools and techniques of psychology, however, are potent and exact; and Talmonides, after exhaustive and rigorous examination of each one of us, has certified that no taint of disloyalty exists among us."

"Which certification is not worth a damn," the burly Officer declared. "What assurance do we have that Talmonides himself is not one of the ringleaders? Mind you, I have no reason to believe that he is not completely loyal. In fact, since he has been one of my best friends for over twenty years, I believe implicitly that he is. Nevertheless the plain fact is, Ariponides, that all the precautions you have taken, and any you can take, are and will be useless insofar as definite knowledge is concerned. The real truth is and will remain unknown."

"You are right," the Psychologist conceded. "And, such being the case, perhaps I should withdraw from the meeting."

"That wouldn't help, either." Artomenes shook his head. "Any competent plotter would be prepared for this, as for any other contingency. One of us others would be the real operator."

"And the fact that our Officer is the one who is splitting hairs so finely could be taken to indicate which one of us the real operator could be," Marxes pointed out, cuttingly.

"Gentlemen! Gentlemen!" Ariponides protested. "While absolute certainty is of course impossible to any finite mind, you all know how Talmonides was tested; you know that in his case there is no reasonable doubt. Such chance as exists, however, must be taken, for if we do not trust each other fully in this undertaking, failure is inevitable. With this word of warning I will get on with my report.

"This world-wide frenzy of unrest followed closely upon the controlled liberation of atomic energy and may be —probably is—traceable to it. It is in no part due to imperialistic aims or acts on the part of Atlantis. This fact cannot be stressed too strongly. We never have been and are not now interested in Empire. It is true that the other nations began as Atlantean colonies, but no attempt was ever made to hold any one of them in colonial status against the wish of its electorate. All nations were and are sister states. We gain or lose together. Atlantis, the parent, was and is a clearing-house, a co-ordinator of effort, but has never claimed or sought authority to rule; all decisions being based upon free debate and free and secret ballot.

"But now! Parties and factions everywhere, even in old Atlantis. Every nation is torn by internal dissensions and strife. Nor is this all. Uighar as a nation is insensately jealous of the Islands of the South, who in turn are jealous of Maya. Maya of Bantu, Bantu of Ekopt, Ekopt of Norheim, and Norheim of Uighar. A vicious circle, worsened by other jealousies and hatreds intercrossing everywhere. Each fears that some other is about to try to seize control of the entire world; and there seems to be spreading rapidly the utterly baseless belief that Atlantis itself is about to reduce all other nations of Earth to vassalage.

"This is a bald statement of the present condition of the world as I see it. Since I can see no other course possible within the constituted framework of our democratic government, I recommend that we continue our present activities, such as the international treaties and agreements upon which we are now at work, intensifying our effort wherever possible. We will now hear from Statesman Cleto."

"You have outlined the situation clearly enough, Faros. My thought, however, is that the principal cause of the trouble is the coming into being of this multiplicity of political parties, particularly those composed principally of crackpots and extremists. The connection with atomic energy is clear: since the atomic bomb gives a small group of people the power to destroy the world, they reason that it thereby confers upon them the authority to dictate to the world. My recommendation is merely a special case of yours; that every effort be made to influence the electorates of Norheim and of Uighar into supporting an effective international control of atomic energy."

"You have your data tabulated in symbolics?" asked Talmonides, from his seat at the keyboard of a calculating machine.

"Yes. Here they are."

"Thanks."

"Minister Philamon," the Faros announced.

"As I see it—as any intelligent man should be able to see it—the principal contribution of atomic energy to this world-wide chaos was the complete demoralization of labor," the gray-haired Minister of Trade stated, flatly. "Output per man-hour should have gone up at least twenty percent, in which case prices would automatically have come down. Instead, short-sighted guilds imposed drastic curbs on production, and now seem to be surprised that as production falls and hourly wages rise, prices also rise and real income drops. Only one course is possible, gentlemen; labor *must* be made to listen to reason. This feather-bedding, this protected loafing, this . . ."

"I protest!" Marxes, Minister of Work, leaped to his feet. "The blame lies squarely with the capitalists. Their greed, their rapacity, their exploitation of . . ."

"One moment, please!" Ariponides rapped the table sharply. "It is highly significant of the deplorable condition of the times that two Ministers of State should speak as you two have just spoken. I take it that neither of you has anything new to contribute to this symposium?"

Both claimed the floor, but both were refused it by vote. "Hand your tabulated data to Talmonides," the Faros directed. "Officer Artomenes?"

"You, our Faros, have more than intimated that our defense program, for which I am primarily responsible, has been largely to blame for what has happened," the grizzled warrior began. "In part, perhaps it was—one must be blind indeed not to see the connection, and biased indeed not to admit it. But what should I have done, knowing that there is no practical defense against the atomic bomb? Every nation has them, and is manufacturing more and more. Every nation is infested with the agents of every other. Should I have tried to keep Atlantis toothless in a world bristling with fangs? And could I—or anyone else—have succeeded in doing so?"

"Probably not. No criticism was intended; we must deal with the situation as it actually exists. Your recommendations, please?"

"I have thought this thing over day and night, and can see no solution which can be made acceptable to our—or to any real—democracy. Nevertheless, I have one recommendation to make. We all know that Norheim and Uighar are the sore spots—particularly Norheim. We have more bombs as of now than both of them together. We know that Uighar's super-sonic jobs are ready. We don't know exactly what Norheim has, since they cut my Intelligence line a while back, but I'm sending over another operative—my best man, too—tonight. If he finds out that we have enough advantage in speed, and I'm pretty sure that we have, I say hit both Norheim and Uighar right then, while we can, before they hit us. And hit them hard—pulverize them. Then set up a world government strong enough to knock out any nation—including Atlantis—that will not cooperate with it. This course of action is flagrantly against all international law and all the principles of democracy, I know; and even it might not work. It is, however, as far as I can see, the only course which *can* work."

"You—we all—perceive its weaknesses." The Faros thought for minutes. "You cannot be sure that your Intelligence has located all of the danger points, and many of them must be so far underground as to be safe from even our heaviest missiles. We all, including you, believe that the Psychologist is right in holding that the reaction of the other nations to such action would be both unfavorable and violent. Your report, please, Talmonides."

"I have already put my data into the integrator." The Psychologist punched a button and the mechanism began to whir and to click. "I have only one new fact of any importance; the name of one of the higher-ups and its corollary implication that there may be some degree of cooperation between Norheim and Uighar . . ."

He broke off as the machine stopped clicking and ejected its report.

"Look at that graph—up ten points in seven days!" Talmonides pointed a finger. "The situation is deteriorating faster and faster. The conclusion is unavoidable—you can see yourselves that this summation line is fast approaching unity —that the outbreaks will become uncontrollable in approximately eight days. With one slight exception—here—you will notice that the lines of organization and purpose are as random as ever. In spite of this conclusive integration I would be tempted to believe that this seeming lack of coherence was due to insufficient data—that back of this whole movement there is a carefully-set-up and completely-integrated plan—except for the fact that the factions and the nations are so evenly matched. But the data are sufficient. It is shown conclusively that no one of the other nations can possibly win, even by totally destroying Atlantis. They would merely destroy each other and our entire Civilization. According to this forecast, in arriving at which the data furnished by our Officer were prime determinants, that will surely be the outcome unless remedial measures be taken at once. You are of course sure of your facts, Artomenes?"

"I am sure. But you said you had a name, and that it indicated a Norheim-Uighar hookup. What is that name?"

"An old friend of yours . . ."

"Lo Sung!" The words as spoken were a curse of fury.

"None other. And, unfortunately, there is as yet no course of action indicated which is at all promising of success."

"Use mine, then!" Artomenes jumped up and banged the table with his fist. "Let me send two flights of rockets over right now that will blow Uigharstoy and Norgrad into radioactive dust and make a thousand square miles around each of them uninhabitable for ten thousand years! If that's the only way they can learn anything, let them learn!"

"Sit down, Officer," Ariponides directed, quietly. "That course, as you have already pointed out, is indefensible. It violates every Prime Basic of our Civilization. Moreover, it would be entirely futile, since this resultant makes it clear that every nation on Earth would be destroyed within the day."

"What, then?" Artomenes demanded, bitterly. "Sit still here and let them annihilate us?"

"Not necessarily. It is to formulate plans that we are here. Talmonides will by now have decided, upon the basis of our pooled knowledge, what must be done."

"The outlook is not good: not good at all," the Psychologist announced, gloomily. "The only course of action which carries any promise whatever of success—and its probability is only point one eight—is the one recommended by the Faros, modified slightly to include Artomenes' suggestion of sending his best operative on the indicated mission. For highest morale, by the way, the Faros should also interview this agent before he sets out. Ordinarily I would not advocate a course of action having so little likelihood of success; but since it is simply a continuation and intensification of what we are already doing, I do not see how we can adopt any other."

"Are we agreed?" Ariponides asked, after a short silence.

They were agreed. Four of the conferees filed out and a brisk young man strode in. Although he did not look at the Faros his eyes asked questions.

"Reporting for orders, sir." He saluted the Officer punctiliously.

"At ease, sir." Artomenes returned the salute. "You were called here for a word from the Faros. Sir, I present Captain Phryges."

"Not orders, son . . . no." Ariponides' right hand rested in greeting upon the captain's left shoulder, wise old eyes probed deeply into gold-flecked, tawny eyes of youth; the Faros saw, without really noticing, a flaming thatch of red-bronze-auburn hair. "I asked you here to wish you well; not only for myself, but for all our nation and perhaps for our entire race. While everything in my being rebels against an unprovoked and unannounced assault, we may be compelled to choose between our Officer's plan of campaign and the destruction of Civilization. Since you already know the vital importance of your mission, I need not enlarge upon it. But I want you to know fully, Captain Phryges, that all Atlantis flies with you this night."

"Th . . . thank you, sir." Phryges gulped twice to steady his voice. "I'll do my best, sir."

And later, in a wingless craft flying toward the airfield, young Phryges broke a long silence. "So *that* is the Faros

. . . I like him, Officer . . . I have never seen him close up
before . . . there's something about him . . . He isn't like my
father, much, but it seems as though I have known him for
a thousand years!"

"Hm . . . m . . . m. Peculiar. You two are a lot alike,
at that, even though you don't look anything like each other.
. . . Can't put a finger on exactly what it is, but it's there."
Although Artomenes nor any other of his time could place
it, the resemblance was indeed there. It was in and back of
the eyes; it was the "look of eagles" which was long later
to become associated with the wearers of Arisia's Lens.
"But here we are, and your ship's ready. Luck, son."

"Thanks, sir. But one more thing. If it should—if I don't
get back—will you see that my wife and the baby are . . . ?"

"I will, son. They will leave for North Maya tomorrow
morning. They will live, whether you and I do or not. Anything else?"

"No, sir. Thanks. Goodbye."

The ship was a tremendous flying wing. A standard commercial job. Empty—passengers, even crewmen, were never
subjected to the brutal accelerations regularly used by un-
manned carriers. Phryges scanned the panel. Tiny motors
were pulling tapes through the controllers. Every light showed
green. Everything was set. Donning a water-proof coverall,
he slid through a flexible valve into his acceleration-tank and
waited.

A siren yelled briefly. Black night turned blinding white
as the harnessed energies of the atom were released. For
five and six-tenths seconds the sharp, hard, beryllium-bronze
leading edge of the back-sweeping V sliced its way through
ever-thinning air.

The vessel seemed to pause momentarily; paused and
bucked viciously. She shuddered and shivered, tried to tear
herself into shreds and chunks; but Phryges in his tank was
unconcerned. Earlier, weaker ships went to pieces against
the solid-seeming wall of atmospheric incompressibility at
the velocity of sound; but this one was built solidly enough,
and powered to hit that wall hard enough, to go through unharmed.

The hellish vibration ceased; the fantastic violence of the
drive subsided to a mere shove; Phryges knew that the vessel had leveled off at its cruising speed of two thousand
miles per hour. He emerged, spilling the least possible amount
of water upon the polished steel floor. He took off his coverall
and stuffed it back through the valve into the tank. He

mopped and polished the floor with towels, which likewise went into the tank.

He drew on a pair of soft gloves and, by manual control, jettisoned the acceleration tank and all the apparatus which had made that unloading possible. This junk would fall into the ocean; would sink; would never be found. He examined the compartment and the hatch minutely. No scratches, no scars, no mars; no tell-tale marks or prints of any kind. Let the Norskies search. So far, so good.

Back toward the trailing edge then, to a small escape-hatch beside which was fastened a dull black ball. The anchoring devices went out first. He gasped as the air rushed out into near-vacuum, but he had been trained to take sudden and violent fluctuations in pressure. He rolled the ball out upon the hatch, where he opened it; two hinged hemispheres, each heavily padded with molded composition resembling sponge rubber. It seemed incredible that a man as big as Phryges, especially when wearing a parachute, could be crammed into a space so small; but that lining had been molded to fit.

This ball *had* to be small. The ship, even though it was on a regularly-scheduled commercial flight, would be scanned intensively and continuously from the moment of entering Norheiman radar range. Since the ball would be invisible on any radar screen, no suspicion would be aroused; particularly since—as far as Atlantean Intelligence had been able to discover—the Norheimans had not yet succeeded in perfecting any device by the use of which a living man could bail out of a super-sonic plane.

Phryges waited—and waited—until the second hand of his watch marked the arrival of zero time. He curled up into one half of the ball; the other half closed over him and locked. The hatch opened. Ball and closely-prisoned man plummeted downward; slowing abruptly, with a horrible deceleration, to terminal velocity. Had the air been any trifle thicker the Atlantean captain would have died then and there; but that, too, had been computed accurately and Phryges lived.

And as the ball bulleted downward on a screaming slant, it *shrank!*

This, too, the Atlanteans hoped, was new—a synthetic which air-friction would erode away, molecule by molecule, so rapidly that no perceptible fragment of it would reach ground.

The casing disappeared, and the yielding porous lining.

And Phryges, still at an altitude of over thirty thousand feet, kicked away the remaining fragments of his cocoon and, by judicious planning, turned himself so that he could see the ground, now dimly visible in the first dull gray of dawn. There was the highway, paralleling his line of flight; he wouldn't miss it more than a hundred yards.

He fought down an almost overwhelming urge to pull his rip-cord too soon. He had to wait—wait until the last possible second—because parachutes were big and Norheiman radar practically swept the ground.

Low enough at last, he pulled the ring. Z-r-r-e-e-k— WHAP! The chute banged open; his harness tightened with a savage jerk, mere seconds before his hard-sprung knees took the shock of landing.

That was close—too close! He was white and shaking, but unhurt, as he gathered in the billowing, fighting sheet and rolled it, together with his harness, into a wad. He broke open a tiny ampoule, and as the drops of liquid touched it the stout fabric began to disappear. It did not burn; it simply disintegrated and vanished. In less than a minute there remained only a few steel snaps and rings, which the Atlantean buried under a meticulously-replaced circle of sod.

He was still on schedule. In less than three minutes the signals would be on the air and he would know where he was—unless the Norsks had succeeded in finding and eliminating the whole Atlantean under-cover group. He pressed a stud on a small instrument; held it down. A line burned green across the dial—flared red—vanished.

"Damn!" he breathed, explosively. The strength of the signal told him that he was within a mile or so of the hide-out—first-class computation—but the red flash warned him to keep away. Kinnexa—*it had better be Kinnexa!*—would come to him.

How? By air? Along the road? Through the woods on foot? He had no way of knowing—talking, even on a tight beam, was out of the question. He made his way to the highway and crouched behind a tree. Here she could come at him by any route of the three. Again he waited, pressing infrequently a stud of his sender.

A long, low-slung ground-car swung around the curve and Phryges' binoculars were at his eyes. It *was* Kinnexa—or a duplicate. At the thought he dropped his glasses and pulled his guns—blaster in right hand, air-pistol in left. But no, that wouldn't do. She'd be suspicious, too—she'd have to be—and that car probably mounted heavy stuff. If he stepped out ready for business she'd fry him, and quick. Maybe not—she might have protection—but he couldn't take the chance.

The car slowed; stopped. The girl got out, examined a front tire, straightened up, and looked down the road, straight at Phryges' hiding place. This time the binoculars brought her up to little more than arm's length. Tall, blonde, beautifully built; the slightly crooked left eyebrow. The threadline of gold betraying a one-tooth bridge and the tiny scar on her upper lip, for both of which he had been responsible —she always did insist on playing cops-and-robbers with boys older and bigger than herself—it *was* Kinnexa! Not even Norheim's science could imitate so perfectly every personalizing characteristic of a girl he had known ever since she was knee-high to a duck!

The girl slid back into her seat and the heavy car began to move. Open-handed, Phryges stepped out into its way. The car stopped.

"Turn around. Back up to me, hands behind you," she directed, crisply.

The man, although surprised, obeyed. Not until he felt a finger exploring the short hair at the back of his neck did he realize what she was seeking—the almost imperceptible scar marking the place where she bit him when she was seven years old!

"Oh, Fry! It *is* you! *Really* you! Thank the gods! I've been ashamed of that all my life, but now . . ."

He whirled and caught her as she slumped, but she did not quite faint.

"Quick! Get in . . . drive on . . . not too fast!" she cautioned, sharply, as the tires began to scream. "The speed limit along here is seventy, and we can't be picked up."

"Easy it is, Kinny. But *give!* What's the score? Where's Kolanides? Or rather, what happened to him?"

"Dead. So are the others, I think. They put him on a psycho-bench and turned him inside out."

"But the blocks?"

"Didn't hold—over here they add such trimmings as skinning and salt to the regular psycho routine. But none of them knew anything about me, nor about how their reports were picked up, or I'd have been dead, too. But it doesn't make any difference, Fry—we're just one week too late."

"What do you mean, too late? Speed it up!" His tone was rough, but the hand he placed on her arm was gentleness itself.

"I'm telling you as fast as I can. I picked up his last report day before yesterday. They have missiles just as big and just as fast as ours—maybe more so—and they are going to fire one at Atlantis tonight at exactly seven o'clock."

"Tonight! Holy gods!" The man's mind raced.

"Yes." Kinnexa's voice was low, uninflected. "And there was nothing in the world that I could do about it. If I approached any one of our places, or tried to use a beam strong enough to reach anywhere, I would simply have got picked up, too. I've thought and thought, but could figure out only one thing that might possibly be of any use, and I couldn't do that alone. But two of us, perhaps . . ."

"Go on. Brief me. Nobody ever accused you of not having a brain, and you know this whole country like the palm of your hand."

"Steal a ship. Be over the ramp at exactly Seven Pay Emma. When the lid opens, go into a full-power dive, beam Artomenes—if I had a second before they blanketed my wave—and meet their rocket head-on in their own launching-tube."

This was stark stuff, but so tense was the moment and so highly keyed up were the two that neither of them saw anything out of the ordinary in it.

"Not bad, if we can't figure out anything better. The joker being, of course, that you didn't see how you could steal a ship?"

"Exactly. I can't carry blasters. No woman in Norheim is wearing a coat or a cloak now, so I can't either. And just look at this dress! Do you see any place where I could hide even one?"

He looked, appreciatively, and she had the grace to blush.

"Can't say that I do," he admitted. "But I'd rather have one of our own ships, if we could make the approach. Could both of us make it, do you suppose?"

"Not a chance. They'd keep at least one man inside all the time. Even if we killed everybody outside, the ship would take off before we could get close enough to open the port with the outside controls."

"Probably. Go on. But first, are you sure that you're in the clear?"

"Positive." She grinned mirthlessly. "The fact that I am still alive is conclusive evidence that they didn't find out anything about me. But I don't want you to work on that idea if you can think of a better one. I've got passports and so on for you to be anything you want to be, from a tube-man up to an Ekoptian banker. Ditto for me, and for us both, as Mr. and Mrs."

"Smart girl." He thought for minutes, then shook his head. "No possible way out that I can see. The sneak-boat isn't due for a week, and from what you've said it probably won't get here. But you might make it, at that. I'll drop you somewhere . . ."

"You will not," she interrupted, quietly but definitely. "Which would *you* rather—go out in a blast like that one will be, beside a good Atlantean, or, after deserting him, be psychoed, skinned, salted, and—still alive—drawn and quartered?"

"Together, then, all the way," he assented. "Man and wife. Tourists—newlyweds—from some town not too far away. Pretty well fixed, to match what we're riding in. Can do?"

"Very simple." She opened a compartment and selected one of a stack of documents. "I can fix this one up in ten minutes. We'll have to dispose of the rest of these, and a lot of other stuff, too. And you had better get out of that leather and into a suit that matches this passport photo."

"Right. Straight road for miles, and nothing in sight either way. Give me the suit and I'll change now. Keep on going or stop?"

"Better stop, I think," the girl decided. "Quicker, and we'll have to find a place to hide or bury this evidence."

While the man changed clothes, Kinnexa collected the contraband, wrapping it up in the discarded jacket. She looked up just as Phryges was adjusting his coat. She glanced at his armpits, then stared.

"Where are your blasters?" she demanded. "They ought to show, at least a little, and even I can't see a sign of them."

He showed her.

"But they're so tiny! I never saw blasters like that!"

"I've got a blaster, but it's in the tail pocket. These aren't. They're air-guns. Poisoned needles. Not worth a damn beyond a hundred feet, but deadly close up. One touch anywhere and the guy dies right then. Two seconds max."

"Nice!" She was no shrinking violet this young Atlantean spy. "You have spares, of course, and I can hide two of them easily enough in leg-holsters. Gimme, and show me how they work."

"Standard controls, pretty much like blasters. Like so." He demonstrated, and as he drove sedately down the highway the girl sewed industriously.

The day wore on, nor was it uneventful. One incident,

in fact—the detailing of which would serve no useful purpose here—was of such a nature that at its end:

"Better pin-point me, don't you think, on that ramp?" Phryges asked, quietly. "Just in case you get scragged in one of these brawls and I don't?"

"Oh! Of course! Forgive me, Fry—it slipped my mind completely that you didn't know where it was. Area six; pin-point four seven three dash six oh five."

"Got it." He repeated the figures.

But neither of the Atlanteans was "scragged", and at six P. M. an allegedly honeymooning couple parked their big roadster in the garage at Norgrad Field and went through the gates. Their papers, tickets included, were in perfect order; they were as inconspicuous and as undemonstrative as newlyweds are wont to be. No more so, and no less.

Strolling idly, gazing eagerly at each new thing, they made their circuitous way toward a certain small hangar. As the girl had said, this field boasted hundreds of super-sonic fighters, so many that servicing was a round-the-clock routine. In that hangar was a sharp-nosed, stubby-V'd flyer, one of Norheim's fastest. It was serviced and ready.

It was too much to hope, of course, that the visitors could actually get into the building unchallenged. Nor did they.

"Back, you!" A guard waved them away. "Get back to the Concourse, where you belong—no visitors allowed out here!"

F-f-t! F-f-t! Phryges' air-gun broke into soft but deadly coughing. Kinnexa whirled—hands flashing down, skirt flying up—and ran. Guards tried to head her off; tried to bring their own weapons to bear. Tried—failed—died.

Phryges, too, ran; ran backward. His blaster was out now and flaming, for no living enemy remained within needle range. A rifle bullet w-h-i-n-g-e-d past his head, making him duck involuntarily and uselessly. Rifles were bad; but their hazard, too, had been considered and had been accepted.

Kinnexa reached the fighter's port, opened it, sprang in. He jumped. She fell against him. He tossed her clear, slammed and dogged the door. He looked at her then, and swore bitterly. A small, round hole marred the bridge of her nose: the back of her head was gone.

He leaped to the controls and the fleet little ship screamed skyward. He cut in transmitter and receiver, keyed and twiddled briefly. No soap. He had been afraid of that. They were already blanketing every frequency he could employ;

using power through which he could not drive even a tight beam a hundred miles.

But he could still crash that missile in its tube. Or—could he? He was not afraid of other Norheiman fighters; he had a long lead and he rode one of their very fastest. But since they were already so suspicious, wouldn't they launch the bomb *before* seven o'clock? He tried vainly to coax another knot out of his wide-open engines.

With all his speed, he neared the pin-point just in time to see a trail of super-heated vapor extending up into and disappearing beyond the stratosphere. He nosed his flyer upward, locked the missile into his sights, and leveled off. Although his ship did not have the giant rocket's acceleration, he could catch it before it got to Atlantis, since he did not need its altitude and since most of its journey would be made without power. What he could do about it after he caught it he did not know, but he'd do *something*.

He caught it; and, by a feat of piloting to be appreciated only by those who have handled planes at super-sonic speeds, he matched its course and velocity. Then, from a distance of barely a hundred feet, he poured his heaviest shells into the missile's war-head. He *couldn't* be missing! It was worse than shooting sitting ducks—it was like dynamiting fish in a bucket! Nevertheless, nothing happened. The thing wasn't fuzed for impact, then, but for time; and the activating mechanism would be shell- and shock-proof.

But there was still a way. He didn't need to call Artomenes now, even if he could get through the interference which the fast-approaching pursuers were still sending out. Atlantean observers would have lined this stuff up long since; the Officer would know exactly what was going on.

Driving ahead and downward, at maximum power, Phryges swung his ship slowly into a right-angle collision course. The fighter's needle nose struck the war-head within a foot of the Atlantean's point of aim, and as he died Phryges knew that he had accomplished his mission. Norheim's missile would not strike Atlantis, but would fall at least ten miles short, and the water there was very deep. Very, *very* deep. Atlantis would not be harmed.

It might have been better, however, if Phryges had died with Kinnexa on Norgrad Field; in which case the continent would probably have endured. As it was, while that one missile did not reach the city, its frightful atomic charge exploded under six hundred fathoms of water, ten scant miles from Atlantis' harbor, and very close to an ancient geological fault.

Artomenes, as Phryges had surmised, had had time in which to act, and he knew much more than Phryges did about what was coming toward Atlantis. Too late, he knew that not one missile, but seven, had been launched from Norheim, and at least five from Uighar. The retaliatory rockets which were to wipe out Norgrad, Uigharstoy, and thousands of square miles of environs were on their way long before either bomb or earthquake destroyed all of the Atlantean launching ramps.

But when equilibrium was at last restored, the ocean rolled serenely where a minor continent had been.

CHAPTER 3

THE FALL OF ROME

1. EDDORE

LIKE TWO HIGH EXECUTIVES OF A TELLURIAN CORPORATION discussing business affairs during a chance meeting at one of their clubs, Eddore's All Highest and Gharlane, his second in command, were having the Eddorian equivalent of an after-business-hours chat.

"You did a nice job on Tellus," the All-Highest commended. "On the other three, too, of course, but Tellus was so far and away the worst of the lot that the excellence of the work stands out. When the Atlantean nations destroyed each other so thoroughly I thought that this thing called 'democracy' was done away with forever, but it seems to be mighty hard to kill. However, I take it that you have this Rome situation entirely under control?"

"Definitely. Mithradates of Pontus was mine. So were both Sulla and Marius. Through them and others I killed practically all of the brains and ability of Rome, and reduced that so-called 'democracy' to a howling, aimless mob. My Nero will end it. Rome will go on by momentum—outwardly,

will even appear to grow—for a few generations, but what
Nero will do can never be undone."

"Good. A difficult task, truly."

"Not difficult, exactly . . . but it's so damned *steady*."
Gharlane's thought was bitter. "But that's the hell of working with such short-lived races. Since each creature lives
only a minute or so, they change so fast that a man can't
take his mind off of them for a second. I've been wanting to
take a little vacation trip back to our old time-space, but it
doesn't look as though I'll be able to do it until after they get
some age and settle down."

"That won't be too long. Life-spans lengthen, you know,
as races approach their norms."

"Yes. But none of the others is having half the trouble
that I am. Most of them, in fact, have things coming along
just about the way they want them. My four planets are
raising more hell than all the rest of both galaxies put together, and I know that it isn't me—next to you, I'm the
most efficient operator we've got. What I'm wondering about
is why I happen to be the goat."

"Precisely because you *are* our most efficient operator."
If an Eddorian can be said to smile, the All-Highest smiled.
"You know, as well as I do, the findings of the Integrator."

"Yes, but I am wondering more and more as to whether to
believe them unreservedly or not. Spores from an extinct
life-form—suitable environments—operation of the laws of
chance—Tommyrot! I am beginning to suspect that chance
is being strained beyond its elastic limit, for my particular
benefit, and as soon as I can find out who is doing that straining there will be one empty place in the Innermost Circle."

"Have a care, Gharlane!" All levity, all casualness disappeared. "Whom do you suspect? Whom do you accuse?"

"Nobody, as yet. The true angle never occurred to me until
just now, while I have been discussing the thing with you.
Nor shall I either suspect or accuse, ever. I shall determine,
then I shall act."

"In defiance of *me?* Of *my* orders?" the All-Highest demanded, his short temper flaring.

"Say, rather, in support," the lieutenant shot back, un-
abashed. "If some one is working on me through my job,
what position are you probably already in, without knowing
it? Assume that I am right, that these four planets of mine
got the way they are because of monkey business inside the
Circle. Who would be next? And how sure are you that
there isn't something similar, but not so far advanced, already

aimed at you? It seems to me that serious thought is in order."

"Perhaps so . . . You may be right . . . There have been a few nonconformable items. Taken separately, they did not seem to be of any importance; but together, and considered in this new light . . ."

Thus was borne out the conclusion of the Arisian Elders that the Eddorians would not at that time deduce Arisia; and thus Eddore lost its chance to begin in time the forging of a weapon with which to oppose effectively Arisia's—Civilization's—Galactic Patrol, so soon to come into being.

If either of the two had been less suspicious, less jealous, less arrogant and domineering—in other words, had not been Eddorians—this History of Civilization might never have been written; or written very differently and by another hand.

Both were, however, Eddorians.

2. ARISIA

In the brief interval between the fall of Atlantis and the rise of Rome to the summit of her power, Eukonidor of Arisia had aged scarcely at all. He was still a youth. He was, and would be for many centuries to come, a Watchman. Although his mind was powerful enough to understand the Elders' visualization of the course of Civilization—in fact, he had already made significant progress in his own visualization of the Cosmic All—he was not sufficiently mature to contemplate unmoved the events which, according to all Arisian visualizations, were bound to occur.

"Your feeling is but natural, Eukonidor." Drounli, the Moulder principally concerned with the planet Tellus, meshed his mind smoothly with that of the young Watchman. "We do not enjoy it ourselves, as you know. It is, however, *necessary*. In no other way can the ultimate triumph of Civilization be assured."

"But can nothing be done to alleviate . . . ?" Eukonidor paused.

Drounli waited. "Have you any suggestions to offer?"

"None," the younger Arisian confessed. "But I thought . . . you, or the Elders, so much older and stronger . . . could . . ."

"We can not. Rome will fall. It must be allowed to fall."

"It will be Nero, then? And we can do nothing?"

"Nero. We can do little enough. Our forms of flesh—Petronius, Acte, and the others—will do whatever they can; but their powers will be exactly the same as those of other human beings of their time. They must be and will be constrained, since any show of unusual powers, either mental or physical, would be detected instantly and would be far too revealing. On the other hand, Nero—that is, Gharlane of Eddore—will be operating much more freely."

"Very much so. Practically unhampered, except in purely physical matters. But, if nothing can be done to stop it . . . If Nero must be allowed to sow his seeds of ruin . . ."

And upon that cheerless note the conference ended.

3. ROME

"But what have you, Livius, or any of us, for that matter, got to live for?" demanded Patroclus the gladiator of his cell-mate. "We are well fed, well kept, well exercised; like horses. But, like horses, we are lower than slaves. Slaves have some freedom of action; most of us have none. We fight—fight whoever or whatever our cursed owners send us against. Those of us who live fight again; but the end is certain and comes soon. I had a wife and children once. So did you. Is there any chance, however slight, that either of us will ever know them again; or learn even whether they live or die? None. At this price, is your life worth living? Mine is not."

Livius the Bithynian, who had been staring out past the bars of the cubicle and over the smooth sand of the arena toward Nero's garlanded and purple-bannered throne, turned and studied his fellow gladiator from toe to crown. The heavily-muscled legs, the narrow waist, the sharply-tapering torso, the enormous shoulders. The leonine head, surmounted by an unkempt shock of red-bronze-auburn hair. And, lastly, the eyes—gold-flecked, tawny eyes—hard and cold now with a ferocity and a purpose not to be concealed.

"I have been more or less expecting something of this sort," Livius said then, quietly. "Nothing overt—you have builded well, Patroclus—but to one who knows gladiators as I know them there has been something in the wind for weeks past. I take it that someone swore his life for me and that I should not ask who that friend might be."

"One did. You should not."

"So be it. To my unknown sponsor, then, and to the gods, I give thanks, for I am wholly with you. Not that I have any hope. Although your tribe breeds men—from your build

and hair and eyes you descend from Spartacus himself—
you know that even he did not succeed. Things now are
worse, infinitely worse, than they were in his day. No one
who has ever plotted against Nero has had any measure
of success; not even his scheming slut of a mother. All have
died, in what fashions you know. Nero is vile, the basest of
the base. Nevertheless, his spies are the most efficient that
the world has ever known. In spite of that, I feel as you do.
If I can take with me two or three of the Praetorians, I die
content. But by your look, your plan is not what I thought,
to storm vainly Nero's podium yonder. Have you, by any
chance, some trace of hope of success?"

"More than a trace; much more." The Thracian's teeth
bared in a wolfish grin. "His spies are, as you say, very good.
But, this time, so are we. Just as hard and just as ruthless.
Many of his spies among us have died; most, if not all,
of the rest are known. They, too, shall die. Glatius, for instance. Once in a while, by the luck of the gods, a man kills
a better man than he is; but Glatius has done it six times
in a row, without getting a scratch. But the next time he fights,
in spite of Nero's protection, Glatius dies. Word has gone out,
and there are gladiators' tricks that Nero never heard of."

"Quite true. One question, and I too may begin to hope.
This is not the first time that gladiators have plotted against
Ahenobarbus. Before the plotters could accomplish anything,
however, they found themselves matched against each other
and the signal was always for death, never for mercy. Has
this . . .?" Livius paused.

"It has not. It is that which gives me the hope I have. Nor
are we gladiators alone in this. We have powerful friends
at court; one of whom has for days been carrying a knife
sharpened especially to slip between Nero's ribs. That he
still carries that knife and that we still live are proofs
enough for me that Ahenobarbus, the matricide and incendiary, has no suspicion whatever of what is going on."

(At this point Nero on his throne burst into a roar of
laughter, his gross body shaking with a merriment which
Petronius and Tigellinus ascribed to the death-throes of a
Christian woman in the arena.)

"Is there any small thing which I should be told in order
to be of greatest use?" Livius asked.

"Several. The prisons and the pits are so crowded with
Christians that they die and stink, and a pestilence threatens.
To mend matters, some scores of hundreds of them are to
be crucified here tomorrow."

"Why not? Everyone knows that they are poisoners of wells and murderers of children, and practitioners of magic. Wizards and witches."

"True enough." Patroclus shrugged his massive shoulders. "But to get on, tomorrow night, at full dark, the remaining hundreds who have not been crucified are to be —have you ever seen sarmentitii and semaxii?"

"Once only. A gorgeous spectacle, truly, almost as thrilling as to feel a man die on your sword. Men and women, wrapped in oil-soaked garments smeared with pitch and chained to posts, make splendid torches indeed. You mean, then, that . . .?"

"Aye. In Caesar's own garden. When the light is brightest Nero will ride in parade. When his chariot passes the tenth torch our ally swings his knife. The Praetorians will rush around, but there will be a few moments of confusion during which we will go into action and the guards will die. At the same time others of our party will take the palace and kill every man, woman, and child adherent to Nero."

"Very nice—in theory." The Bithynian was frankly skeptical. "But just how are we going to get there? A few gladiators—such champions as Patroclus of Thrace—are at times allowed to do pretty much as they please in their free time, and hence could possibly be on hand to take part in such a brawl, but most of us will be under lock and guard."

"That too, has been arranged. Our allies near the throne and certain other nobles and citizens of Rome, who have been winning large sums by our victories, have prevailed upon our masters to give a grand banquet to *all* gladiators tomorrow night, immediately following the mass crucifixion. It is going to be held in the Claudian Grove, just across from Caesar's Gardens."

"Ah!" Livius breathed deep; his eyes flashed. "By Baal and Bacchus! By the round, high breasts of Isis! For the first time in years I begin to live! Our masters die first, then and there . . . but hold—weapons?"

"Will be provided. Bystanders will have them, and armor and shields, under their cloaks. Our owners first, yes; and then the Praetorians. But note, Livius, that Tigellinus, the Commander of the Guard, is mine—mine alone. I, personally, am going to cut his heart out."

"Granted. I heard that he had your wife for a time. But you seem quite confident that you will still be alive tomorrow night. By Baal and Ishtar, I wish I could feel so! With something to live for at last, I can feel my guts turning to water—I can hear Charon's oars. Like as not, now, some toe-dancing stripling of a retiarius will entangle me in his net this very afternoon, and no mercy signal has been or will be given this day. Such is the crowd's temper, from Caesar down, that even you will get 'Pollice verso' if you fall."

"True enough. But you had better get over that feeling, if you want to live. As for me, I'm safe enough. I have made a vow to Jupiter, and he who has protected me so long will not desert me now. Any man or any thing who faces me during these games, dies."

"I hope so, sin . . . but listen! The horns . . . and some-one is coming!"

The door behind them swung open. A lanista, or master of gladiators, laden with arms and armor, entered. The door swung to and was locked from the outside. The visitor was obviously excited, but stared wordlessly at Patroclus for seconds.

"Well, Iron-heart," he burst out finally, "aren't you even curious about what you have got to do today?"

"Not particularly," Patroclus replied, indifferently. "Except to dress to fit. Why? Something special?"

"*Extra* special. The sensation of the year. Fermius himself. Unlimited. Free choice of weapons and armor."

"Fermius!" Livius exclaimed. "Fermius the Gaul? May Athene cover you with her shield!"

"You can say that for me, too," the lanista agreed, callously. "Before I knew who was entered, like a fool, I bet a hundred sesterces on Patroclus here, at odds of only one to two, against the field. But listen, Bronze-head. If you get the best of Fermius, I'll give you a full third of my winnings."

"Thanks. You'll collect. A good man, Fermius, and smart. I've heard a lot about him, but never saw him work. He has seen me, which isn't so good. Both heavy and fast—some-what lighter than I am, and a bit faster. He knows that I always fight Thracian, and that I'd be a fool to try anything else against him. He fights either Thracian or Samnite depending upon the opposition. Against me his best bet would be to go Samnite. Do you know?"

"No. They didn't say. He may not decide until the last moment."

"Unlimited, against me, he'll go Samnite. He'll have to. These unlimiteds are tough, but it gives me a chance to use a new trick I've been working on. I'll take that sword there —no scabbard—and two daggers, besides my gladius. Get me a mace; the lightest real mace they've got in their armory."

"A *mace!* Fighting *Thracian*, against a *Samnite?*"

"Exactly. A mace. Am I going to fight Fermius, or do you want to do it yourself?"

The mace was brought and Patroclus banged it, with a two-handed roundhouse swing, against a stone of the wall. The head remained solid upon the shaft. Good. They waited.

Trumpets blared; the roar of the vast assemblage subsided almost to silence.

"Grand Champion Fermius versus Grand Champion Patroclus," came the raucous announcement. "Single combat. Any weapons that either chooses to use, used in any way possible. No rest, no intermission. Enter!"

Two armored figures strode toward the center of the arena. Patroclus' armor, from towering helmet down, and including the shield, was of dully-gleaming steel, completely bare of ornament. Each piece was marred and scarred; very plainly that armor was for use and had been used. On the other hand, the Samnite half-armor of the Gaul was resplendent with the decorations affected by his race. Fermius' helmet sported three brilliantly-colored plumes, his shield and cuirass, enameled in half the colors of the spectrum, looked as though they were being worn for the first time.

Five yards apart, the gladiators stopped and wheeled to face the podium upon which Nero lolled. The buzz of conversation—the mace had excited no little comment and speculation—ceased. Patroclus heaved his ponderous weapon into the air; the Gaul whirled up his long, sharp sword. They chanted in unison:

"Ave, Caesar Imperator!
Morituri te salutant!"

The starting-flag flashed downward; and at its first sight, long before it struck the ground, both men moved. Fermius whirled and leaped; but, fast as he was, he was not quite fast enough. That mace, which had seemed so heavy in the Thracian's hands a moment before, had become miraculously maneuverable—it was hurtling through the air directly toward the middle of his body! It did not strike its goal—Patroclus hoped that he was the only one there who suspected that he had not expected it to touch his opponent—but in order to dodge the missle Fermius had to break his stride; lost momentarily the fine coordination of his attack. And in that moment Patroclus struck. Struck, and struck again.

But, as has been said, Fermius was both strong and fast.

The first blow, aimed backhand at his bare right leg, struck his shield instead. The left-handed stab, shield-encumbered as the left arm was, ditto. So did the next trial, a vicious forehand cut. The third of the mad flurry of swordcuts, only partially deflected by the sword which Fermius could only then get into play, sheared down and a red, a green, and a white plume floated toward the ground. The two fighters sprang apart and studied each other briefly.

From the gladiators' standpoint, this had been the veriest preliminary skirmishing. That the Gaul had lost his plumes and that his armor showed great streaks of missing enamel meant no more to either than that the Thracian's supposedly surprise attack had failed. Each knew that he faced the deadliest fighter of his world; but if that knowledge affected either man, the other could not perceive it.

But the crowd went wild. Nothing like that first terrific passage-at-arms had ever before been seen. Death, sudden and violent, had been in the air. The arena was saturated with it. Hearts had been ecstatically in throats. Each person there, man or woman, had felt the indescribable thrill of death—vicariously, safely—and every fiber of their lusts demanded more. More! Each spectator knew that one of those men would die that afternoon. None wanted, or would permit them both to live. This was to the death, and death there would be.

Women, their faces blotched and purple with emotion, shrieked and screamed. Men, stamping their feet and waving their arms, yelled and swore. And many, men and women alike, laid wagers.

"Five hundred sesterces on Fermius!" one shouted, tablet and stylus in air.

"Taken!" came an answering yell. "The Gaul is done—Patroclus all but had him there!"

"One thousand, you!" came another challenge. "Patroclus missed his chance and will never get another—a thousand on Fermius!"

"Two thousand!"

"Five thousand!"

"Ten!"

The fighters closed—swung—stabbed. Shields clanged vibrantly under the impact of fended strokes, swords whined and snarled. Back and forth—circling—giving and taking ground—for minute after endless minute that desperately furious exhibition of skill, of speed and of power and of endurance went on. And as it went on, longer and longer past the time expected by even the most optimistic, tension mounted higher and higher.

Blood flowed crimson down the Gaul's bare leg and the crowd screamed its approval. Blood trickled out of the joints of the Thracian's armor and it became a frenzied mob.

No human body could stand that pace for long. Both men were tiring fast, and slowing. With the drive of his weight and armor, Patroclus forced the Gaul to go where he wanted him to go. Then, apparently gathering his every resource for a final effort, the Thracian took one short, choppy step forward and swung straight down, with all his strength.

The blood-smeared hilt turned in his hands; the blade struck flat and broke, its length whining viciously away. Fermius, although staggered by the sheer brute force of the abortive stroke, recovered almost instantly; dropping his sword and snatching at his gladius to take advantage of the wonderful opportunity thus given him.

But that breaking had not been accidental; Patroclus made no attempt to recover his balance. Instead, he ducked *past* the surprised and shaken Gaul. Still stooping, he seized the mace, which everyone except he had forgotten, and swung; swung with all the totalized and synchronized power of hands, wrists, arms, shoulders, and magnificent body.

The iron head of the ponderous weapon struck the center of the Gaul's cuirass, which crunched inward like so much cardboard. Fermius seemed to leave the ground and, folded around the mace, to fly briefly through the air. As he struck the ground, Patroclus was upon him. The Gaul was probably already dead—that blow would have killed an elephant—but that made no difference. If that mob knew that Fermius was dead, they might start yelling for his life, too. Hence, by lifting his head and poising his dirk high in air, he asked of Caesar his Imperial will.

The crowd, already frantic, had gone stark mad at the blow. No thought of mercy could or did exist in that insanely bloodthirsty throng; no thought of clemency for the man who had fought such a magnificent fight. In cooler moments they would have wanted him to live, to thrill them again and yet again; but now, for almost half an hour, they had been loving the hot, the suffocating thrill of death in their throats. Now they wanted, and would have, the ultimate thrill.

"Death!" The solid structure rocked to the crescendo roar of the demand. *"Death!* D E A T H !"

Nero's right thumb pressed horizontally against his chest.

Every vestal was making the same sign. Pollice verso. Death. The strained and strident yelling of the mob grew even louder.

Patroclus lowered his dagger and delivered the unnecessary and unfelt thrust; and—

"Peractum est!" arose one deafening yell.

*   *   *

Thus the red-haired Thracian lived; and also, somewhat to his own surprise, did Livius.

"I'm glad to see you, Bronze-heart, by the white thighs of Ceres, I am!" that worthy exclaimed, when the two met, the following day. Patroclus had never seen the Bithynian so buoyant. "Pallas Athene covered you, like I asked her to. But by the red beak of Thoth and the sacred Zaimph of Tanit, it gave me the horrors when you made that throw so quick and missed it, and I went as crazy as the rest of them when you pulled the real coup. But now, curse it, I suppose that we'll all have to be on the lookout for it—or no, unlimiteds aren't common, thank Ninib the Smiter and his scarlet spears!"

"I hear you didn't do so badly, yourself," Patroclus interrupted his friend's loquacity. "I missed your first two, but I saw you take Kalendios. He's a high-rater—one of the best of the locals—and I was afraid he might snare you, but from the looks of you, you got only a couple of stabs. Nice work."

"Prayer, my boy. Prayer is the stuff. I prayed to 'em in order, and hit the jackpot with Shamash. My guts curled up again, like they belong, and I knew that the portents were all in my favor. Besides, when you were walking out to meet Fermius, did you notice that red-headed Greek posturer making passes at you?"

"Huh? Don't be a fool. I had other things to think of."

"So I figured. So did she, probably, because after a while she came around behind with a lanista and made eyes at me. I must have the next best shape to you here, I guess. What a wench! Anyway, I felt better and better, and before she left I knew that no damn retiarius that ever waved a trident could put a net past my guard. And they couldn't either. A couple more like that and I'll be a Grand Champion myself. But they're digging holes for the crosses and there's the horn that the feast is ready. This show is going to be really good."

They ate, hugely and with unmarred appetite, of the heaped food which Nero had provided. They returned to their assigned places to see crosses, standing as close together as they could be placed and each bearing a suffering Christian, filling the whole vast expanse of the arena.

And, if the truth must be told, those two men enjoyed thoroughly every moment of that long and sickeningly horrible afternoon. They were the hardest products of the hardest school the world has ever known: trained rigorously to deal out death mercilessly at command; to accept death unflinchingly at need. They should not and can not be judged by the higher, finer standards of a softer, gentler day.

The afternoon passed; evening approached. All the gladiators then in Rome assembled in the Claudian Grove, around tables creaking under their loads of food and wine. Women, too, were there in profusion; women for the taking and yearning to be taken; and the tide of revelry ran open, wide, and high. Although all ate and apparently drank with abandon, most of the wine was in fact wasted. And as the sky darkened, most of the gladiators, one by one, began to get rid of their female companions upon one pretext or another and to drift toward the road which separated the festivities from the cloaked and curious throng of lookers-on.

At full dark, a red glare flared into the sky from Caesar's garden and the gladiators, deployed now along the highway, dashed across it and seemed to wrestle briefly with cloaked figures. Then armed, more-or-less-armored men ran back to the scene of their reveling. Swords, daggers, and gladii thrust, stabbed, and cut. Tables and benches ran red; ground and grass grew slippery with blood.

The conspirators turned then and rushed toward the Emperor's brilliantly torch-lit garden. Patroclus, however, was not in the van. He had had trouble in finding a cuirass big enough for him to get into. He had been delayed further by the fact that he had had to kill three strange lanistae before he could get at his owner, the man he really wanted to slay. He was therefore some little distance behind the other gladiators when Petronius rushed up to him and seized him by the arm.

White and trembling, the noble was not now the exquisite Arbiter Elegantiae; nor the imperturbable Augustian.

"Patroclus! In the name of Bacchus, Patroclus, why do the men go there now? No signal was given—I could not get to Nero!"

"What?" the Thracian blazed. "Vulcan and his fiends! It *was* given—I heard it myself! What went wrong?"

"Everything." Petronius licked his lips. "I was standing right beside him. No one else was near enough to interfere. It was—should have been—easy. But after I got my knife out I couldn't move. It was his *eyes*, Patroclus—I swear it, by the white breasts of Venus! He has the evil eye—I couldn't move a muscle, I tell you! Then, although I didn't want to, I turned and ran!"

"How did you find *me* so quick?"

"I—I—I—don't know," the frantic Arbiter stuttered. "I ran and ran, and there you were. But what are we—you—going to do?"

Patroclus' mind raced. He believed implicitly that Jupiter guarded him personally. He believed in the other gods and goddesses of Rome. He more than half believed in the multitudinous deities of Greece, of Egypt, and even of Babylon. The other world was real and close; the evil eye only one of the many inexplicable facts of every-day life. Nevertheless, in spite of his credulity—or perhaps in part because of it—he also believed firmly in himself; in his own powers. Wherefore he soon came to a decision.

"Jupiter, ward from me Ahenobarbus' evil eye!" he called aloud, and turned.

"Where are you going?" Petronius, still shaking, demanded.

"To do the job *you* swore to do, of course—to kill that bloated toad. And then to give Tigellinus what I have owed him so long."

At full run, he soon overtook his fellows, and waded resistlessly into the fray. He was Grand Champion Patroclus, working at his trade; the hard-learned trade which he knew so well. No Praetorian or ordinary soldier could stand before him save momentarily. He did not have all of his Thracian armor, but he had enough. Man after man faced him, and man after man died.

And Nero, sitting at ease with a beautiful boy at his right and a beautiful harlot at his left, gazed appreciatively through his emerald lens at the flaming torches; the while, with a very small fraction of his Eddorian mind, he mused upon the matter of Patroclus and Tigellinus.

Should he let the Thracian kill the Commander of his Guard? Or not? It didn't really matter, one way or the other. In fact, nothing about this whole foul planet—this ultramicroscopic, if offensive, speck of cosmic dust in the Eddorian Scheme of Things—really mattered at all. It would be mildly amusing to watch the gladiator consummate his vengeance by carving the Roman to bits. But, on the other hand, there was such a thing as pride of workmanship. Viewed in that light, the Thracian could not kill Tigellinus, because that bit of corruption had a few more jobs to do. He must descend lower and lower into unspeakable depravity, finally to cut his own throat with a razor. Although Patroclus would not know it—it was better technique not to let him know it—the Thracian's proposed vengeance would have been futility itself compared with that which the luckless Roman was to wreak on himself.

Wherefore a shrewdly-placed blow knocked the helmet from Patroclus' head and a mace crashed down, spattering his brains abroad.

*   *   *

Thus ended the last significant attempt to save the civilization of Rome; in a fiasco so complete that even such meticulous historians as Tacitus and Suetonius mention it merely as a minor disturbance of Nero's garden party.

The planet Tellus circled its sun some twenty hundred times. Sixty-odd generations of men were born and died, but that was not enough. The Arisian program of genetics required more. Therefore the Elders, after due deliberation, agreed that that Civilization, too, must be allowed to fall. And Gharlane of Eddore, recalled to duty from the middle of a much-too-short vacation, found things in very bad shape indeed and went busily to work setting them to rights. He had slain one fellow-member of the Innermost Circle, but there might very well have been more than one Master involved.

BOOK
TWO
THE WORLD WAR

CHAPTER 4

1918

SOBBING FURIOUSLY, CAPTAIN RALPH KINNISON WRENCHED
at his stick—with half of his control surfaces shot away the
crate was hellishly logy. He could step out, of course, the
while saluting the victorious Jerries, but he wasn't on fire—
yet—and hadn't been hit—yet. He ducked and flinched side-
wise as another burst of bullets stitched another seam along
his riddled fuselage and whanged against his dead engine.
Afire? Not yet—good! Maybe he could land the heap,
after all!

Slowly—oh, *so* sluggishly—the Spad began to level off,
toward the edge of the wheatfield and that friendly, inviting
ditch. If the krauts didn't get him with their next pass . . .

He heard a chattering beneath him—Brownings, by God!
—and the expected burst did not come. He knew that he
had been just about over the front when they conked his
engine; it was a toss-up whether he would come down in
enemy territory or not. But now, for the first time in ages, it
seemed, there were machine-guns going that were not aimed
at him!

His landing-gear swished against stubble and he fought
with all his strength of body and of will to keep the Spad's
tail down. He almost succeeded; his speed was almost spent
when he began to nose over. He leaped, then, and as he
struck ground he curled up and rolled—he had been a
motorcycle racer for years—feeling as he did so a wash of
heat: a tracer had found his gas-tank at last! Bullets were
thudding into the ground; one shrieked past his head as,
stooping over, folded into the smallest possible target, he
galloped awkwardly toward the ditch.

The Brownings still yammered, filling the sky with cupro-
nickeled lead; and while Kinnison was flinging himself full
length into the protecting water and mud, he heard a tremendous crash. One of those Huns had been too intent on
murder; had stayed a few seconds too long; had come a few
meters too close.

The clamor of the guns stopped abruptly.

"We got one! We got one!" a yell of exultation.

"Stay down! Keep low, you boneheads!" roared a voice of authority, quite evidently a sergeant's. "Wanna get your blocks shot off? Take down them guns; we gotta get to hell out of here. Hey, you flyer! Are you O.K., or wounded, or maybe dead?"

Kinnison spat out mud until he could talk. "O.K.!" he shouted, and started to lift an eye above the low bank. He stopped, however, as whistling metal, sheeting in from the north, told him that such action would be decidedly unsafe. "But I ain't leaving this ditch right now—sounds mighty hot out there!"

"You said it, brother. It's hotter than the hinges of hell, from behind that ridge over there. But ooze down that ditch a piece, around the first bend. It's pretty well in the clear there, and besides, you'll find a ledge of rocks running straight across the flat. Cross over there and climb the hill— join us by that dead snag up there. We got to get out of here. That sausage over there must have seen this shindig and they'll blow this whole damn area off the map. Snap it up! And you, you goldbricks, get the lead out of your pants!"

Kinnison followed directions. He found the ledge and emerged, scraping thick and sticky mud from his uniform. He crawled across the little plain. An occasional bullet whined through the air, far above him; but, as the sergeant had said, this bit of terrain was "in the clear." He climbed the hill, approached the gaunt, bare tree-trunk. He heard men moving, and cautiously announced himself.

"Ok., fella," came the sergeant's deep bass. "Yeah, it's us. Shake a leg!"

"That's easy!" Kinnison laughed for the first time that day. "I'm shaking already, like a hula-hula dancer's empennage. What outfit is this, and where are we?"

"B R R O O M!" The earth trembled, the air vibrated. Below and to the north, almost exactly where the machine-guns had been, an awe-inspiring cloud billowed majestically into the air; a cloud composed of smoke, vapor, pulverized earth, chunks of rock, and debris of what had been trees. Nor was it alone.

"Crack! Bang! Tweet! Boom! Wham!" Shells of all calibers, high explosive and gas, came down in droves. The landscape disappeared. The little company of Americans, in complete silence and with one mind, devoted themselves to accumulating distance. Finally, when they had to stop for breath:

"Section B, attached to the 76th Field Artillery," the sergeant answered the question as though it had just been asked. "As to where we are, somewhere between Berlin and Paris is about all I can tell you. We got hell knocked out of us yesterday, and have been running around lost ever since. They shot off a rally signal on top of this here hill, though, and we was just going to shove off when we seen the krauts chasing you."

"Thanks. I'd better rally with you, I guess—find out where we are, and what's the chance of getting back to my own outfit."

"Damn slim, I'd say. Boches are all around us here, thicker than fleas on a dog."

They approached the summit, were challenged, were accepted. They saw a gray-haired man—an old man, for such a location—seated calmly upon a rock, smoking a cigarette. His smartly-tailored uniform, which fitted perfectly his not-so-slender figure, was muddy and tattered. One leg of his breeches was torn half away, revealing a blood-soaked bandage. Although he was very evidently an officer, no insignia were visible. As Kinnison and the gunners approached, a first lieutenant—practically spic-and-span—spoke to the man on the rock.

"First thing to do is to settle the matter of rank," he announced, crisply. "I'm First Lieutenant Randolph, of . . ."

"Rank, eh?" The seated one grinned and spat out the butt of his cigarette. "But then, it was important to me, too, when I was a first lieutenant—about the time that you were born. Slayton, Major-General."

"Oh . . . excuse me, sir . . ."

"Skip it. How many men you got, and what are they?"

"Seven, sir. We brought in a wire from Inf . . ."

"A *wire!* Hellanddamnation, why haven't you got it with you, then? Get it!"

The crestfallen officer disappeared; the general turned to Kinnison and the sergeant.

"Have you got any ammunition, sergeant?"

"Yes, sir. About thirty belts."

"Thank God! We can use it, and you. As for you, Captain, I don't know . . ."

The wire came up. The general seized the instrument and cranked.

"Get me Spearmint . . . Spearmint? Slayton—give me Weatherby . . . This is Slayton . . . yes, but . . . No, but I want . . . Hellanddamnation, Weatherby, shut up and let me talk—don't you know that this wire's apt to be cut any second? We're on top of Hill Fo-wer, Ni-yun, Sev-en—that's right—about two hundred men; maybe three. Composite—somebody, apparently, from half the outfits in France. Too fast and too far—both flanks wide open—cut off . . . Hello! Hello! Hello!" He dropped the instrument and turned to Kinnison. "You want to go back, Captain, and I need a runner—bad. Want to try to get through?"

"Yes, sir."

"First phone you come to, get Spearmint—General Weatherby. Tell him Slayton says that we're cut off, but the Germans aren't in much force nor in good position, and for God's sake to get some air and tanks in here to keep them from consolidating. Just a minute. Sergeant, what's your name?" He studied the burly non-com minutely.

"Wells, sir."

"What would you say ought to be done with the machine-guns?"

"Cover that ravine, there, first. Then set up to enfilade if they try to come up over there. Then, if I could find any more guns, I'd . . ."

"Enough. Second Lieutenant Wells, from now. GHQ will confirm. Take charge of all the guns we have. Report when you have made disposition. Now, Kinnison, listen. I can probably hold out until tonight. The enemy doesn't know yet that we're here, but we are due for some action pretty quick now, and when they locate us—if there aren't too many of their own units here, too—they'll flatten this hill like a table. So tell Weatherby to throw a column in here as soon as it gets dark, and to advance Eight and Sixty, so as to consolidate this whole area. Got it?"

"Yes, sir."

"Got a compass?"

"Yes, sir."

"Pick up a tin hat and get going. A hair north of due west, about a kilometer and a half. Keep cover, because the going will be tough. Then you'll come to a road. It's a mess, but it's ours—or was, at last accounts—so the worst of it will be over. On that road, which goes south-west, about two kilometers further, you'll find a Post—you'll know it by the motor-cycles and such. Phone from there. Luck!"

Bullets began to whine and the general dropped to the ground and crawled toward a coppice, bellowing orders as he went. Kinnison crawled, too, straight west, availing himself of all possible cover, until he encountered a sergeant-major reclining against the south side of a great tree.

"Cigarette, buddy?" that wight demanded.

"Sure. Take the pack. I've got another that'll last me—maybe more. But what the hell goes on here? Who ever heard of a major general getting far enough up front to get shot in the leg, and he talks as though he were figuring on licking the whole German army. Is the old bird nuts, or what?"

"Not so you would notice it. Didn'cha ever hear of 'Hell-andamnation' Slayton? You will, buddy, you will. If Pershing doesn't give him three stars after this, he's crazier than hell. He ain't supposed to be on combat at all—he's from GHQ and can make or break anybody in the AEF. Out here on a look-see trip and couldn't get back. But you got to hand it to him—he's getting things organized in great shape. I came in with him—I'm about all that's left of them that did—just waiting for this breeze to die down, but its getting worse. We'd better duck—over there!"

Bullets whistled and stormed, breaking more twigs and branches from the already shattered, practically denuded trees. The two slid precipitately into the indicated shell-hole, into stinking mud. Wells' guns burst into action.

"Damn! I hated to do this," the sergeant grumbled, "On accounta I just got half dry."

"Wise me up," Kinnison directed. "The more I know about things, the more apt I am to get through."

"This is what is left of two battalions, and a lot of casuals. They made objective, but it turns out the outfits on their right and left couldn't, leaving their flanks right out in the open air. Orders come in by blinker to rectify the line by falling back, but by then it couldn't be done. Under observation."

Kinnison nodded. He knew what a barrage would have done to a force trying to cross such open ground in daylight.

"One man could prob'ly make it, though, if he was careful and kept his eyes wide open," the sergeant-major continued. "But you ain't got no binoculars, have you?"

"No."

"Get a pair easy enough. You saw them boots without any hobnails in 'em, sticking out from under some blankets?"

"Yes. I get you." Kinnison knew that combat officers did not wear hobnails, and usually carried binoculars. "How come so many at once?"

"Just about all the officers that got this far. Conniving, my guess is, behind old Slayton's back. Anyway, a kraut aviator

spots 'em and dives. Our machine-guns got him, but not until
after he heaved a bomb. Dead center. Christ, what a mess!
But there's six-seven good glasses in there. I'd grab one myself, but the general would see it—he can see right through
the lid of a mess-kit. Well, the boys have shut those krauts
up, so I'll hunt the old man up and tell him what I found out.
Damn this mud!"

Kinnison emerged sinuously and snaked his way to a row
of blanket covered forms. He lifted a blanket and gasped:
then vomited up everything, it seemed, that he had eaten
for days. But he *had* to have the binoculars.

He got them.

Then, still retching, white and shaken, he crept westward;
availing himself of every possible item of cover.

For some time, from a point somewhere north of his route,
a machine-gun had been intermittently at work. It was close;
but the very loudness of its noise, confused as it was by
resounding echoes, made it impossible to locate at all exactly
the weapon's position. Kinnison crept forward inchwise; scan-
ning every foot of visible terrain through his powerful glass.
He knew by the sound that it was German. More, since
what he did not know about machine-guns could have been
printed in bill-poster type upon the back of his hand, he
knew that it was a Maxim, Model 1907—a mean, mean gun.
He deduced that it was doing plenty of damage to his fellows
back on the hill, and that they had not been able to do much
of anything about it. And it was beautifully hidden; even he,
close as he must be, couldn't see it. But damn it, there *had*
to be a . . .

Minute after minute, unmoving save for the traverse of
his binoculars, he searched, and finally he found. A tiny
plume—the veriest wisp—of vapor, rising from the surface
of the brook. Steam! Steam from the cooling jacket of that
Maxim 1907! And there was the tube!

Cautiously he moved around until he could trace that tube
to its business end—the carefully-hidden emplacement. There
it was! He couldn't maintain his westward course without
them spotting him; nor could he go around far enough. And
besides . . . and besides that, there would be at least a patrol,
if it hadn't gone up the hill already. And there were
grenades available, right close . . .

He crept up to one of the gruesome objects he had been
avoiding, and when he crept away he half-carried, half-dragged
three grenades in a canvas bag. He wormed his way to a

certain boulder. He straightened up, pulled three pins, swung his arm three times.

Bang! Bam! Pow! The camouflage disappeared; so did the shrubbery for yards around. Kinnison had ducked behind the rock, but he ducked still deeper as a chunk of something, its force pretty well spent, clanged against his steel helmet. Another object thudded beside him—a leg, gray-clad and wearing a heavy field boot!

Kinnison wanted to be sick again, but he had neither the time nor the contents.

And damn! What *lousy* throwing! He had never been any good at baseball, but he supposed that he could hit a thing as big as that gun-pit—but not one of his grenades had gone in. The crew would probably be dead—from concussion, if nothing else—but the gun probably wasn't even hurt. He would have to go over there and cripple it himself.

He went—not exactly boldly—forty-five in hand. The Germans looked dead. One of them sprawled on the parapet, right in his way. He gave the body a shove, watched it roll down the slope. As it rolled, however, it came to life and yelled; and at that yell there occurred a thing at which young Kinnison's hair stood straight up inside his iron helmet. On the gray of the blasted hillside hitherto unseen gray forms moved; moved toward their howling comrade. And Kinnison, blessing for the first time in his life his inept throwing arm, hoped fervently that the Maxim was still in good working order.

A few seconds of inspection showed him that it was. The gun had practically a full belt and there was plenty more. He placed a box—he would have no Number Two to help him here—took hold of the grips, shoved off the safety, and squeezed the trip. The gun roared—what a gorgeous, what a heavenly racket that Maxim made! He traversed until he could see where the bullets were striking: then swung the stream of metal to and fro. One belt and the Germans were completely disorganized; two belts and he could see no signs of life.

He pulled the Maxim's block and threw it away; shot the water-jacket full of holes. That gun was done. Nor had he increased his own hazard. Unless more Germans came very soon, nobody would ever know who had done what, or to whom.

He slithered away; resumed earnestly his westward course: going as fast as—sometimes a trifle faster than—caution would permit. But there were no more alarms. He crossed the dangerously open ground; sulked rapidly through the frightfully shattered wood. He reached the road, strode along it around the first bend, and stopped, appalled. He had heard of such things, but he had never seen one; and mere description has always been and always will be completely inadequate. Now he was walking right into it—the thing he was to see in nightmare for all the rest of his ninety-six years of life.

Actually, there was very little to see. The road ended abruptly. What had been a road, what had been wheatfields and farms, what had been woods, were practically indistinguishable, one from the other; were fantastically and impossibly the same. The entire area had been churned. Worse —it was as though the ground and its every surface object had been run through a gargantuan mill and spewed abroad. Spinters of wood, riven chunks of metal, a few scraps of bloody flesh. Kinnison screamed, then, and ran; ran back and around that blasted acreage. And as he ran, his mind built up pictures; pictures which became only the more vivid because of his frantic efforts to wipe them out.

That road, the night before, had been one of the world's most heavily traveled highways. Motorcycles, trucks, bicycles. Ambulances. Kitchens. Staff-cars and other automobiles. Guns; from seventy-fives up to the big boys, whose tremendous weight drove their wide caterpillar treads inches deep into solid ground. Horses. Mules. And people—*especially* people—like himself. Solid columns of men, marching as fast as they could step—there weren't trucks enough to haul them all. That road had been crowded—jammed. Like State and Madison at noon, only more so. Over-jammed with all the personnel, all the instrumentation and incidentalia, all the weaponry, of war.

And upon that teeming, seething highway there had descended a rain of steel-encased high explosive. Possibly some gas, but probably not. The German High Command had given orders to pulverize that particular area at that particular time; and hundreds, or perhaps thousands, of German guns, in a micrometrically-synchronized symphony of firepower, had pulverized it. Just that. Literally. Precisely. No road remained; no farm, no field, no building, no tree or shrub. The bits of flesh might have come from horse or man or mule; few indeed were the scraps of metal which retained enough of their original shape to show what they had once been.

Kinnison ran—or staggered—around that obscene blot and struggled back to the road. It was shell-pocked, but passable.

He hoped that the shell-holes would decrease in number as he went along, but they did not. The enemy had put this whole road out of service. And that farm, the P.C., ought to be around the next bend.

It was, but it was no longer a Post of Command. Either by directed fire—star-shell illumination—or by uncannily accurate chart-work, they had put some heavy shell exactly where they would do the most damage. The buildings were gone; the cellar in which the P.C. had been was now a gaping crater. Parts of motorcycles and of staff cars littered the ground. Stark tree trunks—all bare of leaves, some riven of all except the largest branches, a few stripped even of bark—stood gauntly. In a crotch of one, Kinnison saw with rising horror, hung the limp and shattered naked torso of a man; blown completely out of his clothes.

Shells were—had been, right along—coming over occasionally. Big ones, but high; headed for targets well to the west. Nothing close enough to worry about. Two ambulances, a couple of hundred meters apart, were coming; working their way along the road, between the holes. The first one slowed . . . stopped.

"Seen anybody—Look out! Duck!"

Kinnison had already heard that unmistakable, unforgettable screech, was already diving headlong into the nearest hole. There was a crash as though the world were falling apart. Something smote him; seemed to drive him bodily into the ground. His light went out. When he recovered consciousness he was lying upon a stretcher; two men were bending over him.

"What hit me?" he gasped. "Am I . . .?" He stopped. He was afraid to ask: afraid even to try to move, lest he should find that he didn't have any arms or legs.

"A wheel, and maybe some of the axle, of the other ambulance, is all," one of the men assured him. "Nothing much; you're practically as good as ever. Shoulder and arm bunged up a little and something—maybe shrapnel, though—poked you in the guts. But we've got you all fixed up, so take it easy and . . ."

"What we want to know is," his partner interrupted, "Is there anybody else alive up here?"

"Uh-huh," Kinnison shook his head.

"O.K. Just wanted to be sure. Lots of business back there, and it won't do any harm to have a doctor look at you."

"Get me to a 'phone, as fast as you can," Kinnison directed, in a voice which he thought was strong and full of authority, but which in fact was neither. "I've got an important message for General Weatherby, at Spearmint."

"Better tell us what it is, hadn't you?" The ambulance was now jolting along what had been the road. "They've got phones at the hospital where we're going, but you might faint or something before we get there."

Kinnison told, but fought to retain what consciousness he had. Throughout that long, rough ride he fought. He won. He himself spoke to General Weatherby—the doctors, knowing him to be a Captain of Aviation and realizing that his message should go direct, helped him telephone. He himself received the General's sizzlingly sulphurous assurance that relief would be sent and that that quadruply-qualified line would be rectified that night.

Then someone jabbed him with a needle and he lapsed into a dizzy, fuzzy coma, from which he did not emerge completely for weeks. He had lucid intervals at times, but he did not, at the time or ever, know surely what was real and what was fantasy.

There were doctors, doctors, doctors; operations, operations, operations. There were hospital tents, into which quiet men were carried; from which still quieter men were removed. There was a larger hospital, built of wood. There was a machine that buzzed and white-clad men who studied films and papers. There were scraps of conversation.

"Belly wounds are bad," Kinnison thought—he was never sure—that he heard one of them say. "And such contusions and multiple and compound fractures as those don't help a bit. Prognosis unfavorable—distinctly so—but we'll soon see what we can do. Interesting case . . . fascinating. What would you do, Doctor, if you were doing it?"

"I'd let it alone!" A younger, stronger voice declared, fervently. "Multiple perforations, infection, extravasation, oedema—uh-uh! I am watching, Doctor, and learning!"

Another interlude, and another. Another. And others. Until finally, orders were given which Kinnison did not hear at all.

"Adrenalin! Massage! Massage hell out of him!"

Kinnison again came to—partially to, rather—anguished in every fiber of his being. Somebody was sticking barbed arrows into every square inch of his skin; somebody else was pounding and mauling him all over, taking particular pains to pummel and to wrench at all the places where he hurt the worst. He yelled at the top of his voice; yelled and swore bitterly: "QUIT IT!" being the expurgated gist of his luridly profane protests. He did not make nearly as much noise as he supposed, but he made enough.

"Thank God!" Kinnison heard a lighter, softer voice. Surprised, he stopped swearing and tried to stare. He couldn't see very well, either, but he was pretty sure that there was a middle-aged woman there. There was, and her eyes were not dry. "He is going to live, after all!"

As the days passed, he began really to sleep, naturally and deeply.

He grew hungrier and hungrier, and they would not give him enough to eat. He was by turns sullen, angry, and morose.

In short, he was convalescent.

For Captain Ralph K. Kinnison, THE WAR was over.

CHAPTER 5

1941

CHUBBY, BROWNETTE EUNICE KINNISON SAT IN A ROCKER, reading the Sunday papers and listening to her radio. Her husband Ralph lay sprawled upon the davenport, smoking a cigarette and reading the current issue of EXTRAORDINARY STORIES against an unheard background of music. Mentally, he was far from Tellus, flitting in his super-dreadnaught through parsec after parsec of vacuous space.

The music broke off without warning and there blared out an announcement which yanked Ralph Kinnison back to Earth with a violence almost physical. He jumped up, jammed his hands into his pockets.

"Pearl Harbor!" he blurted. "How in . . . How could they have let them get *that* far?"

"But *Frank!*" the woman gasped. She had not worried much about her husband; but Frank, her son . . . "He'll have to go . . ." Her voice died away.

"Not a chance in the world." Kinnison did not speak to soothe, but as though from sure knowledge. "Designing Engineer for Lockwood? He'll want to, all right, but anyone who was ever even exposed to a course in aeronautical engineering will sit this war out."

"But they say it can't last very long. It can't, can it?"

"I'll say it can. Loose talk. Five years minimum is my guess—not that my guess is any better than anybody else's."

He prowled around the room. His somber expression did not lighten.

"I knew it," the woman said at length. "You, too—even after the last one . . . You haven't said anything, so I thought, perhaps . . ."

"I know I didn't. There was always the chance that we wouldn't get drawn into it. If you say so, though, I'll stay home."

"Am I apt to? I let you go when you were really in danger . . ."

"What do you mean by *that* crack?" he interrupted.

"Regulations. One year too old—Thank Heaven!"

"So what? They'll need technical experts, bad. They'll make exceptions."

"Possibly. Desk jobs. Desk officers don't get killed in action —or even wounded. Why, perhaps, with the children all grown up and married, we won't even have to be separated."

"Another angle—financial."

"Pooh! Who cares about that? Besides, for a man out of a job . . ."

"From you, I'll let that one pass. Thanks, Eunie—you're an ace. I'll shoot 'em a wire."

The telegram was sent. The Kinnisons waited. And waited. Until, about the middle of January, beautifully-phrased and beautifully-mimeographed letters began to arrive.

"The War Department recognizes the value of your previous military experience and appreciates your willingness once again to take up arms in defense of the country . . . Veteran Officer's Questionnaire . . . please fill out completely . . . Form 191A . . . Form 170 in duplicate . . . Form 315 . . . Impossible to forecast the extent to which the War Department may ultimately utilize the services which you and thousands of others have so generously offered . . . Form . . . Form . . . Not to be construed as meaning that you have been permanently rejected . . . Form . . . Advise you that while at the present time the War Department is unable to use you . . ."

"Wouldn't that fry you to a crisp?" Kinnison demanded. "What in hell have they got in their heads—sawdust? They think that because I'm fifty one years old I've got one foot in the grave—I'll bet four dollars that I'm in better shape than that cursed Major General and his whole damned staff!"

"I don't doubt it, dear." Eunice's smile was, however, mostly of relief. "But here's an ad—it's been running for a week."

"CHEMICAL ENGINEERS . . . shell loading plant . . . within seventy-five miles of Townville . . . over five years experience . . . organic chemistry . . . technology . . . explosives . . ."

"They want *you*," Eunice declared, soberly.

"Well, I'm a Ph.D. in Organic. I've had more than five years experience in both organic chemistry and technology. If I don't know something about explosives I did a smart job of fooling Dean Montrose, back at Gosh Whatta University. I'll write 'em a letter."

He wrote. He filled out a form. The telephone rang.

"Kinnison speaking . . . yes . . . Dr. Sumner? Oh, yes, Chief Chemist . . . That's it—one year over age, so I thought . . . Oh, that's a minor matter. We won't starve. If you can't pay a hundred and fifty I'll come for a hundred, or seventy five, or fifty . . . That's all right, too. I'm well enough known in my own field so that a title of Junior Chemical Engineer wouldn't hurt me a bit . . . O.K., I'll see you about one o'clock . . . Stoner and Black, Inc., Operators, Entwhistle Ordnance Plant, Entwhistle, Missikota . . . What! Well, maybe I could, at that . . . Goodbye."

He turned to his wife. "You know what? They want me to come down right away and go to work. Hot Dog! *Am* I glad that I told that louse Hendricks exactly where he could stick that job of mine!"

"He must have known that you wouldn't sign a straight-salary contract after getting a share of the profits so long. Maybe he believed what you always say just before or just after kicking somebody's teeth down their throats; that you're so meek and mild—a regular Milquetoast. Do you really think that they'll want you back, after the war?" It was clear that Eunice was somewhat concerned concerning Kinnison's joblessness; but Kinnison was not.

"Probably. That's the gossip. And I'll come back—when hell freezes over." His square jaw tightened. "I've heard of outfits stupid enough to let their technical brains go because they could sell—for a while—anything they produced, but I didn't know that I was working for one. Maybe I'm not exactly a Timid Soul, but you'll have to admit that I never kicked anybody's teeth out unless they tried to kick mine out first."

*   *   *

Entwhistle Ordnance Plant covered twenty-odd square miles of more or less level land. Ninety-nine percent of its area was "Inside the fence." Most of the buildings within that restricted area, while in reality enormous, were dwarfed by the vast spaces separating them; for safety-distances are not small when TNT and tetryl by the ton are involved. Those structures were built of concrete, steel, glass, transite, and tile.

"Outside the Fence" was different. This was the Administration Area. Its buildings were tremendous wooden barracks, relatively close together, packed with the executive, clerical, and professional personnel appropriate to an organization employing over twenty thousand men and women.

Well inside the fence, but a safety-distance short of the One Line—Loading Line Number One—was a long, low building, quite inadequately named the Chemical Laboratory. "Inadequately" in that the Chief Chemist, a highly capable—if more than a little cantankerous—Explosives Engineer, had already gathered into his Chemical Section most of Development, most of Engineering, and all of Physics, Weights and Measures, and Weather.

One room of the Chemical Laboratory—in the corner most distant from Administration—was separated from the rest of the building by a sixteen-inch wall of concrete and steel extending from foundation to roof without a door, window, or other opening. This was the laboratory of the Chemical Engineers, the boys who played with explosives high and low; any explosion occurring therein could not affect the Chemical Laboratory proper or its personnel.

Entwhistle's main roads were paved; but in February of 1942, such minor items as sidewalks existed only on the blueprints. Entwhistle's soil contained much clay, and at that time the mud was approximately six inches deep. Hence, since there were neither inside doors nor sidewalks, it was only natural that the technologists did not visit at all frequently the polished-tile cleanliness of the Laboratory. It was also natural enough for the far larger group to refer to the segregated ones as exiles and outcasts; and that some witty chemist applied to that isolated place the name "Siberia."

The name stuck. More, the Engineers seized it and acclaimed it. They were Siberians, and proud of it, and Siberians they remained; long after Entwhistle's mud turned into dust. And within the year the Siberians were to become well and favorably known in every ordnance plant in the country, to many high executives who had no idea of how the name originated.

Kinnison became a Siberian as enthusiastically as the youngest man there. The term "youngest" is used in its exact sense, for not one of them was a recent graduate. Each had had at least five years of responsible experience, and "Cappy" Sumner kept on building. He hired extravagantly and fired ruthlessly—to the minds of some, senselessly. But he knew what he was doing. He knew explosives, and he knew men. He was not liked, but he was respected. His building was good.

Being one of the only two "old" men there—and the other did not stay long—Kinnison, as a Junior Chemical Engineer, was not at first accepted without reserve. Apparently he did not notice that fact, but went quietly about his assigned duties. He was meticulously careful with, but very evidently not in any fear of, the materials with which he worked. He pelleted and tested tracer, igniter, and incendiary compositions; he took his turn at burning out rejects. Whenever asked, he went out on the lines with any one of them.

His experimental tetryls always "miked" to size, his TNT melt-pours—introductory to loading forty-millimeter on the Three Line—came out solid, free from checks and cavitations. It became evident to those young but keen minds that he, alone of them all, was on familiar ground. They began to discuss their problems with him. Out of his years of technological experience, and by bringing everyone present into the discussion, he either helped them directly or helped them to help themselves. His stature grew.

Black-haired, black-eyed "Tug" Tugwell, two hundred pounds of ex-football-player in charge of tracer on the Seven Line, called him "Uncle" Ralph, and the habit spread. And in a couple of weeks—at about the same time that "Injun" Abernathy was slightly injured by being blown through a door by a minor explosion of his igniter on the Eight line—he was promoted to full Chemical Engineer; a promotion which went unnoticed, since it involved only changes in title and salary.

Three weeks later, however, he was made Senior Chemical Engineer, in charge of Melt-Pour. At this there was a celebration, led by "Blondie" Wanacek, a sulphuric-acid expert handling tetryl on the Two. Kinnison searched minutely for signs of jealousy or antagonism, but could find none. He went blithely to work on the Six line, where they wanted to start pouring twenty-pound fragmentation bombs, ably assisted by Tug and by two new men. One of these was "Doc" or "Bart" Barton, who, the grapevine said, had been hired by Cappy to be his Assistant. His motto, like that of Rikki-Tikki-Tavi, was to run and find out, and he did so with glee and abandon. He was a good egg. So was the other newcomer, "Charley" Charlevoix, a prematurely gray paint-and-lacquer expert who had also made the Siberian grade.

A few months later, Sumner called Kinnison into the office. The latter went, wondering what the old hard-shell was going to cry about now; for to be called into that office meant only one thing—censure.

"Kinnison, I like your work," the Chief Chemist began, gruffly, and Kinnison's mouth almost dropped open. "Anybody who ever got a Ph.D. under Montrose would have to know explosives, and the F.B.I. report on you showed that you had brains, ability, and guts. But none of that explains how you can get along so well with those damned Siberians. I want to make you Assistant Chief and put you in charge of Siberia. Formally, I mean—actually, you have been for months."

"Why, no . . . I didn't . . . Besides, how about Barton? He's too good a man to kick in the teeth that way."

"Admitted." This *did* surprise Kinnison. He had never thought that the irascible and tempestuous Chief would ever confess to a mistake. This was a Cappy he had never known. "I discussed it with him yesterday. He's a damned good man —but it's decidedly questionable whether he has got whatever it is that made Tugwell, Wanacek and Charlevoix work straight through for seventy two hours, napping now and then on benches and grabbing coffee and sandwiches when they could, until they got that frag bomb straightened out."

Sumner did not mention the fact that Kinnison had worked straight through, too. That was taken for granted.

"Well, I don't know." Kinnison's head was spinning. "I'd like to check with Barton first. O.K.?"

"I expected that. O.K."

Kinnison found Barton and led him out behind the testing shed.

"Bart, Cappy tells me that he figures on kicking you in the face by making me Assistant and that you O.K.'d it. One word and I'll tell the old buzzard just where to stick the job and exactly where to go to do it."

"Reaction, perfect. Yield, one hundred percent." Barton stuck out his hand. "Otherwise, I would tell him all that myself and more. As it is, Uncle Ralph, smooth out the ruffled plumage. They'd go to hell for you, wading in standing straight up—they might do the same with me in the driver's seat, and they might not. Why take a chance? You're IT. Some things about the deal I don't like, of course—but at that, it makes me about the only man working for Stoner and Black who can get a release any time a good permanent job breaks. I'll stick until then. O.K.?" It was unnecessary for Barton to add that as long as he was there he would really work.

"I'll say it's O.K.!" and Kinnison reported to Sumner.

"All right, Chief, I'll try it—if you can square it with the Siberians."

"That will not be too difficult."

Nor was it. The Siberians' reaction brought a lump to Kinnison's throat.

"Ralph the First, Czar of Siberia!" they yelled. "Long live the Czar! Kowtow, serfs and vassals, to Czar Ralph the First!"

Kinnison was still glowing when he got home that night, to the Government Housing Project and to the three-room "mansionette" in which he and Eunice lived. He would never forget the events of that day.

"What a gang! *What* a gang! But listen, ace—they work under their own power—you couldn't *keep* those kids from working. Why should I get the credit for what they do?"

"I haven't the foggiest." Eunice wrinkled her forehead —and her nose—but the corners of her mouth quirked up. "Are you quite sure that you haven't had *anything* to do with it? But supper is ready—let's eat."

More months passed. Work went on. Absorbing work, and highly varied; the details of which are of no importance here. Paul Jones, a big, hard, top-drawer chicle technologist, set up the Four line to pour demolition blocks. Frederick Hinton came in, qualified as a Siberian, and went to work on Anti-Personnel mines.

Kinnison was promoted again: to Chief Chemist. He and Sumner had never been friendly; he made no effort to find out why Cappy had quit, or had been terminated, whichever it was. This promotion made no difference. Barton, now Assistant, ran the whole Chemical Section save for one unit —Siberia—and did a superlative job. The Chief Chemist's secretary worked for Barton, not for Kinnison. Kinnison was the Czar of Siberia.

The Anti-Personnel mines had been giving trouble. Too many men were being killed by prematures, and nobody could find out why. The problem was handed to Siberia. Hinton tackled it, missed, and called for help. The Siberians rallied 'round. Kinnison loaded and tested mines. So did Paul and Tug and Blondie. Kinnison was testing, out in the Firing Area, when he was called to Administration to attend a Staff Meeting. Hinton relieved him. He had not reached the gate, however, when a guard car flagged him down.

"Sorry, sir, but there has been an accident at Pit Five and you are needed out there."

"Accident! Fred Hinton!" Is he . . . ?"

"I'm afraid so, sir."

It is a harrowing thing to have to help gather up what fragments can be found of one of your best friends. Kinnison was white and sick as he got back to the firing station, just in time to hear the Chief Safety Officer say:

"Must have been carelessness—rank carelessness. I warned this man Hinton myself, on one occasion."

"Carelessness, hell!" Kinnison blazed. "You had the guts to warn *me* once, too, and I've forgotten more about safety in explosives than you ever will know. Fred Hinton was *not* careless—if I hadn't been called in, that would have been me."

"What is it, then?"

"I don't know—yet. I tell you now, though, Major Moulton, that I *will* know, and the minute I find out I'll talk to you again."

He went back to Siberia, where he found Tug and Paul, faces still tear-streaked, staring at something that looked like a small piece of wire.

"This is it, Uncle Ralph," Tug said, brokenly. "Don't see how it could be, but it is."

"What is what?" Kinnison demanded.

"Firing pin. Brittle. When you pull the safety, the force of the spring must break it off at this constricted section here."

"But damn it, Tug, it doesn't make sense. It's tension . . . but wait—there'd be some horizontal component, at that. But they'd have to be brittle as glass."

"I know it. It doesn't seem to make much sense. But we were there, you know—and I assembled every one of those God damned mines myself. Nothing else could possibly have made that mine go off just when it did."

"O.K., Tug. We'll test 'em. Call Bart in—he can have the scale-lab boys rig us up a gadget by the time we can get some more of those pins in off the line."

They tested a hundred, under the normal tension of the spring, and three of them broke. They tested another hundred. Five broke. They stared at each other.

"That's it." Kinnison declared. "But this will stink to high Heaven—have Inspection break out a new lot and we'll test a thousand."

Of that thousand pins, thirty two broke.

"Bart, will you dictate a one-page preliminary report to Vera and rush it over to Building One as fast as you can? I'll go over and tell Moulton a few things."

Major Moulton was, as usual, "in conference," but Kinnison was in no mood to wait.

"Tell him," he instructed the Major's private secretary, who had barred his way, "that either he will talk to me right now or I will call District Safety over his head. I'll give him sixty seconds to decide which."

Moulton decided to see him. "I'm very busy, Doctor Kinnison, but . . ."

"I don't give a swivel-eyed tinker's damn how busy you are. I told you that the minute I found out what was the matter with the M2 mine I'd talk to you again. Here I am. Brittle firing pins. Three and two-tenths percent defective. So I'm . . ."

"Very irregular, Doctor. The matter will have to go through channels . . ."

"Not this one. The formal report is going through channels, but as I started to tell you, this is an emergency report to you as Chief of Safety. Since the defect is not covered by specs, neither Process nor Ordnance can reject except by test, and whoever does the testing will very probably be killed. Therefore, as every employee of Stoner and Black is not only authorized but positively instructed to do upon discovering an unsafe condition, I am reporting it direct to Safety. Since my whiskers are a trifle longer than an operator's, I am reporting it direct to the Head of the Safety Division; and I am telling you that if you don't do something about it damned quick—stop production and slap a HOLD order on all the M2AP's you can reach—I'll call District and make you personally responsible for every premature that occurs from now on."

Since any safety man, anywhere, would much rather stop a process than authorize one, and since this particular safety man loved to throw his weight around, Kinnison was surprised that Moulton did not act instantly. The fact that he did not so act should have, but did not, give the naive Kinnison much information as to conditions existing Outside the Fence.

"But they need those mines very badly; they are an item of very heavy production. If we stop them . . . how long? Have you any suggestions?"

"Yes. Call District and have them rush through a change of spec—include heat-treat and a modified Charpy test. In the meantime, we can get back into full production tomorrow if you have District slap a hundred-per-cent inspection onto those pins."

"Excellent! We can do that—very fine work, Doctor! Miss Morgan, get District at once!"

This, too, should have warned Kinnison, but it did not. He went back to the Laboratory.

Tempus fugited.

Orders came to get ready to load M67 H.E., A.T. (105 m/m High Explosive, Armor Tearing) shell on the Nine, and the Siberians went joyously to work upon the new load. The explosive was to be a mixture of TNT and a polysyllabic compound, everything about which was highly confidential and restricted.

"But what the hell's so hush-hush about *that* stuff?" demanded Blondie, who, with five or six others, was crowding around the Czar's desk. Unlike the days of Cappy Sumner, the private office of the Chief Chemist was now as much Siberia as Siberia itself. "The Germans developed it originally, didn't they?"

"Yes, and the Italians used it against the Ethiopians— which was why their bombs were so effective. But it says 'hush-hush,' so that's the way it will be. And if you talk in your sleep, Blondie, tell Betty not to listen."

The Siberians worked. The M67 was put into production. It was such a success that orders for it came in faster than they could be filled. Production was speeded up. Small cavitations began to appear. Nothing serious, since they passed Inspection. Nevertheless, Kinnison protested, in a formal report, receipt of which was formally acknowledged.

General Somebody-or-other, Entwhistle's Commanding Officer, whom none of the Siberians had ever met, was transferred to more active duty, and a colonel—Snodgrass or some such name—took his place. Ordnance got a new Chief Inspector.

An M67, Entwhistle loaded, prematured in a gun-barrel, killing twenty seven men. Kinnison protested again, verbally this time, at a staff meeting. He was assured—verbally— that a formal and thorough investigation was being made. Later he was informed—verbally and without witnesses— that the investigation had been completed and that the loading was not at fault. A new Commanding Officer—Lieutenant-Colonel Franklin—appeared.

The Siberians, too busy to do more than glance at newspapers, paid very little attention to a glider-crash in which several notables were killed. They heard that an investigation was being made, but even the Czar did not know until later that Washington had for once acted fast in correcting a bad situation; that Inspection, which had been under Production, was summarily divorced therefrom. And gossip spread abroad that Stillman, then Head of the Inspection Division, was not a big enough man for the job. Thus it was an entirely unsuspecting Kinnison who was called into the innermost private office of Thomas Keller, the Superintendent of Production.

"Kinnison, how in hell do you handle those Siberians? I never saw anything like them before in my life."

"No, and you never will again. Nothing on Earth except a war could get them together or hold them together. I don't 'handle' them—they can't be 'handled.' I give them a job to do and let them do it. I back them up. That's all."

"Umngpf." Keller grunted. "That's a hell of a formula —if I want anything done right I've got to do it myself. But whatever your system is, it works. But what I wanted to talk to you about is, how'd you like to be Head of the Inspection Divison, which would be enlarged to include your present Chemical Section?"

"Huh?" Kinnison demanded, dumbfounded.

"At a salary well up on the confidential scale." Keller wrote a figure upon a piece of paper, showed it to his visitor, then burned it in an ash-tray.

Kinnison whistled. "I'd like it—for more reasons than that. But I didn't know that you—or have you already checked with the General and Mr. Black?"

"Naturally," came the smooth reply. "In fact, I suggested it to them and have their approval. Perhaps you are curious to know why?"

"I certainly am."

"For two reasons. First, because you have developed a crew of technical experts that is the envy of every technical man in the country. Second, you and your Siberians have done every job I ever asked you to, and done it fast. As a Division Head, you will no longer be under me, but I am right, I think, in assuming that you will work with me just as efficiently as you do now?"

"I can't think of any reason why I wouldn't." This reply was made in all honesty; but later, when he came to understand what Keller had meant, how bitterly Kinnison was to regret its making!

He moved into Stillman's office, and found there what he thought was ample reason for his predecessor's failure to make good. To his way of thinking it was tremendously overstaffed, particularly with Assistant Chief Inspectors. Delegation of authority, so widely preached throughout Entwhistle Ordnance Plant, had not been given even lip service here. Stillman had not made a habit of visiting the lines; nor did the Chief Line Inspectors, the boys who really knew what was going on, ever visit him. They reported to the Assistants, who reported to Stillman, who handed down his Jovian pronouncements.

Kinnison set out, deliberately this time, to mold his key Chief Line Inspectors into just such a group as the Siberians already were. He released the Assistants to more productive work; retaining of Stillman's office staff only a few clerks and his private secretary, one Celeste de St. Aubin, a dynamic, vivacious—at times explosive—brunette. He gave the boys on the Lines full authority; the few who could not handle the load he replaced with men who could. At first the Chief Line Inspectors simply could not believe; but after the affair of the forty millimeter, in which Kinnison rammed the decision of his subordinate past Keller, past the General, past Stoner and Black, and clear up to the Commanding Officer before he made it stick, they were his to a man.

Others of his Section Heads, however, remained aloof. Pettler, whose Technical Section was now part of Inspection, and Wilson, of Gages, were two of those who talked largely and glowingly, but acted obstructively if they acted at all. As weeks went on, Kinnison became wiser and wiser, but made no sign. One day, during a lull, his secretary hung out the "In Conference" sign and went into Kinnison's private office.

"There isn't a reference to any such Investigation anywhere in Central Files." She paused, as if to add something, then turned to leave.

"As you were, Celeste. Sit down. I expected that. Suppressed—if made at all. You're a smart girl, Celeste, and you know the ropes. You know that you can talk to me, don't you?"

"Yes, but this is . . . well, the word is going around that they are going to break you, just as they have broken every other good man on the Reservation."

"I expected that, too." The words were quiet enough, but the man's jaw tightened. "Also, I know how they are going to do it."

"How?"

"This speed-up on the Nine. They know that I won't stand still for the kind of casts that Keller's new procedure, which

goes into effect tonight, is going to produce . . . and this new
C.O. probably will."

Silence fell, broken by the secretary.

"General Sanford, our first C.O., was a soldier, and a
good one," she declared finally. "So was Colonel Snodgrass.
Lieutenant Colonel Franklin wasn't; but he was too much
of a man to do the dir . . ."

"Dirty work," dryly. "Exactly. Go on."

"And Stoner, the New York half—ninety five percent,
really—of Stoner and Black, Inc., is a Big Time Operator. So
we get this damned nincompoop of a major, who doesn't know
a f-u-s-e from a f-u-z-e, direct from a Wall Street desk."

"So what?" One must have heard Ralph Kinnison say
those two words to realize how much meaning they can be
made to carry.

"So what!" the girl blazed, wringing her hands. "Ever since
you have been over here I have been expecting you to blow
up—to smash something—in spite of the dozens of times
you have told me 'a fighter can not slug effectively, Celeste,
until he gets both feet firmly planted.' When—*when*—are you
going to get your feet planted?"

"Never, I'm afraid," he said glumly, and she stared. "So
I'll have to start slugging with at least one foot in the air."

That startled her. "Explain, please?"

"I wanted *proof*. Stuff that I could take to the District
—that I could use to tack some hides out flat on a barn door
with. Do I get it? I do not. Not a shred. Neither can you.
What chance do you think there is of ever getting any real
proof?"

"Very little," Celeste admitted. "But you can at least
smash Pettler, Wilson, and that crowd. *How* I hate those slimy
snakes! I wish that you could smash Tom Keller, the poisonous moron!"

"Not so much moron—although he acts like one at times
—as an ignorant puppet with a head swelled three sizes too
big for his hat. But you can quit yapping about slugging—
fireworks are due to start at two o'clock tomorrow afternoon,
when Drake is going to reject tonight's run of shell."

"Really? But I don't see how either Pettler or Wilson come
in."

"They don't. A fight with those small fry—even smashing
them—wouldn't make enough noise. Keller."

"Keller!" Celeste squealed. "But you'll . . ."

"I know I'll get fired. So what? By tackling him I can
raise enough hell so that the Big Shots will have to cut out

at least some of the rough stuff. You'll probably get fired too, you know—you've been too close to me for your own good."

"Not me." She shook her head vigorously. "The minute they terminate you, I quit. Poof! Who cares? Besides, I can get a better job in Townville."

"Without leaving the Project. That's what I figured. It's the boys I'm worried about. I've been getting them ready for this for weeks."

"But they will quit, too. Your Siberians—your Inspectors—of a surety they will quit, every one!"

"They won't release them; and what Stoner and Black will do to them, even after the war, if they quit without releases, shouldn't be done to a dog. They won't quit, either—at least if they don't try to push them around too much. Keller's mouth is watering to get hold of Siberia, but he'll never make it, nor any one of his stooges . . . I'd better dictate a memorandum to Black on that now, while I'm calm and collected; telling him what he'll have to do to keep my boys from tearing Entwhistle apart."

"But do you think he will pay any attention to it?"

"I'll say he will!" Kinnison snorted. "Don't kid yourself about Black, Celeste. He's a smart man, and before this is done he'll know that he'll have to keep his nose clean."

"But you—how can you do it?" Celeste marveled. "Me, I would urge them on. Few would have the patriotism . . ."

"Patriotism, hell! If that were all, I would have stirred up a revolution long ago. It's for the boys, in years to come. They've got to keep *their* noses clean, too. Get your notebook, please, and take this down. Rough draft—I'm going to polish it up until it has teeth and claws in every line."

And that evening, after supper, he informed Eunice of all the new developments.

"Is it still O.K. with you," he concluded, "for me to get myself fired off of this high-salaried job of mine?"

"Certainly. Being you, how can you do anything else? Oh, how I wish I could wring their necks!" That conversation went on and on, but additional details are not necessary here.

Shortly after two o'clock of the following afternoon, Celeste took a call; and listened shamelessly.

"Kinnison speaking."

"Tug, Uncle Ralph. The casts sectioned just like we thought they would. Dead ringers for Plate D. So Drake hung a red ticket on every tray. Piddy was right there, waiting, and started to raise hell. So I chipped in, and he beat it so fast that I looked to see his coat-tail catch fire. Drake didn't quite like to call you, so I did. If Piddy keeps on going at the rate he left here, he'll be in Keller's office in nothing flat."

"O.K., Tug. Tell Drake that the shell he rejected are going to stay rejected, and to come in right now with his report. Would you like to come along?"

"Would I!" Tugwell hung up and:

"But do you want *him* here, Doc?" Celeste asked, anxiously, without considering whether or not her boss would approve of her eavesdropping.

"I certainly do. If I can keep Tug from blowing his top, the rest of the boys will stay in line."

A few minutes later Tugwell strode in, bringing with him Drake, the Chief Line Inspector of the Nine Line. Shortly thereafter the office door was wrenched open. Keller had come to Kinnison, accompanied by the Superintendent whom the Siberians referred to, somewhat contemptuously, as "Piddy."

"Damn your soul, Kinnison, come out here—I want to talk to you!" Keller roared, and doors snapped open up and down the long corridor.

"Shut up, you God damned louse!" This from Tugwell, who, black eyes almost emitting sparks, was striding purposefully forward. "I'll sock you so damned hard that . . ."

"Pipe down, Tug, I'll handle this." Kinnison's voice was not loud, but it had then a peculiarly carrying and immensely authoritative quality. "Verbally or physically; however he wants to have it."

He turned to Keller, who had jumped backward into the hall to avoid the young Siberian.

"As for you, Keller, if you had the brains that God gave bastard geese in Ireland, you would have had this conference in private. Since you started it in public, however, I'll finish it in public. How you came to pick *me* for a yes-man I'll never know—just one more measure of your stupidity, I suppose."

"Those shell are perfect!" Keller shouted. "Tell Drake here to pass them, right now. If you don't, by God I'll . . ."

"Shut up!" Kinnison's voice cut. "I'll do the talking—you listen. The spec says quote shall be free from objectionable cavitation unquote. The Line Inspectors, who know their stuff, say that those cavitations are objectionable. So do the Chemical Engineers. Therefore, as far as I am concerned, they are objectionable. Those shell are rejected, and they will *stay* rejected."

"That's what *you* think," Keller raged. "But there'll be a

new Head of Inspection, who will pass them, tomorrow morning!"

"In that you may be half right. When you get done licking Black's boots, tell him that I am in my office."

Kinnison re-entered his suite. Keller, swearing, strode away with Piddy. Doors clicked shut.

"I *am* going to quit, Uncle Ralph, law or no law!" Tugwell stormed. "They'll run that bunch of crap through, and then . . ."

"Will you promise not to quit until they do?" Kinnison asked, quietly.

"Huh?" "What?" Tugwell's eyes—and Celeste's—were pools of astonishment. Celeste, being on the inside, understood first.

"Oh—to keep his nose clean—I see!" she exclaimed.

"Exactly. Those shell will not be accepted, nor any like them. On the surface, we got licked. I will get fired. You will find, however, that we won this particular battle. And if you boys stay here and hang together and keep on slugging you can win a lot more."

"Maybe, if we raise enough hell, we can make them fire us, too?" Drake suggested.

"I doubt it. But unless I'm wrong, you can just about write your own ticket from now on, if you play it straight." Kinnison grinned to himself, at something which the young people could not see.

"You told me what Stoner and Black would do to us," Tugwell said, intensely. "What I'm afraid of is that they'll do it to you."

"They can't. Not a chance in the world," Kinnison assured him. "You fellows are young—not established. But I'm well-enough known in my own field so that if they tried to black-ball me they'd just get themselves laughed at, and they know it. So beat it back to the Nine, you kids, and hang red tickets on everything that doesn't cross-section up to standard. Tell the gang goodbye for me—I'll keep you posted."

In less than an hour Kinnison was called into the Office of the President. He was completely at ease; Black was not.

"It has been decided to . . . uh . . . ask for your resignation," the President announced at last.

"Save your breath," Kinnison advised. "I came down here to do a job, and the only way you can keep me from doing that job is to fire me."

"That was not . . . uh . . . entirely unexpected. A difficulty arose, however, in deciding what reason to put on your termination papers."

"I can well believe that. You can put down anything you

like," Kinnison shrugged, "with one exception. Any implication of incompetence and you'll have to prove it in court."

"Incompatibility, say?"

"O.K."

"Miss Briggs—'Incompatibility with the highest echelon of Stoner and Black, Inc.,' please. You may as well wait, Dr. Kinnison; it will take only a moment."

"Fine. I've got a couple of things to say. First, I know as well as you do that you're between Scylla and Charybdis—damned if you do and damned if you don't."

"Certainly not! Ridiculous!" Black blustered, but his eyes wavered. "Where did you get such a preposterous idea? What do you mean?"

"If you ram those sub-standard H.E.A.T. shell through, you are going to have some more prematures. Not many—the stuff is actually almost good enough—one in ten thousand, say: perhaps one in fifty thousand. But you know damned well that you can't afford *any*. What my Siberians and Inspectors know about you and Keller and Piddy and the Nine Line would be enough; but to cap the climax that brainless jackal of yours let the cat completely out of the bag this afternoon, and everybody in Building One was listening. One more premature would blow Entwhistle wide open—would start something that not all the politicians in Washington could stop. On the other hand, if you scrap those lots and go back to pouring good loads, your Mr. Stoner, of New York and Washington, will be very unhappy and will scream bloody murder. I'm sure, however, that you won't offer any Plate D loads to Ordnance—in view of the temper of my boys and girls, and the number of people who heard your dumb stooge give you away, you won't dare to. In fact, I told some of my people that you wouldn't; that you are a smart enough operator to keep your nose clean."

"You *told* them!" Black shouted, in anger and dismay.

"Yes? Why not?" The words were innocent enough, but Kinnison's expression was full of meaning. "I don't want to seem trite, but you are just beginning to find out that honesty and loyalty are a hell of a hard team to beat."

"Get out! Take these termination papers and GET OUT!"

And Doctor Ralph K. Kinnison, head high, strode out of President Black's office and out of Entwhistle Ordnance Plant.

CHAPTER 6

19—?

"THEODORE K. KINNISON!" A CRISP, CLEAR VOICE SNAPPED FROM the speaker of an apparently cold, ordinary-enough-looking radio-television set.

A burly young man caught his breath sharply as he leaped to the instrument and pressed an inconspicuous button.

"Theodore K. Kinnison acknowledging!" The plate remained dark, but he knew that he was being scanned.

"Operation Bullfinch!" the speaker blatted.

Kinnison gulped. "Operation Bullfinch—Off!" he managed to say.

"Off!"

He pushed the button again and turned to face the tall, trim honey-blonde who stood tensely poised in the archway. Her eyes were wide and protesting; both hands clutched at her throat.

"Uh-huh, sweets, they're coming—over the Pole," he gritted. "Two hours, more or less."

"Oh, Ted!" She threw herself into his arms. They kissed, then broke away.

The man picked up two large suitcases, already packed —everything else, including food and water, had been in the car for weeks—and made strides. The girl rushed after him, not bothering even to close the door of the apartment, scooping up *en passant* a leggy boy of four and a chubby, curly-haired girl of two or thereabouts. They ran across the lawn toward a big, low-slung sedan.

"Sure you got your caffeine tablets?" he demanded as they ran.

"Uh-huh."

"You'll need 'em. Drive like the devil—*stay ahead!* You can—this heap has got the legs of a centipede and you've got plenty of gas and oil. Eleven hundred miles from anywhere and a population of one-tenth per square mile—you'll be safe there if anybody is."

"It isn't us I'm worried about—it's you!" she panted.

"Technos' wives get a few minutes' notice ahead of the H-blast—I'll be ahead of the rush and I'll stay ahead. It's you, Ted—*you!*"

"Don't worry, keed. That popcycle of mine has got legs, too, and there won't be so much traffic, the way I'm going."

"Oh, blast! I didn't mean that, and you know it!"

They were at the car. While he jammed the two bags into an exactly-fitting space, she tossed the children into the front seat, slid lithely under the wheel, and started the engine.

"I know you didn't, sweetheart. I'll be back." He kissed her and the little girl, the while shaking hands with his son. "Kidlets, you and mother are going out to visit Grand-dad Kinnison, like we told you all about. Lots of fun. I'll be along later. Now, Lady Lead-Foot, scram—and shovel on the coal!"

The heavy vehicle backed and swung; gravel flew as the accelerator-pedal hit the floor.

Kinnison galloped across the alley and opened the door of a small garage, revealing a long, squat motorcycle. Two deft passes of his hands and two of his three spotlights were no longer white—one flashed a brilliant purple, the other a searing blue. He dropped a perforated metal box into a hanger and flipped a switch—a peculiarly-toned siren began its ululating shriek. He took the alley turn at an angle of forty-five degrees; burned the pavement toward Diversey.

The light was red. No matter—everybody had stopped—that siren could be heard for miles. He barreled into the intersection; his step-plate ground the concrete as he made a screaming left turn.

A siren—creeping up from behind. City tone. Two red spots —city cop—so soon—good! He cut his gun a trifle, the other bike came alongside.

"Is this IT?" the uniformed rider yelled, over the coughing thunder of the competing exhausts.

"Yes!" Kinnison yelled back. "Clear Diversey to the Outer Drive, and the Drive south to Gary and north to Waukegan. Snap it up!"

The white-and-black motorcycle slowed; shot over toward the curb. The officer reached for his microphone.

Kinnison sped on. At Cicero Avenue, although he had a green light, traffic was so heavy that he had to slow down; at Pulaski two policemen waved him through a red. Beyond Sacramento nothing moved on wheels.

Seventy . . . seventy five . . . he took the bridge at eighty, both wheels in air for forty feet. Eighty five . . . ninety . . . that was about all he could do and keep the heap on so rough a road. Also, he did not have Diversey all to himself any more; blue-and-purple-flashing bikes were coming in from every side-street. He slowed to a conservative fifty and went into close formation with the other riders.

The H-blast—the city-wide warning for the planned and supposedly orderly evacuation of all Chicago—sounded, but Kinnison did not hear it.

Across the Park, edging over to the left so that the boys going south would have room to make the turn—even such riders as those need *some* room to make a turn at fifty miles per hour!

Under the viaduct—biting brakes and squealing tires at that sharp, narrow, right-angle left turn—north on the wide, smooth Drive!

That highway was made for speed. So were those machines. Each rider, as he got into the flat, lay down along his tank, tucked his chin behind the cross-bar, and twisted both throttles out against their stops. They were in a hurry. They had a long way to go; and if they did not get there in time to stop those trans-polar atomic missiles, all hell would be out for noon.

Why was all this necessary? This organization, this haste, this split-second timing, this city-wide exhibition of insane hippodrome riding? Why were not all these motorcycle-racers stationed permanently at their posts, so as to be ready for any emergency? Because America, being a democracy, could not strike first, but had to wait—wait in instant readiness—until she was actually attacked. Because every good Techno in America had his assigned place in some American Defense Plan; of which Operation Bullfinch was only one. Because, without the presence of those Technos at their every-day jobs, all ordinary technological work in America would perforce have stopped.

A branch road curved away to the right. Scarcely slowing down, Kinnison bulleted into the turn and through an open, heavily-guarded gate. Here his mount and his lights were passwords enough: the real test would come later. He approached a towering structure of alloy—jammed on his brakes —stopped beside a soldier who, as soon as Kinnison jumped off, mounted the motorcycle and drove it away.

Kinnison dashed up to an apparently blank wall, turned his back upon four commissioned officers holding cocked forty-fives at the ready, and fitted his right eye into a cup. Unlike fingerprints, retinal patterns cannot be imitated, duplicated, or altered; any imposter would have died instantly, without arrest or question. For every man who belonged aboard that rocket had been checked and tested—*how* he had been checked and tested!—since one spy, in any one of those Technos' chairs, could wreak damage untellable.

The port snapped open. Kinnison climbed a ladder into the large, but crowded, Operations Room.

"Hi, Teddy!" a yell arose.

"Hi, Walt! Hi-ya, Red! What-ho, Baldy!" and so on. These men were friends of old.

"Where are they?" he demanded. "Is our stuff getting away? Lemme take a peek at the Ball!"

"I'll say it is! O.K., Ted, squeeze in here!"

He squeezed in. It was not a ball, but a hemisphere, slightly oblate and centered approximately by the North Pole. A multitude of red dots moved slowly—a hundred miles upon that map was a small distance—northward over Canada; a closer-packed, less numerous group of yellowish-greens, already on the American side of the Pole, was coming south.

As had been expected, the Americans had more missiles than did the enemy. The other belief, that America had more adequate defenses and better-trained, more highly skilled defenders, would soon be put to test.

A string of blue lights blazed across the continent, from Nome through Skagway and Wallaston and Churchill and Kaniapiskau to Belle Isle; America's First Line of Defense. Regulars all. Ambers almost blanketed those blues; their combat rockets were already grabbing altitude. The Second Line, from Portland, Seattle, and Vancouver across to Halifax, also showed solid green, with some flashes of amber. Part Regulars; part National Guard.

Chicago was in the Third Line, all National Guard, extending from San Francisco to New York. Green—alert and operating. So were the Fourth, the Fifth, and the Sixth. Operation Bullfinch was clicking; on schedule to the second.

A bell clanged; the men sprang to their stations and strapped down. Every chair was occupied. Combat Rocket Number One Oh Six Eight Five, full-powered by the disintegrating nuclei of unstable isotopes, took off with a whooshing roar which even her thick walls could not mute.

The Technos, crushed down into their form-fitting cushions by three G's of acceleration, clenched their teeth and took it.

Higher! Faster! The rocket shivered and trembled as it hit the wall at the velocity of sound, but it did not pause.

Higher! Faster! Higher! Fifty miles high. One hundred . . . five hundred . . . a thousand . . . fifteen hundred . . . two thousand! Half a radius—the designated altitude at which the Chicago Contingent would go into action.

Acceleration was cut to zero. The Technos, breathing deeply in relief, donned peculiarly-goggled helmets and set up their panels.

Kinnison stared into his plate with everything he could put into his optic nerve. This was not like the Ball, in which the lights were electronically placed, automatically controlled, clear, sharp, and steady. This was radar. A radar considerably different from that of 1948, of course, and greatly improved, but still pitifully inadequate in dealing with objects separated by hundreds of miles and traveling at velocities of thousands of miles per hour!

Nor was this like the practice cruises, in which the targets had been harmless barrels or equally harmless dirigible rockets. This was the real thing; the targets today would be lethal objects indeed. Practice gunnery, with only a place in the Proficiency List at stake, had been exciting enough: this was too exciting—*much* too exciting—for the keenness of brain and the quickness and steadiness of eye and of hand so soon to be required.

A target? Or was it? Yes—three or four of them!

"Target One—Zone Ten," a quiet voice spoke into Kinnison's ear and one of the white specks upon his plate turned yellowish green. The same words, the same lights, were heard and seen by the eleven other Technos of Sector A, of which Kinnison, by virtue of standing at the top of his Combat Rocket's Proficiency List, was Sector Chief. He knew that the voice was that of Sector A's Fire Control Officer, whose duty it was to determine, from courses, velocities, and all other data to be had from ground and lofty observers, the order in which his Sector's targets should be eliminated. And Sector A, an imaginary but sharply-defined cone, was in normal maneuvering the hottest part of the sky. Fire Control's "Zone Ten" had informed him that the object was at extreme range and hence there would be plenty of time. Nevertheless:

"Lawrence—two! Doyle—one! Drummond—stand by with three!" he snapped, at the first word.

In the instant of hearing his name each Techno stabbed down a series of studs and there flowed into his ears a rapid stream of figures—the up-to-the-second data from every point of observation as to every element of motion of his target. He punched the figures into his calculator, which would correct automatically for the motion of his own vessel—glanced once at the printed solution of the problem—tramped down upon a pedal once, twice, or three times, depending upon the number of projectiles he had been directed to handle.

Kinnison had ordered Lawrence, a better shot than Doyle, to launch two torpedoes; neither of which, at such long range, was expected to strike its mark. His second, however, should come close; so close that the instantaneous data sent back to both screens—and to Kinnison's—by the torpedo itself would make the target a sitting duck for Doyle, the less proficient follower.

Drummond, Kinnison's Number Three, would not launch his missiles unless Doyle missed. Nor could both Drummond and Harper, Kinnison's Number Two, be "out" at once. One of the two had to be "in" at all times, to take Kinnison's place in charge of the Sector if the Chief were ordered out. For while Kinnison could order either Harper or Drummond on target, he could not send himself. He could go out only when ordered to do so by Fire Control: Sector Chiefs were reserved for emergency use only.

"Target Two—Zone Nine," Fire Control said.

"Carney, two. French, one. Day, stand by with three!" Kinnison ordered.

"Damn it—missed!" This from Doyle. "Buck fever—no end."

"O.K., boy—that's why we're starting so soon. I'm shaking like a vibrator myself. We'll get over it . . ."

The point of light which represented Target One bulged slightly and went out. Drummond had connected and was back "in".

"Target Three—Zone Eight. Four—eight," Fire Control remarked.

"Target Three—Higgins and Green; Harper stand by. Four —Case and Santos: Lawrence."

After a minute or two of actual combat the Technos of Sector A began to steady down. Stand-by men were no longer required and were no longer assigned.

"Target Forty-one—six," said Fire Control; and:

"Lawrence, two. Doyle, two," ordered Kinnison. This was routine enough, but in a moment:

"Ted!" Lawrence snapped. "Missed—wide—both barrels. Forty-one's dodging—manned or directed—coming like hell —watch it, Doyle—WATCH IT!"

"Kinnison, take it!" Fire Control barked, voice now neither low nor steady, and without waiting to see whether Doyle would hit or miss. "It's in Zone Three already—collision course!"

"Harper! Take over!"

Kinnison got the data, solved the equations, launched five torpedoes at fifty gravities of acceleration. One . . . two— three-four-five; the last three as close together as they could fly without setting off their proximity fuzes.

Communications and mathematics and the electronic brains of calculating machines had done all that they could do; the rest was up to human skill, to the perfection of co-ordination and the speed of reaction of human mind, nerve, and muscle.

Kinnison's glance darted from plate to panel to computer-tape to meter to galvanometer and back to plate; his left hand moved in tiny arcs the knobs whose rotation varied the intensities of two mutually perpendicular components of his torpedoes' drives. He listened attentively to the reports of tri-angulating observers, now giving him data covering his own missiles, as well as the target object. The fingers of his right hand punched almost constantly the keys of his computer; he corrected almost constantly his torpedoes' course.

"Up a hair," he decided. "Left about a point."

The target moved away from its predicted path.

Down two—left three—down a hair—*Right!* The thing was almost through Zone Two; was blasting into Zone One.

He thought for a second that his first torp was going to connect. It almost did—only a last-instant, full-powered side thrust enabled the target to evade it. Two numbers flashed white upon his plate; his actual error, exact to the foot of distance and to the degree on the clock, measured and trans-mitted back to his board by instruments in his torpedo.

Working with instantaneous and exact data, and because the enemy had so little time in which to act, Kinnison's second projectile made a very near miss indeed. His third was a graze; so close that its proximity fuze functioned, detonating the cyclonite-packed warhead. Kinnison knew that his third went off, because the error-figures vanished, almost in the in-stant of their coming into being, as its detecting and trans-mitting instruments were destroyed. That one detonation might have been enough; but Kinnison had had one glimpse of his error—how small it was!—and had a fraction of a second of time. Hence Four and Five slammed home; dead center. What-ever that target had been, it was no longer a threat.

"Kinnison, in," he reported briefly to Fire Control, and took over from Harper the direction of the activities of Sector A.

The battle went on. Kinnison sent Harper and Drummond out time after time. He himself was given three more targets.

The first wave of the enemy—what was left of it—passed. Sector A went into action, again at extreme range, upon the second. Its remains, too, plunged downward and onward toward the distant ground.

The third wave was really tough. Not that it was actually any worse than the first two had been, but the CR10685 was no longer getting the data which her Technos ought to have to do a good job; and every man aboard her knew why. Some enemy stuff had got through, of course; and the observatories, both on the ground and above it—the eye of the whole American Defense—had suffered heavily.

Nevertheless, Kinnison and his fellows were not too perturbed. Such a condition was not entirely unexpected. They were now veterans; they had been tried and had not been found wanting. They had come unscathed through a bath of fire the like of which the world had never before known. Give them any kind of computation at all—or no computation at all except old CR10685's own radar and their own torps, of which they still had plenty—and they could and would take care of anything that could be thrown at them.

The third wave passed. Targets became fewer and fewer. Action slowed down . . . stopped.

The Technos, even the Sector Chiefs, knew nothing whatever of the progress of the battle as a whole. They did not know where their rocket was, or whether it was going north, east, south, or west. They knew when it was going up or down only by the "seats of their pants." They did not even know the nature of the targets they destroyed, since upon their plates all targets looked alike—small, bright, greenish-yellow spots. Hence:

"Give us the dope, Pete, if we've got a minute to spare," Kinnison begged of his Fire Control Officer. "You know more than we do—give!"

"It's coming in now," came the prompt reply. "Six of those targets that did such fancy dodging were atomics, aimed at the Lines. Five were dirigibles, with our number on 'em. You fellows did a swell job. Very little of their stuff got through—not enough, they say, to do much damage to a country as big as the U.S.A. On the other hand, they stopped scarcely any of ours—they apparently didn't have anything to compare with you Technos.

"But all hell seems to be busting loose, all over the world. Our east and west coasts are both being attacked, they say; but are holding. Operation Daisy and Operation Fairfield are clicking, just like we did. Europe, they say, is going to hell—everybody is taking pot-shots at everybody else. One report says that the South American nations are bombing each other . . . Asia, too . . . nothing definite; as straight dope comes in I'll relay it to you.

"We came through in very good shape, considering . . . losses less than anticipated, only seven percent. The First Line—as you know already—took a God-awful shellacking; in fact, the Churchill-Belcher section was practically wiped out, which was what lost us about all of our Observation . . . We are now just about over the southern end of Hudson Bay, heading down and south to join in making a vertical Fleet Formation . . . no more waves coming, but they say to expect attacks from low-flying combat rockets—there goes the alert! On your toes, fellows—but there isn't a thing on Sector A's screen . . ."

There wasn't. Since the CR10685 was diving downward and southward, there wouldn't be. Nevertheless, some observer aboard that rocket saw that atomic missile coming. Some Fire Control Officer yelled orders; some Technos did their best—and failed.

And such is the violence of nuclear fission; so utterly incomprehensible is its speed, that Theodore K. Kinnison died without realizing that anything whatever was happening to his ship or to him.

*Gharlane of Eddore looked upon ruined Earth, his handi-
work, and found it good. Knowing that it would be many
of hundreds of Tellurian years before that planet would again
require his personal attention, he went elsewhere; to Rigel
Four, to Palain Seven, and to the solar system of Velantia,
where he found that his creatures the Overlords were not progressing according to schedule. He spent quite a little time
there, then searched minutely and fruitlessly for evidence of
inimical activity within the Innermost Circle.*

*And upon far Arisia a momentous decision was made:
the time had come to curb sharply the hitherto unhampered
Eddorians.*

*"We are ready, then, to war openly upon them?" Eukoni-
dor asked, somewhat doubtfully. "Again to cleanse the planet
Tellus of dangerous radioactives and of too-noxious forms
of life is of course a simple matter. From our protected areas
in North America a strong but democratic government can
spread to cover the world. That government can be extended
easily enough to include Mars and Venus. But Gharlane,
who is to operate as Roger, who has already planted, in
the Adepts of North Polar Jupiter, the seeds of the Jovian
Wars . . ."*

"Your visualization is sound, youth. Think on."

*"Those interplanetary wars are of course inevitable, and
will serve to strengthen and to unify the government of the
Inner Planets . . . provided that Gharlane does not interfere
. . . Oh, I see. Gharlane will not at first know; since a zone
of compulsion will be held upon him. When he or some
Eddorian fusion perceives that compulsion and breaks it—
at some such time of high stress as the Nevian incident—it
will be too late. Our fusions will be operating. Roger will be
allowed to perform only such acts as will be for Civilization's
eventual good. Nevia was selected as Prime Operator because of its location in a small region of the galaxy which is
almost devoid of solid iron and because of its watery nature;*

its aquatic forms of life being precisely those in which the Eddorians are least interested. They will be given partial neutralization of inertia; they will be able to attain velocities a few times greater than that of light. That covers the situation, I think?"

"Very good, Eukonidor," the Elders approved. "A concise and accurate summation."

Hundreds of Tellurian years passed. The aftermath. Reconstruction. Advancement. One world—two worlds—three worlds—united, harmonious, friendly. The Jovian Wars. A solid, unshakeable union.

Nor did any Eddorian know that such fantastically rapid progress was being made. Indeed, Gharlane knew, as he drove his immense ship of space toward Sol, that he would find Tellus inhabited by peoples little above savagery.

And it should be noted in passing that not once, throughout all those centuries, did a man named Kinnison marry a girl with red-bronze-auburn hair and gold-flecked, tawny eyes.

BOOK
THREE
TRIPLANETARY

CHAPTER 7

PIRATES OF SPACE

APPARENTLY MOTIONLESS TO HER PASSENGERS AND CREW, the Interplanetary liner *Hyperion* bored serenely onward through space at normal acceleration. In the railed-off sanctum in one corner of the control room a bell tinkled, a smothered whirr was heard, and Captain Bradley frowned as he studied the brief message upon the tape of the recorder— a message flashed to his desk from the operator's panel. He beckoned, and the second officer, whose watch it now was, read aloud:

"Reports of scout patrols still negative."

"Still negative." The officer scowled in thought. "They've already searched beyond the widest possible location of wreckage, too. Two unexplained disappearances inside a month—first the *Dione*, then the *Rhea*—and not a plate nor a lifeboat recovered. Looks bad, sir. One might be an accident; two might possibly be a coincidence . . ." His voice died away.

"But at three it would get to be a habit," the captain finished the thought. "And whatever happened, happened quick. Neither of them had time to say a word—their location recorders simply went dead. But of course they didn't have our detector screens nor our armament. According to the observatories we're in clear ether, but I wouldn't trust them from Tellus to Luna. You have given the new orders, of course?"

"Yes, sir. Detectors full out, all three courses of defensive screen on the trips, projectors manned, suits on the hooks. Every object detected to be investigated immediately —if vessels, they are to be warned to stay beyond extreme range. Anything entering the fourth zone is to be rayed."

"Right—we are going through!"

"But no known type of vessel could have made away with them without detection," the second officer argued. "I wonder if there isn't something in those wild rumors we've been hearing lately?"

"Bah! Of course not!" snorted the captain. "Pirates in ships faster than light—sub-ethereal rays—nullification of gravity mass without inertia—ridiculous! Proved impossible, over and over again. No, sir, if pirates are operating in space —and it looks very much like it—they won't get far against a good big battery full of kilowatt-hours behind three courses of heavy screen, and good gunners behind multiplex projectors. They're good enough for anybody. Pirates, Neptunians, angels, or devils—in ships or on broomsticks—if they tackle the *Hyperion* we'll burn them out of the ether!"

Leaving the captain's desk, the watch officer resumed his tour of duty. The six great lookout plates into which the alert observers peered were blank, their far-flung ultra-sensitive detector screens encountering no obstacle—the ether was empty for thousands upon thousands of kilometers. The signal lamps upon the pilot's panel were dark, its warning bells were silent. A brilliant point of white light in the center of the pilot's closely ruled micrometer grating, exactly upon the cross-hairs of his directors, showed that the immense vessel was precisely upon the calculated course, as laid down by the automatic integrating course plotters. Everything was quiet and in order.

"All's well, sir," he reported briefly to Captain Bradley— but all was not well.

Danger—more serious by far in that it was not external— was even then, all unsuspected, gnawing at the great ship's vitals. In a locked and shielded compartment, deep down in the interior of the liner, was the great air purifier. Now a man leaned against the primary duct—the aorta through which flowed the stream of pure air supplying the entire vessel. This man, grotesque in full panoply of space armor, leaned against the duct, and as he leaned a drill bit deeper and deeper into the steel wall of the pipe. Soon it broke through, and the slight rush of air was stopped by the insertion of a tightly fitting rubber tube. The tube terminated in a heavy rubber balloon, which surrounded a frail glass bulb. The man stood tense, one hand holding before his silica-and-steel-helmeted head a large pocket chronometer, the other lightly grasping the balloon. A sneering grin was upon his face as he waited the exact second of action—the carefully predetermined instant when his right hand, closing, would shatter the fragile flask and force its contents into the primary air stream of the *Hyperion!*

*   *   *

Far above, in the main saloon, the regular evening dance was in full swing. The ship's orchestra crashed into silence, there was a patter of applause, and Clio Marsden, radiant belle of the voyage, led her partner out onto the promenade and up to one of the observation plates.

"Oh, we can't see the Earth any more!" she exclaimed. "Which way do you turn this, Mr. Costigan?"

"Like this," and Conway Costigan, burly young First Officer of the liner, turned the dials. "There—this plate is looking back, or down, at Tellus; this other one is looking ahead."

Earth was a brilliantly shining crescent far beneath the flying vessel. Above her, ruddy Mars and silvery Jupiter blazed in splendor ineffable against a background of utterly indescribable blackness—a background thickly besprinkled with dimensionless points of dazzling brilliance which were the stars.

"Oh, isn't it wonderful!" breathed the girl, awed. "Of course, I suppose that it's old stuff to you, but I'm a ground-gripper, you know, and I could look at it forever, I think. That's why I want to come out here after every dance. You know, I . . ."

Her voice broke off suddenly, with a queer, rasping catch, as she seized his arm in a frantic clutch and as quickly went limp. He stared at her sharply, and understood instantly the message written in her eyes—eyes now enlarged, staring, hard, brilliant, and full of soul-searing terror as she slumped down, helpless but for his support. In the act of exhaling as he was, lungs almost entirely empty, yet he held his breath until he had seized the microphone from his belt and had snapped the lever to "emergency."

"Control room!" he gasped then, and every speaker throughout the great cruiser of the void blared out the warning as he forced his already evacuated lungs to absolute emptiness. "Vee-Two Gas! Get tight!"

Writhing and twisting in his fierce struggle to keep his lungs from gulping in a draft of that noxious atmosphere, and with the unconscious form of the girl draped limply over his left arm, Costigan leaped toward the portal of the nearest lifeboat. Orchestra instruments crashed to the floor and dancing couples fell and sprawled inertly while the tortured First Officer swung the door of the lifeboat open and dashed across the tiny room to the air-valves. Throwing them wide open, he put his mouth to the orifice and let his laboring lungs gasp their eager fill of the cold blast roaring from the tanks. Then, air-hunger partially assuaged, he again held his breath, broke open the emergency locker, donned one of the space-suits always kept there, and opened its valves wide in order to flush out of his uniform any lingering trace of the lethal gas.

He then leaped back to his companion. Shutting off the air, he released a stream of pure oxygen, held her face in it, and made shift to force some of it into her lungs by compressing and releasing her chest against his own body. Soon she drew a spasmodic breath, choking and coughing, and he again changed the gaseous stream to one of pure air, speaking urgently as she showed signs of returning consciousness.

"Stand up!" he snapped. "Hang onto this brace and keep your face in this air-stream until I get a suit around you! Got me?"

She nodded weakly, and, assured that she could hold herself at the valve, it was the work of only a minute to encase her in one of the protective coverings. Then, as she sat upon a bench, recovering her strength, he flipped on the lifeboat's visiphone projector and shot its invisible beam up into the control room, where he saw space-armored figures furiously busy at the panels.

"Dirty work at the cross-roads!" he blazed to his captain, man to man—formality disregarded, as it so often was in the Triplanetary service. "There's skulduggery afoot somewhere in our primary air! Maybe that's the way they got those other two ships—pirates! Might have been a timed bomb—don't see how anybody could have stowed away down there through the inspections, and nobody but Franklin can neutralize the shield of the air room—but I'm going to look around, anyway. Then I'll join you fellows up there."

"What was it?" the shaken girl asked. "I think that I remember your saying 'Vee-Two gas.' That's forbidden! Anyway, I owe you my life, Conway, and I'll never forget it—never. Thanks—but the others—how about all the rest of us?"

"It was Vee-Two, and it is forbidden," Costigan replied grimly, eyes fast upon the flashing plate, whose point of projection was now deep in the bowels of the vessel. "The penalty for using it or having it is death on sight. Gangsters and pirates use it, since they have nothing to lose, being on the death list already. As for your life, I haven't saved it yet —you may wish I'd let it ride before we get done. The others are too far gone for oxygen—couldn't have brought even you around in a few more seconds, quick as I got to you. But there's a sure antidote—we all carry it in a lock-box in our armor—and we all know how to use it, because crooks all use Vee-Two and so we're always expecting it. But since the air will be pure again in half an hour we'll be able to revive the others easily enough if we can get by with whatever is going to happen next. There's the bird that did it, right in the air-room. It's the Chief Engineer's suit, but that isn't Franklin that's in it. Some passenger—disguised—slugged the Chief—took his suit and projectors—hole in duct—p-s-s-t! All washed out! Maybe that's all he was scheduled to do to us in this performance, but he'll do nothing else in his life!"

"Don't go down there!" protested the girl. "His armor is *so* much better than that emergency suit you are wearing, and he's got Mr. Franklin's Lewiston, besides!"

"Don't be an idiot!" he snapped. "We can't have a live pirate aboard—we're going to be altogether too busy with outsiders directly. Don't worry, I'm not going to give him a break. I'll take a Standish—I'll rub him out like a blot. Stay right here until I come back after you," he commanded, and the heavy door of the lifeboat clanged shut behind him as he leaped out into the promenade.

Straight across the saloon he made his way, paying no attention to the inert forms scattered here and there. Going up to a blank wall, he manipulated an almost invisible dial set flush with its surface, swung a heavy door aside, and lifted out the Standish—a fearsome weapon. Squat, huge, and heavy, it resembled somewhat an overgrown machine rifle, but one possessing a thick, short telescope, with several opaque condensing lenses and parabolic reflectors. Laboring under the weight of the thing, he strode along corridors and clambered heavily down short stairways. Finally he came to the purifier room, and grinned savagely as he saw the green-ish haze of light obscuring the door and walls—the shield was still in place; the pirate was still inside, still flooding with the terrible Vee Two the *Hyperion's* primary air.

He set his peculiar weapon down, unfolded its three mas-sive legs, crouched down behind it, and threw in a switch. Dull red beams of frightful intensity shot from the reflectors and sparks, almost of lightning proportions, leaped from the shielding screen under their impact. Roaring and snapping, the conflict went on for seconds, then, under the superior force of the Standish, the greenish radiance gave way. Be-hind it the metal of the door ran the gamut of color—red, yellow, blinding white—then literally exploded; molten, vaporized, burned away. Through the aperture thus made Costigan could plainly see the pirate in the space-armor of the chief engineer—an armor which was proof against rifle fire and which could reflect and neutralize for some little time even the terrific beam Costigan was employing. Nor was the pirate unarmed—a vicious flare of incandescence leaped from his Lewiston, to spend its force in spitting, crackling pyrotechnics against the ether-wall of the squat and monstrous Standish. But Costigan's infernal engine did not rely only upon vibratory destruction. At almost the first flash of the pirate's weapon the officer touched a trigger, there was a double report, ear-shattering in that narrowly confined space, and the pirate's body literally flew into mist as a half-kilogram shell tore through his armor and exploded. Costigan shut off his beam, and with not the slightest softening of one hard lineament stared around the air-room; making sure that no serious damage had been done to the vital machinery of the air-purifier—the very lungs of the great spaceship.

Dismounting the Standish, he lugged it back up to the main saloon, replaced it in its safe, and again set the combination lock. Thence to the lifeboat, where Clio cried out in relief as she saw that he was unhurt.

"Oh, Conway, I've been so afraid something would happen to you!" she exclaimed, as he led her rapidly upward toward the control room. "Of course you . . ." she paused.

"Sure," he replied, laconically. "Nothing to it. How do you feel—about back to normal?"

"All right, I think, except for being scared to death and just about out of control. I don't suppose that I'll be good for anything, but whatever I can do, count me in on."

"Fine—you may be needed, at that. Everybody's out, apparently, except those like me, who had a warning and could hold their breath until they got to their suits."

"But how did you know what it was? You can't see it, nor smell it, nor anything."

"You inhaled a second before I did, and I saw your eyes. I've been in it before—and when you see a man get a jolt of that stuff just once, you never forget it. The engineers down below got it first, of course—it must have wiped them out. Then we got it in the saloon. Your passing out warned me, and luckily I had enough breath left to give the word. Quite a few of the fellows up above should have had time to get away—we'll see 'em all in the control room."

"I suppose that was why you revived me—in payment

for so kindly warning you of the gas attack?" The girl laughed; shaky, but game.

"Something like that, probably," he answered, lightly. "Here we are—now we'll soon find out what's going to happen next."

In the control room they saw at least a dozen armored figures; not now rushing about, but seated at their instruments, tense and ready. Fortunate it was that Costigan—veteran of space as he was, though young in years—had been down in the saloon; fortunate that he had been familiar with that horrible outlawed gas; fortunate that he had had presence of mind enough and sheer physical stamina enough to send his warning without allowing one paralyzing trace to enter his own lungs. Captain Bradley, the men on watch, and several other officers in their quarters or in the wardrooms—space-hardened veterans all—had obeyed instantly and without question the amplifiers' gasped command to "get tight". Exhaling or inhaling, their air-passages had snapped shut as that dread "Vee-Two" was heard, and they had literally jumped into their armored suits of space—flushing them out with volume after volume of unquestionable air; holding their breath to the last possible second, until their straining lungs could endure no more.

Costigan waved the girl to a vacant bench, cautiously changing into his own armor from the emergency suit he had been wearing, and approached the captain.

"Anything in sight, sir?" he asked, saluting. "They should have started something before this."

"They've started, but we can't locate them. We tried to send out a general sector alarm, but had hardly started when they blanketed our wave. Look at that!"

Following the captain's eyes, Costigan stared at the high powered set of the ship's operator. Upon the plate, instead of a moving, living, three-dimensional picture, there was a flashing glare of blinding white light; from the speaker, instead of intelligible speech, was issuing a roaring, crackling stream of noise.

"It's impossible!" Bradley burst out, violently. "There's not a gram of metal inside the fourth zone—within a hundred thousand kilometers—and yet they must be close to send such a wave as that. But the Second thinks not—what do you think, Costigan?" The bluff commander, reactionary and of the old school as was his breed, was furious—baffled, raging inwardly to come to grips with the invisible and indetectable foe. Face to face with the inexplicable, however, he listened to the younger men with unusual tolerance.

"It's not only possible; it's quite evident that they've got something we haven't." Costigan's voice was bitter. "But why shouldn't they have? Service ships never get anything until it's been experimented with for years, but pirates and such always get the new stuff as soon as it's discovered. The only good thing I can see is that we got part of a message away, and the scouts can trace that interference out there. But the pirates know that, too—it won't be long now," he concluded, grimly.

He spoke truly. Before another word was said the outer screen flared white under a beam of terrific power, and simultaneously there appeared upon one of the lookout plates a vivid picture of the pirate vessel—a huge, black torpedo of steel, now emitting flaring offensive beams of force.

Instantly the powerful weapons of the *Hyperion* were brought to bear, and in the blast of full-driven beams the stranger's screens flamed incandescent. Heavy guns, under the recoil of whose fierce salvos the frame of the giant globe trembled and shuddered, shot out their tons of high-explosive shell. But the pirate commander had known accurately the strength of the liner, and knew that her armament was impotent against the forces at his command. His screens were invulnerable, the giant shells were exploded harmlessly in mid-space, miles from their objective. And suddenly a frightful pencil of flame stabbed brilliantly from the black hulk of the enemy. Through the empty ether it tore, through the mighty defensive screens, through the tough metal of the outer and inner walls. Every ether-defense of the *Hyperion* vanished, and her acceleration dropped to a quarter of its normal value.

"Right through the battery room!" Bradley groaned. "We're on the emergency drive now. Our rays are done for, and we can't seem to put a shell anywhere near her with our guns!"

But ineffective as the guns were, they were silenced forever as a frightful beam of destruction stabbed relentlessly through the control room, whiffing out of existence the pilot, gunnery, and lookout panels and the men before them. The air rushed into space, and the suits of the three survivors bulged out into drum-head tightness as the pressure in the room decreased.

Costigan pushed the captain lightly toward a wall, then seized the girl and leaped in the same direction.

"Let's get out of here, quick!" he cried, the miniature radio instruments of the helmets automatically taking up the duty of transmitting speech as the sound disks refused to function. "They can't see us—our ether wall is still up and their spy-rays can't get through it from the outside, you know. They're working from blue-prints, and they'll probably take your desk next," and even as they bounded toward the door, now become the outer seal of an airlock, the pirates' beam tore through the space which they had just quitted.

Through the airlock, down through several levels of passengers' quarters they hurried, and into a lifeboat, whose one doorway commanded the full length of the third lounge—an ideal spot, either for defense or for escape outward by means of the miniature cruiser. As they entered their retreat they felt their weight begin to increase. More and more force was applied to the helpless liner, until it was moving at normal acceleration.

"What do you make of that, Costigan?" asked the captain. "Tractor beams?"

"Apparently. They've got something, all right. They're taking us somewhere, fast. I'll go get a couple of Standishes, and another suit of armor—we'd better dig in," and soon the small room became a veritable fortress, housing as it did those two formidable engines of destruction. Then the first officer made another and longer trip, returning with a complete suit of Triplanetary space armor, exactly like those worn by the two men, but considerably smaller.

"Just as an added factor of safety, you'd better put this on, Clio—those emergency suits aren't good for much in a battle. I don't suppose that you ever fired a Standish, did you?"

"No, but I can soon learn how to do it," she replied pluckily.

"Two is all that can work here at once, but you should know how to take hold in case one of us goes out. And while you're changing suits you'd better put on some stuff I've got here—Service Special phones and detectors. Stick this little disk onto your chest with this bit of tape; low down, out of sight. Just under your wishbone is the best place. Take off your wristwatch and wear this one *continuously*—never take it off for a second. Put on these pearls, and wear them all the time, too. Take this capsule and hide it against your skin, some place where it can't be found except by the most rigid search. Swallow it in an emergency—it goes down easily and works just as well inside as outside. It is the most important thing of all—you can get along with it alone if you lose everything else, but without that capsule the whole system's shot to pieces. With that outfit, if we should get separated, you can talk to us—we're both wearing 'em, although in somewhat different forms. You don't need to talk loud—just a mutter will be enough. They're handy little outfits—almost impossible to find, and capable of a lot of things."

"Thanks, Conway—I'll remember that, too," Clio replied, as she turned toward the tiny locker to follow his instructions. "But won't the scouts and patrols be catching us pretty quick? The operator sent a warning."

"Afraid the ether's empty, as far as we're concerned."

Captain Bradley had stood by in silent astonishment during this conversation. His eyes had bulged slightly at Costigan's "we're both wearing 'em," but he had held his peace and as the girl disappeared a look of dawning comprehension came over his face.

"Oh, I see, sir," he said, respectfully—far more respectfully than he had ever before addressed a mere first officer. "Meaning that we both *will be* wearing them shortly, I assume. 'Service Specials'—but you didn't specify exactly *what* Service, did you?"

"Now that you mention it, I don't believe that I did," Costigan grinned.

"That explains several things about you—particularly your recognition of Vee-Two and your uncanny control and speed of reaction. But aren't you . . ."

"No," Costigan interrupted. "This situation is apt to get altogether too serious to overlook any bets. If we get away, I'll take them away from her and she'll never know that they aren't routine equipment. As for you, I know that you can and do keep your mouth shut. That's why I'm hanging this junk on you—I had a lot of stuff in my kit, but I flashed it all with the Standish except what I brought in here for us three. Whether you think so or not, we're in a real jam —our chance of getting away is mighty close to zero. . . ."

He broke off as the girl came back, now to all appearances a small Triplanetary officer, and the three settled down to a long and eventless wait. Hour after hour they flew through the ether, but finally there was a lurching swing and an abrupt increase in their acceleration. After a short consultation Captain Bradley turned on the visiray set and, with the beam at its minimum power, peered cautiously downward, in the direction opposite to that in which he knew the pirate vessel must be. All three stared into the plate, seeing only an infinity of emptiness, marked only by the infinitely remote and coldly brilliant stars. While they stared into space a vast area of the heavens was blotted out and they saw, faintly illuminated by a peculiar blue luminescence,

a vast ball—a sphere so large and so close that they seemed
to be dropping downward toward it as though it were a
world! They came to a stop—paused, weightless—a vast door
slid smoothly aside—they were drawn *upward* through an
airlock and floated quietly in the air above a small, but
brightly-lighted and orderly city of metallic buildings! Gently
the *Hyperion* was lowered, to come to rest in the embracing
arms of a regulation landing cradle.

"Well, wherever it is, we're here," remarked Captain
Bradley, grimly, and:

"And now the fireworks start," assented Costigan, with a
questioning glance at the girl.

"Don't mind me," she answered his unspoken question.
"I don't believe in surrendering, either."

"Right," and both men squatted down behind the ether-
walls of their terrific weapons; the girl prone behind them.

They had not long to wait. A group of human beings—
men and to all appearances Americans—appeared unarmed
in the little lounge. As soon as they were well inside the
room, Bradley and Costigan released upon them without com-
punction the full power of their frightful projectors. From
the reflectors, through the doorway, there tore a concentrated
double beam of pure destruction—but that beam did not
reach its goal. Yards from the men it met a screen of impenetrable density. Instantly the gunners pressed their trig-
gers and a stream of high-explosive shells issued from the
roaring weapons. But shells, also, were futile. They struck
the shield and vanished—vanished without exploding and
without leaving a trace to show that they had ever existed.

Costigan sprang to his feet, but before he could launch
his intended attack a vast tunnel appeared beside him—
something had gone through the entire width of the liner,
cutting effortlessly a smooth cylinder of emptiness. Air
rushed in to fill the vacuum, and the three visitors felt themselves seized by invisible forces and drawn into the tunnel.
Through it they floated, up to and over buildings, finally
slanting downward toward the door of a great high-towered
structure. Doors opened before them and closed behind
them, until at last they stood upright in a room which was
evidently the office of a busy executive. They faced a desk
which, in addition to the usual equipment of the business
man, carried also a bewilderingly complete switchboard and
instrument panel.

Seated impassively at the desk there was a gray man. Not
only was he dressed entirely in gray, but his heavy hair was

gray, his eyes were gray, and even his tanned skin seemed to give the impression of grayness in disguise. His overwhelming personality radiated an aura of grayness—not the gentle gray of the dove, but the resistless, driving gray of the super-dreadnought; the hard, inflexible, brittle gray of the fracture of high-carbon steel.

"Captain Bradley, First Officer Costigan, Miss Marsden," the man spoke quietly, but crisply. "I had not intended you two men to live so long. That is a detail, however, which we will pass by for the moment. You may remove your suits."

Neither officer moved, but both stared back at the speaker, unflinchingly.

"I am not accustomed to repeating instructions," the man at the desk continued; voice still low and level, but instinct with deadly menace. "You may choose between removing those suits and dying in them, here and now."

Costigan moved over to Clio and slowly took off her armor. Then, after a flashing exchange of glances and a muttered word, the two officers threw off their suits simultaneously and fired at the same instant; Bradley with his Lewiston, Costigan with a heavy automatic pistol whose bullets were explosive shells of tremendous power. But the man in gray, surrounded by an impenetrable wall of force, only smiled at the fusillade, tolerantly and maddeningly. Costigan leaped fiercely, only to be hurled backward as he struck that unyielding, invisible wall. A vicious beam snapped him back into place, the weapons were snatched away, and all three captives were held to their former positions.

"I permitted that, as a demonstration of futility," the gray man said, his hard voice becoming harder, "but I will permit no more foolishness. Now I will introduce myself. I am known as Roger. You probably have heard nothing of me: very few Tellurians have, or ever will. Whether or not you two live depends solely upon yourselves. Being something of a student of men, I fear that you will both die shortly. Able and resourceful as you have just shown yourselves to be, you could be valuable to me, but you probably will not—in which case you shall, of course, cease to exist. That, however, in its proper time—you shall be of some slight service to me in the process of being eliminated. In your case, Miss Marsden, I find myself undecided between two courses of action; each highly desirable, but unfortunately mutually exclusive. Your father will be glad to ransom you at an exceedingly high figure, but in spite of that fact I may decide to use you in a research upon sex."

"Yes?" Clio rose magnificently to the occasion. Fear forgotten, her courageous spirit flashed from her clear young eyes and emanated from her taut young body, erect in defiance. "You may think that you can do anything with me that you please, but you can't!"

"Peculiar—highly perplexing—why should that one stimulus, in the case of young females, produce such an entirely disproportionate reaction?" Roger's eyes bored into Clio's; the girl shivered and looked away. "But sex itself, primal and basic, the most widespread concomitant of life in this continuum, is completely illogical and paradoxical. Most baffling—decidedly, this research on sex must go on."

Roger pressed a button and a tall, comely woman appeared—a woman of indefinite age and of uncertain nationality.

"Show Miss Marsden to her apartment," he directed, and as the two women went out a man came in.

"The cargo is unloaded, sir," the newcomer reported. "The two men and the five women indicated have been taken to the hospital."

"Very well, dispose of the others in the usual fashion." The minion went out, and Roger continued, emotionlessly:

"Collectively, the other passengers may be worth a million or so, but it would not be worthwhile to waste time upon them."

"What are you, anyway?" blazed Costigan, helpless but enraged beyond caution. "I have heard of mad scientists who tried to destroy the Earth, and of equally mad geniuses who thought themselves Napoleons capable of conquering even the Solar System. Whichever you are, you should know that you can't get away with it."

"I am neither. I am, however, a scientist, and I direct many other scientists. I am not mad. You have undoubtedly noticed several peculiar features of this place?"

"Yes, particularly the artificial gravity and those screens. An ordinary ether-wall is opaque in one direction, and doesn't bar matter—yours are transparent both ways and something more than impenetrable to matter. How do you do it?"

"You could not understand them if I explained them to you, and they are merely two of our smaller developments. I do not intend to destroy your planet Earth; I have no desire to rule over masses of futile and brainless men. I have, however, certain ends of my own in view. To accomplish my plans I require hundreds of millions in gold and other hundreds of millions in uranium, thorium, and radium; all of which I shall take from the planets of this Solar System before I leave it. I shall take them in spite of the puerile efforts of the fleets of your Triplanetary League.

"This structure was designed by me and built under my direction. It is protected from meteorites by forces of my devising. It is indetectable and invisible—ether waves are bent around it without loss or distortion. I am discussing these points at such length so that you may realize exactly your position. As I have intimated, you can be of assistance to me if you will."

"Now just what could you offer any *man* to make him join your outfit?" demanded Costigan, venomously.

"Many things," Roger's cold tone betrayed no emotion, no recognition of Costigan's open and bitter contempt. "I have under me many men, bound to me by many ties. Needs, wants, longings, and desires differ from man to man, and I can satisfy practically any of them. Many men take delight in the society of young and beautiful women, but there are other urges which I have found quite efficient. Greed, thirst for fame, longing for power, and so on, including many qualities usually regarded as 'noble.' And what I promise, I deliver. I demand only loyalty to me, and that only in certain things and for a relatively short period. In all else, my men do as they please. In conclusion, I can use you two conveniently, but I do not need you. Therefore you may choose now between my service and—the alternative."

"Exactly what is the alternative?"

"We will not go into that. Suffice it to say that it has to do with a minor research, which is not progressing satisfactorily. It will result in your extinction, and perhaps I should mention that that extinction will not be particularly pleasant."

"I say NO, you . . ." Bradley roared. He intended to give an unexpurgated classification, but was rudely interrupted.

"Hold on a minute!" snapped Costigan. "How about Miss Marsden?"

"She has nothing to do with this discussion," returned Roger, icily. "I do not bargain—in fact, I believe that I shall keep her for a time. She has it in mind to destroy herself if I do not allow her to be ransomed, but she will find that door closed to her until I permit it to open."

"In that case, I string along with the Chief—take what he started to say about you and run it clear across the board for me!" barked Costigan.

"Very well. That decision was to be expected from men of your type." The gray man touched two buttons and two of his creatures entered the room. "Put these men into two separate cells on the second level," he ordered. "Search them; all their weapons may not have been in their armor. Seal the doors and mount special guards, tuned to me here."

Imprisoned they were, and carefully searched; but they bore no arms, and nothing had been said concerning communicators. Even if such instruments could be concealed, Roger would detect their use instantly. At least, so ran his thought. But Roger's men had no inkling of the possibility of Costigan's "Service Special" phones, detectors, and spy-ray—instruments of minute size and of infinitesimal power, but yet instruments which, working as they were below the level of the ether, were effective at great distances and caused no vibrations in the ether by which their use could be detected. And what could be more innocent than the regulation personal equipment of every officer of space? The heavy goggles, the wrist-watch and its supplementary pocket chronometer, the flash-lamp, the automatic lighter, the sender, the money-belt?

All these items of equipment were examined with due care; but the cleverest minds of the Triplanetary Service had designed those communicators to pass any ordinary search, however careful, and when Costigan and Bradley were finally locked into the designated cells they still possessed their ultra-instruments.

CHAPTER 8

IN ROGER'S PLANETOID

IN THE HALL CLIO GLANCED AROUND HER WILDLY, SEEKING even the narrowest avenue of escape. Before she could act, however, her body was clamped as though in a vise, and she struggled, motionless.

"It is useless to attempt to escape, or to do anything except what Roger wishes," the guide informed her somberly, snapping off the instrument in her hand and thus restoring to the thoroughly cowed girl her freedom of motion.

"His lightest wish is law," she continued as they walked down a long corridor. "The sooner you realize that you must do exactly as he pleases, in all things, the easier your life will be."

"But I wouldn't *want* to keep on living!" Clio declared, with a flash of spirit. "And I can *always* die, you know."

"You will find that you cannot," the passionless creature returned, monotonously. "If you do not yield, you will long and pray for death, but you will not die unless Roger wills it. Look at me: I cannot die. Here is your apartment. You will stay here until Roger gives further orders concerning you."

The living automaton opened a door and stood silent and impassive while Clio, staring at her in horror, shrank past her and into the sumptuously furnished suite. The door closed soundlessly and utter silence descended as a pall. Not an ordinary silence, but the indescribable perfection of the absolute silence, complete absence of all sound. In that silence Clio stood motionless. Tense and rigid, hopeless, despairing, she stood there in that magnificent room, fighting an almost overwhelming impulse to scream. Suddenly she heard the cold voice of Roger, speaking from the empty air.

"You are over-wrought, Miss Marsden. You can be of no use to yourself or to me in that conditon. I command you to rest; and, to insure that rest, you may pull that cord, which will establish about this room an ether wall: a wall to cut off even this my voice . . ."

The voice ceased as she pulled the cord savagely and threw herself upon a divan in a torrent of gasping, strangling, but rebellious sobs. Then again came a voice, but not to her ears. Deep within her, pervading every bone and muscle, it made itself felt rather than heard.

"Clio?" it asked. "Don't talk yet . . ."

"Conway!" she gasped in relief, every fiber of her being thrilled into new hope at the deep, well-remembered voice of Conway Costigan.

"Keep still!" he snapped. "Don't act so happy! He may have a spy-ray on you. He can't hear me, but he may be able to hear you. When he was talking to you you must have noticed a sort of rough, sandpapery feeling under that necklace I gave you? Since he's got an ether-wall around you the beads are dead now. If you feel anything like that under the wrist-watch, breathe deeply, twice. If you don't feel any-thing there, it's safe for you to talk, as loud as you please."

"I don't feel anything, Conway!" she rejoiced. Tears for-gotten, she was her old, buoyant self again "So that wall *is* real, after all? I only about half believed it."

"Don't trust it too much, because he can cut it off from the outside any time he wants to. Remember what I told you: that necklace will warn you of any spy-ray in the ether, and the watch will detect anything below the level of the ether. It's dead now, of course, since our three phones are direct-connected; I'm in touch with Bradley, too. Don't be too scared; we've got a lot better chance than I thought we had."

"What? You don't mean it!"

"Absolutely. I'm beginning to think that maybe we've got something he doesn't know exists—our ultra-wave. Of course I wasn't surprised when his searchers failed to find our in-struments, but it never occurred to me that I might have a clear field to use them in! I can't quite believe it yet, but I haven't been able to find any indication that he can even detect the bands we are using. I'm going to look around over there with my spy-ray . . . I'm looking at you now—feel it?"

"Yes, the watch feels that way, now."

"Fine! Not a sign of interference over here, either. I can't find a trace of ultra-wave—anything below ether-level, you know—anywhere in the whole place. He's got so much stuff that we've never heard of that I supposed of course he'd have ultra-wave, too; but if he hasn't, that gives us the edge. Well, Bradley and I've got a lot of work to do . . . Wait a minute, I just had a thought. I'll be back in about a second."

There was a brief pause, then the soundless, but clear voice went on:

"Good hunting! That woman that gave you the blue willies isn't alive—she's full of the prettiest machinery and circuits you ever saw!"

"Oh, Conway!" and the girl's voice broke in an engulfing wave of thanksgiving and relief. "It was so unutterably hor-rible, thinking of what must have happened to her and to others like her!"

"He's running a colossal bluff, I think. He's good, all right, but he lacks quite a lot of being omnipotent. But don't get too cocky, either. Plenty has happened to plenty of women here, and men too—and plenty may happen to us unless we put out a few jets. Keep a stiff upper lip, and if you want us, yell. 'Bye!"

The silent voice ceased, the watch upon Clio's wrist again became an unobtrusive timepiece, and Costigan, in his solitary cell far below her tower room, turned his peculiarly goggled eyes toward other scenes. His hands, apparently idle in his pockets, manipulated tiny controls; his keen, highly-trained eyes studied every concealed detail of mechanism of the great globe. Finally, he took off the goggles and spoke in a low voice to Bradley, confined in another windowless room across the hall.

"I think I've got dope enough, Captain. I've found out where he put our armor and guns, and I've located all the main leads, controls, and generators. There are no ether-walls around us here, but every door is shielded, and there are guards outside our doors—one to each of us. They're robots, not men. That makes it harder, since they're undoubtedly connected direct to Roger's desk and will give an alarm at the first hint of abnormal performance. We can't do a thing until he leaves his desk. See that black panel, a little below the cord-switch to the right of your door? That's the conduit cover. When I give you the word, tear that off and you'll see one red wire in the cable. It feeds the shield-generator of your door. Break that wire and join me out in the hall. Sorry I had only one of these ultra-wave spies, but once we're together it won't be so bad. Here's what I thought we could do," and he went over in detail the only course of action which his survey had shown to be possible.

"There, he's left his desk!" Costigan exclaimed after the conversation had continued for almost an hour. "Now as soon as we find out where he's going, we'll start something . . . he's going to see Clio, the swine! This changes things, Bradley!" His hard voice was a curse.

"Somewhat!" blazed the captain. "I know how you two have been getting on all during the cruise. I'm with you, but what can we do?"

"We'll do something," Costigan declared grimly. "If he makes a pass at her I'll get him if I have to blow this whole sphere out of space, with us in it!"

"Don't do that, Conway," Clio's low voice, trembling but determined, was felt by both men. "If there's a chance for you to get away and do anything about fighting him, don't mind me. Maybe he only wants to talk about the ransom, anyway."

"He wouldn't talk ransom to *you*—he's going to talk

something else entirely," Costigan gritted, then his voice changed suddenly. "But say, maybe it's just as well this way. They didn't find our specials when they searched us, you know, and we're going to do plenty of damage right soon now. Roger probably isn't a fast worker—more the cat-and-mouse type, I'd say—and after we get started he'll have something on his mind besides you. Think you can stall him off and keep him interested for about fifteen minutes?"

"I'm sure I can—I'll do *anything* to help us, or you, get away from this horrible..." Her voice ceased as Roger broke the ether-wall of her apartment and walked toward the divan, upon which she crouched in wide-eyed, helpless, trembling terror.

"Get ready, Bradley!" Costigan directed tersely. "He left Clio's ether-wall off, so that any abnormal signals would be relayed to him from his desk—he knows that there's no chance of anyone disturbing him in that room. But I'm holding a beam on that switch, so that the wall is on, full strength. No matter what we do now, he can't get a warning. I'll have to hold the beam exactly in place, though, so you'll have to do the dirty work. Tear out that red wire and kill those two guards. You know how to kill a robot, don't you?"

"Yes—break his eye-lenses and his ear-drums and he'll stop whatever he's doing and send out distress calls ... Got 'em both. Now what?"

"Open my door—the shield switch is to the right."

Costigan's door flew open and the Triplanetary captain leaped into the room.

"Now for our armor!" he cried.

"Not yet!" snapped Costigan. He was standing rigid, goggled eyes staring immovably at a spot on the ceiling. "I can't move a millimeter until you've closed Clio's ether-wall switch. If I take this ray off it for a second we're sunk. Five floors up, straight ahead down a corridor—fourth door on right. When you're at the switch you'll feel my ray on your watch. Snap it up!"

"Right," and the captain leaped away at a pace to be equalled by few men of half his years.

Soon he was back, and after Costigan had tested the ether-wall of the "bridal suite" to make sure that no warning signal from his desk or his servants could reach Roger within it, the two officers hurried away toward the room in which their space-armor was.

"Too bad they don't wear uniforms," panted Bradley,

short of breath from the many flights of stairs. "Might have helped some as disguise."

"I doubt it—with so many robots around, they've probably got signals that we couldn't understand anyway. If we meet anybody it'll mean a battle. Hold it!" Peering through walls with his spy-ray, Costigan had seen two men approaching, blocking an intersecting corridor into which they must turn. "Two of 'em, a man and a robot—the robot's on your side. We'll wait here, right at the corner—when they round it take 'em!" and Costigan put away his goggles in readiness for strife.

All unsuspecting, the two pirates came into view, and as they appeared the two officers struck. Costigan, on the inside, drove a short, hard right low into the human pirate's abdomen. The fiercely-driven fist sank to the wrist into the soft tissues and the stricken man collapsed. But even as the blow landed Costigan had seen that there was a third enemy, following close behind the two he had been watching, a pirate who was even then training a ray projector upon him. Reacting automatically, Costigan swung his unconscious opponent around in front of him, so that it was into an enemy's body that the vicious ray tore, and not into his own. Crouching down into the smallest possible compass, he straightened out with the lashing force of a mighty steel spring, hurling the corpse straight at the flaming mouth of the projector. The weapon crashed to the floor and dead pirate and living went down in a heap. Upon that heap Costigan hurled himself, feeling for the pirate's throat. But the fellow had wriggled clear, and countered with a gouging thrust that would have torn out the eyes of a slower man, following it up instantly with a savage kick for the groin. No automaton this, geared and set to perform certain fixed duties with mechanical precision, but a lithe, strong man in hard training, fighting with every foul trick known to his murderous ilk.

But Costigan was no tyro in the art of dirty fighting. Few indeed were the maiming tricks of foul combat unknown to even the rank and file of the highly efficient under-cover branch of the Triplanetary Service; and Costigan, a Sector Chief, knew them all. Not for pleasure, sportsmanship, nor million-dollar purses did those secret agents use Nature's weapons. They came to grips only when it could not possibly be avoided, but when they were forced to fight in that fashion they went in with but one grim purpose—to kill, and to kill in the shortest possible space of time. Thus it was that Costigan's opening soon came. The pirate launched a vicious *coup de sabot*, which Costigan avoided by a lightning shift. It was a slight shift, barely enough to make the kicker miss, and two powerful hands closed upon that flying foot in midair like the sprung jaws of a bear-trap. Closed and twisted viciously, in the same fleeting instant. There was a shriek, smothered as a heavy boot crashed to its carefully predetermined mark—the pirate was out, definitely and permanently.

The struggle had lasted scarcely ten seconds, coming to its close just as Bradley finished blinding and deafening the robot. Costigan picked up the projector, again donned his spy-ray goggles, and the two hurried on.

"Nice work, Chief—it must be a gift to rough-house the way you do," Bradley exclaimed. "That's why you took the live one?"

"Practice helps some, too—I've been in brawls before, and I'm a lot younger and maybe a bit faster than you are," Costigan explained briefly, penetrant gaze rigidly to the fore as they ran along one corridor after another.

Several more guards, both living and mechanical, were encountered on the way, but they were not permitted to offer any opposition. Costigan saw them first. In the furious beam of the projector of the dead pirate they were riven into nothingness, and the two officers sped on to the room which Costigan had located from afar. The three suits of Triplanetary space armor had been locked up in a cabinet; a cabinet whose doors Costigan literally blew off with a blast of force rather than consume time in tracing the power leads.

"I feel like something now!" Costigan, once more encased in his own armor, heaved a great sigh of relief. "Rough-and-tumble's all right with one or two, but that generator room is full of grief, and we won't have any too much stuff as it is. We've got to take Clio's suit along—we'll carry it down to the door of the power room, drop it there, and pick it up on the way back."

Contemptuous now of possible guards, the armored pair strode toward the power plant—the very heart of the immense fortress of space. Guards were encountered, and captains—officers who signaled frantically to their chief, since he alone could unleash the frightful forces at his command, and who profanely wondered at his unwonted silence—but the enemy beams were impotent against the ether walls of that armor; and the pirates, without armor in the security of their own planetoid as they were, vanished utterly in the ravening beams of the twin Lewistons. As they paused before the door of the power room, both men felt Clio's voice raised in her first and last appeal, an appeal wrung from her against her will by the extremity of her position.

"Conway! Hurry! His eyes—they're tearing me apart! Hurry, dear!" In the horror-filled tones both men read clearly —however inaccurately—the girl's dire extremity. Each saw plainly a happy, carefree young Earth-girl, upon her first trip into space, locked inside an ether-wall with an over-brained, under-conscienced human machine—a super-intelligent, but lecherous and unmoral mechanism of flesh and blood, acknowledging no authority, ruled by nothing save his own scientific drivings and the almost equally powerful urges of his desires and passions! She must have fought with every resource at her command. She must have wept and pleaded, stormed and raged, feigned submission and played for time —and her torment had not touched in the slightest degree the merciless and gloating brain of the being who called himself Roger. Now his tantalizing, ruthless cat-play would be done, the horrible gray-brown face would be close to hers —she wailed her final despairing message to Costigan and attacked that hideous face with the fury of a tigress.

Costigan bit off a bitter imprecation. "Hold him just a second longer, sweetheart!" he cried, and the power room door vanished.

Through the great room the two Lewistons swept at full aperture and at maximum power, two rapidly-opening fans of death and destruction. Here and there a guard, more rapid than his fellows, trained a futile projector—a projector whose magazine exploded at the touch of that frightful field of force, liberating instantaneously its thousands upon thousands of kilowatt-hours of stored-up energy. Through the delicately adjusted, complex mechanisms the destroying beams tore. At their touch armatures burned out, high-tension leads volatilized in crashing, high-voltage arcs, masses of metal smoked and burned in the path of vast forces now seeking the easiest path to neutralization, delicate instruments blew up, copper ran in streams. As the last machine subsided into a semi-molten mass of metal the two wreckers, each grasping a brace, felt themselves become weightless and knew that they had accomplished the first part of their program.

Costigan leaped for the outer door. His the task to go to Clio's aid—Bradley would follow more slowly, bringing the girl's armor and taking care of any possible pursuit. As he sailed through the air he spoke.

"Coming, Clio! All right, girl?" Questioningly, half fear-fully.

"All right, Conway." Her voice was almost unrecogniz-able, broken in retching agony. "When everything went crazy he . . . found out that the ether-wall was up and . . . forgot all about me. He shut it off . . . and seemed to go crazy too . . . he is floundering around like a wild man now . . . I'm trying to keep . . . him from . . . going downstairs."

"Good girl—keep him busy one minute more—he's get-ting all the warnings at once and wants to get back to his board. But what's the matter with you? Did he . . . hurt you, after all?"

"Oh, no, not that—he didn't do anything but look at me —but that was bad enough—but I'm sick—horribly sick. I'm falling . . . I'm so dizzy that I can scarcely see . . . my head is breaking up into little pieces . . . I just *know* I'm going to die, Conway! Oh . . . oh!"

"Oh, is *that* all!" In his sheer relief that they had been in time, Costigan did not think of sympathizing with Clio's very real present distress of mind and body. "I forgot that you're a ground-gripper—that's just a little touch of space-sickness. It'll wear off directly . . . All right, I'm coming! Let go of him and get as far away from him as you can!"

He was now in the street. Perhaps two hundred feet dis-tant and a hundred feet above him was the tower room in which were Clio and Roger. He sprang directly toward its large window, and as he floated "upward" he corrected his course and accelerated his pace by firing backward at various angles with his heavy service pistol, uncaring that at the point of impact of each of those shells a small blast of de-struction erupted. He missed the window a trifle, but that did not matter—his flaming Lewiston opened a way for him, partly through the window, partly through the wall. As he soared through the opening he trained projector and pistol upon Roger, now almost to the door, noticing as he did so that Clio was clinging convulsively to a lamp-bracket upon the wall. Door and wall vanished in the Lewiston's terrific beam, but the pirate stood unharmed. Neither ravening ray nor explosive shell could harm him—he had snapped on the protective shield whose generator was always upon his person.

*   *   *

When Clio reported that Roger seemed to go crazy and was floundering around like a wild man, she had no idea of

how she was understanding the actual situation; for Gharlane of Eddore, then energizing the form of flesh that was
Roger, had for the first time in his prodigiously long life met
in direct conflict with an overwhelming superior force.

Roger had been sublimely confident that he could detect
the use, anywhere in or around his planetoid, of ultra-wave.
He had been equally sure that he could control directly and
absolutely the physical activities of any number of these
semi-intelligent "human beings".

But four Arisians in fusion—Drounli, Brolenteen, Nedanillor, and Kriedigan—had been on guard for weeks. When
the time came to act, they acted.

Roger's first thought, upon discovering what tremendous
and inexplicable damage had already been done, was to
destroy instantly the two men who were doing it. He could
not touch them. His second was to blast out of existence this
supposedly human female, but no more could he touch her.
His fiercest mental bolts spent themselves harmlessly three
millimeters away from her skin; she gazed into his eyes completely unaware of the torrents of energy pouring from them.
He could not even aim a weapon at her! His third was to
call for help to Eddore. He could not. The sub-ether was
closed; nor could he either discover the manner of its closing
or trace the power which was keeping it closed!

His Eddorian body, even if he could recreate it here,
could not withstand the environment—this Roger-thing would
have to do whatever it could, unaided by Gharlane's mental
powers. And, physically, it was a very capable body indeed.
Also, it was armed and armored with mechanisms of Gharlane's own devising; and Eddore's second-in-command was
in no sense a coward.

But Roger, while not exactly a ground-gripper, did not
know how to handle himself without weight; whereas Costigan, given six walls against which to push, was even more efficient in weightless combat than when handicapped by the
force of gravitation. Keeping his projector upon the pirate,
he seized the first club to hand—a long, slender pedestal
of metal—launched himself past the pirate chief. With
all the momentum of his mass and velocity and all the power
of his good right arm he swung the bar at the pirate's head.
That fiercely-driven mass of metal should have taken head
from shoulders, but it did not. Roger's shield of force was
utterly rigid and impenetrable; the only effect of the frightful
blow was to set him spinning, end over end, like the flying
baton of an acrobatic drum-major. As the spinning form

crashed against the opposite wall of the room Bradley floated in, carrying Clio's armor. Without a word the captain loosened the helpless girl's grip upon the bracket and encased her in the suit. Then, supporting her at the window, he held his Lewiston upon the captive's head while Costigan propelled him toward the opening. Both men knew that Roger's shield of force must be threatened every instant—that if he were allowed to release it he probably would bring to bear a hand-weapon even superior to their own.

Braced against the wall, Costigan sighted along Roger's body toward the most distant point of the lofty dome of the artificial planet and gave him a gentle push. Then, each grasping Clio by an arm, the two officers shoved mightily with their feet and the three armored forms darted away toward their only hope of escape—an emergency boat which could be launched through the shell of the great globe. To attempt to reach the *Hyperion* and to escape in one of her lifeboats would have been useless; they could not have forced the great gates of the main airlocks and no other exits existed. As they sailed onward through the air, Costigan keeping the slowly-floating form of Roger enveloped in his beam, Clio began to recover.

"Suppose they get their gravity fixed?" she asked, apprehensively. "And they're raying us and shooting at us!"

"They may have it fixed already. They undoubtedly have spare parts and duplicate generators, but if they turn it on the fall will kill Roger too, and he wouldn't like that. They'll have to get him down with a helicopter or something, and they know that we'll get them as fast as they come up. They can't hurt us with hand-weapons, and before they can bring up any heavy stuff they'll be afraid to use it, because we'll be too close to their shell.

"I wish we could have brought Roger along," he continued, savagely, to Bradley. "But you were right, of course—it'd be altogether too much like a rabbit capturing a wildcat. My Lewiston's about done right now, and there can't be much left of yours—what he'd do to us would be a sin and a shame."

Now at the great wall, the two men heaved mightily upon a lever, the gate of the emergency port swung slowly open, and they entered the miniature cruiser of the void. Costigan, familiar with the mechanism of the craft from careful study from his prison cell, manipulated the controls. Through gate after massive gate they went, until finally they were out in open space, shooting toward distant Tellus at the maximum acceleration of which their small craft was capable.

Costigan cut the other two phones out of circuit and spoke, his attention fixed upon some extremely distant point.

"Samms!" he called sharply. "Costigan. We're out . . . all right . . . yes . . . sure . . . absolutely . . you tell 'em, Sammy, I've got company here."

Through the sound-disks of their helmets the girl and the captain had heard Costigan's share of the conversation. Bradley stared at his erstwhile first officer in amazement, and even Clio had often heard that mighty, half-mythical name. Surely that bewildering young man must rank high, to speak so familiarly to Virgil Samms, the all-powerful head of the space-pervading Service of the Triplanetary League!

"You've turned in a general call-out," Bradley stated, rather than asked.

"Long ago—I've been in touch right along," Costigan answered. "Now that they know what to look for and know that ether-wave detectors are useless, they can find it. Every vessel in seven sectors, clear down to the scout patrols, is concentrating on this point, and the call is out for all battleships and cruisers afloat. There are enough operatives out there with ultra-waves to locate that globe, and once they spot it they'll point it out to all the other vessels."

"But how about the other prisoners?" asked the girl. "They'll be killed, won't they?"

"Hard telling," Costigan shrugged. "Depends on how things turn out. We lack a lot of being safe ourselves yet."

"What's worrying me mostly is our own chance," Bradley assented. "They will chase us, of course."

"Sure, and they'll have more speed than we have. Depends on how far away the nearest Triplanetary vessels are. But we've done everything we can do, for now."

Silence fell, and Costigan cut in Clio's phone and came over to the seat upon which she was reclining, white and stricken—worn out by the horrible and terrifying ordeals of the last few hours. As he seated himself beside her she blushed vividly, but her deep blue eyes met his gray ones steadily.

"Clio, I . . . we . . . you . . . that is," he flushed hotly and stopped. This secret agent, whose clear, keen brain no physical danger could cloud; who had proved over and over again that he was never at a loss in any emergency, however desperate—this quick-witted officer floundered in embarrassment like any schoolboy; but continued, doggedly: "I'm afraid that I gave myself away back there, but . . ."

"We gave ourselves away, you mean," she filled in the

pause. "I did my share, but I won't hold you to it if you don't want—but I *know* that you love me, Conway!"

"*Love* you!" the man groaned, his face lined and hard, his whole body rigid. "That doesn't half tell it, Clio. You don't need to hold me—I'm held for life. There never was a woman who meant anything to me before, and there never will be another. You're the only woman that ever existed. It isn't that. Can't you see that it's impossible?"

"Of course I can't—it isn't impossible, at all." She released her shields, four hands met and tightly clasped, and her low voice thrilled with feeling as she went on: "You love me and I love you. That is all that matters."

"I wish it were," Costigan returned bitterly, "but you don't know what you'd be letting yourself in for. It's who and what you are and who and what I am that's griping me. You, Clio Marsden, Curtis Marsden's daughter. Nineteen years old. You think you've been places and done things. You haven't. You haven't seen or done anything—you don't know what it's all about. And whom am I to love a girl like you? A homeless spacehound who hasn't been on any planet three weeks in three years. A hard-boiled egg. A trouble-shooter and a brawler by instinct and training. A sp . . ." he bit off the word and went on quickly: "Why, you don't know me at all, and there's a lot of me that you never *will* know—that I can't let you know! You'd better lay off me, girl, while you can. It'll be best for you, believe me."

"But I can't, Conway, and neither can you," the girl answered softly, a glorious light in her eyes. "It's too late fo that. On the ship it was just another of those things, but since then we've come really to know each other, and we're sunk. The situation is out of control, and we both know it—and neither of us would change it if we could, and you know that, too. I don't know very much, I admit, but I do know what you thought you'd have to keep from me, and I admire you all the more for it. We all honor the Service, Conway dearest—it is only you men who have made and are keeping the Three Planets fit places to live in—and I know that any one of Virgil Samms' assistants would have to be a man in a thousand million . . ."

"What makes you think that?" he demanded sharply.

"You told me so yourself, indirectly. Who else in the three worlds could possibly call him 'Sammy?' You are hard, of course, but you must be so—and I never did like soft men, anyway. And you brawl in a good cause. You are very much a *man*, my Conway; a real, *real* man, and I love you! Now, if they catch us, all right—we'll die together, at least!" she finished, intensely.

"You're right, sweetheart, of course," he admitted. "I don't believe that I *could* really let you let me go, even though I know you ought to," and their hands locked together even more firmly than before. "If we ever get out of this jam I'm going to kiss you, but this is no time to be taking off your helmet. In fact, I'm taking too many chances with you in keeping your shields off. Snap 'em on again—they ought to be getting fairly close by this time."

Hands released and armor again tight, Costigan went over to join Bradley at the control board.

"How are they coming, Captain?" he asked.

"Not so good. Quite a ways off yet. At least an hour, I'd say, before a cruiser can get within range."

"I'll see if I can locate any of the pirates chasing us. If I do it'll be by accident; this little spy-ray isn't good for much except close work. I'm afraid the first warning we'll have will be when they take hold of us with a tractor or spear us with a needle. Probably a beam, though; this is one of their emergency lifeboats and they wouldn't want to destroy it unless they have to. Also, I imagine that Roger wants us alive pretty badly. He has unfinished business with all three of us, and I can well believe that his 'not particularly pleasant extinction' will be even less so after the way we rooked him."

"I want you to do me a favor, Conway." Clio's face was white with horror at the thought of facing again that unspeakable creature of gray. "Give me a gun or something, please. I don't want him ever to look at me that way again, to say nothing of what else he might do, while I'm alive."

"He won't," Costigan assured her, narrow of eye and grim of jaw. He was, as she had said, hard. "But you don't want a gun. You might get nervous and use it too soon. I'll take care of you at the last possible moment, because if he gets hold of us we won't stand a chance of getting away again."

For minutes there was silence, Costigan surveying the ether in all directions with his ultra-wave device. Suddenly he laughed, and the others stared at him in surprise.

"No, I'm not crazy," he told them. "This is really funny; it had never occurred to me that the ether-walls of all these ships make them invisible. I can see them, of course, with this sub-ether spy, but they can't see us! I knew that they should have overtaken us before this. I've finally found them. They've passed us, and are now tacking around, waiting for us to do something so that they can see us! They're heading right into the Fleet—they think they're safe, of course, but what a surprise they've got coming to them!"

But it was not only the pirates who were to be surprised. Long before the pirate ship had come within extreme visibility range of the Triplanetary Fleet it lost its invisibility and was starkly outlined upon the lookout plates of the three fugitives. For a few seconds the pirate craft seemed unchanged, then it began to glow redly, with a red that seemed to become darker as it grew stronger. Then the sharp outlines blurred, puffs of air burst outward, and the metal of the hull became a viscous, fluid-like something, flowing away in a long, red streamer into seemingly empty space. Costigan turned his ultra-gaze into that space and saw that it was actually far from empty. There lay a vast something, formless and indefinite even to his sub-etheral vision; a something into which the viscid stream of transformed metal plunged. Plunged and vanished.

Powerful interference blanketed his ultra-wave and howled throughout his body; but in the hope that some parts of his message might get through he called Samms, and calmly and clearly he narrated everything that had just happened. He continued his crisp report, neglecting not the smallest detail, while their tiny craft was drawn inexorably toward a redly impermeable veil; continued it until their lifeboat, still intact, shot through that veil and he found himself unable to move. He was conscious, he was breathing normally, his heart was beating; but not a voluntary muscle would obey his will!

CHAPTER 9

FLEET AGAINST PLANETOID

ONE OF THE NEWEST AND FLEETEST OF THE PATROL VESSELS of the Triplanetary League, the heavy cruiser *Chicago* of the North American Division of the Tellurian Contingent, plunged stolidly through interplanetary vacuum. For five long weeks she had patrolled her alloted volume of space. In another week she would report back to the city whose name she bore, where her space-weary crew, worn by their long "tour" in the awesomely oppressive depths of the limitless void, would enjoy to the full their fortnight of refreshing planetary leave.

She was performing certain routine tasks—charting meteorites, watching for derelicts and other obstructions to navigation, checking in constantly with all scheduled spaceships in case of need, and so on—but primarily she was a warship. She was a mighty engine of destruction, hunting for the unauthorized vessels of whatever power or planet it was that had not only defied the Triplanetary League, but was evidently attempting to overthrow it; attempting to plunge the Three Planets back into the ghastly sink of bloodshed and destruction from which they had so recently emerged. Every space-ship within range of her powerful detectors was represented by two brilliant, slowly-moving points of light; one upon a greater micrometer screen, the other in the "tank," the immense, three-dimensional, minutely cubed model of the entire Solar System.

A brilliantly intense red light flared upon a panel and a bell clanged brazenly the furious signals of the sector alarm. Simultaneously a speaker roared forth its message of a ship in dire peril.

"Sector alarm! N. A. T. *Hyperion* gassed with Vee-Two. Nothing detectable in space, but . . ."

The half-uttered message was drowned out in a crackling roar of meaningless noise, the orderly signals of the bell became a hideous clamor, and the two points of light which had marked the location of the liner disappeared in widely spreading flashes of the same high-powered interference. Observers, navigators, and control officers were alike dumbfounded. Even the captain, in the shell-proof, shock-proof, and doubly ray-proof retreat of his conning compartment, was equally at a loss. No ship or thing could *possibly* be close enough to be sending out interfering waves of such tremendous power—yet there they were!

"Maximum acceleration, straight for the point where the *Hyperion* was when her tracers went out," the captain ordered, and through the fringe of that widespread interference he drove a solid beam, reporting concisely to GHQ. Almost instantly the emergency call-out came roaring in— every vessel of the Sector, of whatever class or tonnage, was to concentrate upon the point in space where the ill-fated liner had last been known to be.

Hour after hour the great globe drove on at maximum

acceleration, captain and every control officer alert and at high tension. But in Quartermasters' Department, deep down below the generator rooms, no thought was given to such minor matters as the disappearance of a *Hyperion*. The inventory did not balance, and two Q.M. privates were trying, profanely and without success, to find the discrepancy.

"Charged calls for Mark Twelve Lewistons, none requisitioned, on hand eighteen thous . . ." The droning voice broke off short in the middle of a word and the private stood rigid, in the act of reaching for another slip, every faculty concentrated upon something imperceptible to his companion.

"Come on, Cleve—snap it up!" the second commanded, but was silenced by a vicious wave of the listener's hand.

"What!" the rigid one exclaimed. "Reveal ourselves! Why, it's . . . Oh, all right . . . Oh, that's it . . . uh-huh . . . I see . . . yes, I've got it solid. So long!"

The inventory sheets fell unheeded from his hand, and his fellow private stared after him in amazement as he strode over to the desk of the officer in charge. That officer also stared as the hitherto easy-going and gold-bricking Cleve saluted crisply, showed him something flat in the palm of his left hand, and spoke.

"I've just got some of the funniest orders ever put out, lieutenant, but they came from 'way, 'way up. I'm to join the brass hats in the Center. You'll know all about it directly, I imagine. Cover me up as much as you can, will you?" and he was gone.

Unchallenged he made his way to the control room, and his curt "urgent report for the Captain" admitted him there without question. But when he approached the sacred precincts of the captain's own and inviolate room, he was stopped in no uncertain fashion by no less a personage than the Officer of the Day.

". . . and report yourself under arrest immediately!" the O.D. concluded his brief but pointed speech.

"You were right in stopping me, of course," the intruder conceded, unmoved. "I wanted to get in there without giving everything away, if possible, but it seems that I can't. Well, I've been ordered by Virgil Samms to report to the Captain, at once. See this? Touch it!" He held out a flat, insulated disk, cover thrown back to reveal a tiny golden meteor, at the sight of which the officer's truculent manner altered markedly.

"I've heard of them, of course, but I never saw one before," and the officer touched the shining symbol lightly with his finger, jerking backward as there shot through his whole body a thrilling surge of power, shouting into his very bones an unpronounceable syllable—the password of the Triplanetary Service. "Genuine or not, it gets you to the Captain. He'll know, and if it's a fake you'll be breathing space in five minutes."

Projector at the ready, the Officer of the Day followed Cleve into the Holy of Holies. There the grizzled four-striper touched the golden meteor lightly, then drove his piercing gaze deep into the unflinching eyes of the younger man. But that captain had won his high rank neither by accident nor by "pull"—he understood at once.

"It *must* be an emergency," he growled, half-audibly, still staring at his lowly Q-M clerk, "to make Samms uncover this way." He turned and curtly dismissed the wondering O. D. Then: "All right! Out with it!"

"Serious enough so that every one of us afloat has just received orders to reveal himself to his commanding officer and to anyone else, if necessary to reach that officer at once —orders never before issued. The enemy have been located. They have built a base, and have ships better than our best. Base and ships cannot be seen or detected by any ether wave. However, the Service has been experimenting for years with a new type of communicator beam; and, while pretty crude yet, it was given to us when the *Dione* went out without leaving a trace. One of our men was in the *Hyperion,* managed to stay alive, and has been sending data. I am instructed to attach my new phone set to one of the universal plates in your conning room, and to see what I can find."

"Go to it!" The captain waved his hand and the operative bent to his task.

"Commanders of all vessels of the Fleet!" The Headquarters speaker, receiver sealed upon the wave-length of the Admiral of the Fleet, broke the long silence. "All vessels in sectors L to R, inclusive, will interlock location signals. Some of you have received, or will receive shortly, certain communications from sources which need not be mentioned. Those commanders will at once send out red K4 screens. Vessels so marked will act as temporary flagships. Unmarked vessels will proceed at maximum to the nearest flagship, grouping about it in the regulation squadron cone in order of arrival. Squadrons most distant from objective point designated by flagship observers will proceed toward it at maximum; squadrons nearest it will decelerate or reverse velocity—that point must not be approached until full Fleet formation has been accomplished. Heavy and light cruisers of all other sectors inside the orbit of Mars..." The orders went on, directing the mobilization of the stupendous forces of the League, so that they would be in readiness in the highly improbable event of the failure of the massed power of seven sectors to reduce the pirate base.

In those seven sectors perhaps a dozen vessels threw out enormous spherical screens of intense red light, and as they did so their tracer points upon all the interlocked lookout plates also became ringed about with red. Toward those crimson markers the pilots of the unmarked vessels directed their courses at their utmost power; and while the white lights upon the lookout plates moved slowly toward and clustered about the red ones the ultra-instruments of the Service operatives were probing into space, sweeping the neighborhood of the computed position of the pirate's stronghold.

But the object sought was so far away that the small spy-ray sets of the Service men, intended as they were for close range work, were unable to make contact with the invisible planetoid for which they were seeking. In the captain's sanctum of the *Chicago,* the operative studied his plate for only a minute or two, then shut off his power and fell into a brown study, from which he was rudely aroused.

"Aren't you even going to *try* to find them?" demanded the captain.

"No," Cleve returned shortly. "No use—not half enough power or control. I'm trying to think . . . maybe . . . say, Captain, will you please have the Chief Electrician and a couple of radio men come in here?"

They came, and for hours, while the other ultra-wave men searched the apparently empty ether with their ineffective beams, the three technical experts and the erstwhile Quartermaster's clerk labored upon a huge and complex ultra-wave projector—the three blindly and with doubtful questions; the one with sure knowledge at least of what he was trying to do. Finally the thing was done, the crude, but efficient graduated circles were set, and the tubes glowed redly as their massed output drove into a tight beam of ultra-vibration.

"There it is, sir," Cleve reported, after some ten minutes of manipulation, and the vast structure of the miniature world flashed into being upon his plate. "You may notify the fleet —coordinates H 11.62, RA 124-31-16, and Dx about 173.2."

The report made and the assistants out of the room, the captain turned to the observer and saluted gravely.

"We have always known, sir, that the Service had *men;* but I had no idea that any one man could possibly do, on the spur of the moment, what you have just done—unless that man happened to be Lyman Cleveland."

"Oh, it doesn't . . ." the observer began, but broke off, muttering unintelligibly at intervals; then swung the visiray beam toward the Earth. Soon a face appeared upon the plate; the keen, but careworn face of Virgil Samms!

"Hello, Lyman," his voice came clearly from the speaker, and the Captain gasped—his ultra-wave observer and some-time clerk was Lyman Cleveland himself, probably the greatest living expert in beam transmission! "I knew that you'd do something, if it could be done. How about it—can the others install similar sets on their ships? I'm betting that they can't."

"Probably not," Cleveland frowned in thought. "This is a patchwork affair, made of gunny sacks and hay-wire. I'm holding it together by main strength and awkwardness, and even at that, it's apt to go to pieces any minute."

"Can you rig it up for photography?"

"I think so. Just a minute—yes, I can. Why?"

"Because there's something going on out there that neither we nor apparently the pirates know anything about. The Admiralty seems to think that it's the Jovians again, but we don't see how it can be—if it is, they have developed a lot of stuff that none of our agents has even suspected," and he recounted briefly what Costigan had reported to him, concluding: "Then there was a burst of interference—on the *ultra-band,* mind you—and I've heard nothing from him since. Therefore I want you to stay out of the battle entirely. Stay as far away from it as you can and still get good pictures of everything that happens. I will see that orders are issued to the *Chicago* to that effect."

"But listen . . ."

"Those are orders!" snapped Samms. "It is of the utmost importance that we know every detail of what is going to happen. The answer is pictures. The only possibility of obtaining pictures is that machine you have just developed. If the fleet wins, nothing will be lost. If the fleet loses—and I am not half as confident of success as the Admiral is—the *Chicago* doesn't carry enough power to decide the issue, and we will have the pictures to study, which is all-important. Besides, we have probably lost Conway Costigan today, and we don't want to lose *you,* too."

Cleveland remained silent, pondering this startling news, but the grizzled Captain, veteran of the Fourth Jovian War that he was, was not convinced.

"We'll blow them out of space, Mr. Samms!" he declared.

"You just think you will, Captain. I have suggested, as forcibly as possible, that the general attack be withheld until after a thorough investigation is made, but the Admiralty will not listen. They see the advisibility of withdrawing a camera ship, but that is as far as they will go."

"And that's plenty far enough!" growled the *Chicago's* commander, as the beam snapped off. "Mr. Cleveland, I don't like the idea of running away under fire, and I won't do it without direct orders from the Admiral."

"Of course you won't—that's why you are going . . ."

He was interrupted by a voice from the Headquarters speaker. The captain stepped up to the plate and, upon being recognized, he received the exact orders which had been requested by the Chief of the Triplanetary Service.

Thus it was that the *Chicago* reversed her acceleration, cut off her red screen, and fell rapidly behind, while the vessels following her shot away toward another crimson-flaring loader. Farther and farther back she dropped, back to the limiting range of the mechanism upon which Cleveland and his highly-trained assistants were hard at work. And during all this time the forces of the seven sectors had been concentrating. The pilot vessels, with their flaming red screens, each followed by a cone of space-ships, drew closer and closer together, approaching the *Fearless*—the British super-dreadnought which was to be the flagship of the Fleet—the mightiest and heaviest space-ship which had yet lifted her stupendous mass into the ether.

Now, systematically and precisely, the great Cone of Battle was coming into being; a formation developed during the Jovian Wars while the forces of the Three Planets were fighting in space for their very civilizations' existence, and one never used since the last space-fleets of Jupiter's murderous hordes had been wiped out.

The mouth of that enormous hollow cone was a ring of scout patrols, the smallest and most agile vessels of the fleet. Behind them came a somewhat smaller ring of light cruisers, then rings of heavy cruisers and of light battleships, and finally of heavy battleships. At the apex of the cone, protected by all the other vessels of the formation and in best position to direct the battle, was the flagship. In this formation every vessel was free to use her every weapon, with a minimum of danger to her sister ships; and yet, when the gigantic main projectors were operated along the axis of the formation, from the entire vast circle of the cone's mouth there flamed a cylindrical field of force of such intolerable

intensity that in it no conceivable substance could endure for
a moment!

The artifical planet of metal was now close enough so that
it was visible to the ultra-vision of the Service men, so plainly
visible that the cigar-shaped warships of the pirates were seen
issuing from the enormous air-locks. As each vessel shot out
into space it sped straight for the approaching fleet without
waiting to go into any formation—gray Roger believed his
structures invisible to Triplanetary eyes, thought that the presence of the fleet was the result of mathematical calculations,
and was convinced that his mighty vessels of the void would
destroy even that vast fleet without themselves becoming
known. He was wrong. The foremost vessels were allowed
actually to enter the mouth of that conical trap before an
offensive move was made. Then the vice-admiral in command
of the fleet touched a button, and simultaneously every generator in every Triplanetary vessel burst into furious activity.
Instantly the hollow volume of the immense cone became a
coruscating hell of resistless energy, an inferno which with
the velocity of light extended itself into a far-reaching cylinder
of rapacious destruction. Ether-waves they were, it is true, but
vibrations driven with such fierce intensity that the screens of
deflection surrounding the pirate vessels could not handle even
a fraction of their awful power. Invisibility lost, their defensive
screens flared briefly; but even the enormous force backing
Roger's inventions, far greater than that of any single Triplanetary vessel, could not hold off the incredible violence
of the massed attack of the hundreds of mighty vessels com-
posing the Fleet. Their defensive screens flared briefly, then
went down; their great hulls first glowing red, then shining
white, then in a brief moment exploding into flying masses of
red hot, molten, and gaseous metal.

A full two-thirds of Roger's force was caught in that raging,
incandescent beam; caught and obliterated: but the remainder
did not retreat to the planetoid. Darting out around the edge
of the cone at a stupendous acceleration, they attacked its
flanks and the engagement became general. But now, since
enough beams were kept upon each ship of the enemy so that
invisibility could not be restored, each Triplanetary war vessel
could attack with full efficiency. Magnesium flares and star-
shells illuminated space for a thousand miles, and from every
unit of both fleets was being hurled every item of solid, explosive and vibratory destruction known to the warfare of
that age. Offensive beams, rods and daggers of frightful power
struck and were neutralized by defensive screens equally cap-

able; the long range and furious dodging made ordinary solid, or even atomic-explosive projectiles useless; and both sides were filling all space with such a volume of blanketing frequencies that such radio-dirigible atomics as were launched could not be controlled, but darted madly and erratically hither and thither, finally to be exploded or volatilized harmlessly in mid-space by the touch of some fiercely insistant, probing beam of force.

Individually, however, the pirate vessels were far more powerful than those of the fleet, and that superiority soon began to make itself felt. The power of the smaller ships began to fail as their accumulators became discharged under the awful drain of the battle, and vessel after vessel of the Triplanetary fleet was hurled into nothingness by the concentrated blasts of the pirates' rays. But the Triplanetary forces had one great advantage. In furious haste the Service men had been altering the controls of the dirigible atomic torpedoes, so that they would respond to ultra-wave control; and, few in number though they were, each was highly effective.

A hard-eyed observer, face almost against his plate and both hands and both feet manipulating controls, hurled the first torpedo. Propelling rockets viciously aflame, it twisted and looped around the incandescent rods of destruction so thickly and starkly outlined, under perfect control; unaffected by the hideous distortion of all ether-borne signals. Through a pirate screen it went, and under the terrific blast of its detonation the entire midsection of the stricken battleship vanished. It should have been out, cold—but to the amazement of the observers, both ends kept on fighting with scarcely lessened power! Two more of the frightful bombs had to be launched —each remaining section had to be blown to bits—before those terrible beams went out! Not a man in that great fleet had even an inkling of the truth; that those great vessels, those awful engines of destruction, did not contain a single living creature: that they were manned and fought by automatons; robots controlled by keen-eyed, space-hardened veterans inside the pirates' planetoid!

But they were to receive an inkling of it. As ship after ship of the pirate fleet was destroyed, Roger realized that his navy was beaten, and forthwith all his surviving vessels darted toward the apex of the cone, where the heaviest battleships were stationed. There each hurled itself upon a Triplanetary warship, crashing to its own destruction, but in that destruction insuring the loss of one of the heaviest vessels of the enemy. Thus passed the *Fearless*, and twenty of the finest space-ships of the fleet as well. But the ranking officer assumed command, the war-cone was re-formed, and, yawning maw to the fore, the great formation shot toward the pirate stronghold, now near at hand. It again launched its stupendous cylinder of annihilation, but even as the mighty defensive screens of the planetoid flared into incandescently furious defense, the battle was interrupted and pirates and Triplanetarians learned alike that they were not alone in the ether.

Space became suffused with a redly impenetrable opacity, and through that indescribable pall there came reaching huge arms of force incredible; writhing, coruscating beams of power which glowed a baleful, although almost imperceptible, red. A vessel of unheard-of armament and power, hailing from the then unknown solar system of Nevia, had come to rest in that space. For months her commander had been searching for one ultra-precious substance. Now his detectors had found it; and, feeling neither fear of Triplanetarian weapons nor reluctance to sacrifice those thousands of Triplanetarian lives, he was about to take it!

CHAPTER 10

WITHIN THE RED VEIL

NEVIA, THE HOME PLANET OF THE MARAUDING SPACE-SHIP, would have appeared peculiar indeed to Terrestrial senses. High in the deep red heavens a fervent blue sun poured down its flood of brilliant purplish light upon a world of water. Not a cloud was to be seen in that flaming sky, and through that dustless atmosphere the eye could see the horizon—a horizon three times as distant as the one to which we are accustomed —with a distinctness and clarity impossible in our Terra's dust-filled air. As that mighty sun dropped below the horizon the sky would fill suddenly with clouds and rain would fall violently and steadily until midnight. Then the clouds would vanish as suddenly as they had come into being, the torrential downpour would cease, and through that huge world's wonderfully transparent gaseous envelope the full glory of the firmament would be revealed. Not the firmament as we know it— for that hot blue sun and Nevia, her one planet-child, were light-years distant from Old Sol and his numerous brood—but a strange and glorious firmament containing few constellations familiar to Earthly eyes.

Out of the vacuum of space a fish-shaped vessel of the void—the vessel that was to attack so boldly both the massed fleet of Triplanetary and Roger's planetoid—plunged into the rarefied outer atmosphere, and crimson beams of force tore shriekingly through the thin air as it braked its terrific speed. A third of the circumference of Nevia's mighty globe was traversed before the velocity of the craft could be reduced sufficiently to make a landing possible. Then, approaching the twilight zone, the vessel dived vertically downward, and it became evident that Nevia was neither entirely aqueous nor devoid of intelligent life. For the blunt nose of the space-ship was pointing toward what was evidently a half-submerged city, a city whose buildings were flat-topped, hexagonal towers, exactly alike in size, shape, color, and material. These buildings were arranged as the cells of a honeycomb would be if each cell were separated from its neighbors by a relatively narrow channel of water, and all were built of the same white metal. Many bridges and more tubes extended through the air from building to building, and the watery "streets" teemed with swimmers, with surface craft, and with submarines.

The pilot, stationed immediately below the conical prow of the space-ship, peered intently through thick windows which afforded unobstructed vision in every direction. His four huge and contractile eyes were active, each operating independently in sending its own message to his peculiar but capable brain. One was watching the instruments, the others scanned narrowly the immense, swelling curve of the ship's belly, the water upon which his vessel was to land, and the floating dock to which it was to be moored. Four hands—if hands they could be called—manipulated levers and wheels with infinite delicacy of touch, and with scarcely a splash the immense mass of the Nevian vessel struck the water and glided to a stop within a foot of its exact berth.

Four mooring bars dropped neatly into their sockets and the captain-pilot, after locking his controls in neutral, released his safety straps and leaped lightly from his padded bench to the floor. Scuttling across the floor and down a runway upon his four short, powerful, heavily scaled legs, he slipped smoothly into the water and flashed away, far below the surface. For Nevians are true amphibians. Their blood is cold; they use with equal comfort and efficiency gills and lungs for breathing; their scaly bodies are equally at home in the water or in the air; their broad, flat feet serve equally well for running about upon a solid surface or for driving their streamlined bodies through the water at a pace few fishes can equal.

Through the water the Nevian commander darted along, steering his course accurately by means of his short, vaned tail. Through an opening in a wall he sped and along a submarine hallway, emerging upon a broad ramp. He scurried up the incline and into an elevator which lifted him to the top of the hexagon, directly into the office of the Secretary of Commerce of all Nevia.

"Welcome, Captain Nerado!" The Secretary waved a tentacular arm and the visitor sprang lightly upon a softly cushioned bench, where he lay at ease, facing the official across his low, flat "desk." "We congratulate you upon the success of your final trial flight. We received all your reports, even while you were traveling at ten times the velocity of light. With the last difficulties overcome, you are now ready to start?"

"We are ready," the captain-scientist replied, soberly. "Mechanically, the ship is as nearly perfect as our finest minds can make her. She is stocked for two years. All the iron-bearing suns within reach have been plotted. Everything is ready except the iron. Of course the Council refused to allow us any of the national supply—how much were you able to purchase for us in the market?"

"Nearly ten pounds . . ."

"Ten pounds! Why, the securities we left with you could not have bought two pounds, even at the price then prevailing!"

"No, but you have friends. Many of us believe in you, and have dipped into our own resources. You and your fellow scientists of the expedition have each contributed his entire personal fortune; why should not some of the rest of us also contribute, as private citizens?"

"Wonderful—we thank you. Ten pounds!" The captain's great triangular eyes glowed with an intense violet light. "At least a year of cruising. But . . . what if, after all, we should be wrong?"

"In that case you shall have consumed ten pounds of irreplaceable metal." The Secretary was unmoved. "That is the viewpoint of the Council and of almost everyone else. It is not the waste of treasure they object to; it is the fact that ten pounds of iron will be forever lost."

"A high price, truly," the Columbus of Nevia assented. "And after all, I may be wrong."

"You probably are wrong," his host made startling answer. "It is practically certain—it is almost a demonstrable mathematical fact—that no other sun within hundreds of thousands of light-years of our own has a planet. In all probability Nevia is the only planet in the entire Universe. We are very probably the only intelligent life in the Universe. There is only one chance in numberless millions that anywhere within the cruising range of your newly perfected space-ship there may be an iron-bearing planet upon which you can effect a landing. There is a larger chance, however, that you may be able to find a small, cold, iron-bearing cosmic body—small enough so that you can capture it. Although there are no mathematics by which to evaluate the probability of such an occurrence, it is upon that larger chance that some of us are staking a portion of our wealth. We expect no return whatever, but if you *should* by some miracle happen to succeed, what then? Deep seas being made shallow, civilization extending itself over the globe, science advancing by leaps and bounds, Nevia becoming populated as she should be peopled —that, my friend, is a chance well worth taking!"

The Secretary called in a group of guards, who escorted the small package of priceless metal to the space-ship. Before the massive door was sealed the friends bade each other farewell.

". . . I will keep in touch with you on the ultra-wave," the Captain concluded. "After all, I do not blame the Council for refusing to allow the other ship to go out. Ten pounds of iron will be a fearful loss to the world. If we *should* find iron, however, see to it that she loses no time in following us."

"No fear of that! If you find iron she will set out at once, and all space will soon be full of vessels. Good-bye."

The last opening was sealed and Nerado shot the great vessel into the air. Up and up, out beyond the last tenuous trace of atmosphere, on and on through space it flew with ever-increasing velocity until Nevia's gigantic blue sun had been left so far behind that it became a splendid blue-white star. Then, projectors cut off to save the precious iron whose disintegration furnished them power, for week after week Captain Nerado and his venturesome crew of scientists drifted idly through the illimitable void.

There is no need to describe in detail Nerado's tremendous voyage. Suffice it to say that he found a G-type dwarf star possessing planets—not one planet only, but six . . . seven . . . eight . . . yes, at least nine! And most of those worlds were themselves centers of attraction around which were circling one or more worldlets! Nerado thrilled with joy as he applied a full retarding force, and every creature aboard that great vessel had to peer into a plate or through a telescope before he could believe that planets other than Nevia did in reality exist!

Velocity checked to the merest crawl, as space-speeds go, and with electro-magnetic detector screens full out, the Nevian vessel crept toward our sun. Finally the detectors encountered an obstacle, a conductive substance which the patterns showed conclusively to be practically pure iron. Iron—an enormous mass of it—floating alone out in space! Without waiting to investigate the nature, appearance, or structure of the precious mass, Nerado ordered power into the converters and drove an enormous softening field of force upon the object—a force of such a nature that it would condense the metallic iron into an allotropic modification of much smaller bulk; a red, viscous, extremely dense and heavy liquid which could be stored conveniently in his tanks.

No sooner had the precious fluid been stored away than the detectors again broke into an uproar. In one direction was an enormous mass of iron, scarcely detectable; in another a great number of smaller masses; in a third an isolated mass, comparatively small in size. Space seemed to be full of iron, and Nerado drove his most powerful beam toward distant Nevia and sent an exultant message.

"We have found iron—easily obtained and in unthinkable quantity—not in fractions of milligrams, but in millions upon unmeasured millions of tons! Send our sister ship here at once!"

"Nerado!" The captain was called to one of the observation plates as soon as he had opened his key. "I have been investigating the mass of iron now nearest us, the small one. It is an artificial structure, a small space-boat, and there are three creatures in it—monstrosities certainly, but they must possess some intelligence or they could not be navigating space."

"What? Impossible!" exclaimed the chief explorer. "Probably, then, the other was—but no matter, we had to have the iron. Bring the boat in without converting it, so that we may study at our leisure both the beings and their mechanisms," and Nerado swung his own visiray beam into the emergency boat, seeing there the armored figures of Clio Marsden and the two Triplanetary officers.,

"They are indeed intelligent," Nerado commented, as he detected and silenced Costigan's ultra-beam communicator. "Not, however, as intelligent as I had supposed," he went on, after studying the peculiar creatures and their tiny spaceship more in detail. "They have immense stores of iron, yet use it for nothing other than building material. They make little and inefficient use of atomic energy. They apparently have a rudimentary knowledge of ultra-waves, but do not use them intelligently—they cannot neutralize even these ordinary forces we are now employing. They are of course more intelligent than the lower ganoids, or even than some of the higher fishes, but by no stretch of the imagination can they be compared to us. I am quite relieved—I was afraid that in my haste I might have slain members of a highly developed race."

The helpless boat, all her forces neutralized, was brought up close to the immense flying fish. There flaming knives of force sliced her neatly into sections and the three rigid armored figures, after being bereft of their external weapons, were brought through the airlocks and into the control room, while the pieces of their boat were stored away for future study. The Nevian scientists first analyzed the air inside the space-suits of the Terrestrials, then carefully removed the protective coverings of the captives.

Costigan—fully conscious through it all and now able to move a little, since the peculiar temporary paralysis was wearing off—braced himself for he knew not what shock, but it was needless; their grotesque captors were not torturers. The air, while somewhat more dense than Earth's and of a peculiar odor, was eminently breathable, and even though the vessel was motionless in space an almost-normal gravitation gave them a large fraction of their usual weight.

After the three had been relieved of their pistols and other articles which the Nevians thought might prove to be weapons, the strange paralysis was lifted entirely. The Earthly clothing puzzled the captors immensely, but so strenuous were the objections raised to its removal that they did not press the point, but fell back to study their find in detail.

Then faced each other the representatives of the civilizations of two widely separated solar systems. The Nevians studied the human beings with interest and curiosity blended largely with loathing and repulsion; the three Terrestrials regarded the unmoving, expressionless "faces"—if those coned heads could be said to possess such thing—with horror and disgust, as well as with other emotions, each according to his type and training. For to human eyes the Nevian is a fearful thing. Even today there are few Terrestrials—or Solarians, for that matter—who can look at a Nevian, eye to eye, without feeling a creeping of the skin and experiencing a "gone" sensation in the pit of the stomach. The horny, wrinkled, drought-resisting Martian, whom we all know and rather like, is a hideous being indeed. The bat-eyed, colorless, hairless, practically skinless Venerian is worse. But they both are, after all, remote cousins of Terra's humanity, and we get along with them quite well whenever we are compelled to visit Mars or Venus. But the Nevians—

The horizontal, flat, fish-like body is not so bad, even supported as it is by four short, powerful, scaly, flat-footed legs; and terminating as it does in the weird, four-vaned tail. The neck, even, is endurable, although it is long and flexible, heavily scaled, and is carried in whatever eye-wringing loops or curves the owner considers most convenient or ornamental at the time. Even the smell of a Nevian—a maladorous reek of over-ripe fish—does in time become tolerable, especially if sufficiently disguised with creosote, which purely Terrestrial chemical is the most highly prized perfume of Nevia. But the head! It is that member that makes the Nevian so appalling to Earthly eyes, for it is a thing utterly foreign to all Solarian history or experience. As most Tellurians already know, it is fundamentally a massive cone, covered with scales, based spearhead-like upon the neck. Four great sea-green, triangular eyes are spaced equidistant from each other about half way up the cone. The pupils are contractile at will, like the eyes of the cat, permitting the Nevian to see equally well in any ordinary extreme of light or darkness. Immediately below each eye springs out a long, jointless, boneless, tentacular arm; an arm which at its extremity divides into eight delicate and sensitive, but very strong, "fingers." Below each arm is a mouth: a beaked, needle-tusked orifice of dire potentialities. Finally, under the overhanging edge of the cone-shaped head are the delicately-frilled organs which serve either as gills or as nostrils and lungs, as may be desired. To other Nevians the eyes and other features are highly expressive, but to us they appear utterly cold and unmoving. Terrestrial senses can detect no changes of expression in a Nevian's "face." Such were the frightful beings at whom the three prisoners stared with sinking hearts.

But if we human beings have always considered Nevians grotesque and repulsive, the feeling has always been mutual. For those "monstrous" beings are a highly intelligent and extremely sensitive race, and our—to us—trim and graceful human forms seem to them the very quintessence of malformation and hideousness.

"Good Heavens, Conway!" Clio exclaimed, shrinking against Costigan as his left arm flashed around her. "What horrible monstrosities! And they can't talk—not one of them has made a sound—suppose they can be deaf and dumb?"

But at the same time Nerado was addressing his fellows.

"What hideous, deformed creatures they are! Truly a low form of life, even though they do possess some intelligence. They cannot talk, and have made no signs of having heard our words to them—do you suppose that they communicate by sight? That those weird contortions of their peculiarly placed organs serve as speech?"

Thus both sides, neither realizing that the other had spoken. For the Nevian voice is pitched so high that the lowest note audible to them is far above our limit of hearing. The shrillest note of a Terrestrial piccolo is to them so profoundly low that it cannot be heard.

"We have much to do." Nerado turned away from the captives. "We must postpone further study of the specimens until we have taken aboard a full cargo of the iron which is so plentiful here."

"What shall we do with them, sir?" asked one of the Nevian officers. "Lock them in one of the storage rooms?"

"Oh, no! They might die there, and we must by all means keep them in good condition, to be studied most carefully by the fellows of the College of Science. What a commotion there will be when we bring in this group of strange creatures, living proof that there are other suns possessing planets; planets which are supporting organic and intelligent life! You may put them in three communicating rooms, say in the fourth section—they will undoubtedly require light and exercise. Lock all the exits, of course, but it would be best to leave the doors between the rooms unlocked, so that they can be together or apart, as they choose. Since the smallest one, the female, stays so close to the larger male, it may be that they are mates. But since we know nothing of their habits or customs, it will be best to give them all possible freedom compatible with safety."

Nerado turned back to his instruments and three of the frightful crew came up to the human beings. One walked away, waving a couple of arms in an unmistakable signal that the prisoners were to follow him. The three obediently set out after him, the other two guards falling behind.

"Now's our best chance!" Costigan muttered, as they passed through a low doorway and entered a narrow corridor. "Watch that one ahead of you, Clio—hold him for a second if you can. Bradley, you and I will take the two behind us—now!"

Costigan stooped and whirled. Seizing a cable-like arm, he pulled the outlandish head down, the while the full power of his mighty right leg drove a heavy service boot into the place where scaly neck and head joined. The Nevian fell, and instantly Costigan leaped at the leader, ahead of the girl. Leaped; but dropped to the floor, again paralyzed. For the Nevian leader had been alert, his four eyes covering the entire circle of vision, and he had acted rapidly. Not in time to stop Costigan's first berserk attack—the First Officer's reactions were practically instantaneous and he moved fast— but in time to retain command of the situation. Another Nevian appeared, and while the stricken guard was recovering, all four arms wrapped tightly around his convulsively looping, writhing neck, the three helpless Terrestrials were lifted into the air and carried bodily into the quarters to which Nerado had assigned them. Not until they had been placed upon cushions in the middle room and the heavy metal doors had been locked upon them did they again find themselves able to use arms or legs.

"Well, that's another round we lose," Costigan commented, cheerfully. "A guy can't mix it very well when he can neither kick, strike, nor bite. I expected those lizards to rough me up then, but they didn't."

"They don't want to hurt us. They want to take us home with them, wherever that is, as curiosities, like wild animals or something," decided the girl, shrewdly. "They're pretty bad, of course, but I like them a lot better than I do Roger and his robots, anyway."

"I think you have the right idea, Miss Marsden," Bradley rumbled. "That's it, exactly. I feel like a bear in a cage. I should think you'd feel worse than ever. What chance has an animal of escaping from a menagerie?"

"These animals, lots. I'm feeling better and better all the time," Clio declared, and her serene bearing bore out her words. "You two got us out of that horrible place of Roger's, and I'm pretty sure that you will get us away from here, somehow or other. They may think we're stupid animals, but before you two and the Triplanetary Patrol and the Service get done with them they'll have another think coming."

"That's the old fight, Clio!" cheered Costigan. "I haven't got it figured out as close as you have, but I get about the same answer. These four-legged fish carry considerably heavier stuff than Roger did, I'm thinking; but they'll be up against something themselves pretty quick that is *no* light-weight, believe me!"

"Do you know something, or are you just whistling in the dark?" Bradley demanded.

"I know a little; not much. Engineering and Research have been working on a new ship for a long time; a ship to travel so much faster than light that it can go anywhere in the Galaxy and back in a month or so. New sub-ether drive, new atomic power, new armament, new everything. Only bad thing about it is that it doesn't work so good yet—it's fuller of bugs than a Venerian's kitchen. It has blown up five times that I know of, and has killed twenty-nine men. But when they get it licked they'll *have something!*"

"When, or if?" asked Bradley, pessimistically.

"I said *when!*" snapped Costigan, his voice cutting. "When the Service goes after anything they get it, and when they get it it *stays . . .*" He broke off abruptly and his voice lost its edge. "Sorry. Didn't mean to get high, but I think we'll have help, if we can keep our heads up a while. And it looks good—these are first-class cages they've given us. All the comforts of home, even to lookout plates. Let's see what's going on, shall we?"

After some experimenting with the unfamiliar controls Costigan learned how to operate the Nevian visiray, and upon the plate they saw the Cone of Battle hurling itself toward Roger's planetoid. They saw the pirate fleet rush out to do battle with Triplanetary's massed forces, and with bated breath they watched every maneuver of that epic battle to its savagely sacrificial end. And that same battle was being watched, also with the most intense interest, by the Nevians in their control room.

"It is indeed a bloodthirsty combat," mused Nerado at his observation plate. "And it is peculiar—or rather, probably only to be expected from a race of such a low stage of development—that they employ only ether-borne forces. Warfare seems universal among primitive types—indeed, it is not so long ago that our own cities, few in number though they are, ceased fighting each other and combined against the semicivilized fishes of the greater deeps."

He fell silent, and for many minutes watched the furious battle between the two navies of the void. That conflict ended, he watched the Triplanetary fleet reform its battle cone and rush upon the planetoid.

"Destruction, always destruction," he sighed, adjusting his power switches. "Since they are bent upon mutual destruction I can see no purpose in refraining from destroying all of them. We need the iron, and they are a useless race."

He launched his softening, converting field of dull red energy. Vast as that field was, it could not encompass the whole fleet, but half of the lip of the gigantic cone soon disappeared, its component vessels subsiding into a sluggishly flowing stream of allotropic iron. The fleet, abandoning its attack upon the planetoid, swung its cone around, to bring the flame-erupting axis to bear upon the formless something dimly perceptible to the ultra-vision of Samms' observers. Furiously the gigantic composite beam of the massed fleet was hurled, nor was it alone.

For Gharlane had known, ever since the easy escape of his human prisoners, that something was occurring which was completely beyond his experience, although not beyond his theoretical knowledge. He had found the sub-ether closed; he had been unable to make his sub-ethereal weapons operative against either the three captives or the war-vessels of the Triplanetary Patrol. Now, however, he could work in the sub-ethereal murk of the newcomers; a light trial showed him that if he so wished he could use sub-ethereal offenses against them. What was the real meaning of those facts?

He had become convinced that those three persons were no more human than was Roger himself. Who or what was activating them? It was definitely not Eddorian workmanship; no Eddorian would have developed those particular techniques, nor could possibly have developed them without his knowledge. What, then? To do what had been done necessitated the existence of a race as old and as capable as the Eddorians, but of an entirely different nature; and, according to Eddore's vast Information Center, no such race existed or ever had existed.

Those visitors, possessing mechanisms supposedly known only to the science of Eddore, would also be expected to possess the mental powers which had been exhibited. Were they recent arrivals from some other space-time continuum? Probably not—Eddorian surveys had found no trace of any such life in any reachable plenum. Since it would be utterly fantastic to postulate the unheralded appearance of two such races at practically the same moment, the conclusion seemed unavoidable that these as yet unknown beings were the protectors—the activators, rather—of the two Triplanetary officers and the woman. This view was supported by the fact that while the strangers had attacked Triplanetary's fleet and had killed thousands of Triplanetary's men, they had actually rescued those three supposedly human beings. The planetoid, then would be attacked next. Very well, he would join Triplanetary in attacking them—with weapons no more dangerous to them than Triplanetary's own—the while preparing his real attack, which would come later. Roger issued orders; and waited; and thought more and more intensely upon one point which remained obsure—why, when the strangers themselves destroyed Triplanetary's fleet, had Roger been unable to use his most potent weapons against that fleet?

Thus, then, for the first time in Triplanetary's history, the forces of law and order joined hands with those of piracy and banditry against a common foe. Rods, beams, planes, and stilettos of unbearable energy the doomed fleet launched, in addition to its terrifically destructive main beam: Roger hurled every material weapon at his command. But bombs, high-explosive shells, even the ultra-deadly atomic torpedoes, alike were ineffective; alike simply vanished in the redly murky veil of nothingness. And the fleet was being melted. In quick succession the vessels flamed red, shrank together, gave out their air, and merged their component iron into the intensely crimson, sullenly viscous stream which was flowing through the impenetrable veil against which both Triplanetarians and pirates were directing their terrific offense.

The last vessel of the attacking cone having been converted and the resulting metal stored away, the Nevians—as Roger had anticipated—turned their attention toward the planetoid. But that structure was no feeble warship. It had been designed by, and built under the personal supervision of, Gharlane of Eddore. It was powered, equipped, and armed to meet any emergency which Gharlane's tremendous mind had been able to envision. Its entire bulk was protected by the shield whose qualities had so surprised Costigan; a shield far more effective than any Tellurian scientist or engineer would have believed possible.

The voracious converting beam of the Nevians, below the level of the ether though it was, struck that shield and rebounded; defeated and futile. Struck again, again rebounded; then struck and clung hungrily, licking out over that impermeable surface in darting tongues of flame as the surprised Nerado doubled and then quadrupled his power. Fiercer and fiercer the Nevian flood of force drove in. The whole immense globe of the planetoid became one scintillant ball of raw, red energy; but still the pirates' shield remained intact.

Gray Roger sat coldly montionless at his great desk, the top of which was now swung up to become a panel of massed and tiered instruments and controls. He could carry this load forever—but unless he was very wrong, this load would change shortly. What then? The essence that was Gharlane could not be killed—could not even be hurt—by any physical, chemical, or nuclear force. Should he stay with the planetoid to its end, and thus perforce return to Eddore with no material evidence whatever? He would not. Too much remained undone. Any report based upon his present information could be neither complete nor conclusive, and reports submitted by Gharlane of Eddore to the coldly cynical and ruthlessly analytical innermost Circle had always been and always would be both.

It was a fact that there existed at least one non-Eddorian mind which was the equal of his own. If one, there would be a race of such minds. The thought was galling; but to deny the existence of a fact would be the essence of stupidity. Since power of mind was a function of time, that race must be of approximately the same age as his own. Therefore the Eddorian Information Center, which by the inference of its completeness denied the existence of such a race, was wrong. It was not complete.

Why was it not complete? The only possible reason for two such races remaining unaware of the existence of each other would be the deliberate intent of one of them. Therefore, at some time in the past, the two races had been in contact for at least an instant of time. All Eddorian knowledge of that meeting had been suppressed and no more contacts had been allowed to occur.

The conclusion reached by Gharlane was a disturbing thing indeed; but, being an Eddorian, he faced it squarely. He did not have to wonder how such a suppression could have been accomplished—he knew. He also knew that his own mind contained everything known to his every ancestor since the first Eddorian was: the probability was exceedingly great that if any such contact had ever been made his mind would still contain at least some information concerning it, however carefully suppressed that knowledge had been.

He thought. Back . . . back . . . farther back . . . farther still . . .

And as he thought, an interfering force began to pluck at him; as though palpable tongs were pulling out of line the mental probe with which he was exploring the hitherto unplumbed recesses of his mind.

"Ah . . . so you do not want me to remember?" Roger asked aloud, with no change in any lineament of his hard, gray face. "I wonder . . . do you really believe that you can keep me from remembering? I must abandon this search for the moment, but rest assured that I shall finish it very shortly."

*   *   *

"Here is the analysis of his screen, sir." A Nevian computer handed his chief a sheet of metal, bearing rows of symbols.

"Ah, a polycyclic . . . complete coverage . . . a screen of that type was scarcely to have been expected from such a low form of life," Nerado commented, and began to adjust dials and controls.

As he did so the character of the clinging mantle of force changed. From red it flamed quickly through the spectrum, became unbearably violet, then disappeared; and as it disappeared the shielding wall began to give way. It did not cave in abruptly, but softened locally, sagging into a peculiar grouping of valleys and ridges—contesting stubbornly every inch of position lost.

Roger experimented briefly with inertialessness. No use. As he had expected, they were prepared for that. He summoned a few of the ablest of his scientist-slaves and issued instructions. For minutes a host of robots toiled mightily, then a portion of the shield bulged out and became a tube extending beyond the attacking layers of force; a tube from which there erupted a beam of violence incredible. A beam behind which was every erg of energy that the gigantic mechanisms of the planetoid could yield. A beam that tore a hole through the redly impenetrable Nevian field and hurled itself upon the inner screen of the fish-shaped cruiser in frenzied incandesence. And was there, or was there not, a lesser eruption upon the other side— -an almost imperceptible flash, as though something had shot from the doomed planetoid out into space?

Nerado's neck writhed convulsively as his tortured drivers whined and shrieked at the terrific overload; but Roger's effort was far too intense to be long maintained. Generator after generator burned out, the defensive screen collapsed, and the red converter beam attacked voraciously the unresisting metal of those prodigious walls. Soon there was a terrific explosion as the pent-up air of the planetoid broke through its weakening container, and the sluggish river of allotropic iron flowed in an ever larger stream, ever faster.

"It is well that we had an unlimited supply of iron." Nerado almost tied a knot in his neck as he spoke in huge relief. "With but the seven pounds remaining of our original supply, I fear that it would have been difficult to parry that last thrust."

"Difficult?" asked the second in command. "We would now be free atoms in space. But what shall I do with this iron? Our reservoirs will not hold more than half of it. And how about that one ship which remains untouched?"

"Jettison enough supplies from the lower holds to make room for this lot. As for that one ship, let it go. We will be overloaded as it is, and it is of the utmost importance that we get back to Nevia as soon as possible."

This, if Gharlane could have heard it, would have answered his question. All Arisia knew that it was *necessary* for the camera-ship to survive. The Nevians were interested only in iron; but the Eddorian, being a perfectionist, would not have been satisfied with anything less than the complete destruction of every vessel of Triplanetary's fleet.

The Nevian space-ship moved away, sluggishly now because of its prodigious load. In their quarters in the fourth section the three Terrestrials, who had watched with strained attention the downfall and absorption of the planetoid, stared at each other with drawn faces. Clio broke the silence.

"Oh, Conway, this is ghastly! It's . . . it's just simply too damned perfectly horrible!" she gasped, then recovered a measure of her customary spirit as she stared in surprise at Costigan's face. For it was thoughtful, his eyes were bright and keen—no trace of fear or disorganization was visible in any line of his hard young face.

"It's not so good," he admitted frankly. "I wish I wasn't such a dumb cluck—if Lyman Cleveland or Fred Rodebush were here they could help a lot, but I don't know enough about any of their stuff to flag a hand-car. I can't even interpret that funny flash—if it really was a flash—that we saw."

"Why bother about one little flash, after all that really did happen?" asked Clio, curiously.

"You think Roger launched something? He couldn't have —I didn't see a thing," Bradley argued.

"I don't know what to think. I've never seen anything material sent out so fast that I couldn't trace it with an ultrawave—but on the other hand, Roger's got a lot of stuff that I never saw anywhere else. However, I don't see that it has anything to do with the fix we're in right now—but at that, we might be worse off. We're still breathing air, you notice, and if they don't blanket my wave I can still talk."

He put both hands into his pockets and spoke.

"Samms? Costigan. Put me on a recorder, quick—I probably haven't got much time," and for ten minutes he talked, concisely and as rapidly as he could utter words, reporting clearly and exactly everything that had transpired. Suddenly he broke off, writhing in agony. Frantically he tore his shirt open and hurled a tiny object across the room.

"Wow!" he exclaimed. "They may be deaf, but they can certainly detect an ultra-wave, and what an interference they can set up on it! No, I'm not hurt," he reassured the anxious girl, now at his side, "but it's a good thing I had you out of circuit—it would have jolted you loose from six or seven of your back teeth."

"Have you any idea where they're taking us?" she asked soberly.

"No," he answered flatly, looking deep into her steadfast eyes. "No use lying to you—if I know you at all you'd rather take it standing up. That talk of Jovians or Neptunians is the bunk—nothing like that ever grew in our Solarian system. All the signs say that we're going for a long ride."

CHAPTER 11

NEVIAN STRIFE

THE NEVIAN SPACE-SHIP WAS HURTLING UPON ITS WAY. Space-navigators both, the two Terrestrial officers soon discovered that it was even then moving with a velocity far above that of light and that it must be accelerating at a high rate, even though to them it seemed stationary—they could feel only a gravitational force somewhat less than that of their native Earth.

Bradley, seasoned old campaigner that he was, had retired promptly as soon as he had completed a series of observations, and was sleeping soundly upon a pile of cushions in the first of the three inter-connecting rooms. In the middle room, which was to be Clio's, Costigan was standing very close to the girl, but was not touching her. His body was rigid, his face was tense and drawn.

"You are wrong, Conway; all wrong," Clio was saying, very seriously. "I know how you feel, but it's false chivalry."

"That isn't it, at all," he insisted, stubbornly. "It isn't only that I've got you out here in space, in danger and alone, that's stopping me. I know you and I know myself well enough to know that what we start now we'll go through with for life. It doesn't make any difference, that way, whether I start making love to you now or whether I wait until we're back on Tellus; but I'm telling you that for your own good you'd better pass me up entirely. I've got enough horsepower to keep away from you if you tell me to—not otherwise."

"I know it, both ways, dear, but . . ."

"But nothing!" he interrupted. "Can't you get it into your skull what you'll be letting yourself in for if you marry me? Assume that we get back, which isn't sure, by any means. But even if we do, some day—and maybe soon, too, you can't tell—somebody is going to collect fifty grams of radium for my head."

"Fifty grams—and everybody knows that Samms himself is rated at only sixty? I *knew* that you were somebody, Conway!" Clio exclaimed, undeterred. "But at that, something tells me that any pirate will earn even that much reward several times over before he collects it. Don't be silly, my dear —goodnight."

She tipped her hand back, holding up to him her red, sweetly curved, smiling lips, and his arms swept around her. Her arms went up around his neck and they stood, clasped together in the motionless ecstasy of love's first embrace.

"Girl, girl, how I love you!" Costigan's voice was husky, his usually hard eyes were glowing with a tender light. "That settles that. I'll really *live* now, anyway, while . . ."

"Stop it!" she commanded, sharply. "You're going to live until you die of old age—see if you don't. You'll simply *have* to, Conway!"

"That's so, too—no percentage in dying now. All the pirates between Tellus and Andromeda couldn't take me after this— I've got too much to live for. Well, goodnight, sweetheart, I'd better beat it—you need some sleep."

The lovers' parting was not as simple and straightforward a procedure as Costigan's speech would indicate, but finally he did seek his own room and relaxed upon a pile of cushions, his stern visage transformed. Instead of the low metal ceiling he saw a beautiful, oval, tanned young face, framed in a golden-blonde corona of hair. His gaze sank into the depths of loyal, honest, dark blue eyes; and looking deeper and deeper into those blue wells he fell asleep. Upon his face, too set and grim by far for a man of his years—the lives of Sector Chiefs of the Triplanetary Service were not easy, nor as a rule were they long—there lingered as he slept that newly-acquired softness of expression, the reflection of his transcendent happiness.

For eight hours he slept soundly, as was his wont, then, also according to his habit and training he came wide awake, with no intermediate stage of napping.

"Clio?" he whispered. "Awake, girl?"

"Awake!" her voice come through the ultra phone, relief in every syllable. "Good heavens, I thought you were going to sleep until we got to wherever it is that we're going! Come on in, you two—I don't see how you can possibly sleep, just as though you were home in bed."

"You've got to learn to sleep anywhere if you expect to keep in . . . " Costigan broke off as he opened the door and saw Clio's wan face. She had evidently spent a sleepless and wracking eight hours. "Good Lord, Clio, why didn't you call me?"

"Oh, I'm all right, except for being a little jittery. No need of asking how *you* feel, is there?"

"No—I feel hungry," he answered cheerfully. "I'm going to see what we can do about it—or say, guess I'll see whether they're still interfering on Samms' wave."

He took out the small, insulated case and touched the contact stud lightly with his finger. His arm jerked away powerfully.

"Still at it," he gave the unnecessary explanation. "They don't seem to want us to talk outside, but his interference is as good as my talking—they can trace it, of course. Now I'll see what I can find out about our breakfast."

He stepped over to the plate and shot its projector beam forward into the control room, where he saw Nerado lying, doglike, at his instrument panel. As Costigan's beam entered the room a blue light flashed on and the Nevian turned an eye and an arm toward his own small observation plate. Knowing that they were now in visual communication, Costigan beckoned an invitation and pointed to his mouth in what he hoped was the universal sign of hunger. The Nevian waved an arm and fingered controls, and as he did so a wide section of the floor of Clio's room slid aside. The opening thus made revealed a table which rose upon its low pedestal, a table equipped with three softly-cushioned benches and spread with a glittering array of silver and glassware.

Bowls and platters of a dazzlingly white metal, narrow-waisted goblets of sheerest crystal; all were hexagonal, beautifully and intricately carved or etched in apparently conventional marine designs. And the table utensils of this strange race were peculiar indeed. There were tearing forceps of sixteen needle-sharp curved teeth; there were flexible spatulas;

there were deep and shallow ladles with flexible edges; there were many other peculiarly-curved instruments at whose uses the Terrestrials could not even guess; all having delicately-fashioned handles to fit the long slender fingers of the Nevians.

But if the table and its appointments were surprising to the Terrestrials, revealing as they did a degree of culture which none of them had expected to find in a race of beings so monstrous, the food was even more surprising, although in another sense. For the wonderful crystal goblets were filled with a grayish-green slime of a nauseous and over-powering odor, the smaller bowls were full of living sea spiders and other such delicacies; and each large platter contained a fish fully a foot long, raw and whole, garnished tastefully with red, purple, and green strands of seaweed!

Clio looked once, then gasped, shutting her eyes and turning away from the table, but Costigan flipped the three fish into a platter and set it aside before he turned back to the visiplate.

"They'll go good fried," he remarked to Bradley, signaling vigorously to Nerado that the meal was not acceptable and that he wanted to talk to him, *in person*. Finally he made himself clear, the table sank down out of sight, and the Nevian commander cautiously entered the room.

At Costigan's insistance, he came up to the visiplate, leaving near the door three alert and fully-armed guards. The man then shot the beam into the galley of the pirate's lifeboat, suggesting that they should be allowed to live there. For some time the argument of arms and fingers raged—though not exactly fluent conversation, both sides managed to convey their meanings quite clearly. Nerado would not allow the Terrestrials to visit their own ship—he was taking no chances —but after a thorough ultra-ray inspection he did finally order some of his men to bring into the middle room the electric range and a supply of Terrestrial food. Soon the Nevian fish were sizzling in a pan and the appetizing odors of coffee and browning biscuit permeated the room. But at the first appearance of those odors the Nevians departed hastily, content to watch the remainder of the curious and repulsive procedure in their visiray plates.

Breakfast over and everything made tidy and ship-shape, Costigan turned to Clio.

"Look here, girl; you've got to learn how to sleep. You're all in. Your eyes look like you've been on a Martian picnic and you didn't eat half enough breakfast. You've got to sleep and eat to keep fit. We don't want you passing out on us, so I'll put out this light, and you'll lie down here and sleep until noon."

"Oh, no, don't bother. I'll sleep tonight. I'm quite . . ."

"You'll sleep now," he informed her, levelly. "I never thought of you being nervous, with Bradley and me on each side of you. We're both right here now, though, and we'll stay here. We'll watch over you like a couple of old hens with one chick between them. Come on; lie down and go bye-bye."

Clio laughed at the simile, but lay down obediently. Costigan sat upon the edge of the great divan holding her hand, and they chatted idly. The silences grew longer, Clio's remarks became fewer, and soon her long-lashed eyelids fell and her deep, regular breathing showed that she was sound asleep. The man stared at her, his very heart in his eyes. So young, so beautiful, so lovely—and *how* he did love her! He was not formally religious, but his every thought was a prayer. If he could only get her out of this mess . . . he wasn't fit to live on the same planet with her, but . . . just give him one chance, God . . . just one!

But Costigan had been laboring for days under a terrific strain, and had been going very short on sleep. Half hypnotized by his own mixed emotions and by his staring at the smooth curves of Clio's cheek, his own eyes closed and, still holding her hand, he sank down into the soft cushions beside her and into oblivion.

Thus sleeping hand in hand like two children Bradley found them, and a tender, fatherly expression came over his face as he looked down at them.

"Nice little girl, Clio," he mused, "and when they made Costigan they broke the mold. They'll do—about as fine a couple of kids as old Tellus ever produced. I could do with some more sleep myself." He yawned prodigiously, lay down at Clio's left, and in minutes was himself asleep.

Hours later, both men were awakened by a merry peal of laughter. Clio was sitting up, regarding them with sparkling eyes. She was refreshed, buoyant, ravenously hungry and highly amused. Costigan was amazed and annoyed at what he considered a failure in a self-appointed task; Bradley was calm and matter-of-fact.

"Thanks for being such a nice body-guard, you two." Clio laughed again, but sobered quickly. "I slept wonderfully well, but I wonder if I can sleep tonight without making you hold my hand all night?"

"Oh, he doesn't mind doing that," Bradley commented.

"Mind it!" Costigan exclaimed, and his eyes and his tone spoke volumes.

They prepared and ate another meal, one to which Clio did full justice. Rested and refreshed, they had begun to discuss possibilities of escape when Nerado and his three armed guards entered the room. The Nevian scientist placed a box upon a table and began to make adjustments upon its panels, eyeing the Terrestrials attentively after each setting. After a time a staccato burst of articulate speech issued from the box, and Costigan saw a great light.

"You've got it—hold it!" he exclaimed, waving his arms excitedly. "You see, Clio, their voices are pitched either higher or lower than ours—probably higher—and they've built an audio-frequency changer. He's nobody's fool, that lizard!"

Nerado heard Costigan's voice, there was no doubt of that. His long neck looped and twisted in Nevian gratification; and although neither side could understand the other, both knew that intelligent speech and hearing were attributes common to the two races. This fact altered markedly the relations between captors and captives. The Nevians admitted among themselves that the strange bipeds might be quite intelligent, after all; and the Terrestrials at once became more hopeful.

"It isn't so bad, if they can talk," Costigan summed up the situation. "We might as well take it easy and make the best of it, particularly since we haven't been able to figure out any possible way of getting away from them. They can talk and hear, and we can learn their language in time. Maybe we can make some kind of a deal with them to take us back to our own system, if we can't make a break."

The Nevians being as eager as the Terrestrials to establish communication, Nerado kept the newly devised frequency changer in constant use. There is no need of describing at length the details of that interchange of languages. Suffice it to say that starting at the very bottom they learned as babies learn, but with the great advantage over babies of possessing fully developed and capable brains. And while the human beings were learning the tongue of Nevia, several of the amphibians (and incidentally Clio Marsden) were learning Triplanetarian; the two officers knowing well that it would be much easier for the Nevians to learn the logically-built common language of the Three Planets than to master the senseless intricacies of English.

In a short time the two parties were able to understand each other after a fashion, by using a weird mixture of both languages. As soon as a few ideas had been exchanged, the Nevian scientists built transformers small enough to be worn collar-like by the Terrestrials, and the captives were allowed to roam at will throughout the great vessel; only the compartment in which was stored the dismembered pirate lifeboat being sealed to them. Thus it was that they were not left long in doubt when another fish-shaped cruiser of the void was revealed upon their lookout plates in the awful emptiness of interstellar space.

"This is our sister-ship going to your Solarian system for a cargo of the iron which is so plentiful there," Nerado explained to his involuntary guests.

"I hope the gang has got the bugs worked out of our super-ship!" Costigan muttered savagely to his companions as Nerado turned away. "If they have, that outfit will get something more than a load of iron when they get there!"

More time passed, during which a blue-white star separated itself from the infinitely distant firmament and began to show a perceptible disk. Larger and larger it grew, becoming bluer and bluer as the flying space-ship approached it, until finally Nevia could be seen, apparently close beside her parent orb.

Heavily laden though the vessel was, such was her power that she was soon dropping vertically downward toward a large lagoon in the middle of the Nevian city. That bit of open water was devoid of life, for this was to be no ordinary landing. Under the terrific power of the beams braking the descent of that unimaginable load of allotropic iron the water seethed and boiled; and instead of floating gracefully upon the surface of the sea, this time the huge ship of space sank like a plummet to the bottom. Having accomplished the delicate feat of docking the vessel safely in the immense cradle prepared for her, Nerado turned to the Tellurians, who, now under guard, had been brought before him.

"While our cargo of iron is being discharged, I am to take you three specimens to the College of Science, where you are to undergo a thorough physical and psychological examination. Follow me."

"Wait a minute!" protested Costigan, with a quick and furtive wink at his companions. "Do you expect us to go through *water*, and at this frightful depth?"

"Certainly," replied the Nevian, in surprise. "You are air-breathers, of course, but you must be able to swim a little, and this slight depth—but little more than thirty of your meters—will not trouble you."

"You are wrong, twice," declared the Terrestrial, convincingly. "If by 'swimming' you mean propelling yourself in or through the water, we know nothing of it. In water over our heads we drown helplessly in a minute or two, and the pressure at this depth would kill us instantly."

"Well, I could take a lifeboat, of course, but that . . ." the Nevian Captain began, doubtfully, but broke off at the sound of a staccato call from his signal panel.

"Captain Nerado, attention!"

"Nerado," he acknowledged into a microphone.

"The Third City is being attacked by the fishes of the greater deeps. They have developed new and powerful mobile fortresses mounting unheard-of weapons and the city reports that it cannot long withstand their attack. They are asking for all possible help. Your vessel not only has vast stores of iron, but also mounts weapons of power. You are requested to proceed to their aid at the earliest possible moment."

Nerado snapped out orders and the liquid iron fell in streams from wide-open ports, forming a vast, red pool in the bottom of the dock. In a short time the great vessel was in equilibrium with the water she displaced, and as soon as she had attained a slight buoyancy the ports snapped shut and Nerado threw on the power.

"Go back to your own quarters and stay there until I send for you," the Nevian directed, and as the Terrestrials obeyed the curt orders the cruiser tore herself from the water and flashed up into the crimson sky.

"What a barefaced liar!" Bradley exclaimed. The three, transformers cut off, were back in the middle room of their suite. "You can outswim an otter, and I happen to know that you came up out of the old DZ83 from a depth of . . ."

"Maybe I did exaggerate a trifle," Costigan interrupted, "but the more helpless he thinks we are the better for us. And we want to stay out of any of their cities as long as we can, because they may be hard places to get out of. I've got a couple of ideas, but they aren't ripe enough to pick yet . . . Wow! How this bird's been traveling! We're there already! If he hits the water going like this, he'll split himself, sure!"

With undiminished velocity they were flashing downward in a long slant toward the beleaguered Third City, and from the flying vessel there was launched toward the city's central lagoon a torpedo. No missile this, but a capsule containing a full ton of allotropic iron, which would be of more use to the Nevian defenders than millions of men. For the Third City was sore pressed indeed. Around it was one unbroken ring of boiling, exploding water—water billowing upward in searing, blinding bursts of super-heated steam, or being hurled bodily in all directions in solid masses by the cataclysmic forces being released by the embattled fishes of the greater deeps. Her outer defenses were already down, and even as the Terrestrials stared in amazement another of the immense hexagonal buildings burst into fragments; its upper structure flying wildly into scrap metal, its lower half subsiding drunkenly below the surface of the boiling sea.

The three Earth-people seized whatever supports were at hand as the Nevian space-ship struck the water with undiminished speed, but the precaution was needless—Nerado knew thoroughly his vessel, its strength and its capabilities. There was a mighty splash, but that was all. The artificial gravity was unchanged by the impact; to the passengers the vessel was still motionless and on even keel as, now a submarine, she snapped around like a very fish and attacked the rear of the nearest fortress.

For fortresses they were; vast structures of green metal, plowing forward implacably upon immense caterpillar treads. And as they crawled they destroyed, and Costigan, exploring the strange submarine with his visiray beam, watched and marveled. For the fortresses were full of water; water artificially cooled and aerated, entirely separate from the boiling flood through which they moved. They were manned by fish some five feet in length. Fish with huge, goggling eyes; fish plentifully equipped with long, armlike tentacles; fish poised before control panels or darting about intent upon their various duties. Fish with brains, waging war!

Nor was their warfare ineffectual. Their heat-rays boiled the water for hundreds of yards before them and their torpedoes were exploding against the Nevian defenses in one appallingly continuous concussion. But most potent of all was a weapon unknown to Triplanetary warfare. From a fortress there would shoot out, with the speed of a meteor, a long, jointed, telescopic rod; tipped with a tiny, brilliantly-shining ball. Whenever that glowing tip encountered any obstacle, that obstacle disappeared in an explosion world-wracking in its intensity. Then what was left of the rod, dark now, would be retracted into the fortress—only to emerge again in a moment with a tip once more shining and potent.

Nerado, apparently as unfamiliar with the peculiar weapon as were the Terrestrials, attacked cautiously; sending out far to the fore his murkily impenetrable screens of red. But the submarine was entirely non-ferrous, and its officers were apparently quite familiar with Nevian beams which licked at and clung to the green walls in impotent fury. Through the red veil came stabbing ball after ball, and only the most frantic dodging saved the space-ship from destruction in those first few furious seconds. And now the Nevian defenders of the Third City had secured and were employing the vast store of allotropic iron so opportunely delivered by Nerado.

From the city there pushed out immense nets of metal, extending from the surface of the ocean to its bottom; nets radiating such terrific forces that the very water itself was beaten back and stood motionless in vertical, glassy walls. Torpedoes were futile against that wall of energy. The most fiercely driven rays of the fishes flamed incandescent against it, in vain. Even the incredible violence of a concentration of every available force-ball against one point could not break through. At that unimaginable explosion water was hurled for miles. The bed of the ocean was not only exposed, but in it there was blown a crater at whose dimensions the Terrestrials dared not even guess. The crawling fortresses themselves were thrown backward violently and the very world was rocked to its core by the concussion, but that iron-driven wall held. The massive nets swayed and gave back, and tidal waves hurled their mountainously destructive masses through the Third City, but the mighty barrier remained intact. And Nerado, still attacking two of the powerful tanks with his every weapon, was still dodging those flashing balls charged with the quintessence of destruction. The fishes could not see through the subethereal veil, but all the gunners of the two fortresses were combing it thoroughly with ever-lengthening, ever-thrusting rods, in a desperate attempt to wipe out the new and apparently all-powerful Nevian submarine whose sheer power was slowly but inexorably crushing even their gigantic walls.

"Well, I think that right now's the best chance we'll ever have of doing something for ourselves." Costigan turned away from the absorbing scenes pictured upon the visiplate and faced his two companions.

"But what can we possibly do?" asked Clio.

"Whatever it is, we'll try it!" Bradley exclaimed.

"Anything's better than staying here and letting them analyze us—no telling what they'd do to us," Costigan went on.

"I know a lot more about things than they think I do. They never did catch me using my spy-ray—it's on an awfully narrow beam, you know, and uses almost no power at all—so I've been able to dope out quite a lot of stuff. I can open most of their locks, and I know how to run their small boats. This battle, fantastic as it is, is deadly stuff, and it isn't one-sided, by any means, either, so that every one of them, from Nerado down, seems to be on emergency duty. There are no guards watching us, or stationed where we want to go—our way out is open. And once out, this battle is giving us our best possible chance to get away from them. There's so much emission out there already that they probably couldn't detect the driving force of the lifeboat, and they'll be too busy to chase us, anyway."

"Once out, then what?" asked Bradley."

"We'll have to decide that before we start, of course. I'd say make a break back for Earth. We know the direction and we'll have plenty of power."

"But good Heavens, Conway, it's so far!" exclaimed Clio. "How about food, water, and air—would we ever get there?"

"You know as much about that as I do. I think so, but of course anything might happen. This ship is none too big, is considerably slower than the big space-ship, and we're a long ways from home. Another bad thing is the food question. The boat is well stocked according to Nevian ideas, but it's pretty foul stuff for us to eat. However, it's nourishing, and we'll have to eat it, since we can't carry enough of our own supplies to the boat to last long. Even so, we may have to go on short rations, but I think that we'll be able to make it. On the other hand, what happens if we stay here? They will find us sooner or later, and we don't know any too much about these ultra-weapons. We are land-dwellers, and there is little if any land on this planet. Then, too, we don't know where to look for what land there may be, and even if we could find it, we know that it is all over-run with amphibians already. There's a lot of things that might be better, but they might be a lot worse, too. How about it? Do we try or do we stay here?"

"We try it!" exclaimed Clio and Bradley, as one.

"All right. I'd better not waste any more time talking— let's go!"

Stepping up to the locked and shielded door, he took out a peculiarly built torch and pointed it at the Nevian lock. There was no light, no noise, but the massive portal swung smoothly open. They stepped out and Costigan relocked and reshielded the entrance.

"How . . . what . . ." Clio demanded.

"I've been going to school for the last few weeks," Costigan grinned, "and I've picked up quite a few things here and there —literally, as well as figuratively. Snap it up, guys! Our armor is stored with the pieces of the pirates' lifeboat, and I'll feel a lot better when we've got it on and have hold of a few Lewistons."

They hurried down corridors, up ramps, and along hallways, with Costigan's spy-ray investigating the course ahead for chance Nevians. Bradley and Clio were unarmed, but the operative had found a piece of flat metal and had ground it to a razor edge.

"I think I can throw this thing straight enough and fast enough to chop off a Nevian's head before he can put a paralyzing ray on us," he explained grimly, but he was not called upon to show his skill with the improvised cleaver.

As he had concluded from his careful survey, every Nevian was at some control or weapon, doing his part in that frightful combat with the denizens of the greater deeps. Their path was open; they were neither molested nor detected as they ran toward the compartment within which was sealed all their belongings. The door of that room opened, as had the other, to Costigan's knowing beam; and all three set hastily to work. They made up packs of food, filled their capacious pockets with emergency rations, buckled on Lewistons and automatics, donned their armor, and clamped into their external holsters a full complement of additional weapons.

"Now comes the ticklish part of the business," Costigan informed the others. His helmet was slowly turning this way and that, and the others knew that through his spy-ray goggles he was studying their route. "There's only one boat we stand a chance of reaching, and somebody's mighty apt to see us. There's a lot of detectors up there, and we'll have to cross a corridor full of communicator beams. There, that line's off—scoot!"

At his word they dashed out into the hall and hurried along for minutes, dodging sharply to right or left as the leader snapped out orders. Finally he stopped.

"Here's those beams I told you about. We'll have to roll under 'em. They're less than waist high—right there's the lowest one. Watch me do it, and when I give you the word, one at a time, you do the same. *Keep low*—don't let an arm or a leg get up into a ray or they may see us."

He threw himself flat, rolled upon the floor a yard or so, and scrambled to his feet. He gazed intently at the blank wall for a space.

"Bradley—now!" he snapped, and the captain duplicated his performance.

But Clio, unused to the heavy and cumbersome space-armor she was wearing, could not roll in it with any degree of success. When Costigan barked his order she tried, but stopped, floundering almost directly below the network of invisible beams. As she struggled one mailed arm went up, and Costigan saw in his ultra-goggles the faint flash as the beam encountered the interfering field. But already he had acted. Crouching low, he struck down the arm, seized it, and dragged the girl out of the zone of visibility. Then in furious haste he opened a nearby door and all three sprang into a tiny compartment.

"Shut off all the fields of your suits, so that they can't interfere!" he hissed into the utter darkness. "Not that I'd mind killing a few of them, but if they start an organized search we're sunk. But even if they did get a warning by touching your glove, Clio, they probably won't suspect us. Our rooms are still shielded, and the chances are that they're too busy to bother much about us, anyway."

He was right. A few beams darted here and there, but the Nevians saw nothing amiss and ascribed the interference to the falling into the beam of some chance bit of charged metal. With no further misadventures the fugitives gained entrance to the Nevian lifeboat, where Costigan's first act was to disconnect one steel boot from his armor of space. With a sigh of relief he pulled his foot out of it, and from it carefully poured into the small power-tank of the craft fully thirty pounds of allotropic iron!

"I pinched it off them," he explained, in answer to amazed and inquiring looks, "and maybe you don't think it's a relief to get it out of that boot! I couldn't steal a flask to carry it in, so this was the only place I could put it. These lifeboats are equipped with only a couple of grams of iron apiece, you know, and we couldn't get half-way back to Tellus on that, even with smooth going; and we may have to fight. With this much to go on, though, we could go to Andromeda, fighting all the way. Well, we'd better break away."

Costigan watched his plate closely; and, when the maneuvering of the great vessel brought his exit port as far away as possible from the Third City and the warring tanks, he shot the little cruiser out and away. Straight out into the ocean it sped, through the murky red veil, and darted upward toward the surface. The three wanderers sat tense, hardly daring to breathe, staring into the plates—Clio and Bradley pushing at mental levers and stepping down hard upon mental brakes in unconscious efforts to help Costigan dodge the beams and rods of death flashing so appallingly close upon all sides. Out of the water and into the air the darting, dodging lifeboat flashed in safety; but in the air, supposedly free from menace, came disaster. There was a crunching, grating shock and the vessel was thrown into a dizzy spiral, from which Costigan finally leveled it into headlong flight away from the scene of battle. Watching the pyrometers which recorded the temperature of the outer shell, he drove the lifeboat ahead at the highest safe atmospheric speed while Bradley went to inspect the damage.

"Pretty bad, but better than I thought," the captain reported. "Outer and inner plates broken away on a seam. We wouldn't hold cotton waste, let alone air. Any tools aboard?"

"Some—and what we haven't got we'll make," Costigan declared. "We'll put a lot of distance behind us, then we'll fix her up and get away from here."

"What are those fish, anyway, Conway?" Clio asked, as the lifeboat tore along. "The Nevians are bad enough, Heaven knows, but the very idea of intelligent and educated *fish* is enough to drive one mad!"

"You know Nerado mentioned several times the 'semicivilized fishes of the greater deeps'?" he reminded her. "I gather that there are at least three intelligent races here. We know two—the Nevians, who are amphibians, and the fishes of the greater deeps. The fishes of the lesser deeps are also intelligent. As I get it, the Nevian cities were originally built in very shallow water, or perhaps were upon islands. The development of machinery and tools gave them a big edge on the fish; and those living in the shallow seas, nearest the Islands, gradually became tributary nations, if not actually slaves. Those fish not only serve as food, but work in the mines, hatcheries, and plantations, and do all kinds of work for the Nevians. Those so-called 'lesser deeps' were conquered first, of course, and all their races of fish are docile enough now. But the deep-sea breeds, who live in water so deep that the Nevians can hardly stand the pressure down there, were more intelligent to start with, and more stubborn besides. But the most valuable metals here are deep down—this planet is very light for its size, you know—so the Nevians kept at it until they conquered some of the deep-sea fish, too, and put 'em to work. But those high-pressure boys were nobody's fools. They realized that as time went on the amphibians would get further and further ahead of them in development, so they let themselves be conquered, learned how to use the Nevians' tools and everything else they could get hold of, developed a lot of new stuff of their own, and now they're out to wipe the amphibians off the map completely, before they get too far ahead of them to handle."

"And the Nevians are afraid of them, and want to kill them all, as fast as they possibly can," guessed Clio.

"That would be the logical thing, of course," commented Bradley. "Got pretty nearly enough distance now, Costigan?"

"There isn't enough distance on the planet to suit me," Costigan replied. "We'll need all we can get. A full diameter away from that crew of amphibians is too close for comfort—their detectors are keen."

"Then they can detect us?" Clio asked. "Oh, I wish they hadn't hit us—we'd have been away from here long ago."

"So do I," Costigan agreed, feelingly. "But they did—no use squawking. We can rivet and weld those seams, and things could be a lot worse—we are still breathing air!"

In silence the lifeboat flashed onward, and half of Nevia's mighty globe was traversed before it was brought to a halt. Then in furious haste the two officers set to work, again to make their small craft sound and spaceworthy.

CHAPTER 12

WORM, SUBMARINE, AND FREEDOM

SINCE BOTH COSTIGAN AND BRADLEY HAD OFTEN WATCHED their captors at work during the long voyage from the Solar System to Nevia, they were quite familiar with the machine tools of the amphibians. Their stolen lifeboat, being an emergency craft, of course carried full repair equipment; and to such good purpose did the two officers labor that even before their air-tanks were fully charged, all the damage had been repaired.

The lifeboat lay motionless upon the mirror-smooth surface of the ocean. Captain Bradley had opened the upper port and the three stood in the opening, gazing in silence toward the incredibly distant horizon, while powerful pumps were forcing the last possible ounces of air into the storage cylinders. Mile upon strangely flat mile stretched that waveless, unbroken expanse of water, merging finally into the violent redness of the Nevian sky. The sun was setting; a vast ball of purple flame dropping rapidly toward the horizon. Darkness came suddenly as that seething ball disappeared, and the air became bitterly cold, in sharp contrast to the pleasant warmth of a moment before. And as suddenly clouds appeared in blackly banked masses and a cold, driving rain began to beat down.

"Br-r-r, it's cold! Let's go in—Oh! *Shut the door!*" Clio shrieked, and leaped wildly down into the compartment below, out of Costigan's way, for he and Bradley had also seen slithering toward them the frightful arm of the Thing.

Almost before the girl had spoken Costigan had leaped to the controls, and not an instant too soon; for the tip of that horrible tentacle flashed into the rapidly narrowing crack just before the door clanged shut. As the powerful toggles forced the heavy wedges into engagement and drove the massive disk home, that grisly tip fell severed to the floor of the compartment and lay there, twitching and writhing with a loathsome and unearthly vigor. Two feet long the piece was, and larger than a strong man's leg. It was armed with spiked and jointed metallic scales, and instead of sucking disks it was equipped with a series of *mouths*—mouths filled with sharp metallic teeth which gnashed and ground together furiously, even though sundered from the horrible organism which they were designed to feed.

The little submarine shuddered in every plate and member as monstrous coils encircled her and tightened inexorably in terrific, rippling surges eloquent of mastodonic power; and a strident vibration smote sickeningly upon Terrestrial eardrums as the metal spikes of the monstrosity crunched and ground upon the outer plating of their small vessel. Costigan stood unmoved at the plate, watching intently; hands ready upon the controls. Due to the artificial gravity of the lifeboat it seemed perfectly stationary to its occupants. Only the weird gyrations of the pictures upon the lookout screens showed that the craft was being shaken and thrown about like a rat in the jaws of a terrier; only the gauges revealed that they were almost a mile below the surface of the ocean already, and were still going downward at an appalling rate. Finally Clio could stand no more.

"Aren't you going to do something, Conway?" she cried. "Not unless I have to," he replied, composedly. "I don't believe that he can really hurt us, and if I use force of any kind I'm afraid that it will kick up enough disturbance to bring Nerado down on us like a hawk onto a chicken. However, if he takes us much deeper I'll have to go to work on him. We're getting down pretty close to our limit, and the bottom's a long ways down yet."

Deeper and deeper the lifeboat was dragged by its dreadful opponent, whose spiked teeth still tore savagely at the tough outer plating of the craft, until Costigan reluctantly threw in his power switches. Against the full propellant thrust the monster could draw them no lower, but neither could the lifeboat make any headway toward the surface. The pilot then turned on his beams, but found that they were ineffective. So closely was the creature wrapped around the submarine that his weapons could not be brought to bear upon it.

"What can it possibly be, anyway, and what can we do about it?" Clio asked.

"I thought at first it was something like a devilfish, or possibly an overgrown starfish, but it isn't," Costigan made answer. "It must be a kind of flat worm. That doesn't sound reasonable—the thing must be all of a hundred meters long—but there it is. The only thing left to do that I can think of is to try to boil him alive."

He closed other circuits, diffusing a terrific beam of pure heat, and the water all about them burst into furious clouds of steam. The boat leaped upward as the metallic fins of the gigantic worm fanned vapor instead of water, but the creature neither released its hold nor ceased its relentlessly grinding attack. Minute after minute went by, but finally the worm dropped limply away—cooked through and through; vanquished only by death.

"Now we've put our foot in it, clear to the neck!" Costigan exclaimed, as he shot the lifeboat upward at its maximum power. "Look at that! I knew that Nerado could trace us, but I didn't have any idea that *they* could!"

Staring with Costigan into the plate, Bradley and the girl saw, not the Nevian sky-rover they had expected, but a fast submarine cruiser, manned by the frightful fishes of the greater deeps. It was coming directly toward the lifeboat, and even as Costigan hurled the little vessel off at an angle and then sped upward into the air, one of the deadly offensive rods, tipped with its glowing ball of pure destruction, flashed through the spot where they would have been had they held their former course.

But powerful as were the propellant forces of the lifeboat and fiercely though Costigan applied them, the denizens of the deep clamped a tractor beam upon the flying vessel before it had gained a mile of altitude. Costigan aligned his every driving projector as his vessel came to an abrupt halt in the invisible grip of the beam, then experimented with various dials.

"There ought to be some way of cutting that beam," he pondered audibly, "but I don't know enough about their system to do it, and I'm afraid to monkey around with things too much, because I might accidentally release the screens we've already got out, and they're stopping altogether too much stuff for us to do without them right now."

He frowned as he studied the flaring defensive screens, now radiating an incandescent violet under the concentration of forces being hurled against them by the warlike fishes, then stiffened suddenly.

"I thought so—they *can* shoot 'em!" he exclaimed, throwing the lifeboat into a furious corkscrew turn, and the very air blazed into flaming splendor as a dazzlingly scintillating ball of energy sped past them and high into the air beyond.

Then for minutes a spectacular battle raged. The twisting, turning, leaping airship, small as she was and agile, kept on eluding the explosive projectiles of the fishes, and her screens neutralized and re-radiated the full power of the attacking beams. More—since Costigan did not need to think of sparing his iron, the ocean around the great submarine began furiously to boil under the full-driven offensive beams of the tiny Nevian ship. But escape Costigan could not. He could not cut that tractor beam and the utmost power of his drivers could not wrest the lifeboat from its tenacious clutch. And slowly but inexorably the ship of space was being drawn downward toward the ship of ocean's depths. Downward, in spite of the utmost possible effort of every projector and generator; and Clio and Bradley, sick at heart, looked once at each other. Then they looked at Costigan, who, jaw hard set and eyes unflinchingly upon his plate, was concentrating his attack upon one turret of the green monster as they settled lower and lower.

"If this is . . . if our number is going up, Conway," Clio began, unsteadily.

"Not yet, it isn't!" he snapped. "Keep a stiff upper lip, girl. We're still breathing air, and the battle's not over yet!"

Nor was it; but it was not Costigan's efforts, mighty though they were, that ended the attack of the fishes of the greater deeps. The tractor beams snapped without warning, and so prodigious were the forces being exerted by the lifeboat that as it hurled itself away the three passengers were thrown violently to the floor, in spite of the powerful gravity controls. Scrambling up on hands and knees, bracing himself as best he could against the terrific forces, Costigan managed finally to force a hand up to his panel. He was barely in time; for even as he cut the driving power to its normal value the outer shell of the lifeboat was blazing at white heat from the friction of the atmosphere through which it had been tearing with such an insane acceleration!

"Oh, I see—Nerado to the rescue," Costigan commented, after a glance into the plate. "I hope that those fish blow him clear out of the Galaxy!"

"Why?" demanded Clio. "I should think that you'd . . ."

"Think again," he advised her. "The worse Nerado gets licked the better for us. I don't really expect that, but if they can keep him busy long enough, we can get far enough away so that he won't bother about us any more."

As the lifeboat tore upward through the air at the highest permissible atmospheric velocity Bradley and Clio peered over Costigan's shoulders into the plate, watching in fascinated interest the scene which was being kept in focus upon it. The Nevian ship of space was plunging downward in a long, slanting dive, her terrific beams of force screaming out ahead of her. The beams of the little lifeboat had boiled the waters of the ocean; those of the parent craft seemed literally to blast them out of existence. All about the green submarine there had been volumes of furiously-boiling water and dense clouds of vapor; now water and fog alike disappeared, converted into transparent superheated steam by the blasts of Nevian energy. Through that tenuous gas the enormous mass of the submarine fell like a plummet, her defensive screens flaming an almost invisible violet, her every offensive weapon vomiting forth solid and vibratory destruction toward the Nevian cruiser so high in the angry, scarlet heavens.

For miles the submarine dropped, until the frightful pressure of the depth drove water into Nerado's beam faster than his forces could volatilize it. Then in that seething funnel there was waged a starkly fantastic conflict. At its wildly turbulent bottom lay the submarine, now apparently trying to escape, but held fast by the tractors of the spaceship; at its top, smothered almost to the point of invisibility by billowing masses of steam, hung poised the Nevian cruiser.

As the atmosphere had grown thinner and thinner with

increasing altitude Costigan had regulated his velocity accordingly, keeping the outer shell of the vessel at the highest temperature consistent with safety. Now beyond measurable atmospheric pressure, the shell cooled rapidly and he applied full touring acceleration. At an appalling and constantly increasing speed the miniature space-ship shot away from the strange, red planet; and smaller and smaller upon the plate became its picture. The great vessel of the void had long since plunged beneath the surface of the sea, to come more closely to grips with the vessel of the fishes; for a long time nothing of the battle had been visible save immense clouds of steam, blanketing hundreds of square miles of the ocean's surface. But just before the picture became too small to reveal details a few tiny dark spots appeared above the banks of cloud, now brilliantly illuminated by the rays of the rising sun—dots which might have been fragments of either vessel, blown bodily from the depths of the ocean and, riven asunder, hurled high into the air by the incredible forces at the command of the other.

Nevia a tiny moon and the fierce blue sun rapidly growing smaller in the distance, Costigan swung his visiray beam into the line of travel and turned to his companions.

"Well, we're off," he said, scowling. "I hope it was Nerado that got blown up back there, but I'm afraid it wasn't. He whipped two of those submarines that we know of, and probably half their fleet besides. There's no particular reason why that one should be able to take him, so it's my idea that we should get ready for great gobs of trouble. They'll chase us, of course; and I'm afraid that with their power, they'll catch us."

"But what can we do, Conway?" asked Clio.

"Several things," he grinned. "I managed to get quite a lot of dope on that paralyzing ray and some of their other stuff, and we can install the necessary equipment in our suits easily enough."

They removed their armor, and Costigan explained in detail the changes which must be made in the Triplanetary field generators. All three set vigorously to work—the two officers deftly and surely; Clio uncertainly and with many questions, but with undaunted spirit. Finally, having done everything they could do to strengthen their position, they settled down to the watchful routine of the flight, with every possible instrument set to detect any sign of the pursuit they so feared.

CHAPTER 13

THE HILL

THE HEAVY CRUISER CHICAGO HUNG MOTIONLESS IN SPACE, thousands of miles distant from the warring fleets of spaceships so viciously attacking and so stubbornly defending Roger's planetoid. In the captain's sanctum Lyman Cleveland crouched tensely above his ultracameras, his sensitive fingers touching lightly their micrometric dials. His body was rigid, his face was set and drawn. Only his eyes moved; flashing back and forth between his instruments and the smoothly-running strands of spring-steel wire upon which were being recorded the frightful scenes of carnage and destruction.

Silent and bitterly absorbed, though surrounded by staring officers whose fervent, almost unconscious cursing was prayerful in its intensity, the visiray expert kept his ultra-instruments upon that awful struggle to its dire conclusion. Flawlessly those instruments noted every detail of the destruction of Roger's fleet, of the transformation of the armada of Triplanetary into an unknown fluid, and finally of the dissolution of the gigantic planetoid itself. Then furiously Cleveland drove his beam against the crimsonly opaque obscurity into which the peculiar, viscous stream of substance was disappearing. Time after time he applied his every watt of power, with no result. A vast volume of space, roughly ellipsoidal in shape, was closed to him by forces entirely beyond his experience or comprehension. But suddenly, while his rays were still trying to pierce that impenetrable murk, it disappeared instantly and without warning: the illimitable infinity of space once more lay revealed upon his plates and his beams flashed unimpeded through the void.

"Back to Tellus, sir?" The *Chicago's* captain broke the strained silence.

"I wouldn't say so, if I had the say." Cleveland, baffled and frustrated, straightened up and shut off his cameras. "We should report back as soon as possible, of course, but there seems to be a lot of wreckage out there yet that we can't photograph in detail at this distance. A close study of it might help us a lot in understanding what they did and how they did it. I'd say that we should get close-ups of whatever is left, and do it right away, before it gets scattered all over space; but of course I can't give you orders."

"You can, though," the captain made surprising answer. "My orders are that you are in command of this vessel."

"In that case we will proceed at full emergency acceleration to investigate the wreckage," Cleveland replied, and the cruiser —sole survivor of Triplanetary's supposedly invincible force —shot away with every projector delivering its maximum blast.

As the scene of the disaster was approached there was revealed upon the plates a confused mass of debris; a mass whose individual units were apparently moving at random, yet which was as a whole still following the orbit of Roger's planetoid. Space was full of machine parts, structural members, furniture, flotsam of all kinds; and everywhere were the bodies of men. Some were encased in space-suits, and it was to these that the rescuers turned first—space-hardened veterans though the men of the *Chicago* were, they did not care even to look at the others. Strangely enough, however, not one of the floating figures spoke or moved, and space-line men were hurriedly sent out to investigate.

"All dead." Quickly the dread report came back. "Been dead a long time. The armor is all stripped off the suits, and all the generators and other apparatus are all shot. Something funny about it, too—none of them seem to have been touched, but the machinery of the suits seems to be about half missing."

"I've got it all on the reels, sir." Cleveland, his close-up survey of the wreckage finished, turned to the captain. "What they've just reported checks up with what I have photographed everywhere. I've got an idea of what might have happened, but it's so new that I'll have to have some evidence before I'll believe it myself. You might have them bring in a few of the armored bodies, a couple of those switchboards and panels floating around out there, and half a dozen miscellaneous pieces of junk—the nearest things they get hold of, whatever they happen to be."

"Then back to Tellus at maximum?"

"Right—back to Tellus, as fast as we can possibly get there."

While the *Chicago* hurtled through space at full power, Cleveland and the ranking officers of the vessel grouped themselves about the salvaged wreckage. Familiar with space-wrecks as were they all, none of them had ever seen anything like the material before them. For every part and instrument was weirdly and meaninglessly disintegrated. There were no breaks, no marks of violence, and yet nothing was intact. Bolt-holes stared empty, cores, shielding cases and needles had disappeared, the vital parts of every instrument hung awry, disorganization reigned rampant and supreme.

"I never imagined such a mess," the captain said, after a long and silent study of the objects. "If you have a theory to cover *that*, Cleveland, I would like to hear it!"

"I want you to notice something first," the expert replied. "But don't look for what's there—look for what *isn't* there."

"Well, the armor is gone. So are the shielding cases, shafts, spindles, the housings and stems . . ." the captain's voice died away as his eyes raced over the collection. "Why everything that was made of wood, bakelite, copper, aluminum, silver, bronze, or anything but steel hasn't been touched, and every bit of that is gone. But that doesn't make sense—what does it mean?"

"I don't know—yet," Cleveland replied, slowly. "But I'm afraid that there's more, and worse." He opened a space-suit reverently, revealing the face; a face calm and peaceful, but utterly, sickeningly white. Still reverently, he made a deep incision in the brawny neck, severing the jugular vein, then went on, soberly:

"You never imagined such a thing as *white* blood, either, but it all checks up. Someway, somehow, every atom of free or combined iron in this whole volume of space was made off with."

"Huh? How come? And above all, *why?*" from the amazed and staring officers.

"You know as much as I do," grimly, ponderingly. "If it were not for the fact that there are solid asteroids of iron out beyond Mars, I would say that somebody wanted iron badly enough to wipe out the fleet and the planetoid to get it. But anyway, whoever they were, they carried enough power so that our armament didn't bother them at all. They simply took the metal they wanted and went away with it—so fast that I couldn't trace them with an ultra-beam. There's only one thing plain; but that's so plain that it scares me stiff. This whole affair spells intelligence, with a capital 'I', and that intelligence is anything but friendly. I want to put Fred Rodebush at work on this just as fast as I can get him."

He stepped over to his ultra-projector and put in a call for Virgil Samms, whose face soon appeared upon his screen.

"We got it all, Virgil," he reported. "It's something extra-ordinary—bigger, wider, and deeper than any of us dreamed. It may be urgent, too, so I think I had better shoot the stuff in on an ultra-beam and save some time. Fred has a telemagneto recorder there that he can synchronize with this outfit easily enough. Right?"

"Right. Good work, Lyman—thanks," came back terse approval and appreciation, and soon the steel wires were again flashing from reel to reel. This time, however, their varying magnetic charges were so modulating ultra-waves that every detail of that calamitous battle of the void was being screened and recorded in the innermost private laboratory of the Triplanetary Service.

Eager though he naturally was to join his fellow-scientists, Cleveland was not impatient during the long, but uneventful journey back to Earth. There was much to study, many improvements to be made in his comparatively crude first ultra-camera. Then, too, there were long conferences with Samms, and particularly with Rodebush, the nuclear physicist, who would have to do much of the work involved in solving the riddles of the energies and weapons of the Nevians. Thus it did not seem long before green Terra grew large beneath the flying sphere of the *Chicago.*

"Going to have to circle it once, aren't you?" Cleveland asked the chief pilot. He had been watching that officer closely for minutes, admiring the delicacy and precision with which the great vessel was being maneuvered preliminary to entering the Earth's atmosphere.

"Yes," the pilot replied. "We had to come in in the shortest possible time, and that meant a velocity here that we can't check without a spiral. However, even at that we saved a lot of time. You can save quite a bit more, though, by having a rocket-plane come out to meet us somewhere around fifteen or twenty thousand kilometers, depending upon where you want to land. With their drives they can match our velocity and still make the drop direct."

"Guess I'll do that—thanks," and the operative called his chief, only to learn that his suggestion had already been acted upon.

"We beat you to it, Lyman," Samms smiled. "The *Silver Sliver* is out there now, looping to match your course, acceleraction, and velocity at twenty two thousand kilometers. You'll be ready to transfer?"

"I'll be ready," and the Quartermaster's ex-clerk went to his quarters and packed his dunnage-bag.

In due time the long, slender body of the rocket-plane came into view, creeping "down" upon the space-ship from "above," and Cleveland bade his friends goodbye. Donning a space-suit, he stationed himself in the starboard airlock. Its atmosphere was withdrawn, the outer door opened, and he glanced across a bare hundred feet of space at the rocket-plane which, keel ports fiercely aflame, was braking her terrific speed to match the slower pace of the gigantic sphere of war. Shaped like a toothpick, needle-pointed fore and aft, with ultra-stubby wings and vanes, with flush-set rocket ports everywhere, built of a lustrous, silvery alloy of noble and almost infusible metals—such was the private speedboat of Triplanetary's head man. The fastest thing known, whether in planetary air, the stratosphere, or the vacuous depth of interplanetary space, her first flashing trial spins had won her the nickname of the *Silver Sliver*. She had had a more formal name, but that title had long since been buried in the Departmental files.

Lower and lower dropped the speed-boat, her rockets flaming ever brighter, until her slender length lay level with the airlock door. Then her blasting discharges subsided to the power necessary to match exactly the *Chicago's* acceleration.

"Ready to cut, *Chicago!* Give me a three-second call!" snapped from the pilot room of the *Sliver.*

"Ready to cut!" the pilot of the *Chicago* replied. "Seconds! Three! Two! One! CUT!"

At the last word the power of both vessels was instantly cut off and everything in them became weightless. In the tiny airlock of the slender plane crouched a space-line man with coiled cable in readiness, but he was not needed. As the flaring exhausts ceased Cleveland swung out his heavy bag and stepped lightly off into space, and in a right line he floated directly into the open port of the rocket-plane. The door clanged shut behind him and in a matter or moments he stood in the control room of the racer, divested of his armor and shaking hands with his friend and co-laborer, Frederick Rodebush.

"Well, Fritz, what do you know?" Cleveland asked, as soon as greetings had been exchanged. "How do the various reports dovetail together? I know that you couldn't tell me anything on the wave, but there's no danger of eavesdroppers *here.*"

"You can't tell," Rodebush soberly replied. "We're just beginning to wake up to the fact that there are a lot of things we don't know anything about. Better wait until we're back at the Hill. We have a full set of ultra screens around there now. There's a couple of other good reasons, too—it would be better for both of us to go over the whole thing with Virgil, from the ground up; and we can't do any more talking, anyway. Our orders are to get back there at maximum, and you know what that means aboard the *Sliver*. Strap yourself solid in that shock-absorber there, and here's a pair of ear-plugs."

"When the *Sliver* really cuts loose it means a rough party, all right." Cleveland assented, snapping about his body the heavy spring-straps of his deeply cushioned seat, "but I'm just as anxious to get back to the Hill as anybody can be to get me there. All set."

Rodebush waved his hand at the pilot and the purring whisper of the exhausts changed instantly to a deafening, continuous explosion. The men were pressed deeply into their shock-absorbing chairs as the *Silver Sliver* spun around her longitudinal axis and darted away from the *Chicago* with such a tremendous acceleration that the spherical warship seemed to be standing still in space. In due time the calculated midpoint was reached, the slim space-plane rolled over again, and, mad acceleration now reversed, rushed on toward the Earth, but with constantly diminishing speed. Finally a measurable atmospheric pressure was encountered, the needle prow dipped downward, and the *Silver Sliver* shot forward upon her tiny wings and vanes, nose-rockets now drumming in staccato thunder. Her metal grew hot; dull red, bright red, yellow, blinding white; but it neither melted nor burned. The pilot's calculations had been sound, and though the limiting point of safety of temperature was reached and steadily held, it was not exceeded. As the density of the air increased so decreased the velocity of the man-made meteorite. So it was that a dazzling lance of fire sped high over Seattle, lower over Spokane, and hurled itself eastward, a furiously flaming arrow; slanting downward in a long, screaming dive toward the heart of the Rockies. As the now rapidly cooling greyhound of the skies passed over the western ranges of the Bitter Roots it became apparent that her goal was a vast, flat-topped, conical mountain, shrouded in violet light; a mountain whose height awed even its stupendous neighbors.

While not artificial, the Hill had been altered markedly by the engineers who had built into it the headquarters of the Triplanetary Service. Its mile-wide top was a jointless expanse of gray armor steel; the steep, smooth surface of the truncated cone was a continuation of the same immensely thick sheet of metal. No known vehicle could climb that smooth, hard, forbidding slope of steel; no known projectile could mar that armor; no known craft could even approach the Hill without detection. Could not approach it at all, in fact, for it was constantly inclosed in a vast hemisphere of lambent violet flame through which neither material substance nor destructive ray could pass.

As the *Silver Sliver*, crawling along at a bare five hundred miles an hour, approached that transparent, brilliantly violet wall of destruction, a light of the same color filled her control room and as suddenly went out; flashing on and off again and again.

"Giving us the once-over, eh?" Cleveland asked. "That's something new, isn't it?"

"Yes, it's a high-powered ultra-wave spy," Rodebush returned. "The light is simply a warning, which can be carried if desired. It can also carry voice and vision . . ."

"Like this," Samms' voice interrupted from a speaker upon the pilot's panel and his clear-cut face appeared upon the television screen. "I don't suppose Fred thought to mention it, but this is one of his inventions of the last few days. We are just trying it out on you. It doesn't mean a thing though, as far as the *Sliver* is concerned. Come ahead!"

A circular opening appeared on the wall of force, an opening which disappeared as soon as the plane had darted through it; and at the same time her landing-cradle rose into the air through a great trap-door. Slowly and gracefully the space-plane settled downward into that cushioned embrace. Then cradle and nestled *Sliver* sank from view and, turning smoothly upon mighty trunnions, the plug of armor drove solidly back into its place in the metal pavement of the mountain's lofty summit. The cradle-elevator dropped rapidly, coming to rest many levels down in the heart of the Hill, and Cleveland and Rodebush leaped lightly out of their transport, through her still hot outer walls. A door opened before them and they found themselves in a large room of unshadowed daylight illumination; the office of the Chief of the Triplanetary Service. Calmly efficient executives sat at their desks, concentrating upon problems or at ease, according to the demands of the moment; agents, secretaries, and clerks, men and women, went about their wonted tasks; televisotypes and recorders flashed busily but silently—each person and machine an integral part of the Service which for so many years had been carrying an ever-increasing share of the load of governing the three planets.

"Right of way, Norma?" Rodebush paused before the desk of Virgil Samms' private secretary. She pressed a button and the door behind her swung wide.

"You two do not need to be announced," the attractive young woman smiled. "Go right in."

Samms met them at the door eagerly, shaking hands particularly vigorously with Cleveland.

"Congratulations on that camera, Lyman!" he exclaimed. "You did a wonderful piece of work on that. Help yourselves to smokes and sit down—there are a lot of things we want to talk over. Your pictures carried most of the story, but they would have left us pretty much at sea without Costigan's reports. But as it was, Fred here and his crew worked out most of the answers from the dope the two of you got; and what few they haven't got yet they soon will have."

"Nothing new on Conway?" Cleveland was almost afraid to ask the question.

"No." A shadow came over Samms' face. "I'm afraid . . . but I'm hoping it's only that those creatures, whatever they are, have taken him so far away he can't reach us."

"They certainly are so far away that we can't reach them," Rodebush volunteered. "We can't even get their ultra-wave interference any more."

"Yes, that's a hopeful sign," Samms went on. "I hate to think of Conway Costigan checking out. There, fellows, was a real observer. He was the only man I have ever known who combined the two qualities of the perfect witness. He could actually see everything he looked at, and could report it truly, to the last, least detail. Take all this stuff, for instance; especially their ability to transform iron into a fluid allotrope, and in that form to use its atomic—nuclear?—energy as power. Something brand new, and yet he described their converters and projectors so minutely that Fred was able to work out the underlying theory in three days, and to tie it in with our own super-ship. My first thought was that we'd have to rebuild it iron-free, but Fred showed me my error—you found it first yourself, of course."

"It wouldn't do any good to make the ship non-ferrous unless you could so change our blood chemistry that we could get along without hemoglobin, and that would be quite a feat," Cleveland agreed. "Then, too, our most vital electrical machinery is built around iron cores. We'll also have to develop a screen for those forces—screens, rather, so powerful that they can't drive anything through them."

"We've been working along those lines ever since you reported," Rodebush said, "and we're beginning to see light. And in that same connection it's no wonder that we couldn't handle our super-ship. We had some good ideas, but they were wrongly applied. However, things look quite promising now. We have the transformation of iron all worked out in theory, and as soon as we get a generator going we can straightened out everything else in short order. And think what that unlimited power means! All the power we want—power enough even to try out such hitherto purely theoretical possibilities as the neutralization of the inertia of matter!"

"Hold on!" protested Samms. "You certainly can't do *that!* Inertia is—*must* be—a basic attribute of matter, and surely cannot be done away with without destroying the matter itself. Don't start anything like that, Fred—I don't want to lose you and Lyman, too."

"Don't worry about us, Chief," Rodebush replied with a smile. "If you will tell me what matter is, fundamentally, I may agree with you . . . No? Well, then, don't be surprised at anything that happens. We are going to do a lot of things that nobody on the Three Planets ever thought of doing before."

Thus for a long time the argument and discussion went on, to be interrupted by the voice of the secretary.

"Sorry to disturb you, Mr. Samms, but some things have come up that you will have to handle. Knobos is calling from Mars. He has caught the *Endymion,* and has killed about half her crew doing it. Milton has finally reported from Venus, after being out of touch for five days. He trailed the Wintons into Thalleron swamp. They crashed him there, and he won out and has what he went after. And just now I got a flash from Fletcher, in the asteroid belt. I think that he has finally traced that dope line. But Knobos is on now—what do you want him to do about the *Endymion?*"

"Tell him to—no, put him on here, I'd better tell him myself," Samms directed, and his face hardened in ruthless decision as the horny, misshapen face of the Martian lieutenant appeared upon the screen. "What do you think, Knobos? Shall they come to trial or not?"

"Not."

"I don't think so, either. It is better that a few gangsters should disappear in space than that the Patrol should have to put down another uprising. See to it."

"Right." The screen darkened and Samms spoke to his secretary. "Put Milton and Fletcher on whenever they come in." He turned to his guests. "We've covered the ground quite thoroughly. Goodbye—I wish I could go with you, but I'll be pretty well tied up for the next week or two."

" 'Tied up' doesn't half express it," Rodebush remarked as the two scientists walked along a corridor toward an elevator. "He probably is the busiest man on three planets."

"As well as the most powerful," Cleveland supplemented. "And very few men could use his power as fairly—but he's welcome to it, as far as I'm concerned. I'd have the pink fantods for a month if I had to do only once what he's just done—and to him it's just part of a day's work."

"You mean the *Endymion?* What else could he do?"

"Nothing—that's the hell of it. It had to be done, since bringing them to trial would mean killing half the people of Morseca; but at the same time it's a ghastly thing to order a job of deliberate, cold-blooded, and illegal murder."

"You're right, of course, but you would . . ." he broke off, unable to put his thoughts into words. For while inarticulate, manlike, concerning their deepest emotions, in both men was ingrained the code of the organization; both knew that to every man chosen for it THE SERVICE was everything, himself nothing.

"But enough of that, we'll have plenty of grief of our own right here." Rodebush changed the subject abruptly as they stepped into a vast room, almost filled by the immense bulk of the *Boise*—the sinister space-ship which, although never flown, had already lined with black so many pages of Triplanetary's roster. She was now, however, the center of a furious activity. Men swarmed over her and through her, in the orderly confusion of a fiercely driven but carefully planned program of reconstruction.

"I hope your dope is right, Fritz!" Cleveland called, as the two scientists separated to go to their respective laboratories. "If it is, we'll make a perfect lady out of this unmanageable man-killer yet!"

CHAPTER 14

THE SUPER-SHIP IS LAUNCHED

AFTER WEEKS OF CEASELESS WORK, DURING WHICH WAS LAV-
ished upon her every resource of mind and material afforded
by three planets, the *Boise* was ready for her maiden
flight. As nearly ready, that is, as the thought and labor of
man could make her. Rodebush and Cleveland had finished
their last rigid inspection of the aircraft and, standing beside
the center door of the main airlock, were talking with their
chief.

"You say that you think that it's safe, and yet you won't
take a crew," Samms argued. "In that case it isn't safe enough
for you two, either. We need you too badly to permit you
to take such chances."

"You've *got* to let us go, because we are the only ones
who are at all familiar with her theory," Rodebush insisted.
"I said, and I still say, that I *think* it is safe. I can't prove it,
however, even mathematically; because she's altogether too
full of too many new and untried mechanisms, too many
extrapolations beyond all existing or possible data. Theoretic-
ally, she is sound, but you know that theory can go only so
far, and that mathematically negligible factors may become
operative at those velocities. We do not need a crew for a
short trip. We can take care of any minor mishaps, and if
our fundamental theories are wrong, all the crews between
here and Jupiter wouldn't do any good. Therefore we two
are going—alone.

"Well, be very careful, anyway. I wish that you could
start out slow and take it easy."

"In a way, so do I, but she wasn't designed to neutralize
half of gravity, nor half of the inertia of matter—it's got to
be everything or nothing, as soon as the neutralizers go on.
We could start out on the projectors, of course, instead of on
the neutralizers, but that wouldn't prove anything and
would only prolong the agony."

"Well, then, be as careful as you can."

"We'll do that, Chief," Cleveland put in. "We think as

much of us as anybody else does—maybe more—and we aren't committing suicide if we can help it. And remember about everybody staying inside when we take off—it's barely possible that we'll take up a lot of room. Goodbye!"

"Goodbye, fellows!"

The massive insulating doors were shut, the metal side of the mountain opened, and huge, squat caterpillar tractors came roaring and clanking into the room. Chains and cables were made fast and, mighty steel rails groaning under the load, the space-ship upon her rolling ways was dragged out of the Hill and far out upon the level floor of the valley before the tractors cast off and returned to the fortress.

"Everybody is under cover," Samms informed Rodebush. The Chief was staring intently into his plate, upon which was revealed the control room of the untried super-ship. He heard Rodebush speak to Cleveland; heard the observer's brief reply; saw the navigator push the switch-button—then the communicator plate went blank. Not the ordinary blankness of a cut-off, but a peculiarly disquieting fading out into darkness. And where the great space-ship had rested there was for an instant nothing. Exactly nothing—a vacuum. Vessel, falsework, rollers, trucks, the enormous steel I-beams of the tracks, even the deep-set concrete piers and foundations and a vast hemisphere of the solid ground; all disappeared utterly and instantaneously. But almost as suddenly as it had been formed the vacuum was filled by a cyclonic rush of air. There was a detonation as of a hundred vicious thunderclaps made one, and through the howling, shrieking blasts of wind there rained down upon valley, plain, and metaled mountain a veritable avalanche of debris; bent, twisted, and broken rails and beams, splintered timbers, masses of concrete, and thousands of cubic yards of soil and rock. For the atomic-powered "Rodebush-Cleveland" neutralizers were more powerful by far, and had a vastly greater radius of action, than the calculations of their designers had shown; and for a moment everything within a hundred yards or so of the *Boise* behaved as though it were an integral part of the vessel. Then, left behind immediately by the super-ship's almost infinite velocity, all this material had again become subject to all of Nature's everyday laws and had crashed back to the ground.

"Could you hold your beam, Randolph?" Samms' voice cut sharply through the daze of stupefaction which held spellbound most of the denizens of the Hill. But all were not so held—no conceivable emergency could take the attention of the chief ultra-wave operator from his instruments.

"No, sir," Radio Center shot back. "It faded out and I couldn't recover it. I put everything I've got behind a tracer on that beam, but haven't been able to lift a single needle off the pin."

"And no wreckage of the vessel itself," Samms went on, half audibly. "Either they have succeeded far beyond their wildest hopes or else . . . more probably . . ." He fell silent and switched off the plate. Were his two friends, those intrepid scientists, alive and triumphant, or had they gone to lengthen the list of victims of that man-killing space-ship? Reason told him that they were gone. They *must* be gone, or else the ultra-beams—energies of such unthinkable velocity of propagation that man's most sensitive instruments had never been able even to estimate it—would have held the ship's transmitter in spite of any velocity attainable by matter under any conceivable conditions. The ship must have been disintegrated as soon as Rodebush released his forces. And yet, had not the physicist dimly foreseen the possibility of such an actual velocity—or had he? However, individuals could come and go, but the Service went on. Samms squared his shoulders unconsciously; and slowly, grimly, made his way back to his private office.

"Mr. Fairchild would like to have a moment as soon as possible, sir," his secretary informed him even before he sat down. "Senator Morgan has been here all day, you know, and he insists on seeing you personally."

"Oh, that kind, eh? All right, I'll see him. Get Fairchild, please . . . Dick? Can you talk, or is he there listening?"

"No, he's heckling Saunders at the moment. He's been here long enough. Can you take a minute and throw him out?"

"Of course, if you say so, but why not throw the hooks into him yourself, as usual?"

"He wants to lay down the law to you, personally. He's a Big Shot, you know, and his group is kicking up quite a row, so it might be better to have it come straight from the top. Besides, you've got a unique knack—when you throw a harpoon, the harpoonee doesn't forget it."

"All right. He's the uplifter and leveler-off. Down with Triplanetary, up with National Sovereignty. We're power-mad dictators—iron-heel-on-the-necks-of-the-people, and so on. But what's he like, personally? Thick-skinned, of course —got a brain?"

"Rhinoceros. He's got a brain, but it's definitely weaseloid. Bear down—sink it in full length, and then twist it."

"O.K. You've got a harpoon, of course?"

"Three of 'em!" Fairchild, Head of Triplanetary's Public Relations, grinned with relish. "Boss Jim Towne owns him in fee simple. The number of his hot lock box is N469T414. His subbest sub-rosa girl-friend is Fi-Chi le Bay . . . yes, everything that the name implies. She got a super-deluxe fur coat—Martian tekkyl, no less—out of that Mackenzie River power deal. Triple play, you might say—Clander to Morgan to le Bay."

"Nice. Bring him in."

"Senator Morgan, Mr. Samms," Fairchild made the introduction and the two men sized each other up in lightning glances. Samms saw a big man, florid, somewhat inclined toward corpulence, with the surface geniality—and the shrewd calculating eyes—of the successful politician. The senator saw a tall, hard-trained man in his forties; a lean, keen, smooth-shaven face; a shock of red-bronze-auburn hair a couple of weeks overdue for a cutting; a pair of gold-flecked tawny eyes too penetrant for comfort.

"I trust, Senator, that Fairchild has taken care of you satisfactorily?"

"With one or two exceptions, yes." Since Samms did not ask what the exceptions could be, Morgan was forced to continue. "I am here, as you know, in my official capacity as Chairman of the Pernicious Activities Committee of the North American Senate. It has been observed for years that the published reports of your organization have left much unsaid. It is common knowledge that high-handed outrages have been perpetrated; if not by your men themselves, in such circumstances that your agents could not have been ignorant of them. Therefore it has been decided to make a first-hand and comprehensive investigation, in which matter your Mr. Fairchild has not been at all cooperative."

"Who decided to make this investigation?"

"Why, the North American Senate, of course, through its Pernicious Activities . . ."

"I thought so." Samms interrupted. "Don't you know, Senator, that the Hill is not a part of the North American Continent? That the Triplanetary Service is responsible only to the Triplanetary Council?"

"Quibbling, sir, and outmoded! This, sir, is a democracy!" the Senator began to orate. "All that will be changed very shortly, and if you are as smart as you are believed to be,

I need only say that you and those of your staff who co-operate . . ."

"You need say nothing at all." Samms' voice cut. "It has not been changed yet. The Government of North America rules its continent, as do the other Continental Governments. The combined Continental Governments of the Three Planets form the Triplanetary Council, which is a non-political body, the members of which hold office for life and which is the supreme authority in any matter, small or large, affecting more than one Continental Government. The Council has two principal operating agencies; the Triplanetary Patrol, which enforces its decisions, rules, and regulations, and the Triplanetary Service, which performs such other tasks as the Council directs. We have no interest in the purely internal affairs of North America. Have you any information to the contrary?"

"More quibbling!" the Senator thundered. "This is not the first time in history that a ruthless dictatorship has operated in the disguise of a democracy. Sir, I *demand* full access to your files, so that I can spread before the North American Senate the full facts of the various matters which I mentioned to Fairchild—one of which was the affair of the *Pelarion*. In a democracy, sir, facts should not be hidden; the people must and shall be kept completely informed upon any matter which affects their welfare or their political lives!"

"Is that so? If I should ask, then, for the purpose of keeping the Triplanetary Council, and through it your constituents, fully informed as to the political situation in North America, you would undoubtedly give me the key to safe-deposit box N469T414? For it is common knowledge, in the Council at least, that there is a certain amount of—shall we say turbidity?—in the supposedly pellucid reaches of North American politics."

"What? Preposterous!" Morgan made a heroic effort, but could not quite maintain his poise. "Private papers only, sir!"

"Perhaps. Certain of the Councillors believe, however mistakenly, that there are several things of interest there: such as the record of certain transactions involving one James F. Towne; references to and details concerning dealings—not to say deals—with Mackenzie Power, specifically with Mackenzie Power's Mr. Clander; and perhaps a juicy bit or two concerning a person known as le Bay and a tekkyl coat. Of interest no end, don't you think, to the dear people of North America?"

As Samms drove the harpoon in and twisted it, the big man suffered visibly. Nevertheless:

"You refuse to cooperate, eh?" he blustered. "Very well, I will go—but you have not heard the last of me, Samms!"

"No? Probably not. But remember, before you do any more rabble-rousing, that this lock-box thing is merely a sample. We of the Service know a lot of things that we do not mention to anybody—except in self-defense."

"I am holding Fletcher, Mr. Samms. Shall I put him on now?" Norma asked, as the completely deflated Morgan went out.

"Yes, please . . . Hello, Sid; mighty glad to see you—we were scared for a while. How did you make out, and what was it?"

"Hi, Chief! Mostly hadive. Some heroin, and quite a bit of Martian ladolian. Lousy job, though—three of the gang got away, and took about a quarter of the loot with them. That was what I want to talk to you about in such a hurry—fake meteors; the first I ever saw."

Samms straightened up in his chair.

"Just a second. Norma, put Redmond on here with us . . . Listen, Harry. Now, Fletcher, did you see that fake meteor yourself? Touch it?"

"Both. In fact, I've still got it. One of the runners, pretending to be a Service man, flashed it on *me*. It's really good, too, Chief. Even now, I can't tell it from my own except that mine is in my pocket. Shall I send it in?"

"By all means; to Dr. H. D. Redmond, Head of Research. Keep on slugging, Sid—goodbye. Now, Harry, what do you think? It *could* be one of our own, you know."

"Could be, but probably isn't. We'll know as soon as we get it in the lab. Chances are, though, that they have caught up with us again. After all, that was to be expected—anything that science can synthesize, science can analyze; and whatever the morals and ethics of the pirates may be, they have got brains."

"And you haven't been able to devise anything better?"

"Variations only, which wouldn't take much time to solve. Fundamentally, the present meteor is the best we know."

"Got anybody you would like to put on it, immediately?"

"Of course. One of the new boys will be perfect for the job, I think. Name of Bergenholm. Quite a character. Brilliant, erratic, flashes of sheer genius that he can't explain, even to us. I'll put him on it right away."

"Thanks a lot. And now, Norma, please keep everybody off my neck that you can. I want to think."

And think he did; keen eyes clouded, staring unseeingly at the papers littering his desk. Triplanetary needed a symbol—a something—which would identify a Service man anywhere, at any time, under any circumstances, without doubt or question . . . something that could not be counterfeited or imitated, to say nothing of being duplicated . . . something that no scientist not of Triplanetary Service could *possibly* imitate . . . better yet, something that no one not of Triplanetary could even wear . . .

Samms grinned fleetingly at that thought. A tall order one calling for a *deus ex machina* with a vengeance . . . But damn it, there ought to be *some* way to . . .

"Excuse me, sir." His secretary's voice, usually so calm and cool, trembled as she broke in on his thinking. "Commissioner Kinnison is calling. Something terrible is going on again, out toward Orion. Here he is," and there appeared upon Samms' screen the face of the Commissioner of Public Safety, the commander-in-chief of Triplanetary's every armed force; whether of land or of water, of air or of empty space.

"They've come back, Virgil!" The Commissioner rapped out without preliminary or greeting. "Four vessels gone—a freighter and a passenger liner, with her escort of two heavy cruisers. All in Sector M, Dx about 151. I have ordered all traffic out of space for the duration of the emergency, and since even our warships seem useless, every ship is making for the nearest dock at maximum. How about that new flyer of yours—got anything that will do us any good?" No one beyond the "Hill's" shielding screens knew that the *Boise* had already been launched.

"I don't know. We don't even know whether we have a super-ship or not," and Samms described briefly the beginning—and very probably the ending—of the trial flight, concluding: "It looks bad, but if there was any possible way of handling her, Rodebush and Cleveland did it. All our tracers are negative yet, so nothing definite has . . ."

He broke off as a frantic call came in from the Pittsburgh station for the Commissioner; a call which Samms both heard and saw.

"The city is being attacked!" came the urgent message. "We need all the reenforcements you can send us!" and a picture of the beleaguered city appeared in ghastly detail upon the screens of the observers; a view being recorded from the air. It required only seconds for the commissioner to order every available man and engine of war to the seat of conflict; then, having done everything they could do, Kinnison and Samms stared in helpless, fascinated horror into their plates, watching the scenes of carnage and destruction depicted there.

The Nevian vessel—the sister-ship, the craft which Costigan had seen in mid-space as it hurtled Earthward in response to Nerado's summons—hung poised in full visibility high above the metropolis. Scornful of the pitiful weapons wielded by man, she hung there, her sinister beauty of line sharply defined against the cloudless sky. From her shining hull there reached down a tenuous but rigid rod of crimson energy; a rod which slowly swept hither and thither as the Nevians searched out the richest deposits of the precious metal for which they had come so far. Iron, once solid, now a viscous red liquid, was sluggishly flowing in an ever-thickening stream up that intangible crimson duct and into the capacious storage tanks of the Nevian raider; and wherever that flaming beam went there went also ruin, destruction and death. Office buildings, skyscrapers towering majestically in their architectural symmetry and beauty, collapsed into heaps of debris as their steel skeletons were abstracted. Deep into the ground the beam bored; flood, fire, and explosion following in its wake as the mazes of underground piping disappeared. And the humanity of the buildings died: instantaneously and painlessly, never knowing what struck them, as the life-bearing iron of their bodies went to swell the Nevian stream.

Pittsburgh's defenses had been feeble indeed. A few antiquated railway rifles had hurled their shells upward in futile defiance, and had been quietly absorbed. The district planes of Triplanetary, newly armed with iron-driven ultra-beams, had assembled hurriedly and had attacked the invader in formation, with but little more success. Under the impact of their beams, the stranger's screens had flared white, then poised ship and flying squadron had alike been lost to view in a murkily opaque shroud of crimson flame. The cloud had soon dissolved, and from the place where the planes had been there floated or crashed down a litter of non-ferrous wreckage. And now the cone of space-ships from the Buffalo base of Triplanetary was approaching Pittsburgh hurling itself toward the Nevian plunderer and toward known, gruesome, and hopeless defeat.

"Stop them, Rod!" Samms cried. "It's sheer slaughter! They haven't got a thing—they aren't even equipped yet with the iron drive!"

"I know it," the commissioner groaned, "and Admiral Barnes knows it as well as we do, but it can't be helped—wait a minute! The Washington cone is reporting. They're as close as the other, and they have the new armament. Philadelphia is close behind, and so is New York. Now perhaps we can do something!"

The Buffalo flotilla slowed and stopped, and in a matter of minutes the detachments from the other bases arrived. The cone was formed and, iron-driven vessels in the van, the old-type craft far in the rear, it bore down upon the Nevian, vomiting from its hollow front a solid cylinder of annihilation. Once more the screens of the Nevian flared into brilliance, once more the red cloud of destruction was flung abroad. But these vessels were not entirely defenseless. Their iron-driven ultra-generators threw out screens of the Nevians' own formulae, screens of prodigious power to which the energies of the amphibians clung and at which they clawed and tore in baffled, wildly coruscant displays of power unthinkable. For minutes the furious conflict raged, while the inconceivable energy being dissipated by those straining screens hurled itself in terribly destructive bolts of lightning upon the city far beneath.

No battle of such incredible violence could long endure. Triplanetary's ships were already exerting their utmost power, while the Nevians, contemptuous of Solarian science, had not yet uncovered their full strength. Thus the last desperate effort of mankind was proved futile as the invaders forced their beams deeper and deeper into the overloaded defensive screens of the war-vessels; and one by one the supposedly invincible space-ships of humanity dropped in horribly dismembered ruin upon the ruins of what had once been Pittsburgh.

CHAPTER 15

SPECIMENS

ONLY TOO WELL FOUNDED WAS COSTIGAN'S CONVICTION THAT the submarine of the deep-sea fishes had not been able to prevail against Nerado's formidable engines of destruction.

For days the Nevian lifeboat with its three Terrestrial passengers hurtled through the interstellar void without incident, but finally the operative's fears were realized—his far flung detector screens reacted; upon his observation plate they could see Nerado's mammoth space-ship, in full pursuit of its fleeing life-boat!

"On your toes, folks—it won't be long now!" Costigan called, and Bradley and Clio hurried into the tiny control room.

Armor donned and tested, the three Terrestrials stared into the observation plates, watching the rapidly-enlarging picture of the Nevian space-ship. Nerado had traced them and was following them, and such was the power of the great vessel that the now inconceivable velocity of the lifeboat was the veriest crawl in comparison to that of the pursuing cruiser.

"And we've hardly started to cover the distance back to Tellus. Of course you couldn't get in touch with anybody yet?" Bradley stated, rather than asked.

"I kept trying, of course, until they blanketed my wave, but all negative. Thousands of times too far for my transmitter. Our only hope of reaching anybody was the mighty slim chance that our super-ship might be prowling around out here already, but it isn't, of course. Here they are!"

Reaching out to the control panel, Costigan viciously shot out against the great vessel wave after wave of lethal vibrations, under whose fiercely clinging impacts the Nevian defensive screens flared white; but, strangely enough, their own screens did not radiate. As if contemptuous of any weapons the lifeboat might wield, the mother ship simply defended herself from the attacking beams, in much the same fashion as a wildcat mother wards off the claws and teeth of her spitting, snarling kitten who is resenting a touch of needed maternal discipline.

"They probably wouldn't fight us, at that," Clio first understood the situation. "This is their own lifeboat, and they want us alive, you know."

"There's one more thing we can try—hang on!" Costigan snapped, as he released his screens and threw all his power into one enormous pressor beam.

The three were thrown to the floor and held there by an awful weight as the lifeboat darted away at the stupendous acceleration of the beam's reaction against the unimaginable mass of the Nevian sky-rover; but the flight was of short duration. Along that pressor beam there crept a dull red rod of energy, which surrounded the fugitive shell and brought it slowly to a halt. Furiously then Costigan set and reset his controls, launching his every driving force and his every weapon, but no beam could penetrate that red murk, and the lifeboat remained motionless in space. No, not motionless —the red rod was shortening, drawing the truant craft back toward the launching port from which she had so hopefully emerged a few days before. Back and back it was drawn; Costigan's utmost efforts futile to affect by a hair's breadth its line of motion. Through the open port the boat slipped neatly, and as it came to a halt in its original position within the multi-layered skin of the monster, the prisoners heard the heavy doors clang shut behind them, one after another.

And then sheets of blue fire snapped and crackled about the three suits of Triplanetary armor—the two large human figures and the small ones were outlined starkly in blinding blue flame.

"That's the first thing that has come off according to schedule." Costigan laughed, a short, fierce bark. "That is their paralyzing ray, we've got it stopped cold, and we've each got enough iron to hold it forever."

"But it looks as though the best we can do is a stalemate," Bradley argued. "Even if they can't paralyze us, we can't hurt them, and we are heading back for Nevia."

"I think Nerado will come in for a conference, and we'll be able to make terms of some kind. He must know what these Lewistons will do, and he knows that we'll get a chance to use them, some way or other, before he gets to us again," Costigan asserted, confidently—but again he was wrong.

The door opened, and through it there waddled, rolled, or crawled a metal-clad monstrosity—a thing with wheels, legs and writhing tentacles of jointed bronze; a thing possessed of defensive screens sufficiently powerful to absorb the full blast of the Triplanetary projectors without effort. Three brazen tentacles reached out through the ravening beams of the Lewistons, smashed them to bits, and wrapped themselves in unbreakable shackles about the armored forms of the three human beings. Through the door the machine or creature carried its helpless load, and out into and along a main corridor. And soon the three Terrestrials, without arms, without armor, and almost without clothing, were standing in the control room, again facing the calm and unmoved Nerado. To the surprise of the impetuous Costigan, the Nevian commander was entirely without rancor.

"The desire for freedom is perhaps common to all forms of animate life," he commented, through the transformer. "As I told you before, however, you are specimens to be studied by the College of Science, and you shall be so studied in spite of anything you may do. Resign yourselves to that."

"Well, say that we don't try to make any more trouble; that we cooperate in the examination and give you whatever information we can," Costigan suggested. "Then you will probably be willing to give us a ship and let us go back to our own world?"

"You will not be allowed to cause any more trouble," the amphibian declared, coldly. "Your cooperation will not be required. We will take from you whatever knowledge and information we wish. In all probability you will never be allowed to return to your own system, because as specimens you are too unique to lose. But enough of this idle chatter—take them back to their quarters!"

Back to their three inter-communicating rooms the prisoners were led under heavy guard; and, true to his word, Nerado made certain that they had no more opportunities to escape. To Nevia the space-ship sped without incident, and in manacles the Terrestrials were taken to the College of Science, there to undergo the physical and psychical examinations which Nerado had promised them.

Nor had the Nevian scientist-captain erred in stating that their cooperation was neither needed nor desired. Furious but impotent, the human beings were studied in laboratory after laboratory by the coldly analytical, unfeeling scientists of Nevia, to whom they were nothing more or less than specimens; and in full measure they came to know what it meant to play the part of an unknown, lowly organism in a biological research. They were photographed, externally and internally. Every bone, muscle, organ, vessel, and nerve was studied and charted. Every reflex and reaction was noted and discussed. Meters registered every impulse and recorders filmed every thought, every idea, and every sensation. Endlessly, day after day, the nerve-wracking torture went on, until the frantic subjects could bear no more. White-faced and shaking, Clio finally screamed wildly, hysterically, as she was being strapped down upon a laboratory bench; and at the sound Costigan's nerves, already at the breaking point, gave way in an outburst of berserk fury.

The man's struggles and the girl's shrieks were alike futile, but the surprised Nevians, after a consultation, decided to give the specimens a vacation. To that end they were installed, together with their Earthly belongings, in a three-roomed structure of transparent metal, floating in the large central lagoon of the city. There they were left undisturbed for a time—undisturbed, that is, except by the continuous gaze of the crowd of hundreds of amphibians which constantly surrounded the floating cottage.

"First we're bugs under a microscope," Bradley growled, "then we're goldfish in a bowl. I don't know that . . ."

He broke off as two of their jailers entered the room. Without a word into the transformers they seized Bradley and Clio. As those tentacular arms stretched out toward the girl, Costigan leaped. A vain attempt. In midair the paralyzing beam of the Nevians touched him and he crashed heavily to the crystal floor; and from that floor he looked on in helpless, raging fury while his sweetheart and his captain were carried out of their prison and into a waiting submarine.

CHAPTER 16

SUPER-SHIP IN ACTION

DOCTOR FREDERICK RODEBUSH SAT AT THE CONTROL PANEL of Triplanetary's newly reconstructed super-ship; one finger poised over a small black button. Facing the unknown though the physicist was, yet he grinned whimsically at his friend.

"Something, whatever it is, is about to occur. The *Boise* is about to take off. Ready, Cleve?"

"Shoot!" laconically. Cleveland also was constitutionally unable to voice his deeper sentiments in time of stress.

Rodebush drove his finger down, and instantly over both men there came a sensation akin to a tremendously intensified vertigo; but a vertigo as far beyond the space-sickness of weightlessness as that horrible sensation is beyond mere Earthly dizziness. The pilot reached weakly toward the board, but his leaden hands refused utterly to obey the dictates of his reeling mind. His brain was a writhing, convulsive mass of torment indescribable; expanding, exploding, swelling out with an unendurable pressure against its confining skull. Fiery spirals, laced with streaming, darting lances of black and green, flamed inside his bursting eyeballs. The Universe spun and whirled in mad gyrations about him as he reeled drunkenly to his feet, staggering and sprawling. He fell. He realized that he was falling, yet he could not fall! Thrashing wildly, grotesquely in agony, he struggled madly and blindly across the room, directly toward the thick steel wall. The tip of one hair of his unruly thatch touched the wall, and the slim length of that single hair did not even bend as its slight strength brought to an instant halt the hundred-and-eighty-odd pounds of mass—mass now entirely without inertia—that was his body.

But finally the sheer brain power of the man began to triumph over his physical torture. By force of will he compelled his grasping hands to seize a life-line, almost meaningless to his dazed intelligence; and through that nightmare incarnate of hellish torture he fought his way back to the control board. Hooking one leg around a standard, he made a seemingly enormous effort and depressed a red button; then fell flat upon the floor, weakly but in a wave of relief and thankfulness, as his racked body felt again the wonted phenomena of weight and of inertia. White, trembling, frankly and openly sick, the two men stared at each other in half-amazed joy.

"It worked," Cleveland smiled wanly as he recovered sufficiently to speak, then leaped to his feet. "Snap it up, Fred! We must be falling fast—we'll be wrecked when we hit!"

"We're not falling anywhere." Rodebush, foreboding in his eyes, walked over to the main observation plate and scanned the heavens. "However, it's not as bad as I was afraid it might be. I can still recognize a few of the constellations, even though they are all pretty badly distorted. That means that we can't be more than a couple of light-years or so away from the Solar System. Of course, since we had so little thrust on, practically all of our energy and time was taken up in getting out of the atmosphere. Even at that, though, it's a good thing that space isn't a perfect vacuum, or we would have been clear out of the Universe by this time."

"Huh? What are you talking about? Impossible! Where are we, anyway? Then we must be making mil . . . Oh, I see!" Cleveland exclaimed, somewhat incoherently, as he also stared into the plate.

"Right. We aren't traveling at all—*now*." Rodebush replied. "We are perfectly stationary relative to Tellus, since we made that hop without inertia. We must have attained one

hundred percent neutralization—one hundred point oh
oh oh oh oh—which we didn't quite expect. Therefore we
must have stopped instantaneously when our inertia was restored. Incidentally, that original, pre-inertialess velocity
'intrinsic' velocity, suppose we could call it?—is going to
introduce plenty of complications, but we don't have to
worry about them right now. Also, it isn't *where* we are that
is worrying me—we can get fixes on enough recognizable
stars to find that out in short order—it's *when*."

"That's right, too. Say we're two light years away from
home. You think maybe that we're two years older now than
we were ten minutes ago? Interesting no end—and distinctly
possible. Maybe even probable—I wouldn't know—there's
been a lot of discussion on that theory, and as far as I
know we're the first ones who ever had a chance to prove
or disprove it absolutely. Let's snap back to Tellus and find
out, right now."

"We'll do that, after a little more experimenting. You see,
I had no intention of giving us such a long push. I was going
to throw the switches in and out, but you know what happened. However, there's one good thing about it—it's worth
two years of anybody's life to settle that relativity-time
thing definitely, one way or the other."

"I'll say it is. But say, we've got a lot of power on our
ultra-wave; enough to reach Tellus, I think. Let's locate the
sun and get in touch with Samms."

"Let's work on these controls a little first, so we'll have
something to report. Out here's a fine place to try the ship
out—nothing in the way."

"All right with me. But I *would* like to find out whether
I'm two years older than I think I am, or not!"

Then for four hours they put the great super-ship through
her paces, just as test-pilots check up on every detail of performance of an airplane of new and radical design. They
found that the horrible vertigo could be endured, perhaps in
time even conquered as space-sickness could be conquered,
by a strong will in a sound body; and that their new con-
veyance had possibilities of which even Rodebush had never
dreamed. Finally, their most pressing questions answered,
they turned their most powerful ultra-beam communicator
toward the yellowish star which they knew to be Old Sol.

"Samms . . . Samms." Cleveland spoke slowly and distinctly. "Rodebush and Cleveland reporting from the 'Space-
Eating Wampus', now directly in line with Beta Ursae Minoris
from the sun, distance about two point two light years. It

will take six bands of tubes on your tightest beam, LSV3, to reach us. Barring a touch of an unusually severe type of space-sickness, everything worked beautifully; even better than either of us dared to believe. There's something we want to know right away—have we been gone four hours and some odd minutes, or better than two years?"

He turned to Rodebush and went on:

"Nobody knows how fast this ultra-wave travels, but if it goes as fast as we did coming out it's no creeper. I'll give him about thirty minutes, then shoot in another . . ."

But, interrupting Cleveland's remark, the care-ravaged face of Virgil Samms appeared sharp and clear upon the plate and his voice snapped curtly from the speaker.

"Thank God you're alive, and twice that that the ship works!" he exclaimed. "You've been gone four hours, eleven minutes, and forty one seconds, but never mind about abstract theorizing. Get back here, to Pittsburgh, as fast as you can drive. That Nevian vessel or another one like her is mopping up the city, and has destroyed half the Fleet already!"

"We'll be back there in nine minutes!" Rodebush snapped into the transmitter. "Two to get from here to atmosphere, four from Atmosphere down to the Hill, and three to cool off. Notify the full four-shift crew—everybody we've picked out. Don't need anybody else. Ship, equipment, and armament are *ready!*"

"Two minutes to atmosphere? Think you can do it?" Cleveland asked, as Rodebush flipped off the power and leaped to the control panel. "You might, though, at that."

"We could do it in less than that if we had to. We used scarcely any power at all coming out, and I'm going to use quite a lot going back," the physicist explained rapidly, as he set the dials which would determine their flashing course.

The master switches were thrown and the pangs of inertialessness again assailed them—but weaker far this time than ever before—and upon their lookout plates they beheld a spectacle never before seen by eye of man. For the ultra-beam, with its heterodyned vision, is not distorted by any velocity yet attained, as are the ether-borne rays of light. Converted into light only at the plate, it showed their progress as truly as though they had been traveling at a pace to be expressed in the ordinary terms of miles per hour. The yellow star that was the sun detached itself from the firmament and leaped toward them, swelling visibly, momently, into a blinding monster of incandescence. And toward them also flung the Earth, enlarging with such indescribable rapidity that Cleveland protested involuntarily, in spite of his knowledge of the peculiar mechanics of the vessel in which they were.

"Hold it, Fred, hold it! Way 'nuff!" he exclaimed.

"I'm using only a few thousand kilograms of thrust, and I'll cut that as soon as we touch atmosphere, long before she can even begin to heat," Rodebush explained. "Looks bad, but we'll stop without a jar."

"What would you call this kind of flight, Fritz?" Cleveland asked. "What's the opposite of 'inert'?"

"Damned if I know. Isn't any, I guess. Light? No . . . how would 'free' be?"

"Not bad. 'Free' and 'Inert' maneuvering, eh? O.K."

Flying "free", then, the super-ship came from her practically infinite velocity to an almost instantaneous halt in the outermost, most tenuous layer of the Earth's atmosphere. Her halt was but momentary. Inertia restored, she dropped at a sharp angle downward. More than dropped; she was forced downward by one full battery of projectors; projectors driven by iron-powered generators. Soon they were over the Hill, whose violet screens went down at a word.

Flaming a dazzling white from the friction of the atmosphere through which she had torn her way, the *Boise* slowed abruptly as she neared the ground, plunging toward the surface of the small but deep artificial lake below the Hill's steel apron. Into the cold waters the space-ship dove, and even before they could close over her, furious geysers of steam and boiling water erupted as the stubborn alloy gave up its heat to the cooling liquid. Endlessly the three necessary minutes dragged their slow way into time, but finally the water ceased boiling and Rodebush tore the ship from the lake and hurled her into the gaping doorway of her dock. The massive doors of the air-locks opened, and while the full crew of picked men hurried aboard with their personal equipment, Samms talked earnestly to the two scientists in the control room.

". . . and about half the fleet is still in the air. They aren't attacking; they are just trying to keep her from doing much more damage until you can get there. How about your take-off? We can't launch you again—the tracks are gone—but you handled her easily enough coming in?"

"That was all my fault," Rodebush admitted. "I had no idea that the fields would extend beyond the hull. We'll take her out on the projectors this time, though, the same as we brought her in—she handles like a bicycle. The projector blast tears things up a little, but nothing serious. Have you got that Pittsburgh beam for me yet? We're about ready to go."

"Here it is, Doctor Rodebush," came Norma's voice, and upon the screen there flashed into being the view of the events transpiring above that doomed city. "The dock is empty and sealed against your blast."

"Goodbye, and power to your tubes!" came Samms' ringing voice.

As the words were being spoken mighty blasts of power raved from the driving projectors, and the immense mass of the super-ship shot out through the portals and upward into the stratosphere. Through the tenuous atmosphere the huge globe rushed with ever-mounting speed, and while the hope of Triplanetary drove eastward Rodebush studied the ever-changing scene of battle upon his plate and issued detailed instructions to the highly trained specialists manning every offensive and defensive weapon.

But the Nevians did not wait to join battle until the new-comers arrived. Their detectors were sensitive—operative over untold thousands of miles—and the ultra-screen of the Hill had already been noted by the invaders as the Earth's only possible source of trouble. Thus the departure of the *Boise* had not gone unnoticed, and the fact that not even with his most penetrant rays could he see into her interior had already given the Nevian commander some slight concern. Therefore as soon as it was determined that the great globe was being directed toward Pittsburgh the fish-shaped cruiser of the void went into action.

High in the stratosphere, speeding eastward, the immense mass of the *Boise* slowed abruptly, although no projector had slackened its effort. Cleveland, eyes upon interferometer grating and spectrophotometer charts, fingers flying over calculator keys, grinned as he turned toward Rodebush.

"Just as you thought, Skipper; an ultra-band pusher. C4V-63L29. Shall I give him a little pull?"

"Not yet; let's feel him out a little before we force a close-up. We've got plenty of mass. See what he does when I put full push on the projectors."

As the full power of the Tellurian vessel was applied the Nevian was forced backward, away from the threatened city, against the full drive of her every projector. Soon, however, the advance was again checked, and both scientists read the reason upon their plates. The enemy had put down re-enforcing rods of tremendous power. Three compression members spread out fanwise behind her, bracing her against a low mountainside, while one huge tractor beam was thrust directly downward, holding in an unbreakable grip a cylinder of earth extending deep down into bedrock.

"Two can play at that game!" and Rodebush drove down similar beams, and forward-reaching tractors as well. "Strap yourselves in solid, everybody!" he sounded in general warning. "Something is going to give way somewhere soon, and when it does we'll get a jolt!"

And the promised jolt did indeed come soon. Prodigiously massive and powerful as the Nevian was, the *Boise* was even more massive and more powerful; and as the already enormous energy feeding the tractors, pushers, and projectors was raised to its inconceivable maximum, the vessel of the enemy was hurled upward, backward; and that of Earth shot ahead with a bounding leap that threatened to strain even her mighty members. The Nevian anchor rods had not broken; they had simply pulled up the vast cylinders of solid rock that had formed their anchorages.

"Grab him now!" Rodebush yelled, and even while an avalanche of falling rock was burying the countryside Cleveland snapped a tractor ray upon the flying fish and pulled tentatively.

Nor did the Nevian now seem averse to coming to grips. The two warring super-dreadnoughts darted toward each other, and from the invader there flooded out the dread crimson opacity which had theretofore meant the doom of all things Solarian. Flooded out and engulfed the immense globe of humanity's hope in its spreading cloud of redly impenetrable murk. But not for long. Triplanetary's super-ship boasted no ordinary Terrestrial defense, but was sheathed in screen after screen of ultra-vibrations: imponderable walls, it is true, but barriers impenetrable to any unfriendly wave. To the outer screen the red veil of the Nevians clung tenaciously, licking greedily at every square inch of the shielding sphere of force, but unable to find an opening through which to feed upon the steel of the *Boise's* armor.

"Get back—'way back! Go back and help Pittsburgh!" Rodebush drove an ultra communicator beam through the murk to the instruments of the Terrestrial admiral; for the surviving warships of the fleet—its most powerful units— were hurling themselves forward, to plunge into that red destruction. "None of you will last a second in this red field. And watch out for a violet field pretty soon—it'll be worse than this. We can handle them alone, I think; but if we can't, there's nothing in the System that can help us!"

And now the hitherto passive screen of the super-ship became active. At first invisible, it began to glow in fierce violet light, and as the glow brightened to unbearable intensity the entire spherical shield began to increase in size. Driven outward from the super-ship as a center, its advancing surface of seething energy consumed the crimson murk as a billow of blast-furnace heat consumes the cloud of snow-flakes in the air above its cupola. Nor was the red death-mist all that was consumed. Between that ravening surface and the armor skin of the *Boise* there was nothing. No debris, no atmosphere, no vapor, no single atom of material substance—the first time in Terrestrial experience that an absolute vacuum had ever been attained!

Stubbornly contesting every foot of way lost, the Nevian fog retreated before the violet sphere of nothingness. Back and back it fell, disappearing altogether from all space as the violet tide engulfed the enemy vessel; but the flying fish did not disappear. Her triple screens flashed into furiously incandescent splendor and she entered unscathed that vacuous sphere, which collapsed instantly into an enormously elongated ellipsoid, at each focus a madly warring ship of space.

Then in that tube of vacuum was waged a spectacular duel of ultra-weapons—weapons impotent in air, but deadly in empty space. Beams, rays, and rods of Titanic power smote cracklingly against ultra-screens equally capable. Time after time each contestant ran the gamut of the spectrum with his every available ultra-force, only to find all channels closed. For minutes the terrible struggle went on, then:

"Cooper, Adlington, Spencer, Dutton!" Rodebush called into his transmitter. "Ready? Can't touch him on the ultra, so I'm going onto the macro-bands. Give him everything you have as soon as I collapse the violet. Go!"

At the word the violet barrier went down, and with a crash as of a disrupting Universe the atmosphere rushed into the void. And through the hurricane there shot out the deadliest material weapons of Triplanetary. Torpedoes—non-ferrous, ultra-screened, beam-dirigible torpedoes charged with the most effective forms of material destruction known to man. Cooper hurled his canisters of penetrating gas, Adlington his allotropic-iron atomic bombs, Spencer his indestructible armor-piercing projectiles, and Dutton his shatterable flasks of the quintessence of corrosion—a sticky, tacky liquid of such dire potency that only one rare Solarian element could contain it. Ten, twenty, fifty, a hundred were thrown as fast as the automatic machinery could launch them; and the Nevians found them adversaries not to be despised. Size for size, their screens were quite as capable as those of the *Boise*. The Nevians' destructive rays glanced harmlessly from their shields, and the Nevians' elaborate screens, neutralized at impact by those of the torpedoes, were impotent to impede their progress. Each projectile must needs be caught and crushed individually by beams of the most prodigious power; and while one was being annihilated dozens more were rushing to the attack. Then while the twisting, dodging invader was busiest with the tiny but relentless destroyers, Rodebush launched his heaviest weapon.

The macro-beams! Prodigious streamers of bluish-green flame which tore savagely through course after course of Nevian screen! Malevolent fangs, driven with such power and velocity that they were biting into the very walls of the enemy vessel before the amphibians knew that their defensive shells of force had been punctured! And the emergency screens of the invaders were equally futile. Course after course was sent out, only to flare viciously through the spectrum and to go black.

Outfought at every turn, the now frantically dodging Nevian leaped away in headlong flight, only to be brought to a staggering, crashing halt as Cleveland nailed her with a tractor beam. But the Tellurians were to learn that the Nevians held in reserve a means of retreat. The tractor snapped —sheared off squarely by a sizzling plane of force—and the fish-shaped cruiser faded from Cleveland's sight, just as the *Boise* had disappeared from the communicator plates of Radio Center, back in the Hill, when she was launched. But though the plates in the control room could not hold the Nevian, she did not vanish beyond the ken of Randolph, now Communications Officer in the super-ship. For, warned and humiliated by his losing one speeding vessel from his plates in Radio Center, he was now ready for any emergency. Therefore as the Nevian fled Randolph's spy-ray held her, automatically behind it as there was the full output of twelve special banks of iron-driven power tubes; and thus it was that the vengeful Earthmen flashed immediately along the Nevians' line of flight. Inertialess now, pausing briefly from time to time to enable the crew to accustom themselves to the new sensations, Triplanetary's super-ship pursued the invader; hurtling through the void with a velocity unthinkable.

"He was easier to take than I thought he would be," Cleveland grunted, staring into the plate.

"I thought he had more stuff, too," Rodebush assented, "but I guess Costigan got almost everything they had. If so, with all our own stuff and most of theirs besides, we should be able to take them. Conway's data indicated that they have only partial neutralization of inertia—if it's one hundred percent we'll never catch them—but it isn't—there they are!"

"And this time I'm going to hold her or burn out all our generators trying," Cleveland declared, grimly. "Are you fellows down there able to handle yourselves yet? Fine! Start throwing out your cans!"

Space-hardened veterans, all, the other Tellurian officers had fought off the horrible nausea of inertialessness, just as Rodebush and Cleveland had done. Again the ravening green macro-beams tore at the flying cruiser, again the mighty frames of the two space-ships shuddered sickeningly as Cleveland clamped on his tractor rod, again the highly dirigible torpedoes dashed out with their freights of death and destruction. And again the Nevian shear-plane of force slashed at the Boise's tractor beam; but this time the mighty puller did not give way. Sparkling and spitting high-tension sparks, the plane bit deeply into the stubborn rod of energy. Brighter, thicker, and longer grew the discharges as the gnawing plane drew more and more power; but in direct ratio to that power the rod grew larger, denser, and ever harder to cut. More and more vivid became the pyrotechnic display, until suddenly the entire tractor rod disappeared. At the same instant a blast of intolerable flame erupted from the Boise's flank and the whole enormous fabric of her shook and quivered under the force of a terrific detonation.

"Randolph! I don't see them! Are they attacking or running?" Rodebush demanded. He was the first to realize what had happened.

"Running—fast!"

"Just as well, perhaps, but get their line. Adlington!"

"Here!"

"Good! Was afraid you were gone—that was one of your bombs, wasn't it?"

"Yes. Well launched, just inside the screens. Don't see how it could have detonated unless something hot and hard struck it in the tube; it would need about that much time to explode. Good thing it didn't go off any sooner, or none of us would have been here. As it is, Area Six is pretty well done in, but the bulkheads held the damage to Six. What happened?"

"We don't know, exactly. Both generators on the tractor beam went out. At first, I thought that was all, but my neutralizers are dead and I don't know what else. When the G-4's went out the fusion must have shorted the neutralizers. They would make a mess; it must have burned a hole down into number six tube. Cleveland and I will come down, and we'll all look around."

Donning space-suits, the scientists let themselves into the damaged compartment through the emergency air-locks, and what a sight they saw! Both outer and inner walls of alloy armor had been blown away by the awful force of the explosion. Jagged plates hung awry; bent, twisted and broken. The great torpedo tube, with all its intricate automatic machinery, had been driven violently backward and lay piled in hideous confusion against the backing bulkheads. Practically nothing remained whole in the entire compartment.

"Nothing much we can do here," Rodebush said finally, through his transmitter. "Let's go see what number four generator looks like."

That room, although not affected by the explosion from without, had been quite as effectively wrecked from within. It was still stiflingly hot; its air was still reeking with the stench of burning lubricant, insulation, and metal; its floor was half covered by a semi-molten mass of what had once been vital machinery. For with the burning out of the generator bars the energy of the disintegrating allotropic iron had had no outlet, and had built up until it had broken through its insulation and in an irresistible flood of power had torn through all obstacles in its path to neutralization.

"Hm . . m . . . m. Should have had an automatic shut-off—one detail we overlooked," Rodebush mused. "The electricians can rebuild this stuff here, though—that hole in the hull is something else again."

"I'll say it's something else," the grizzled Chief Engineer agreed. "She's lost all her spherical strength—anchoring a tractor with this ship now would turn her inside out. Back to the nearest Triplanetary shop for us, I would say."

"Come again, Chief!" Cleveland advised the engineer. "None of us would live long enough to get there. We can't travel inertialess until the repairs are made, so if they can't be made without very much traveling, it's just too bad."

"I don't see how we could support our jacks . . . " the engineer paused, then went on: "If you can't give me Mars or Tellus, how about some other planet? I don't care about atmosphere, or about anything but mass. I can stiffen her up in three or four days if I can sit down on something heavy enough to hold our jacks and presses; but if we have to rig up space-cradles around the ship herself it'll take a long time— months, probably. Haven't got a spare planet on hand, have you?"

"We might have, at that," Rodebush made surprising answer. "A couple of seconds before we engaged we were heading toward a sun with at least two planets. I was just getting ready to dodge them when we cut the neutralizers, so they should be fairly close somewhere—yes, there's the sun, right over there. Rather pale and small; but it's close, comparatively speaking. We'll go back up into the control room and find out about the planets."

The strange sun was found to have three large and easily located children, and observation showed that the crippled space-ship could reach the nearest of these in about five days. Power was therefore fed to the driving projectors, and each scientist, electrician, and mechanic bent to the task of repairing the ruined generators; rebuilding them to handle any load which the converters could possibly put upon them. For two days the *Boise* drove on, then her acceleration was reversed, and finally a landing was effected upon the forbidding, rocky soil of the strange world.

It was larger than the Earth, and of a somewhat stronger gravitation. Although its climate was bitterly cold, even in its short daytime, it supported a luxuriant but outlandish vegetation. Its atmosphere, while rich enough in oxygen and not really poisonous, was so rank with indescribably fetid vapors as to be scarcely breatheable. But these things bothered the engineers not at all. Paying no attention to temperature or to scenery and without waiting for chemical analysis of the air, the space-suited mechanics leaped to their tasks; and in only a little more time than had been mentioned by the chief engineer the hull and giant frame of the super-ship were as staunch as of yore.

"All right, Skipper!" came finally the welcome word. "You might try her out with a fast hop around this world before you shove off in earnest."

Under the fierce blast of her projectors the vessel leaped ahead, and time after time, as Rodebush hurled her mass upon tractor beam or pressor, the engineers sought in vain for any sign of weakness. The strange planet half girdled and the severest tests passed flawlessly, Rodebush reached for his neutralizer switches. Reached and paused, dumbfounded, for a brilliant purple light had sprung into being upon his panel and a bell rang out insistently.

"What the hell!" Rodebush shot out an exploring beam along the detector line and gasped. He stared, mouth open, then yelled:

"*Roger* is here, rebuilding his planetoid! STATIONS ALL!"

CHAPTER 17

ROGER CARRIES ON

As HAS BEEN INTIMATED, GRAY ROGER DID NOT PERISH IN THE floods of Nevian energy which destroyed his planetoid. While those terrific streamers of force emanating from the crimson obscurity surrounding the amphibians' space-ship were driving into his defensive screens he sat impassive and immobile at his desk, his hard gray eyes moving methodically over his instruments and recorders.

When the clinging mantle of force changed from deep red into shorter and even shorter wave-lengths, however:

"Baxter, Hartkopf, Chatelier, Anandrusung, Penrose, Nishimura, Mirsky . . ." he called off a list of names. "Report to me here at once!"

"The planetoid is lost," he informed his select group of scientists when they had assembled, "and we must abandon it in exactly fifteen minutes, which will be the time required for the robots to fill this first section with our most necessary machinery and instruments. Pack each of you one box of the things he most wishes to take with him, and report back here in not more than thirteen minutes. Say nothing to anyone else."

They filed out calmly, and as they passed out into the hall Baxter, perhaps a trifle less case-hardened than his fellows, at least voiced a thought for those they were so brutally deserting.

"I say, it seems a bit thick to dash off this way and leave the rest of them; but still, I suppose . . ."

"You suppose correctly." Bland and heartless Nishimura

filled in the pause. "A small part of the planetoid may be able to escape; which, to me at least, is pleasantly surprising news. It cannot carry all our men and mechanisms, therefore only the most important of both are saved. What would you? For the rest it is simply what you call 'the fortune of war,' no?"

"But the beautiful . . ." began the amorous Chatelier.

"Hush, fool!" snorted Hartkopf. "One word of that to the ear of Roger and you too left behind are. Of such non-essentials the Universe full is, to be collected in times of ease, but in times hard to be disregarded. Und this is a time of *schrecklichkeit* indeed!"

The group broke up, each man going to his own quarters; to meet again in the First Section a minute or so before the zero time. Roger's "office" was now packed so tightly with machinery and supplies that but little room was left for the scientists. The gray monstrosity still sat unmoved behind his dials.

"But of what use is it, Roger?" the Russian physicist demanded. "Those waves are of some ultra-band, of a frequency immensely higher than anything heretofore known. Our screens should not have stopped them for an instant. It is a mystery that they have held so long, and certainly this single section will not be permitted to leave the planetoid without being destroyed."

"There are many things you do not know, Mirsky," came the cold and level answer. "Our screens, which you think are of your own devising, have several improvements of my own in the formulae, and would hold forever had I the power to drive them. The screens of this section, being smaller, can be held as long as will be found necessary."

"Power!" the dumbfounded Russian exclaimed. "Why, we have almost infinite power—unlimited—sufficient for a lifetime of high expenditure!"

But Roger made no reply, for the time of departure was at hand. He pressed down a tiny lever, and a mechanism in the power room threw in the gigantic plunger switches which launched against the Nevians the stupendous beam which so upset the complacence of Nerado the amphibian— the beam into which was poured recklessly every resource of power afforded by the planetoid, careless alike of burnout and of exhaustion. Then, while all of the attention of the Nevians and practically all of their maximum possible power output was being devoted to the neutralization of that last desperate thrust, the metal wall of the planetoid opened and the First Section shot out into space. Full-driven as they were, Roger's screens flared white as he drove through the temporarily lessened attack of the Nevians; but in their preoccupation the amphibians did not notice the additional disturbance and the section tore on, unobserved and undetected.

Far out in space, Roger raised his eyes from the instrument panel and continued the conversation as though it had not been interrupted.

"Everything is relative, Mirsky, and you have misused gravely the term 'unlimited.' Our power was, and is, very definitely limited. True, it then seemed ample for our needs, and is far superior to that possessed by the inhabitants of any solar system with which I am familiar; but the beings behind that red screen, whoever they are, have sources of power as far above ours as ours are above those of the Solarians."

"How do you know?"

"That power, what is it?"

"We have, then, the analyses of those fields recorded!" came simultaneous questions and exclamations.

"Their source of power is the intra-atomic energy of iron. Complete; not the partial liberation incidental to the nuclear fission of such unstable isotopes as those of thorium, uranium, plutonium, and so on. Therefore much remains to be done before I can proceed with my plan—I must have the most powerful structure in the macrocosmic universe."

Roger thought for minutes, nor did any one of his minions break the silence. Gharlane of Eddore did not have to wonder why such incredible advancement could have been made without his knowledge: after the fact, he knew. He had been and was still being hampered by a mind of power; a mind with which, in due time, he would come to grips.

"I now know what to do," he went on presently. "In the light of what I have learned, the losses of time, life, and treasure—even the loss of the planetoid—are completely insignificant."

"But what can you do about it?" growled the Russian.

"Many things. From the charts of the recorders we can compute their fields of force, and from that point it is only a step to their method of liberating the energy. We shall build robots. They shall build other robots, who shall in turn construct another planetoid; one this time that, wielding the theoretical maximum of power, will be suited to my needs."

"And where will you build it? We are marked. Invisibility now is useless. Triplanetary will find us, even if we take up an orbit beyond that of Pluto!"

"We have already left your Solarian system far behind. We are going to another system; one far enough removed so that the spy-rays of Triplanetary will never find us, and yet one that we can reach in a reasonable length of time with the energies at our command. Some five days will be required for the journey, however, and our quarters are cramped. Therefore make places for yourselves wherever you can, and lessen the tedium of those days by working upon whatever problems are most pressing in your respective researches."

The gray monster fell silent, immersed in what thoughts no one knew, and the scientists set out to obey his orders. Baxter, the British chemist, followed Penrose, the lantern-jawed, saturnine American engineer and inventor, as he made his way to the furthermost cubicle of the section.

"I say, Penrose, I'd like to ask you a couple of questions, if you don't mind?"

"Go ahead. Ordinarily it's dangerous to be a cackling hen anywhere around *him*, but I don't imagine that he can hear anything here now. His system must be pretty well shot to pieces. You want to know all I know about Roger?"

"Exactly so. You have been with him so much longer than I have, you know. In some ways he impresses one as being scarcely human, if you know what I mean. Ridiculous, of course, but of late I have been wondering whether he really *is* human. He knows too much, about too many things. He seems to be acquainted with many solar systems, to visit which would require lifetimes. Then, too, he has dropped remarks which would imply that he actually saw things that happened long before any living man could possibly have been born. Finally, he looks—well, peculiar—and certainly does not act human. I have been wondering, and have been able to learn nothing about him; as you have said, such talk as this aboard the planetoid was not advisable."

"You needn't worry about being paid your price; that's one thing. If we live—and that was part of the agreement, you know—we will get what we sold out for. You will become a belted earl. I have already made millions, and shall make many more. Similarly, Chatelier has had and will have his women, Anandrusung and Nishimura their cherished revenges, Hartkopf his power, and so on." He eyed the other speculatively, then went on:

"I might as well spill it all, since I'll never have a better chance and since you should know as much as the rest of us do. You're in the same boat with us and tarred with the same brush. There's a lot of gossip, that may or may not be true, but I know one very startling fact. Here it is. My great-great-grandfather left some notes which, taken in connection with certain things I myself saw on the planetoid, prove beyond question that our Roger went to Harvard University at the same time he did. Roger was a grown man then, and the elder Penrose noted that he was marked, like this," and the American sketched a cabalistic design.

"What!" Baxter exclaimed. "An adept of North Polar Jupiter—*then?*"

"Yes. That was before the First Jovian War, you know, and it was those medicine-men—really high-caliber scientists—that prolonged that war so . . ."

"But I say, Penrose, that's really a bit thick. When they were wiped out it was proved a lot of hocus-pocus . . ."

"*If* they were wiped out," Penrose interrupted in turn. "Some of it may have been hocus-pocus, but most of it certainly was not. I'm not asking you to believe anything except that one fact; I'm just telling you the rest of it. But it is also a fact that those adepts knew things and did things that take a lot of explaining. Now for the gossip, none of which is guaranteed. Roger is supposed to be of Tellurian parentage, and the story is that his father was a moon-pirate, his mother a Greek adventuress. When the pirates were chased off the moon they went to Ganymede, you know, and some of them were captured by the Jovians. It seems that Roger was born at an instant of time sacred to the adepts, so they took him on. He worked his way up through the Forbidden Society as all adepts did, by various kinds of murder and job lots of assorted deviltries, until he got clear to the top— the seventy-seventh mystery . . ."

"The secret of eternal youth!" gasped Baxter, awed in spite of himself.

"Right, and he stayed Chief Devil, in spite of all the efforts of all his ambitious sub-devils to kill him, until the turning-point of the First Jovian War. He cut away then in a space-ship, and ever since then he has been working—and working hard—on some stupendous plan of his own that nobody else has ever got even an inkling of. That's the story. True or not, it explains a lot of things that no other theory can touch. And now I think you'd better shuffle along; enough of this is a great plenty!"

Baxter went to his own cubby, and each man of gray Roger's cold-blooded crew methodically took up his task. True to prediction, in five days a planet loomed beneath them and their vessel settled through a reeking atmosphere toward a rocky and forbidding plain. Then for hours they plunged along, a few thousand feet above the surface of that strange world, while Roger with his analytical detectors sought the most favorable location from which to wrest the materials necessary for his program of construction.

It was a world of cold; its sun was distant, pale, and wan. It had monstrous forms of vegetation, of which each branch and member writhed and fought with a grotesque and horrible individual activity. Ever and anon a struggling part broke from its parent plant and darted away in independent existence; leaping upon and consuming or being consumed by a fellow creature equally monstrous. This flora was of a uniform color, a lurid, sickly yellow. In form some of it was fern-like, some cactus-like, some vaguely tree-like; but it was all outrageous, inherently repulsive to all Solarian senses. And no less hideous were the animal-like forms of life which slithered and slunk rapaciously through that fantastic pseudo-vegetation. Snake-like, reptile-like, bat-like, the creatures squirmed, crawled, and flew; each covered with a dankly oozing yellow hide and each motivated by twin common impulses—to kill and insatiably and indiscriminately to devour. Over this reeking wilderness Roger drove his vessel, untouched by its disgusting, its appalling ferocity and horror.

"There should be intelligence, of a kind," he mused, and swept the surface ot the planet with an exploring beam. "Ah, yes, there is a city, of sorts," and in a few minutes the outlaws were looking down upon a metal-walled city of roundly conical buildings.

Inside these structures and between and around them there scuttled formless blobs of matter, one of which Roger brought up into his vessel by means of a tractor. Held immovable by the beam it lay upon the floor, a strangely extensile, amoeba-like, metal-studded mass of leathery substance. Of eyes, ears, limbs, or organs it apparently had none, yet it radiated an intensely hostile aura; a mental effluvium concentrated of rage and of hatred.

"Apparently the ruling intelligence of the planet," Roger commented. "Such creatures are useless to us; we can build machines in half the time that would be required for their subjugation and training. Still, it should not be permitted to carry back what it may have learned of us." As he spoke the adept threw the peculiar being out into the air and dispassionately rayed it out of existence.

"That thing reminds me of a man I used to know, back in Penobscot." Penrose was as coldly callous as his unfeeling master. "The evenest-tempered man in town—mad all the time!"

Eventually Roger found a location which satisfied his requirements of raw materials, and made a landing upon that unfriendly soil. Sweeping beams denuded a great circle of life, and into that circle leaped robots. Robots requiring neither rest nor food, but only lubricants and power; robots insensible alike to that bitter cold and to that noxious atmosphere.

But the outlaws were not to win a foothold upon that inimical planet easily, nor were they to hold it without effort. Through the weird vegetation of the circle's bare edge there scuttled and poured along a horde of the metal-studded men—if "men" they might be called—who, ferocity incarnate, rushed the robot line. Mowed down by hundreds, still they came on; willing, it seemed to spend any number of lives in order that one living creature might once touch a robot with one outthrust metallic stud. Whenever that happened there was a flash of lightning, the heavy smoke of burning insulation, grease, and metal, and the robot went down out of control. Recalling his remaining automatons, Roger sent out a shielding screen, against which the defenders of their planet raged in impotent fury. For days they hurled themselves and their every force against that impenetrable barrier, then withdrew: temporarily stopped, but by no means acknowledging defeat.

Then while Roger and his cohorts directed affairs from within their comfortable and now sufficiently roomy vessel, there came into being around it an industrial city of metal peopled by metallic and insensate mechanisms. Mines were sunk, furnaces were blown in, smelters belched forth into the already unbearable air their sulphurous fumes, rolling mills and machine shops were built and were equipped; and as fast as new enterprises were completed additional robots were ready to man them. In record time the heavy work of girders, members, and plates was well under way; and shortly thereafter light, deft, multi-fingered mechanisms began to build and to install the prodigious amount of precise machinery required by the vastness of the structure.

As soon as he was sure that he would be completely

free for a sufficient length of time, Roger-Gharlane assembled, boiled down and concentrated, his every mental force. He probed then, very gently, for whatever it was that had been and was still blocking him. He found it—synchronized with it—and in the instant hurled against it the fiercest thrust possible for his Eddorian mind to generate: a bolt whose twin had slain more than one member of Eddore's Innermost Circle; a bolt whose energies, he had previously felt sure, would slay any living thing save only His Ultimate Supremacy, the All-Highest of Eddore.

Now, however, and not completely to his surprise, that blast of force was ineffective; and the instantaneous riposte was of such intensity as to require for its parrying everything that Gharlane had. He parried it, however barely, and directed a thought at his unknown opponent.

"You, whoever you may be, have found out that you cannot kill me. No more can I kill you. So be it. Do you still believe that you can keep me from remembering whatever it was that my ancestor was compelled to forget?"

"Now that you have obtained a focal point we cannot prevent you from remembering; and merely to hinder you would be pointless. You may remember in peace."

Back and back went Gharlane's mind. Centuries . . . millenia . . . cycles . . . eons. The trace grew dim, almost imperceptible, deeply buried beneath layer upon layer of accretions of knowledge, experience, and sensation which no one of many hundreds of his ancestors had even so much as disturbed. But every iota of knowledge that any of his progenitors had ever had was still his. However dim, however deeply buried, however suppressed and camouflaged by inimical force, he could now find it.

He found it, and in the instant of its finding it was as though Enphilistor the Arisian spoke directly to him; as though the fused Elders of Arisia tried—vainly now—to erase from his own mind all knowledge of Arisia's existence. The fact that such a race as the Arisians had existed so long ago was bad enough. That the Arisians had been aware throughout all those ages of the Eddorians, and had been able to keep their own existence secret, was worse. The crowning fact that the Arisians had had all this time in which to work unopposed against his own race made even Gharlane's indomitable ego quail.

This was *important.* Such minor matters as the wiping out of non-conforming cultures—the extraordinarily rapid growth of which was now explained—must wait. Eddore must revise its thinking completely; the pooled and integrated mind of the Innermost Circle must scrutinize every fact, every implication and connotation, of this new-old knowledge. Should he flash back to Eddore, or should he wait and take the planetoid, with its highly varied and extremely valuable contents? He would wait; a few moments more would be a completely negligible addition to the eons of time which had already elapsed since action should have been begun.

The rebuilding of the planetoid, then, went on. Roger had no reason to suspect that there was anything physically dangerous within hundreds of millions of miles. Nevertheless, since he knew that he could no longer depend upon his own mental powers to keep him informed as to all that was going on around him, it was his custom to scan, from time to time, all nearby space by means of ether-borne detectors. Thus it came about that one day, as he sent out his beam, his hard gray eyes grew even harder.

"Mirsky! Nishimura! Penrose! Come here!" he ordered, and showed them upon his plate an enormous sphere of steel, its offensive beams flaming viciously. "Is there any doubt whatever in your minds as to the System to which that ship belongs?"

"None at all—Solarian," replied the Russian. "To narrow it still further, Triplanetarian. While larger than any I have ever seen before, its construction is unmistakable. They managed to trace us, and are testing out their weapons before attacking. Do we attack or do we run away?"

"If Triplanetarian, and it surely is, we attack," coldly. "This one section is armed and powered to defeat Triplanetary's entire navy. We shall take that ship, and shall add its slight resources to our own. And it may even be that they have picked up the three who escaped me . . . I have never been balked for long. Yes, we shall take that vessel. And those three sooner or later. Except for the fact that their excape from me is a matter which should be corrected, I care nothing whatever about either Bradley or the woman. Costigan, however, is in a different category . . . Costigan *handled* me . . ." Diamond-hard eyes glared balefully at the urge of thoughts to a clean and normal mind unthinkable.

"To your posts," he ordered. "The machines will continue to function under their automatic controls during the short time it will require to abate this nuisance."

"One moment!" A strange voice roared from the speakers. "Consider yourselves under arrest, by order of the Triplanetary Council! Surrender and you shall receive impartial hearing; fight us and you shall never come to trial. From what we have learned of Roger, we do not expect him to surrender, but if any of you other men wish to avoid immediate death, leave your vessel at once. We will come back for you later."

"Any of you wishing to leave this vessel have my full permission to do so," Roger announced, disdaining any reply to the challenge of the *Boise.* "Any such, however, will not be allowed inside the planetoid area after the rest of us return from wiping out that patrol. We attack in one minute."

"Would not one do better by stopping on?" Baxter, in the quarters of the American, was in doubt as to the most profitable course to pursue. "I should leave immediately if I thought that that ship could win; but I do not fancy that it can, do you?"

"That ship? *One* Triplanetary ship against *us?*" Penrose laughed raucously. "Do as you please. I'd go in a minute if I thought that there was any chance of us losing; but there isn't, so I'm staying. I know which side *my* bread's buttered on. Those cops are bluffing, that's all. Not bluffing exactly, either, because they'll go through with it as long as they last. Foolish, but it's a way they have—they'll die trying every time instead of running away, even when they know they're licked before they start. They don't use good judgment."

"None of you are leaving? Very well, you each know what to do," came Roger's emotionless voice. The stipulated minute having elapsed, he advanced a lever and the outlaw cruiser slid quietly into the air.

Toward the poised *Boise* Roger steered. Within range, he flung out a weapon new-learned and supposedly irresistible to any ferrous thing or creature, the red converter-field of the Nevians. For Roger's analytical detector had stood him in good stead during those frightful minutes in the course of which the planetoid had borne the brunt of Nerado's superhuman attack; in such good stead that from the records of those ingenious instruments he and his scientists had been able to reconstruct not only the generators of the attacking forces, but also the screens employed by the amphibians in the neutralization of similar beams. With a vastly inferior armament the smallest of Roger's vessels had defeated the most powerful battleships of Triplanetary; what had he to fear in such a heavy craft as the one he now was driving, one so superlatively armed and powered? It was just as well for his peace of mind that he had no inkling that the harmless-looking sphere he was so blithely attacking was in reality the much-discussed, half-mythical super-ship upon which the Triplanetary Service had been at work so long; nor that its already unprecedented armament had been reenforced, thanks to that hated Costigan, with Roger's own every worth-while idea, as well as with every weapon and defense known to that arch-Nevian, Nerado!

Unknowing and contemptuous, Roger launched his converter field, and instantly found himself fighting for his very life. For from Rodebush at the controls down, the men of the *Boise* countered with wave after wave and with salvo after salvo of vibratory and material destruction. No thought of mercy for the men of the pirate ship could enter their minds. The outlaws had each been given a chance to surrender, and each had refused it. Refusing, they knew, as the Triplanetarians knew and as all modern readers know, meant that they were staking their lives upon victory. For with modern armaments few indeed are the men who live through the defeat in battle of a war-vessel of space.

Roger launched his field of red opacity, but it did not reach even the *Boise's* screens. All space seemed to explode into violet splendor as Rodebush neutralized it, drove it back with his obliterating zone of force; but even that all-devouring zone could not touch Roger's peculiarly efficient screen. The outlaw vessel stood out, unharmed. Ultra-violet, infra-red, pure heat, infra-sound, solid beams of high-tension, high-frequency stuff in whose paths the most stubborn metals would be volatilized instantly, all iron-driven; every deadly and torturing vibration known was hurled against that screen: but it, too, was iron-driven, and it held. Even the awful force of the macro-beam was dissipated by it—reflected, hurled away on all sides in coruscating torrents of blinding, dazzling energy. Cooper, Adlington, Spencer, and Dutton hurled against it their bombs and torpedoes—and still it held. But Roger's fiercest blasts and heaviest projectiles were equally impotent against the force-shields of the super-ship. The adept, having no liking for a battle upon equal terms, then sought safety in flight, only to be brought to a crashing, stunning halt by a massive tractor beam.

"That must be that polycyclic screen that Conway reported on." Cleveland frowned in thought. "I've been doing a lot of work on that, and I think I've calculated an opener for it, Fred, but I'll have to have number ten projector and the whole output of number ten power room. Can you let me play with that much juice for a while? All right, Blake, tune her up to fifty-five thousand—there, hold it! Now, you other fellows, listen! I'm going to try to drill a hole through that screen with a hollow, quasi-solid beam; like a diamond drill cutting out a core. You won't be able to shove anything into the hole from outside the beam, so you'll have to steer your cans out through the central orifice of number ten projector—that'll be cold, since I'm going to use only the outer ring. I don't know how long I'll be able to hold the hole open, though, so shoot them along as fast as you can. Ready? Here goes!"

He pressed a series of contacts. Far below, in number ten converter room, massive switches drove home and the enormous mass of the vessel quivered under the terrific reaction of the newly-calculated, semi-material beam of energy that was hurled out, backed by the mightiest of all the mighty converters and generators of Triplanetary's superdreadnaught. That beam, a pipe-like hollow cylinder of intolerable energy, flashed out, and there was a rending, tearing crash as it struck Roger's hitherto impenetrable wall. Struck and clung, grinding, boring in, while from the raging inferno that marked the circle of contact of cylinder and shield the pirate's screen radiated scintillating torrents of crackling, streaming sparks, lightning like in length and in intensity.

Deeper and deeper the gigantic drill was driven. It was through! Pierced Roger's polycyclic screen; exposed the bare metal of Roger's walls! And now, concentrated upon one point, flamed out in seemingly redoubled fury Triplanetary's raging beams—in vain. For even as they could not penetrate the screen, neither could they penetrate the wall of Cleveland's drill, but rebounded from it in the cascaded brilliance of thwarted lightning.

"Oh, what a dumb-bell I am!" groaned Cleveland. "Why, oh *why* didn't I have somebody rig up a secondary SX7 beam on Ten's inner rings? Hop to it, will you, Blake, so that we'll have it in case they are able to stop the cans?"

But the pirates could not stop all of Triplanetary's projectiles, now hurrying along inside the pipe as fast as they could be driven. In fact, for a few minutes gray Roger, knowing that he faced the first real defeat of his long life, paid no attention to them at all, nor to any of his useless offensive weapons: he struggled only to break away from the savage grip of the *Boise's* tractor rod. Futile. He could neither cut nor stretch that inexorably anchoring beam. Then he devoted his every resource to the closing of that unbelievable breach in his shield. Equally futile. His most desperate efforts resulted only in more frenzied displays of incandescence along the curved surface of contact of that penetrant cylinder. And through that terrific conduit came speeding package after package of distruction. Bombs, armor-piercing shells, gas shells of poisonous and corrosive fluids followed each other in close succession. The surviving scientists of the planetoid, expert gunners and ray-men all, destroyed many of the projectiles, but it was not humanly possible to cope with them all. And the breach could not be forced shut against the all but irresistible force of Cleveland's "opener". And with all his power Roger could not shift his vessel's position in the grip of Triplanetary's tractors sufficiently to bring a projector to bear upon the super-ship along the now unprotected axis of that narrow, but deadly tube.

Thus it was that the end came soon. A war-head touched steel plating and there ensued a space-wracking explosion of atomic iron. Gaping wide, helpless, with all defenses down, other torpedoes entered the stricken hulk and completed its destruction even before they could be recalled. Atomic bombs literally volatilized most of the pirate vessel; vials of pure corrosion began to dissolve the solid fragments of her substance into dripping corruption. Reeking gasses filled every cranny of circumambient space as what was left of Roger's battle cruiser began the long plunge to the ground. The super-ship followed the wreckage down, and Rodebush sent out an exploring spy-ray.

". . . resistance was such that it was necessary to employ corrosive, and ship and contents were completely disinte grated," he dictated, a little later, into his vessel's log. "While there were of course no remains recognizable as human, it is certain that Roger and his last eleven men died; since it is clear that the circumstances and conditions were such that no life could possibly have survived."

*   *   *

It is true that the form of flesh which had been known as Roger was destroyed. The solids and liquids of its substance were resolved into their component molecules or atoms. That which had energized that form of flesh, however, could not be harmed by any physical force, however applied. Therefore that which made Roger what he was; the essence which was Gharlane of Eddore; was actually back upon his native planet even before Rodebush completed his study of what was left of the pirates' vessel.

The Innermost Circle met, and for a space of time which would have been very long indeed for any Earthly mind those monstrous being considered as one multi-ply intelligence every newly-exposed phase and facet of the truth. At the end, they knew the Arisians as well as the Arisians knew them. The All-Highest then called a meeting of all the minds of Eddore.

". . . hence it is clear that these Arisians, while possessing minds of tremendous latent capability, are basically soft, and therefore inefficient," he concluded. "Not weak, mind you, but scrupulous and unrealistic; and it is by taking advantage of these characteristics that we shall ultimately triumph."

"A few details, All-Highest, if Your Ultimate Supremacy would deign," a lesser Eddorian requested. "Some of us have not been able to perceive at all clearly the optimum lines of action."

"While detailed plans of campaign have not yet been worked out, there will be several main lines of attack. A purely military undertaking will of course be one, but it will not be the most important. Political action, by means of subversive elements and obstructive minorities, will prove much more useful. Most productive of all, however, will be the operations of relatively small but highly organized groups whose functions will be to negate, to tear down and destroy, every bulwark of what the weak and spineless adherents of Civilization consider the finest things in life—love, truth, honor, loyalty, purity, altruism, decency, and so on."

"Ah, love . . . extremely interesting. Supremacy, this thing they call sex," Gharlane offered. "What a silly, what a meaningless thing it is! I have studied it intensively, but am not yet fully enough informed to submit a complete and conclusive report. I do know, however, that we can and will use it. In our hands, vice will become a potent weapon indeed. Vice . . . drugs . . . greed . . . gambling . . . extortion . . . blackmail . . . lust . . . abduction . . . assassination . . . ah-h-h!"

"Exactly. There will be room, and need, for the fullest powers of every Eddorian. Let me caution you all, however, that little or none of this work is to be done by any of us in person. We must work through echelon upon echelon of higher and lower executives and supervisors if we are to control efficiently the activities of the thousands of billions of operators which we must and will have at work. Each echelon of control will be vastly greater in number than the one immediately above it, but correspondingly lower in the individual power of its component personnel. The sphere of activity of each supervisor, however small or great, will be clearly and sharply defined. Rank, from the operators at planetary-population levels up to and including the Eddorian Directorate, will be a linear function of ability. Absolute authority will be delegated. Full responsibility will be assumed. Those who succeed will receive advancement and satisfaction of desire; those who fail will die.

"Since the personnel of the lower echelons will be of small value and easy of replacement, it is of little moment whether or not they become involved in reverses affecting the still lower echelons whose activities they direct. The echelon immediately below us of Eddore, however—and incidentally, it is my thought that the Ploorans will best serve as our immediate underlings—must never, under any conditions, allow any hint of any of its real business to become known either to any member of any lower echelon or to any adherent of Civilization. This point is vital; everyone here must realize that only in that way can our own safety remain assured, and must take pains to see to it that any violator of this rule is put instantly to death.

"Those of you who are engineers will design ever more powerful mechanisms to use against the Arisians. Psychologists will devise and put into practice new methods and techniques, both to use against the able minds of the Arisians and to control the activities of mentally weaker entities. Each Eddorian, whatever his field or his ability, will be given the task he is best fitted to perform. That is all."

*   *   *

And upon Arisia, too, while there was no surprise, a general conference was held. While some of the young Watchmen may have been glad that the open conflict for which they had been preparing so long was now about to break, Arisia as a whole was neither glad nor sorry. In the Great Scheme of Things which was the Cosmic All, this whole affair was an infinitesimal incident. It had been foreseen. It had come. Each Arisian would do to the fullest extent of his ability that which the very fact of his being an Arisian would compel him to do. It would pass.

"In effect, then, our situation has not really changed," Eukonidor stated, rather than asked, after the Elders had again spread their Visualization for public inspection and discussion. "This killing, it seems, must go on. This stumbling, falling, and rising; this blind groping; this futility; this frustration; this welter of crime, disaster, and bloodshed. Why? It seems to me that it would be much better—cleaner, simpler, faster, more efficient, and involving infinitely less bloodshed and suffering—for us to take now a direct and active part, as the Eddorians have done and will continue to do."

"Cleaner, youth, yes; and simpler. Easier; less bloody. It would not, however, be better; or even good; because no end-point would ever be attained. Young civilizations advance only by overcoming obstacles. Each obstacle surmounted, each step of progress made, carries its suffering as well as its reward. We could negate the efforts of any echelon below the Eddorians themselves, it is true. We could so protect and shield each one of our protege races that not a war would be waged and not a law would be broken. But to what end? Further contemplation will show you immature thinkers that in such a case not one of our races would develop into what the presence of the Eddorians has made it necessary for them to become.

"From this it follows that we would never be able to overcome Eddore; nor would our conflict with that race remain indefinitely at stalemate. Given sufficient time during which to work against us, they will be able to win. However, if every Arisian follows his line of action as it is laid out in this Visualization, all will be well. Are there any more questions?"

"None. The blanks which you may have left can be filled in by a mind of very moderate power."

*   *   *

"Look here, Fred." Cleveland called attention to the plate, upon which was pictured a horde of the peculiar inhabitants of that ghastly planet, wreaking their frenzied electrical wrath upon everything within the circle bared of native life by Roger's destructive beams. "I was just going to suggest that we clean up the planetoid that Roger started to build, but I see that the local boys and girls are attending to it."

"Just as well, perhaps. I would like to stay and study these people a little while, but we must get back onto the trail of the Nevians," and the *Boise* leaped away into space, toward the line of flight of the amphibians.

They reached that line and along it they traveled at full normal blast. As they traveled their detecting receivers and amplifiers were reaching out with their utmost power; ultra-instruments capable of rendering audible any signal originating within many light-years of them, upon any possible communications band. And constantly at least two men, with every sense concentrated in their ears, were listening to those instruments.

Listening—straining to distinguish in the deafening roar of background noise from the over-driven tubes any sign of voice or of signal:

Listening—while, millions upon millions of miles beyond even the prodigious reach of those ultra-instruments, three human beings were even then sending out into empty space an almost hopeless appeal for the help so desperately needed!

CHAPTER 18

THE SPECIMENS ESCAPE

KNOWING WELL THAT CONVERSATION WITH ITS FELLOWS IS one of the greatest needs of any intelligent being, the Nevians had permitted the Terrestrial specimens to retain possession of their ultra-beam communicators. Thus it was that Costigan had been able to keep in touch with his sweetheart and with Bradley. He learned that each had been placed upon exhibition in a different Nevian city; that the three had been separated in response to an insistent popular demand for such a distribution of the peculiar, but highly interesting creatures from a distant solar system. They had not been harmed. In fact, each was visited daily by a specialist, who made sure that his charge was being kept in the pink of condition.

As soon as he became aware of this condition of things Costigan became morose. He sat still, drooped, and pined away visibly. He refused to eat, and of the worried specialist he demanded liberty. Then, failing in that as he knew he would fail, he demanded something to *do*. They pointed out to him, reasonably enough, that in such a civilization as theirs there was nothing he could do. They assured him that they would do anything they could to alleviate his mental suffering, but that since he was a museum piece he must see, himself, that he must be kept on display for a short time. Wouldn't he please behave himself and eat, as a reasoning being should? Costigan sulked a little longer, then wavered. Finally he agreed to compromise. He would eat and exercise if they would fit up a laboratory in his apartment, so that he could continue the studies he had begun upon his own native planet. To this they agreed, and thus it came about that one day the following conversation was held:

"Clio? Bradley? I've got something to tell you this time. Haven't said anything before, for fear things might not work out, but they did. I went on a hunger strike and made them give me a complete laboratory. As a chemist I'm a damn good electrician; but luckily, with the sea-water they've got here, it's a very simple thing to make . . ."

"Hold on!" snapped Bradley. "Somebody may be listening in on us!"

"They aren't. They can't, without my knowing it, and I'll cut off the second anybody tries to synchronize with my beam. To resume—making Vee-Two is a very simple process, and I've got everything around here that's hollow clear full of it . . ."

"How come they let you?" asked Clio.

"Oh, they don't know what I'm doing. They watched me for a few days, and all I did was make up and bottle the weirdest messes imaginable. Then I finally managed to separate oxygen and nitrogen, after trying hard all of one day; and when they saw that I didn't know anything about either one of them or what to do with them after I had them, they gave me up in disgust as a plain dumb ape and haven't paid any attention to me since. So I've got me plenty of kilograms of liquid Vee-Two, all ready to touch off. I'm getting out of here in about three minutes and a half, and I'm coming over after you folks, in a new, iron-powered space-speedster that they don't know I know anything about. They've just given it its final tests, and it's the slickest thing you ever saw."

"But Conway, dearest, you can't possibly rescue me," Clio's voice broke. "Why, there are thousands of them, all around here. If you can get away, go, dear, but don't . . ."

"I said I was coming after you, and if I get away I'll be there. A good whiff of this stuff will lay out a thousand of them just as easily as it will one. Here's the idea. I've made a gas mask for myself, since I'll be in it where it's thick, but you two won't need any. It's soluble enough in water so that three or four thicknesses of wet cloth over your noses will be enough. I'll tell you when to wet down. We're going to break away or go out trying—there aren't enough amphibians between here and Andromeda to keep us humans cooped up like menagerie animals forever! But here comes my specialist with the keys to the city; time for the overture to start. See you later!"

The Nevian physician directed his key tube upon the transparent wall of the chamber and an opening appeared, an opening which vanished as soon as he had stepped through it; Costigan kicked a valve open; and from various innocent tubes there belched forth into the water of the central lagoon and into the air over it a flood of deadly vapor. As the Nevian turned toward the prisoner there was an almost inaudible hiss and a tiny jet of the frightful, outlawed stuff struck his open gills, just below his huge, conical head. He tensed momentarily, twitched convulsively just once, and fell motionless to the floor. And outside, the streams of avidly soluble liquefied gas rushed out into air and into water. It spread, dissolved, and diffused with the extreme mobility which is one of its characteristics; and as it diffused and was borne outward the Nevians in their massed hundreds died. Died not knowing what killed them, not knowing even that they died. Costigan, bitterly resentful of the inhuman treatment accorded the three and fiercely anxious for the success of his plan of escape, held his breath and, grimly alert, watched the amphibians die. When he could see no more motion anywhere he donned his gas-mask, strapped upon his back a large canister of the poison—his capacious pockets were already full of smaller containers—and two savagely exultant sentences escaped him.

"I am a poor, ignorant speciman of ape that can be let play with apparatus, am I?" he rasped, as he picked up the key tube of the specialist and opened the door of his prison. "They'll learn now that it ain't safe to judge by the looks of a flea how far he can jump!"

He stepped out through the opening into the water, and, burdened as he was, made shift to swim to the nearest ramp. Up it he ran, toward a main corridor. But ahead of him there was wafted a breath of dread Vee-Two, and where that breath went, went also unconsciousness—an unconsciousness which would deepen gradually into permanent oblivion save for the prompt intervention of one who possessed, not only the necessary antidote, but the equally important knowledge of exactly how to use it. Upon the floor of that corridor were strewn Nevians, who had dropped in their tracks. Past or over their bodies Costigan strode, pausing only to direct a jet of lethal vapor into whatever branching corridor or open door caught his eye. He was going to the intake of the city's ventilation plant, and no unmasked creature dependent for life upon oxygen could bar his path. He reached the intake, tore the canister from his back, and released its full, vast volume

of horrid contents into the primary air stream of the entire
city.

And all throughout that doomed city Nevians dropped;
quietly and without a struggle, unknowing. Busy executives
dropped upon their cushioned, flat-topped desks; hurrying
travelers and messengers dropped upon the floors of the corridors or relaxed in the noxious waters of the ways; look-
outs and observers dropped before their flashing screens;
central operators of communications dropped under the
winking lights of their panels. Observers and centrals in the
outlying sections of the city wondered briefly at the unwonted universal motionlessness and stagnation; then the
racing taint in water and in air reached them, too, and they
ceased wondering—forever.

Then through those quiet halls Costigan stalked to a certain
storage room, where with all due precaution he donned his
own suit of Triplanetary armor. Making an ungainly bundle
of the other Solarian equipment stored there, he dragged it
along behind him as he clanked back toward his prison, until
he neared the dock at which was moored the Nevian space-
speedster which he was determined to take. Here, he knew,
was the first of many critical points. The crew of the
vessel was aboard, and, with its independent air-supply, unharmed. They had weapons, were undoubtedly alarmed, and
were very probably highly suspicious. They, too, had ultra-
beams and might see him, but his very closeness to them
would tend to protect him from ultra-beam observation.
Therefore he crouched tensely behind a buttress, staring
through his spy-ray goggles, waiting for a moment when
none of the Nevians would be near the entrance, but grimly
resolved to act instantly should he feel any touch of a spying
ultra-beam.

"Here's where the pinch comes," he growled to himself.
"I know the combinations, but if they're suspicious enough
and act quick enough they can seal that door on me before
I can get it open, and then rub me out like a blot; but . . . ah!"

The moment had arrived, before the touch of any revealing ray. He trained the key-tube, the entrance opened,
and through that opening in the instant of its appearance
there shot a brittle bulb of glass, whose breaking meant
death. It crashed into fragments against a metallic wall and
Costigan, entering the vessel, consigned its erstwhile crew
one by one to the already crowded waters of the lagoon. He
then leaped to the controls and drove the captured speedster
through the air, to plunge it down upon the surface of the

lagoon beside the door of the isolated structure which had for so long been his prison. Carefully he transferred to the vessel the motley assortment of containers of Vee-Two, and after a quick check-up to make sure that he had overlooked nothing, he shot his craft straight up into the air. Then only did he close his ultra-wave circuits and speak.

"Clio, Bradley—I got away clean, without a bit of trouble. Now I'm coming after you, Clio."

"Oh, it's wonderful that you got away, Conway!" the girl exclaimed. "But hadn't you better get Captain Bradley first? Then, if anything should happen, he would be of some use, while I . . ."

"I'll knock him into an outside loop if he does!" the captain snorted, and Costigan went on:

"You won't need to. You come first, Clio, of course. But you're too far away for me to see you with my spy, and I don't want to use the high-powered beam of this boat for fear of detection; so you'd better keep on talking, so that I can trace you."

"That's one thing I *am* good at!" Clio laughed in sheer relief. "If talking were music, I'd be a full brass band!" and she kept up a flow of inconsequential chatter until Costigan told her that it was no longer necessary; that he had established the line.

"Any excitement around there yet?" he asked her then.

"Nothing unusual that I can see," she replied. "Why? Should there be some?"

"I hope not, but when I made my getaway I couldn't kill them all, of course, and I thought maybe they might connect things up with my jail-break and tell the other cities to take steps about you two. But I guess they're pretty well disorganized back there yet, since they can't know who hit them, or what with, or why. I must have got about everybody that wasn't sealed up somewhere, and it doesn't stand to reason that those who are left can check up very closely for a while yet. But they're nobody's fools—they'll certainly get conscious when I snatch you, maybe before . . . there, I see your city, I think."

"What are you going to do?"

"Same as I did back there, if I can. Poison their primary air and all the water I can reach . . ."

"Oh, Conway!" Her voice rose to a scream. "They must know—they're all getting out of the water and are rushing inside the buildings as fast as they possibly can!"

"I see they are," grimly. "I'm right over you now, 'way

up. Been locating their primary intake. They've got a dozen ships around it, and have guards posted all along the corridors leading to it; and *those guards are wearing masks!* They're clever birds, all right, those amphibians—they know what they got back there and how they got it. That changes things, girl! If we use gas here we won't stand a chance in the world of getting old Bradley. Stand by to jump when I open that door!"

"Hurry, dear! They are coming out here after me!"

"Sure they are." Costigan had already seen the two Nevians swimming out toward Clio's cage, and had hurled his vessel downward in a screaming power dive. "You're too valuable a specimen for them to let you be gassed, but if they can get there before I do they're traveling fools!"

He miscalculated slightly, so that instead of coming to a halt at the surface of the liquid medium the speedster struck with a crash that hurled solid masses of water for hundreds of yards. But no ordinary crash could harm that vessel's structure, her gravity controls were not overloaded, and she shot back to the surface; gallant ship and reckless pilot alike unharmed. Costigan trained his key-tube upon the doorway of Clio's cell, then tossed it aside.

"Different combination over here!" he barked. "Got to cut you out—lie down in that far corner!"

His hands flashed over the panel, and as Clio fell prone without hesitation or question a heavy beam literally blasted away a large portion of the roof of the structure. The speedster shot into the air and dropped down until she rested upon the tops of opposite walls; walls still glowing, semi-molten. The girl piled a stool upon the table and stood upon it, reached upward and seized the mailed hands extended downward toward her. Costigan heaved her up into the vessel with a powerful jerk, slammed the door shut, leaped to the controls, and the speedster darted away.

"Your armor's in that bundle there. Better put it on, and check your Lewistons and pistols—no telling what kind of jams we'll get into," he snapped, without turning. "Bradley, start talking . . . all right, I've got your line. Better get your wet rags ready and get organized generally—every second will count by the time we get there. We're coming so fast that our outer plating's white hot, but it may not be fast enough, at that."

"It isn't fast enough, quite," Bradley announced, calmly. "They're coming out after me now."

"Don't fight them and probably they won't paralyze you.

Keep on talking, so that I can find out where they take you."

"No good, Costigan." The voice of the old spacehound did not reveal a sign of emotion as he made his dread announcement. "They have it all figured out. They're not taking any chances at all—they're going to paral . . ." His voice broke off in the middle of the word.

With a bitter imprecation Costigan flashed on the powerful ultra-beam projector of the speedster and focused the plate upon Bradley's prison; careless now of detection, since the Nevians were already warned. Upon that plate he watched the Nevians carry the helpless body of the captain into a small boat, and continued to watch as they bore it into one of the largest buildings of the city. Up a series of ramps they took the still form, placing it finally upon a soft couch in an enormous and heavily guarded central hall. Costigan turned to his companion, and even through the helmets she could see plainly the white agony of his expression. He moistened his lips and tried twice to speak—tried and failed; but he made no move either to cut off their power or to change their direction.

"Of course," she approved steadily. "We are going through. I know that you *want* to run with me, but if you actually did it I would never want to see you or hear of you again, and you would hate me forever."

"Hardly that." The anguish did not leave his eyes and his voice was hoarse and strained, but his hands did not vary the course of the speedster by so much as a hair's breadth. "You're the finest little fellow that ever waved a plume, and I would love you no matter what happened. I'd trade my immortal soul to the devil if it would get you out of this mess, but we're both in it up to our necks and we can't back out now. If they kill him we beat it—he and I both knew that it was on the chance of that happening that I took you first—but as long as all three of us are alive it's all three or none."

"Of course," she said again, as steadily, thrilled this time to the depths of her being by the sheer manhood of him who had thus simply voiced his Code; a man of such fiber that neither love of life nor his infinitely greater love for her could make him lower its high standard. "We are going through. Forget that I am a woman. We are three human beings, fighting a world full of monsters. I am simply one of us three. I will steer your ship, fire your projectors, or throw your bombs. What can I do best?"

"Throw bombs," he directed, briefly. He knew what must be done were they to have even the slightest chance of winning clear. "I'm going to blast a hole down into that auditorium, and when I do you stand by that port and start dropping bottles of perfume. Throw a couple of big ones right down the shaft I make, and the rest of them most anywhere, after I cut the wall open. They'll do good wherever they hit, land or water."

"But Captain Bradley—he'll be gassed, too." Her fine eyes were troubled.

"Can't be helped. I've got the antidote, and it'll work any time under an hour. That'll be lots of time—if we aren't gone in less than ten minutes we'll be staying here. They're bringing in platoons of militia in full armor, and if we don't beat those boys to it we're in for plenty of grief. All right—start throwing!"

The speedster had come to a halt directly over the imposing edifice within which Bradley was incarcerated, and a mighty beam had flared downward, digging a fiery well through floor after floor of stubborn metal. The ceiling of the amphitheater was pierced. The beam expired. Down into that assembly hall there dropped two canisters of Vee-Two, to crash and to fill its atmosphere with imperceptible death. Then the beam flashed on again, this time at maximum power, and with it Costigan burned away half of the entire building. Burned it away until room above room gaped open, shelf-like, to outer atmosphere; the great hall now resembling a over-size pigeon-hole surrounded by smaller ones. Into that largest pigeon-hole the speedster darted, and cushioned desks and benches crashed down; crushed flat under its enormous weight as it came to rest upon the floor.

Every available guard had been thrown into that room, regardless of customary occupation or of equipment. Most of them had been ordinary watchmen, not even wearing masks, and all such were already down. Many, however, were masked, and a few were dressed in full armor. But no portable armor could mount defenses of sufficient power to withstand the awful force of the speedster's weapons, and one flashing swing of a projector swept the hall almost clear of life.

"Can't shoot very close to Bradley with this big beam, but I'll mop up on the rest of them by hand. Stay here and cover me, Clio!" Costigan ordered, and went to open the port.

"I can't—I won't!" Clio replied instantly. "I don't know the controls well enough. I'd kill you or Captain Bradley, sure; but I *can* shoot, and I'm going to!" and she leaped out, close upon his heels.

Thus, flaming Lewiston in one hand and barking automatic in the other, the two mailed figures advanced toward Bradley, now doubly helpless; paralyzed by his enemies and gassed by his friends. For a time the Nevians melted away before them, but as they approached more nearly the couch upon which the captain was they encountered six figures encased in armor fully as capable as their own. The beams of the Lewistons rebounded from that armor in futile pyrotechnics, the bullets of the automatics spattered and exploded impotently against it. And behind that single line of armored guards were massed perhaps twenty unarmored, but masked, soldiers; and scuttling up the ramps leading into the hall were coming the platoons of heavily armored figures which Costigan had previously seen.

Decision instantly made, Costigan ran back toward the speedster, but he was not deserting his companions. "Keep the good work up!" he instructed the girl as he ran. "I'll pick those jaspers off with a pencil and then stand off the bunch that's coming while you rub out the rest of that crew there and drag Bradley back here."

Back at the control panel, he trained a narrow, but intensely dense beam—quasi-solid lightning—and one by one the six armored figures fell. Then, knowing that Clio could handle the remaining opposition, he devoted his attention to the reenforcements so rapidly approaching from the sides. Again and again the heavy beam lashed out, now upon this side, now upon that, and in its flaming path Nevians disappeared. And not only Nevians—in the incredible energy of that beam's blast floor, walls, ramps, and every material thing vanished in clouds of thick and brilliant vapor. The room temporarily clear of foes, he sprang again to Clio's assistance, but her task was nearly done. She had "rubbed out" all opposition and, tugging lustily at Bradley's feet, had already dragged him almost to the side of the speedster.

"At-a-girl, Clio!" cheered Costigan, as he picked up the burly captain and tossed him through the doorway. "Highly useful, girl of my dreams, as well as ornamental. In with you, and we'll go places!"

But getting the speedster out of the now completely ruined hall proved to be much more of a task than driving it in had been, for scarcely had Costigan closed his locks than a section of the building collapsed behind them, cutting off their retreat. Nevian submarines and airships were beginning to arrive upon the scene, and were beaming the building viciously in an attempt to entrap or to crush the foreigners in its ruins

Costigan managed finally to blast his way out, but the Nevians had had time to assemble in force and he was met by a concentrated storm of beams and of metal from every inimical weapon within range.

But not for nothing had Conway Costigan selected for his dash for liberty the craft which, save only for the two immense interstellar cruisers, was the most powerful vessel ever built upon red Nevia. And not for nothing had he studied minutely and to the last, least detail every item of its controls and of its armament during wearily long days and nights of solitary imprisonment. He had studied it under test, in action, and at rest; studied it until he knew thoroughly its every possibility—and what a ship it was! The atomic-powered generators of his shielding screens handled with ease the terrific load of the Nevians' assault, his polycyclic screens were proof against any material projectile, and the machines supplying his offensive weapons with power were more than equal to their tasks. Driven now at full rating those frightful beams lashed out against the Nevians' blocking the way, and under their impacts her screens flared brilliantly through the spectrum and went down. And in the instant of their failure the enemy vessel was literally blown into nothingness—no unprotected metal, however resistant, could exist for a moment in the pathway of those iron-driven tornadoes of pure energy.

Ship after ship of the Nevians plunged toward the speedster in desperately suicidal attempts to ram her down, but each met the same flaming fate before it could reach its target. Then from the grouped submarines far below there reached up red rods of force, which seized the space-ship and began relentlessly to draw her down.

"What are they doing that for, Conway? *They* can't fight us!"

"They don't want to fight us. They want to hold us, but I know what to do about that, too," and the powerful tractor rods snapped as a plane of pure force knifed through them. Upward now at the highest permissible velocity the speedster leaped, and past the few ships remaining above her she dodged; nothing now between her and the freedom of boundless space.

"You did it, Conway; you did it!" Clio exulted. "Oh, Conway, you're just simply wonderful!"

"I haven't done it yet," Costigan cautioned her. "The worst is yet to come. Nerado. He's why they wanted to hold us back, and why I was in such a hurry to get away. That boat of his is bad medicine, girl, and we want to put plenty of kilometers behind us before he gets started."

"But do you think he will chase us?

"*Think* so? I *know* so! The mere facts that we are rare specimens and that he told us that we were going to stay there all the rest of our lives would make him chase us clear to Lundmark's Nebula. Besides that, we stepped on their toes pretty heavily before we left. We know altogether too much now to be let get back to Tellus; and finally, they'd all die of acute enlargement of the spleen if we get away with this prize ship of theirs. I hope to tell you they'll chase us!"

He fell silent, devoting his whole attention to his piloting, driving his craft onward at such velocity that its outer plating held steadily at the highest point of temperature compatible with safety. Soon they were out in open space, hurtling toward the sun under the drive of every possible watt of power, and Costigan took off his armor and turned toward the helpless body of the captain.

"He looks so . . . so . . . so *dead,* Conway! Are you really sure that you can bring him to?"

"Absolutely. Lots of time yet. Just three simple squirts in the right places will do the trick." He took from a locked compartment of his armor a small steel box, which housed a surgeon's hypodermic and three vials. One, two, three, he injected small, but precisely measured amounts of the fluids into the three vital localities, then placed the inert form upon a deeply cushioned couch.

"There! That'll take care of the gas in five or six hours. The paralysis will wear off long before that, so he'll be all right when he wakes up; and we're going away from here with everything we can put out. I've done everything I know how to do, for the present."

Then only did Costigan turn and look down, directly into Clio's eyes. Wide, eloquent blue eyes that gazed back up into his, tender and unafraid; eyes freighted with the oldest message of woman to chosen man. His hard young face softened wonderfully as he stared at her; there were two quick steps and they were in each other's arms. Lips upon eager lips, blue eyes to gray, motionless they stood clasped in ecstasy; thinking nothing of the dreadful past, nothing of the fearful future, conscious only of the glorious, wonderful present.

"Clio mine . . . darling . . . girl, girl, how I love you!" Costigan's deep voice was husky with emotion. "I haven't kissed you for seven thousand years! I don't rate you, by a million steps; but if I can just get you out of this mess, I swear by all the gods of interplanetary space . . ."

"You needn't, lover. Rate *me?* Good Heavens, Conway! It's just the other way . . ."

"Stop it!" he commanded in her ear. "I'm still dizzy at the idea of your loving me at all, to say nothing of loving me *this* way! But you do, and that's all I ask, here or hereafter."

"Love you? *Love* you!" Their mutual embrace tightened and her low voice thrilled brokenly as she went on: "Conway dearest . . . I can't say a thing, but you know . . . Oh, Conway!"

After a time Clio drew a long and tremulous, but supremely happy breath as the realities of their predicament once more obtruded themselves upon her consciousness. She released herself gently from Costigan's arms.

"Do you really think that there is a chance of us getting back to the Earth, so that we can be together . . . always?"

"A chance, yes. A probability, no," he replied, unequivocally. "It depends upon two things. First, how much of a start we got on Nerado. His ship is the biggest and fastest thing I ever saw, and if he strips her down and drives her—which he will—he'll catch us long before we can make Tellus. On the other hand, I gave Rodebush a lot of data, and if he and Lyman Cleveland can add it to their own stuff and get that super-ship of ours rebuilt in time, they'll be out here on the prowl; and they'll have what it takes to give even Nerado plenty of argument. No use worrying about it, anyway. We won't know anything until we can detect one or the other of them, and then will be the time to do something about it."

"If Nerado catches us, will you . . ." She paused.

"Rub you out? I will not. Even if he does catch us, and takes us back to Nevia, I won't. There's lots more time coming onto the clock. Nerado won't hurt either of us badly enough to leave scars, either physical, mental, or moral. I'd kill you in a second if it were Roger; he's dirty. He's mean —he's thoroughly bad. But Nerado's a good enough old scout, in his way. He's big and he's clean. You know, I could really like that fish if I could meet him on terms of equality sometime?"

"*I* couldn't!" she declared vigorously. "He's crawly and scaly and snaky; and he smells so . . . so . . ."

"So rank and fishy?" Costigan laughed deeply. "Details, girl; mere details. I've seen people who looked like money in the bank and who smelled like a bouquet of violets that you couldn't trust half the length of Nerado's neck."

"But look what he did to us!" she protested. "And they weren't trying to recapture us back there; they were trying to kill us."

"That was perfectly all right, what he did and what they did—what else could they have done?" he wanted to know. "And while you're looking, look at what we did to them— plenty, I'd say. But we all had it to do, and neither side will blame the other for doing it. He's a square shooter, I tell you."

"Well, maybe, but I don't like him a bit, and let's not talk about him any more. Let's talk about us. Remember what you said once, when you advised me to 'let you lay,' or whatever it was?" Woman-like, she wished to dip again lightly into the waters of pure emotion, even though she had such a short time before led the man out of their profoundest depths. But Costigan, into whose hard life love of woman had never before entered, had not yet recovered sufficiently from his soul-shaking plunge to follow her lead. Inarticulate, distrusting his newly found supreme happiness, he must needs stay out of those enchanted waters or plunge again. And he was afraid to plunge—diffident, still deeming himself unworthy of the miracle of this wonder-girl's love—even though every fiber of his being shrieked its demand to feel again that slender body in his arms. He did not consciously think those thoughts. He acted them without thinking; they were prime basics in that which made Conway Costigan what he was.

"I do remember, and I still think it's a sound idea, even though I am too far gone now to let you put it into effect," he assured her, half seriously. He kissed her, tenderly and reverently, then studied her carefully. "But you look as though you'd been on a Martian picnic. When did you eat last?"

"I don't remember, exactly. This morning, I think."

"Or maybe last night, or yesterday morning? I thought so! Bradley and I can eat anything that's chewable, and drink anything that will pour, but you can't. I'll scout around and see if I can't fix up something that you'll be able to eat."

He rummaged through the store-rooms, emerging with sundry viands from which he prepared a highly satisfactory meal.

"Think you can sleep now, sweetheart?" After supper, once more within the circle of Costigan's arms, Clio nodded her head against his shoulder.

"Of course I can, dear. Now that you are with me, out here alone, I'm not a bit afraid any more. You will get us back to Earth some way, sometime; I just know that you will. Good-night, Conway."

"Good-night, Clio . . . little sweetheart," he whispered, and went back to Bradley's side.

In due time the captain recovered consciousness, and slept. Then for days the speedster flashed on toward our distant solar system; days during which her wide-flung detector screens remained cold.

"I don't know whether I'm afraid they'll hit something or afraid that they won't," Costigan remarked more than once, but finally those tenuous sentinels did in fact encounter an interfering vibration. Along the detector line a visibeam sped, and Costigan's face hardened as he saw the unmistakable outline of Nerado's interstellar cruiser, far behind them.

"Well, a stern chase always was a long one," Costigan said finally. "He can't catch us for plenty of days yet . . . now what?" for the alarms of the detectors had broken out anew. There was still another point of interference to be investigated. Costigan traced it, and there, almost dead ahead of them, between them and their sun, nearing them at the incomprehensible rate of the sum of the two vessels' velocities, came another cruiser of the Nevians!

"Must be the sister-ship, coming back from our System with a load of iron," Costigan deduced. "Heavily loaded as she is, we may be able to dodge her; and she's coming so fast that if we can stay out of her range we'll be all right—he won't be able to stop for probably three or four days. But if our super-ship is anywhere in these parts, now's the time for her to rally 'round!"

He gave the speedster all the side-thrust she would take; then, putting every available communicator tube behind a tight beam, he aimed it at Sol and began sending out a long-continued call to his fellows of the Triplanetary Service.

Nearer and nearer the Nevian flashed, trying with all her power to intercept the speedster; and it soon became evident that, heavily laden though she was, she could make enough sideway to bring her within range at the time of meeting.

"Of course, they've got partial neutralization of inertia, the same as we have," Costigan cogitated, "and by the way he's coming I'd say that he had orders to blow us out of the ether—he knows as well as we do that he can't capture us alive at anything like the relative velocities we've got now. I can't give her any more side thrust without overloading the gravity controls, so overloaded they've got to be. Strap down, you two, because they may go out entirely!"

"Do you think that you can pull away from them, Conway?" Clio was staring in horrified fascination into the plate, watching the pictured vessel increase in size, moment by moment.

"I don't know whether I can or not, but I'm going to try. Just in case we don't, though, I'm going to keep on yelling for help. In solid? All right, boat, DO YOUR STUFF!"

CHAPTER 19

GIANTS MEET

"CHECK YOUR BLAST, FRED, I THINK THAT I HEAR SOMETHING trying to come through!" Cleveland called out, sharply. For days the *Boise* had torn through the illimitable reaches of empty space, and now the long vigil of the keen-eared listeners was to be ended. Rodebush cut off his power, and through the crackling roar of tube noise an almost inaudible voice made itself heard.

". . . all the help you can give us. Samms—Cleveland—Rodebush — anybody of Triplanetary who can hear me, listen! This is Costigan, with Miss Marsden and Captain Bradley, heading for where we think the sun is, from right ascension about six hours, declination about plus fourteen degrees. Distance unknown, but probably a good many light-years. Trace my call. One Nevian ship is overhauling us slowly, another is coming toward us from the sun. We may or may not be able to dodge it, but we need all the help you can give us. Samms—Rodebush—Cleveland—anybody of Triplanetary . . ."

Endlessly the faint, faint voice went on, but Rodebush and Cleveland were no longer listening. Sensitive ultra-loops had been swung, and along the indicated line shot Triplanetary's super-ship at a velocity which she had never before even approached; the utterly incomprehensible, almost incalculable velocity attained by inertialess matter driven through an almost perfect vacuum by the *Boise's* maximum projector blasts—a blast which would lift her stupendous normal tonnage against a gravity five times that of Earth. At the full frightful measure of that velocity the super-ship literally annihilated distance, while ahead of her the furiously driven spy-ray beam fanned out in quest of the three Triplanetarians who were callling for help.

"Got any idea how fast we're going?" Rodebush demanded, glancing up for an instant from the observation plate. "We should be able to see him, since we could hear him, and our range is certainly as great as anything he can have."

"No. Can't figure velocity without any reliable data on how many atoms of matter exist per cubic meter out here." Cleveland was staring at the calculator. "It's constant, of course, at the value at which the friction of the medium is equal to our thrust. Incidentally, we can't hold it too long. We're running a temperature, which shows that we're stepping along faster than anybody ever computed before. Also, it points out the necessity for something that none of us ever anticipated needing in an open-space drive—refrigerators or radiating wall-shields or repellers or something of the sort. But to get back to our velocity—taking Throckmorton's estimates it figures somewhere near the order of magnitude of ten to the twenty-seventh. Fast enough, anyway, so that you'd better bend an eye on that plate. Even after you see them you won't know where they really are, because we don't know any of the velocities involved—our own, theirs, or that of the beam—and we may be right on top of them."

"Or, if we happen to be outrunning the beam, we won't see them at all. That makes it nice piloting."

"How are you going to handle things when we get there?"

"Lock to them and take them aboard, if we're in time. If not, if they are fighting already—*there they are!*"

The picture of the speedster's control room flashed upon the speaker.

"Hi, Fritz! Hi, Cleve! Welcome to our city! Where are you?"

"We don't know," Cleveland snapped back, "and we don't know where you are, either. Can't figure anything without data. I see you're still breathing air. Where are the Nevians? How much time have we got yet?"

"Not enough, I'm afraid. By the looks of things they will be within range of us in a couple of hours, and you haven't even touched our detector screen yet."

"A couple of *hours!*" In his relief Cleveland shouted the words. "That's time to burn—we can be just about out of the Galaxy in that . . ." He broke off at a yell from Rodebush.

"Broadcast, Spud, BROADCAST!" the physicist had cried, as Costigan's image had disappeared utterly from his plate.

He cut off the *Boise's* power, stopping her instantaneously in mid-space, but the connection had been broken. Costigan could not possibly have heard the orders to change his beam signal to a broadcast, so that they could pick it up; nor would it have done any good if he had heard and had obeyed. So immeasurably great had been their velocity that they had flashed past the speedster and were now un- known thousands—or millions—of miles beyond the fugitives they had come so far to help; far beyond the range of any possible broadcast. But Cleveland understood instantly what had happened. He now had a little data upon which to work, and his hands flew over the keys of the calculator.

"Back blast, at maximum, seventeen seconds!" he directed crisply. "Not exact, of course, but that will put us close enough so that we can find 'em with our detectors."

For the calculated seventeen seconds the super-ship re- traced her path, at the same awful speed with which she had come so far. The blast expired and there, plainly limned upon the observation plates, was the Nevian speedster.

"As a computer, you're good, Cleve," Rodebush ap- plauded. "So close that we can't use the neutralizers to catch him. If we use one dyne of drive we'll overshoot a million kilometers before I could snap the switch."

"And yet he's so far away and going so fast that if we keep our inertia on it'll take all day at full blast to overtake —no, wait a minute—we could *never* catch him." Cleve- land was puzzled. "What to do? Shunt in a potentiometer?"

"No, we don't need it." Rodebush turned to the trans- mitter. "Costigan! We are going to take hold of you with a very light tractor—a tracer, really—and whatever you do, DON'T CUT IT, or we can't reach you in time. It may look like a collision, but it won't be—we'll just touch you, without even a jar."

"A tractor—inertialess?" Cleveland wondered.

"Sure. Why not?" Rodebush set up the beam at its abso- lute minimum of power and threw in the switch.

While hundreds of thousands of miles separated the two vessels and the attractor was exerting the least effort of which it was capable, yet the super-ship leaped toward the smaller craft at a pace which covered the intervening distance in almost no time at all. So rapidly were the objectives en- larging upon the plates that the automatic focusing devices could scarcely function rapidly enough to keep them in place. Cleveland flinched involuntarily and seized his arm-rests in a spasmodic clutch as he watched this, the first inertialess space-approach; and even Rodebush, who knew better than anyone else what to expect, held his breath and swallowed hard at the unbelievable rate at which the two vessels were rushing together.

And if these two, who had rebuilt the super-ship, could hardly control themselves, what of the three in the speedster, who knew nothing whatever of the wonder-craft's potentialities? Clio, staring into the plate with Costigan, uttered one piercing shriek as she sank her fingers into his shoulders. Bradley swore a mighty deep-space oath and braced himself against certain annihilation. Costigan stared for an instant, unable to believe his eyes; then, in spite of the warning, his hand darted toward the studs which would cut the beam. Too late. Before his flying fingers could reach the buttons the *Boise* was upon them; had struck the speedster in direct central impact. Moving at the full measure of her unthinkable velocity though the super-ship was in the instant of impact, yet the most delicate recording instruments of the speedster could not detect the slightest shock as the enormous globe struck the comparatively tiny torpedo and clung to it; accommodating instantaneously and effortlessly her own terrific pace to that of the smaller and infinitely slower craft. Clio sobbed in relief and Costigan, one arm around her, sighed hugely.

"Hey, you spacelugs!" he cried. "Glad to see you, and all that, but you might as well kill a man outright as scare him to death! So *that's* the super-ship, huh? *Some* ship!"

"Hi-ya, Murf! Hi, Spud!" came from the speaker.

"Murf? Spud? How come?" Clio, practically recovered now, glanced upward questioningly. It was plain that she did not quite know whether or not to like the nicknames which the rescuers were calling her Conway.

"My middle name is Murphy, so they've called me things like that ever since I was so high." Costigan indicated a length of approximately twelve inches. "And now you'll probably live long enough—I hope—to hear me called a lot worse stuff than that."

"Don't *talk* that way—we're safe now, Con . . . Spud? It's nice that they like you so much—but they would, of course." She snuggled even closer, and both listened to what Rodebush was saying.

". . . realize myself that it would look so bad; it scared me as much as it did anybody. Yes, this is IT. She really works—thanks more than somewhat to Conway Costigan, by the way. But you had better transfer. If you'll get your things . . ."

"'Things' is good!" Costigan laughed, and Clio giggled sunnily.

"We've made so many transfers already that what you see is all we've got," Bradley explained. "We'll bring ourselves, and we'll hurry. That Nevian is coming up fast."

"Is there anything on this ship you fellows want?" Costigan asked.

"There may be, but we haven't any locks big enough to let her inside and we haven't time to study her now. You might leave her controls in neutral, so that we can calculate her position if we should want her later on."

"All right." The three armor-clad figures stepped into the *Boise's* open lock, the tractor beam was cut off, and the speedster flashed away from the now stationary super-ship.

"Better let formalities go for a while," Captain Bradley interrupted the general introductions taking place. "I was scared out of nine years' growth when I saw you coming at us, and maybe I've still got the humps; but that Nevian is coming up fast, and if you don't already know it I can tell you that she's *no* light cruiser."

"That's so, too," Costigan agreed. "Have you fellows got enough stuff so that you think you can take him? You've got the legs on him, anyway—you can certainly run if you want to!"

"Run?" Cleveland laughed. "We have a bone of our own to pick with that ship. We licked her to a standstill once, until we burned out a sct of generators, and since we got them fixed we've been chasing her all over space. We were chasing her when we picked up your call. See there? She's doing the running."

The Nevian was running, in truth. Her commander had seen and had recognized the great vessel which had flashed out of nowhere to the rescue of the three fugitives from Nevia; and, having once been at grips with that vengeful super-dreadnaught, he had little stomach for another encounter. Therefore his side-thrust was now being exerted in the opposite direction; he was frankly trying to put as much distance as possible between himself and Triplanetary's formidable warship. In vain. A light tractor was clamped on and the *Boise* flashed up to close range before Rodebush restored her inertia and Cleveland brought the two vessels relatively to rest by increasing gradually his tractor's pull. And this time the Nevian could not cut the tractor. Again that shearing plane of force bit into it and tore at it, but it neither yielded nor broke. The rebuilt generators of Number Four were designed to carry the load, and they carried it. And again Triplanetary's every mighty weapon was brought into play.

The "cans" were thrown, ultra- and infra-beams were driven, the furious macro-beam gnawed hungrily at the Nevian's defenses; and one by one those defenses went down. In desperation the enemy commander threw his every generator behind a polycyclic screen; only to see Cleveland's even more powerful drill bore relentlessly through it. After that puncturing, the end came soon. A secondary SX7 beam was now in place on mighty Ten's inner rings, and one fierce blast blew a hole completely through the Nevian cruiser. Into that hole entered Adlington's terrific bombs and their gruesome fellows, and where they entered, life departed. All defenses vanished, and under the blasts of the *Boise's* batteries, now unopposed, the metal of the Nevian vessel exploded into a widely spreading cloud of vapor. Sparkling vapor, with perhaps here and there a droplet or two of material which had been only liquified.

So passed the sister-ship, and Rodebush turned his plates upon the vessel of Nerado. But that highly intelligent amphibian had seen all that had occurred. He had long since given over the pursuit of the speedster, and he did not rush in to do hopeless battle beside his fellow Nevians against the Tellurians. His analytical detectors had written down each detail of every weapon and of every screen employed; and even while prodigious streamers of force were raving out from his vessel, braking her terrific progress and swinging her around in an immnese circle back toward far Nevia, his scientists and mechanics were doubling and redoubling the power of his already Titanic installations, to match and if possible to overmatch those of Triplanetary's super-dreadnaught.

"Do we kill him now or do we let him suffer a while longer?" Costigan demanded.

"I don't think so, yet," Rodebush replied. "Would you, Cleve?"

"Not yet," said Cleveland, grimly, reading the other's thought and agreeing with it. "Let him pilot us to Nevia; we might not be able to find it without a guide. While we're at it we want to so pulverize that crowd that if they never come near the Solarian system again they'll think it's twenty minutes too soon."

Thus it was that the *Boise*, increasing her few dynes of

driving force at a rate just sufficient to match her quarry's acceleration, pursued the Nevian ship. Apparently exerting every effort, she never came quite within range of the fleeing raider; yet never was she so far behind that the Nevian space-ship was not in clear register upon her observation plates.

Nor was Nerado alone in strengthening his vessel. Costigan knew well and respected highly the Nevian scientist-captain, and at his suggestion much time was spent in reenforcing the super-ship's armament to the iron-driven limit of theoretical and mechanical possibility.

In mid-space, however, the Nevian slowed down.

"What gives?" Rodebush demanded of the group at large. "Not turn-over time already, is it?"

"No." Cleveland shook his head. "Not for at least a day yet."

"Cooking up something on Nevia, is my guess," Costigan put in. "If I know that lizard at all, he wired ahead—specifications for the welcoming committee. We're getting there too fast, so he's stalling. Check?"

"Check." Rodebush agreed. "But there's no use of us waiting, if you're sure you know which one of those stars up ahead is Nevia. Do you, Cleve?"

"Definitely."

"The only other thing is, then, shall we blow them out of the ether first?"

"You might try," Costigan remarked. "That is, if you're damned sure that you can run if you have to."

"Huh? *Run?*" demanded Rodebush.

"Just that. It's spelled R-U-N, run. I know those freaks better than you do. Believe me, Fritz, they've got what it takes."

"Could be, at that," Rodebush admitted. "We'll play it safe."

The *Boise* leaped upon the Nevian, every weapon aflame. But, as Costigan had expected, Nerado's vessel was completely ready for any emergency. And, unlike her sister-ship, she was manned by scientists well versed in the fundamental theory of the weapons with which they fought. Beams, rods, and lances of energy flamed and flared; planes and pencils cut, slashed, and stabbed; defensive screens glowed redly or flashed suddenly into intensely brilliant, coruscating incandescence. Crimson opacity struggled sullenly against violet curtain of annihilation. Material projectiles and torpedoes were launched under full beam control; only to be exploded harmlessly in mid-space, to be blasted into nothingness, or to disappear innocuously against impenetrable polycyclic screens. Even Cleveland's drill was ineffective. Both vessels were equipped completely with iron-driven mechanisms; both were manned by scientists capable of wringing the highest possible measure of power from their installations. Neither could harm the other.

The *Boise* flashed away; reached Nevia in minutes. Down into the crimson atmosphere she dropped, down toward the city which Costigan knew was Nerado's home port.

"Hold up a bit!" Costigan cautioned, sharply. "There's something down there that I don't like!"

As he spoke there shot upward from the city a multitude of flashing balls. The Nevians had mastered the secret of the explosive of the fishes of the greater deeps, and were launching it in a veritable storm against the Tellurian visitor.

"Those?" asked Rodebush, calmly. The detonating balls of destruction were literally annihilating even the atmosphere beyond the polycyclic screen, but that barrier was scarcely affected.

"No. That." Costigan pointed out a hemispherical dome which, redly translucent, surrounded a group of buildings towering high above their neighbors. "Neither those high towers nor those screens were there the last time I was in this town. Nerado *was* stalling for time, and that's what they're doing down there—that's all those fire-balls are for. Good sign, too—they aren't ready for us yet. We'd better take 'em while the taking's good. If they *were* ready for us, our play would be to get out of here while we're all in one piece."

Nerado had been in touch with the scientists of his city; he had been instructing them in the construction of converters and generators of such weight and power that they could crush even the defenses of the super-ship. The mechanisms were not, however, ready; the entirely unsuspected possibilities of speed inherent in absolute inertialessness had not entered into Nerado's calculations.

"Better drop a few cans down onto that dome, fellows," Rodebush suggested to his gunners.

"We can't," came Adlington's instant reply. "No use trying it—that's a polycyclic screen. Can you drill it? If you can, I've got a real bomb here—that special we built—that will do the trick if you can protect it from them until it gets down into the water."

"I'll try it," Cleveland answered, at a nod from the

physicist. "I couldn't drill Nerado's polycyclics, but I couldn't use any momentum on him. Couldn't ram him—he fell back with my thrust. But that screen down there can't back away from us, so maybe I can work on it. Get your special ready. Hang on, everybody!"

The *Boise* looped upward, and from an altitude of miles dove straight down through a storm of force-balls, beams, and shells; a dive checked abruptly as the hollow tube of energy which was Cleveland's drill snarled savagely down ahead of her and struck the shielding hemisphere with a grinding, lightning-spitting shock. As it struck, backed by all the enormous momentum of the plunging space ship and driven by the full power of her prodigious generators it bored in, clawing and gouging viciously through the tissues of that rigid and unyielding barrier of pure energy. Then, mighty drill and plunging mass against iron-driven wall, eye-tearing and furiously spectacular warfare was waged.

Well it was for Triplanetary that day that its super-ship carried ample supplies of allotropic iron; well it was that her originally Gargantuan converters and generators had been doubled and quadrupled in power on the long Nevian way! For that ocean-girdled fortress was powered to withstand any conceivable assault—but the *Boise's* power and momentum were now inconceivable; and every watt and every dyne was solidly behind that hellishly flaming, that voraciously tearing, that irresistibly ravening cylinder of energy incredible!

Through the Nevian shield that cylinder gnawed its frightful way, and down its protecting length there drove Adlington's "Special" bomb. "Special" it was indeed; so great of girth that it could barely pass through the central orifice of Ten's mighty projector, so heavily charged with sensitized atomic iron that its detonation upon any planet would not have been considered for an instant if that planet's integrity meant anything to its attackers. Down the shielding pipe of force the "Special" screamed under full propulsion, and beneath the surface of Nevia's ocean it plunged.

"Cut!" yelled Adlington, and as the scintillating drill expired the bomber pressed his detonating switch.

For moments the effect of the explosion seemed unimportant. A dull, low rumble was all that was to be heard of a concussion that jarred red Nevia to her very center; and all that could be seen was a slow heaving of the water. But that heaving did not cease. Slowly, *so* slowly it seemed to the observers now high in the heavens, the waters rose up and parted; revealing a vast chasm blown deep into the ocean's rocky bed. Higher and higher the lazy mountains of water reared; effortlessly to pick up, to smash, to grind into fragments, and finally to toss aside every building, every structure, every scrap of material substance pertaining to the whole Nevian city.

Flattened out, driven backward for miles, the buffeted waters were pressed, leaving exposed bare ground and broken rock where once had been the ocean's busy floor. Tremendous blasts of incandescent gas raved upward, jarring even the enormous mass of the super-ship poised so high above the site of the explosion. Then the displaced millions of tons of water rushed to make even more complete the already total destruction of the city. The raging torrents poured into that yawning cavern, filled it, and piled mountainously above it; receding and piling up, again and again; causing tidal waves which swept a full half of Nevia's mighty, watery globe. That city was silenced—forever.

"MY . . . GOD!" Cleveland was the first to break the awed, the stunned, silence. He licked his lips. "But we had it to do . . . and at that, it's not as bad as what they did to Pittsburgh—they would have evacuated all except military personnel."

"Of course . . . what next?" asked Rodebush. "Look around, I suppose, to see if they have any more . . ."

"Oh, no, Conway—no! Don't let them!" Clio was sobbing openly. "I'm going to my room and crawl under the bed—I'll see that sight all the rest of my life!"

"Steady, Clio." Costigan's arm tightened around her. "We'll have to look, but we won't find any more. One—if they could have finished it—would have been enough."

Again and again the *Boise* circled the world. No more super-powered installations were being built. And, surprisingly enough, the Nevians made no demonstration of hostility.

"I wonder why?" Rodebush mused. "Of course, we aren't attacking them, either, but you'd think . . . do you suppose that they are waiting for Nerado?"

"Probably." Costigan paused in thought. "We'd better wait for him, too. We can't leave things this way."

"But if we can't force engagement . . . a stalemate . . ." Cleveland's voice was troubled.

"We'll do *something!*" Costigan declared. "This thing has got to be settled, some way or other, before we leave here. First, try talking. I've got an idea that . . . anyway, it can't do any harm, and I know that he can hear and understand you."

Nerado arrived. Instead of attacking, his ship hung quietly poised, a mile or two away from the equally undemonstrative *Boise*. Rodebush directed a beam.

"Captain Nerado, I am Rodebush of Triplanetary. What do you wish to do about this situation?"

"I wish to talk to you." The Nevian's voice came clearly from the speaker. "You are, I now perceive, a much higher form of life than any of us had thought possible; a form perhaps as high in evolution as our own. It is a pity that we did not take the time for a full meeting of minds when wc first neared your planet, so that much life, both Tellurian and Nevian, might have been spared. But what is past cannot be recalled. As reasoning beings, however, you will see the futility of continuing a combat in which neither is capable of winning victory over the other. You may, of course, destroy more of our Nevian cities, in which case I should be compelled to go and destroy similarly upon your Earth; but, to reasoning minds, such a course would be sheerest stupidity."

Rodebush cut the communicator beam.

"Does he mean it?" he demanded of Costigan. "It sounds perfectly reasonable, but . . ."

"But fishy!" Cleveland broke in. "Altogether too reasonable to be true!"

"He means it. He means every word of it," Costigan assured his fellows. "I had an idea that he would take it that way. That's the way they are. Reasonable, passionless. Funny—they lack a lot of things that we have; but they've got stuff that I wish more of us Tellurians had, too. Give me the plate—I'll talk for Triplanetary," and the beam was restored.

"Captain Nerado," he greeted the Nevian commander. "Having been with you and among your people, I know that you mean what you say and that you speak for your race. Similarly, I believe that I can speak for the Triplanetary Council—the governing body of three of the planets of our solar system—in saying that there is no need for any more conflict between our peoples. I also was compelled by circumstances to do certain things which I now wish could be undone; but as you have said, the past is past. Our two races have much to gain from each other by friendly exchanges of materials and of ideas, while we can expect nothing except mutual extermination if we elect to continue this warfare. I offer you the friendship of Triplanetary. Will you release your screens and come aboard to sign a treaty?"

"My screens are down. I will come." Rodebush likewise cut off his power, although somewhat apprehensively, and a Nevian lifeboat entered the main air-lock of the *Boise*.

Then, at a table in the control room of Triplanetary's first super-ship, there was written the first Inter-Systemic Treaty. Upon one side were the three Nevians; amphibious, cone-headed, loop-necked, scaly, four-legged things to us monstrosities: upon the other were human beings; air-breathing, round-headed, short-necked, smooth-bodied, two-legged creatures equally monstrous to the fastidious Nevians. Yet each of these representatives of two races so different felt respect for the other race increase within him minute by minute as the conversation went on.

The Nevians had destroyed Pittsburgh, but Adlington's bomb had blown an important Nevian city completely out of existence. One Nevian vessel had wiped out a Triplanetarian fleet; but Costigan had depopulated one Nevian city, had seriously damaged another, and had beamed down many Nevian ships. Therefore loss of life and material damage could be balanced off. The Solarian System was rich in iron, to which the Nevians were welcome; red Nevia possessed abundant stores of substances which upon Earth were either rare or of vital importance, or both. Therefore commerce was to be encouraged. The Nevians had knowledges and skills unknown to Earthly science, but were entirely ignorant of many things commonplace to us. Therefore interchange of students and of books was highly desirable. And so on.

Thus was signed the Triplanetario-Nevian Treaty of Eternal Peace. Nerado and his two companions were escorted ceremoniously to their vessel, and the *Boise* took off inertialess for Earth, bearing the good news that the Nevian menace was no more.

Clio, now a hardened spacehound, immune even to the horrible nausea of inertialessness, wriggled lithely in the curve of Costigan's arm and laughed up at him.

"You can talk all you want to, Conway Murphy Spud Costigan, but I don't like them the least little bit. They give me goose-bumps all over. I suppose that they are really estimable folks; talented, cultured, and everything; but just the same I'll bet that it will be a long, long time before anybody on Earth will really, truly *like* them!"